"What's a nice girl like you . . ."

Claude Rainwater slapped his hands against his jeans, raising dust as he approached. May Rose's heart hammered in her chest. It was now or never.

"I've come to talk to you about getting married," she said.

Claude's laughter filled the barn. "Little girl, does your daddy know where you are? You're gonna get a whippin' if he ever finds out you been in a barn with a Rainwater." He gazed at her. "You in trouble?"

May Rose gasped. "No!"

"Then what the hell you doin' here? How come a good girl like you likes me?"

"You kissed me once. I never forgot it."

There was a long silence. "You've got a real pretty mouth."

A knot formed in her throat and she couldn't speak. When his mouth covered hers, a tingling shot through her.

Claude felt it, too. Amazed, he pulled back, staring at the girl-woman in front of him. It had taken a lot of courage for her to come and speak to him, but her courage was quickly running out. If he wanted her, he'd better say so fast. . . .

Books by Mardi Oakley Medawar

The Glory Days of Buffalo Egbert
a.k.a. People of the Whistling Waters

Remembering the Osage Kid

Rainwater on the White Road
a.k.a. The Misty Hills of Home

Tay-Bodal *series*
Death at Rainy Mountain
Witch of the Palo Duros

For more information
visit: www.SpeakingVolumes.us

Rainwater on the White Road

Mardi Oakley Medawar

SPEAKING VOLUMES, LLC
NAPLES, FLORIDA
2019

Rainwater on the White Road
a.k.a. The Misty Hills of Home

ISBN 978-1-61232-774-7

For Tom

Chapter One

Osage County, Oklahoma
July 1920

May Rose Fallen Hawk was in love with Claude Rainwater. This was not something to be discussed or debated. It was simply a thing that was. And no amount of *talking sense*, as her father continually did, would ever change the unchangeable.

"That whole mess of Rainwaters ain't worth the snot outta my nose!" Walter Fallen Hawk yelled into the set face of his sixteen-year-old, stubborn as a dyspeptic mule, daughter.

And now it was being put about the town of Urainia that Claude Rainwater was to marry Carl-Betty Le Fleur. Actually, her name was not Carl-Betty, but Charlotte Elizabeth. She had been called Carl-Betty as an adorable baby, and was stuck with it for a lifetime.

Carl-Betty was everything May Rose was not. She was an older woman (nineteen), needing no one's permission to marry. She was beautiful. She was French-Osage with light creamy skin, pretty Gallic features. She was also a slut. There was a little behind-the-hand saying among the men: Saturday night just ain't Saturday night without Carl-Betty an' beer.

Well, May Rose reckoned as she pulled on her brother's "borrowed" pair of dungarees (with any luck she'd be home in two hours and have them back in his room before he realized he'd been a lender), an old cotton shirt, a pair of hand-me-down boots—we'll just see who Carl-Betty is going to marry and who she isn't.

May Rose escaped out of the back porch without slamming the screened door and legged it across the field of breeze soughing waist-high buffalo grass.

The early morning sun beamed a bluish halo off the top of May Rose's head as she stomped along the single-track dirt farm road toward Delbert Black Eagle's holdings. Delbert was a contrary man, but the general opinion was one of grudging admiration. He did not allow anyone from an oil company anywhere near any of his allotted acres. He didn't care how rich the Osage Nation became, or how well-to-do individual Osage families became from the oil puddled just below their feet. That was their business. In the same way growing wheat and raising a few head of cattle was his business. When he went into town to do his shopping, he traveled there the same way he'd traveled as a boy. The way God intended, in a horse-drawn wagon. But it did gall him when his wagon was passed by automobiles and trucks, and Osage drivers honked and waved. Obstinately, he stuck with his horse and wagon because he knew how often those cars and trucks broke down. He should. Those were the only times his horse and wagon were given the opportunity to pass the faster-moving vehicles.

"Hey, Del!" was the usual cry from some fool with

a flat tire or stuck up to the hubs in mud. "Give us a hand with this thing?"

Delbert flicked the reins and clicked his tongue to the horse, and the animal kept plodding. "Nope. You bought the problem, you work it out."

As Delbert Black Eagle's wagon topped a rise in the beaten road, he saw little May Rose Fallen Hawk clogging straight toward him—and in pants!

Her momma is gonna wear her bottom out if she catches her in those britches.

Delbert pulled hard on the thick reins, calling whoa to the horse.

"May Rose!" Delbert shouted. "What in the world are you doin', girl? Do you know how snaky it is out on this back track? There's rattlers long as trees slimin' around in these grasses. They'll bite you on the butt, girl, an' you'll swell all up an' then you'll never get them britches off."

"Afternoon, Mr. Black Eagle," May Rose panted. Without waiting to be invited, she clambered aboard the buckboard and sat beside him on the seat.

Delbert's black eyes glittered out of hooded sockets. His face was partially shaded by the brim of his well-worn hat. He had the face of an escarpment, flinty and thoroughly lined. No one knew for certain how old Delbert was. Some said forties, some said fifties. Actually, he was sixty-three. Being the redman's answer to Dorian Grey, when Delbert hit fifty-five, he realized that this age pleased him more than any of his previous ages, and so he just stayed with it. He did, however, have the typical middle-aged *dunlap*—"My chest quit being my chest an' started dunlappin' over my belt." Otherwise, there wasn't

3

any other sign of increased age. His six-three frame was as hard as his face.

"I don't suppose you'd give me a ride to your place."

Delbert's head snapped back on his neck. "You mean to tell me that you expect me to turn this here rig around an' go all the way back home."

"Yes, sir."

"Why would I do that?"

May Rose pushed blowing hair away from her face. "Maybe to save me from being bitten on my butt."

Delbert rumbled a chesty laugh. Without further argument he turned the resting horse's head. As the wagon creaked over the ruts and dippy holes of the hardpan road, Delbert, without looking at his passenger, said somberly, "May Rose, if we're elopin', I gotta tell you right off, I've had me four wives already an' I never let one of 'em wear britches."

May Rose's eyes slew to the corners and caught Delbert's mischievous grin. She smiled softly, but her voice was solemn. "You know why I gotta get to your place, don'tcha?"

"I'm sorta figurin' your reason stands a bit taller than me an's as skinny as a ten-penny nail."

"Yes, sir. That's the one."

Delbert nodded. "When your momma's finished with you about them britches, your daddy's gonna get on you about that long-legged nail."

"I don't care."

"Didn't figure you did."

Delbert reined up on the horse a few moments after the wagon entered the dusty yard. His place was a world-weary bachelor's haven. He had himself a nice three-room house with a covered veranda where he sat in the evenings listening to the prairie night sounds. There was a large barn to the back and a host of outbuildings. Chickens roamed freely without a trace of fear of the old dog lying in the shade of a cottonwood. They pecked the ground all around where the feeble bloodhound lay. One hen even pecked at the splayed ear. The dog acknowledged the treatment with a raised brow. It looked at the wagon in the yard with a waning interest, glanced at the hen, now sticking its feathered back end toward the hound's face, then the dog closed its eyes.

Delbert, having climbed down from the wagon and gone around to the passenger side, put his gloved hands on May Rose's waist, lifting her down off the wagon.

"You know I've lifted grain sacks heavier than you?" After setting her down, he pushed his hat back on his head. With the sun shining fully on his face, he did seem ageless. He wore long braids, the dark hair shot with rivers of silver. "May," he said seriously, "he's over in the field behind the barn. I got him bustin' clods on the fallow acres. We're gonna be muckin' before first frost. Since your daddy's real happy bein' an oily Osage, not doing nothing but sitting back and countin' his headright money, you probably don't even know what muckin' is, do ya?"

"No, sir."

"Well, that's when ya take all the cow pies ya been savin' in one god-all-mighty heap until it's hot and steamier than it ever was inside the cow, an' ya spread it."

5

May Rose puckered her face in disgust.

"An' now you know how I feel about oil rigs." Delbert laughed. "A little cow mud never hurt nobody, but you take it from me, this oil business is gonna kill the whole world one of these here days. An' then everybody in the Nation is gonna come to me an' say, 'Oh, Delbert, you wise old sonofabitch, we're so sorry we got greedy.' An' then I'm gonna say, 'Get off my land.' "

May Rose laughed, snorting lightly. Delbert grinned at her, cocking his head to one side and studying her. When he spoke again, his eyes were narrowed. "You *sure* you didn't come out this way to elope with me, May?"

May Rose put her hand lightly against Delbert's chest. The heartbeat beneath her palm was strong and steady. "If *he* turns me down, you're next."

"Well, okay, but remember what I said about them britches."

Claude Rainwater was the great-great-grandson of chiefs. Chiefs who had known the wild forest country of Missouri, then the Flint Hills and flat plains of Kansas. When the Osage were resettled in Oklahoma, the descendants of these chiefs fell in love with liquor and outlawry. Rainwaters had subsequently gone to prison; three had been hanged. Then the twentieth-century oil boom hit, and the lucrative benefit of headright money exacerbated their inherent weakness. As fast as the oil shot up the wooden derricks and rained down wealth, the Rainwaters drank, fought among themselves and everyone else.

Claude was just as bad, but he had one saving grace. He actually liked to work. It felt good to him.

Rainwater on the White Road

The only man with enough guts to give him any work was Delbert, because no one else was brave enough to allow a Rainwater on their property. Basically because the Rainwaters weren't known for their forgiving natures. They had an ugly habit of getting even whenever they felt they had been wronged, no matter how slight the injury. Allowing a Rainwater onto your land for any reason was comparable to throwing your hands in the air and shouting, *"Here's my barn! Burn it, burn it!"*

Delbert wasn't afraid of the Rainwaters. "I've shot better" was all he said. The townspeople of Urainia were still waiting for the predictable outcome of Delbert's foolish employment of a Rainwater. After a year the town was confused as to why the wait was proving to be so lengthy.

Claude was driving the two-mule plow team toward the barn. The back acres had been turned. He'd been plowing since sunrise. He was dirty from it, tired and shiny with sweat. His long black hair was pulled into a single ponytail trailing the length of his bare back. Jeans hung loosely around narrow hipbones. On his feet were a pair of oversize boots. After tending the needs of the mules he would leave his usual note on the nail jutting from the post of the veranda. *It's done.* And then he would be off home.

Notes were the way Delbert and Claude communicated. In the mornings when he arrived, hot coffee would be waiting on the table on the porch. A piece of paper listing the day's chores hung from the nail. Claude would drink a cup of coffee as he slowly read the list, mouthing each word he read. He had gone to the agency school, but the priest had beaten him more than the nuns had taught him. At twenty he added, subtracted, and read on a third-grade level. When he had turned fifteen and stood six feet, he'd beaten the hell out of the Jesuit and his career as a student had duly ended.

May Rose knew every bit of this. She would have had to have been deaf, dumb, and blind from birth not to know. Claude Rainwater was not considered marriage material for a girl from a good family. May Rose Fallen Hawk was from a good family. Carl-Betty's rumored engagement to him should have amused her as much as it amused everyone else. But May Rose had been in love with Claude ever since she was thirteen years old, coming out of the general store to find Claude lolling on the wooden sidewalk with his brothers and cousins. He had looked at her clutching the small bag of penny candies, smiled a blindingly handsome smile, saying, "Hey, kid. Give me some sugars, an' I'll give you a kissy."

She'd given him the entire bag. And felt his kiss on her mouth the remainder of the week, her mind closed to everything else, including the mocking laughter of Claude's brothers and cousins while he kissed her.

From that point on she couldn't grow up fast enough. While she struggled and strained to lose her childhood, he ran wilder than tornado winds, drinking, womanizing, going to jail for months at a stretch. When he was out of jail, he walked the main street of Urainia oblivious to the girl-child watching him with adoration shining in her eyes.

Her puppy love for such a no-good scandalized her mother and infuriated her father. Claude Rainwater might be ignorant of her feelings, but her family was only too aware of them. Especially after she had received a box Kodak camera at her recent sweet sixteen birthday party. In the last two weeks she had used up an entire roll of film snapping Claude, without his knowledge, purposely going wherever he might be to accomplish this. Her father had torn up every one of those pictures except for one she kept hidden and kissed lovingly every night before slipping it under her pillow.

Oh, how her father had glowed a the supper table last night as he ladled string beans onto his plate, passing the bowl to his eldest son, nineteen-year-old Danny, saying, "So, Carl-Betty's marrying Claude Rainwater is she?"

"Yep." Danny laughed. He accepted the bowl of snap beans from his father and, dishing them out onto his plate, he was careful not to let a single string bean near the slab of roast. Danny didn't like his foods to touch. He didn't even like to think of them getting all mixed up inside his stomach. It reminded him too much of the night he'd been sick, hanging out of his bedroom window like an L while he heaved. He became sick all over again looking down at the mess on the grass. After that he was fussy. Meat, potatoes, greens, always had to be on separate sections of his plate. And if he thought his mother would have gone along with it, he would have demanded separate plates for each serving.

"It's all over town," Danny continued. May Rose nibbled buttered cornbread and eyed her brother furtively. "Carl-Betty's in the family way. The father's either Claude or his brother Bernie. Carl-Betty don't want Bernie 'cause he's passed out drunk more than he's awake, so she's takin' Claude."

Everyone, her three brothers, her father, and even

9

her mother, laughed. May Rose's ears and face burned. She imagined other families sitting around their supper tables laughing too. And why not? The Rainwaters invited scorn, didn't they?

Her father broke into her thoughts, glaring at her from his place at the head of the table. "At least that wedding will put an end to other foolishness. Now maybe when Charlie Redlands comes to call, a certain young lady won't be so rude."

Danny grimaced as Walter Fallen Hawk shoveled a fork full of mixed-up mashed potatoes, gravy, and string beans into his mouth. May Rose threw the wedge of cornbread onto her plate.

"Charlie Redlands is *old*," she cried.

Walter Fallen Hawk didn't look up as he worked the fork against the plate, metal scrapping china. "Twenty-seven is not old," he said mildly.

"I don't like him."

"You'll get to like him once you're wed." Her father lifted his face, his eyes boring into her. "An' you will wed him. Mark me, girl. It's been promised."

A small figure stood in the shade of the barn. Claude squinted his eyes, but he couldn't make out who that person was. The two mules, anxious to be at their rations of grain and water, dragged Claude behind them. As animals and man entered the shade, the cooling darkness enveloping them, Claude vaguely recognized the young girl he passed. He looked at her curiously as he and the mules ambled through the opened double doorway. May Rose fell in beside Claude, walking with him toward the stalls.

"Hey," he said in surprise, "don't I know you?"

"Yes."

"Old Walt Fallen Hawk's girl, right?"

"Right."

"What you doing here?"

"Come to talk."

Claude halted the mules, beginning to unharness them. "Think you can help while you're talkin'?"

"What do I do?" May Rose asked in a brightening voice.

"See them nosebags hanging yonder? An' them opened grain sacks leanin' by the wall?"

"Yes."

"Well, go put two measures outta each grain sack in the bags for me."

May Rose scampered off, doing exactly as she was told while Claude put the mules into the stalls and hung up the harness. When she brought the nosebags to him, he was tossing hay into the stall bins. He took the bags from her, and she watched fascinated as the mules drank from the shared trough, sucking up great loads of water.

"Hey, Boss," Claude said to one mule, clipping the animal's face. "That's enough." The mule stood obediently as Claude fitted the feed bag over the mule's muzzle and strapped it behind the ears of the lowered head. He went to the next one. "Jenny-Lynn," he crooned, "you worked good today. Ole Boss gets tired easy. It's good of ya to take care of him the way you do."

Leaving the stalls, he slapped his hands against his jeans, raising dust as he approached May Rose. He smelled sweaty. He towered over her. She stood five feet five. He was six-five. Working as a field hand had muscled him. He didn't own one ounce of fat. He had the reputation of a demon, but he had the

11

face of an angel. As she looked up into it, her heart trip hammered in her chest. It was now or absolutely never.

"I've come to talk to you about getting married," she said flatly.

Claude eyed her speculatively. "Carl-Betty send you?"

"No."

Claude tossed his head back as he grunted, "Wouldn't do her no good no how. I'll say to you exactly what I said to her. I ain't gettin' married to no hussy."

May Rose smiled, her face radiant.

Claude let go a laugh that filled the barn. "Little girl, does your daddy know where you are? You know you're gonna get a whippin' if he ever finds out you been in a barn with a Rainwater."

May Rose laughed nervously, working her hands as if she were soaping them. "My daddy would have my hide for just *talkin'* to you. But I had to talk to you, so I'll worry about Daddy later."

Claude rapidly scratched the back of his head. "Well, you got some sand, I'll say that for ya." He stuck his hands to his narrow hips and stared at her for a long moment. In a low voice touched with—what? concern?—he asked, "You in trouble?"

"I told you he doesn't know where I am!"

Claude waved an irritated hand. "I ain't talkin' about that no more. Keep up, kid. I'm askin' if you're in trouble like Carl-Betty's in trouble?"

May Rose's eyes flared wide and she gasped. "No!"

"Then what the hell you doin' here?" Claude yelled. "I ain't exactly the kind of guy a girl comes lookin' for if she ain't in trouble an' got nowhere else to go."

May Rose's cheeks flamed. Anger took over where nerve was beginning to fail. "Claude Rainwater, I am not Carl-Betty! Do you know Charlie Redlands?"

"Yeah." Claude shrugged.

"Well, my daddy says I've got to marry him. And I don't like Charlie Redlands. I like you. And when I heard you were going to marry Carl-Betty, I just figured I'd better find you fast and tell you how I feel before we both got stuck with people neither one of us want."

"You think I don't want Carl-Betty?"

"I know you don't," she fired. "You just told me so yourself."

"When?"

"When you asked me if she'd sent me to talk you around."

Claude turned away from her, pursing his lips as he idly toed the earthen barn floor. "Oh, yeah," he said softly. "I did, didn't I?" He snapped his head back in her direction, squinting his eyes as he stared at her. "How come a good girl like you likes me?"

"You kissed me once."

Claude's eyes widened. "I did?"

"Yes, you did."

"Was I drunk?"

"No."

"Then how come I don't remember?"

"It was a long time ago."

"Oh." He angled his head, appraising her with new interest. "You must have been just a little girl, 'cause you ain't more'n a drip of water now."

13

"I was."

Claude's grin turned into a mocking leer. He wriggled his eyebrows. There was long silence as he continued to study her. "You've got a real pretty mouth. I bet if I kissed you now, I'd never forget doin' it."

A knot formed in her throat. It was so tight she couldn't speak around it as he slowly approached, gently placed his hands on her quaking shoulders. He lowered his head until she had to close her eyes against the doubled vision of him. When his mouth covered hers, a tingling shot through her. If she had placed a wet finger in a wall socket, she couldn't have been more zapped.

Claude felt it too. Amazed, he pulled back, staring at the girl-woman in front of him with open-mouthed wonder. "Where'd you learn to kiss like that?" he barked.

"I-I," she stammered. "I've only been kissed twice. And both times by you."

Claude turned away from her, pushing his hand over his forehead, skull, letting it rest on the back of his neck as he turned his head in her direction. "You sure I wasn't drunk that first time?"

"You didn't seem drunk. You traded me a kiss for my candies."

Claude tilted his head, laughing loudly. "Hell, I was drunk. I hate candy." With his head back, his hand still on his neck, he gazed sightlessly at the barn rafters, his teeth scraping the corner of his mouth as he thought.

A good girl. I got a good girl to like me. Damn. If I was to marry her . . . He allowed that thought to trail off as new thoughts tumbled pell-mell through his brain. Thoughts of escaping Carl-Betty. Thoughts of escaping the life he knew and hated. Walter Fallen Hawk was an esteemed man with a nice house, nice family. *I'd never do better than this girl if I was to look for the rest of my whole life. If I was to marry her, I'd have something besides getting drunk on Saturday nights and drying out on Mondays walkin' behind Delbert's mules. And she does kiss good. She kisses real good.*

He took a deep breath, expelled it. When he looked at her, he could see that she was anxious and almost on the verge of tears. It had taken a lot of courage for her to come and speak to him, but she was only a little girl and her courage was quickly running out. If he wanted her, he'd better say so fast or she would take off like a scalded hare.

"I think I'd best get cleaned up an' go have a talk with your daddy."

A smile so sunny it lit the dreary interior of the barn flashed from her face. "I'll come with you. We'll talk to him together."

It was a long walk to the Rainwater place. She walked every rolling mile of it holding his hand. He talked the entire time, words pouring out of him, each word alive with his hopes and dreams for the future. Their future. May Rose hung on to each word as tightly as she held onto his hand.

She'd heard a lot about the Rainwaters, how clanny they were, how they lived. Still, the large falling-down house with its swaybacked roof came as a shock. Swing tires hung from tree limbs, the only recreational activity for the children who lived in that rough house. Dogs were everywhere. The Fallen Hawks had dogs too. Two of them. Black retrievers. Her father had gotten them in Tulsa. The retrievers were always well fed, and they were sleek and glowing with health. The Rainwater dogs were mangy, skinny, and mean. May Rose eyed the dogs warily and clung desperately to Claude as they walked through the littered and weedy yard. The dogs crowded and sniffed her. Claude absently bent down and picked up a long stick. Instead of throwing it, as her brothers did for their dogs, Claude threatened the mongrels with it.

"Back off!" he shouted, raising the stick. A few of the curs cowered, some whimpered, others growled warnings. "Back off or I'll beat the hell out of ya!"

One dog, as if testing the mettle of the human, bared its teeth and made an awkward lunge. Claude kicked it in the face. Yelping, the dog ran off. The others fell back, then turned and chased after the injured dog.

"The truck's here. I'm puttin' you in it. You stay inside no matter what happens. Got it, May?"

May Rose nodded her head rapidly, both hands holding onto his arm for dear life.

May Rose scooted inside the Model T truck, Claude slamming the door, talking to her through the glass window.

"Remember. Stay put!"

He hadn't gone three feet when the front door of the house opened and people literally waterfalled out onto the slouching porch. It looked like a comedy. A family joke. But it wasn't a joke. This was not a funny greeting for Claude returning from a long day's work. These people were chasing Bernie, Claude's older brother and father-most-likely of Carl-Betty's unborn baby. A huge woman was straining to hold onto the collar of Bernie's shirt. Women were scream-

ing, children were wailing, and men were cursing as
Bernie tried to escape.

Her mouth agape, May Rose watched family life
Rainwater style. The young girls of the family were
strikingly pretty. So were all of the young men, including the strangling Bernie. The older men looked
as if they had just given up, whipped so badly by
life they just naturally walked in a bowed posture.
The only ones who looked well fed were the older
women.

May had seen several of these women many times
walking through town, if walking was the word.
Plodding was closer to the mark. They moved on
tree-trunk legs, swaying rumps so wide that the simple cotton dresses they wore rode their hind-ends
like oil slicks, undulating and retreating with the ebb
and flow of the water the oil covered.

Claude turned on his heel and raced back toward
the truck. Bernie was falling down drunk, but still
lucid enough to recognize Claude and realize what
Claude was planning. Enraged, Bernie turned on the
woman, his aunt by marriage, punching her in the
face. She immediately let go her hold on his tearing
shirt, howling as both hands covered her bleeding
nose. Bernie made a dash after Claude, stumbled,
and lay sprawled in the dirt. With a roar he scrambled awkwardly to his feet, and dash-reeled toward
the family truck.

Claude was in the cab next to May Rose, pressing
the starter button and frantically pumping the gas
pedal when Bernie splashed himself against the driver's door, his head craning through the opened window frame.

May Rose was out of her mind with fear, but a

17

little voice somewhere inside her said, *He looks so much like Claude. They could be twins.*

Slurring his shouted words, Bernie stood on the running board and leaned in through the driver's window. "What ya doing, Claude!"

"I'm taking the truck." Claude answered, mentally begging the truck to start.

"The hell you are, Claude!" A long string of drool hung from Bernie's mouth. "You take this truck an' I'll kill you!"

Claude raised his hand, pressed it firmly into the twin face, and pushed, sending Bernie backward. Bernie immediately disappeared from sight, a brown dust cloud momentarily taking his place.

May Rose let go a scream as the woman with the bleeding nose and three other substantial women appeared at the passenger side. The bleeding woman banged a fist against the window. She was looking past May Rose, her attention fixed on Claude.

"You gotta stop him, Claudie! He's gone crazy this time. He's swearin' up an' down he's gonna cut up Carl-Betty!"

"That's her look-out!" Claude shouted. "I got my own woman to worry about."

"What woman?" the aunt screamed, slamming a ham fist on the tinny top of the truck. The sound echoed around the cab and rang painfully in May Rose's ears.

"You got eyes, Aunt Edith. She's sittin' right here. Me an' her's gettin' married."

Aunt Edith, her face smeared with gummy blood, looked for the first time at the startled face in front of her. May Rose's saucer-wide eyes peered back at her. She looked like a trapped live pheasant under

18

glass. Aunt Edith let go a high-pitched whoop. Then she started laughing as the other women crowded in to get a closer look at May Rose. Meanwhile, Claude pumped the gas pedal and cussed the truck.

"Do you know who that is?" Aunt Edith squealed. "That's the Fallen Hawk girl. Our Claudie is marryin' a Fallen Hawk." Aunt Edith looked back at May Rose as if (too late) she were putting the best family foot forward. "Roll down the winda, honey, an' give your Auntie Edith a big kissy."

May Rose looked worriedly at Claude. He squeezed her cold, bloodless hand and said softly, both of them ignoring Auntie Edith steadily banging on the window, "Don't do it. Sit tight. I gotta play with the engine a minute. I'll get ya outta here just as fast as I can." As if to seal the promise, he leaned in and kissed her quivering mouth. "I won't let anyone hurt you, May."

May Rose screamed a blast that nearly cost Claude his hearing when Bernie's maniacally grinning face suddenly appeared behind Claude. For that one split second Claude's shoulders seemed to have two heads. And one of them was crazy.

When Claude realized Bernie was laughing because he had almost scared the pee out of May Rose, Claude was filled with rage. His fist shot through the opened window and connected with Bernie's face. Bernie stumbled from the blow, Claude leaped out of the cab and punched him again.

May Rose raked her fingers along the sides of her face as Rainwater bedlam reached new heights. Claude was kicking the tar out of his older brother, people were shouting and screaming, children were climbing trees like monkeys, either to get out of the

19

way of the battling adults or have a better view of the fight. The dogs were back and baying like a wolf pack. And a bloody-faced Auntie Edith continued chatting amiably through the glass window.

"Your momma's named Mona. I 'member her. She's a little younger than me, so we were in different classes. That was back when the Major still ran everything. The Major was a good man. He didn't allow young girls to get married like they used to marry us off in the old-timey days. He said girls need education just same as the boys. Do you still go to school, honey? You gonna quit after you marry Claudie?"

Men were pulling "Claudie" off of Bernie, who was clearly unconscious, trying to cool Claude down before he stomped all of the life out of his fallen brother. Presumably this was typical fare at the Rainwater place, because other than making a stab at wiping her face clean on the sleeve of her dress, Auntie Edith didn't turn a hair.

"Aunt Edith!" Claude roared. "Get in the truck and sit with May while I clean off."

Claude stomped off toward the house while the rest of the family dealt with Bernie, dragging him off to do God only knew what. From the look of him, he needed to be rushed to a hospital. Instead he was being dragged by his ankles around the side of the house.

Aunt Edith waggled her fingers at the departing Claude, calling after him, "Don't you worry, Claudie. I'll stay right with her." To May Rose she said sympathetically, "Poor li'l old thing. You're scared, ain't ya?" As Aunt Edith hauled her bulk around the front of the truck, she screamed at one of the other women, "Gretchen! Fetch our new daughter a glass of tea!"

The woman called Gretchen scowled darkly over a rounded shoulder. "We ain't got no tea!"

"Then fix some," Edith screeched as she clambered inside the cab and slammed the door. Turning to the recoiling May Rose, Aunt Edith whispered, "She's an idiot, but she does make good tea. Puts lots of lemon in it."

Hours seemed to pass. May Rose sipped the bitter tea, holding onto the glass with both hands so that her shaking would not spill it. She was beginning to have serious doubts about the love of her life when he emerged, and the sight of him, cleaned up in a fresh pair of jeans and reasonably nice shirt, banished nearly all of the nightmare events. Edith blathered on, May Rose not listening to a word as Claude raised one side of the engine hood, the metal frame forming a tepee. He bent over the fender and fiddled with engine things. That was as technical as May Rose's knowledge of mechanics went.

"Try the starter, Aunt Edith."

Still talking, Edith complied, and the thing clattered to life, the truck shaking and hopping on its narrow tires. Edith relieved May of the tea glass, then climbed out. Missing now her considerable weight, the truck shuddered and danced with a real frenzy. It was only after Claude climbed in and geared into reverse, looking over his shoulder as he drove out of the yard, that the truck settled down, behaving normally.

At a whiplash-threatening twenty-five miles per, the couple escaped.

"I want ya to remember one thing, May," Claude

21

yelled over the rumble of the truck. The tires hit a rut, and both young people bounced and rolled with it. "You're marryin' me, not them. We ain't never gonna live around 'em. An' our kids ain't never gonna play with their kids. Our name will be Rainwater, but we ain't gonna ever *be* Rainwaters. Got it?"

"Thank you, Claude," May shouted back.

Claude glanced at her and read the uncertainty on her face. He became fearful of her having second thoughts. If she changed her mind, demanded to be dropped a mile or two from her house, making certain no one saw her with him, she wouldn't lose a thing. She could still marry Charlie Redlands and have a nice life. Claude, on the other hand, would lose the one chance life had ever thrown his way. If he continued to live as he lived now, in twenty years he would look and behave exactly the way his father and uncles behaved. And he'd still be in that damn house listening to neglected babies screaming and angry men fighting. He did not want that. He wanted more. Therefore, he could not afford to lose the one and only decent girl ever to look twice at him. He had to do something drastic, especially after everything she'd seen, or she just might get away.

There was an old, rarely used dirt track to the left. Claude abruptly turned onto it and drove the truck into the shade of a few scrub oaks, killing the engine.

"W-what are we doing?" May Rose squeaked.

"We're gonna neck, May."

"What's that?"

"Ain't you never heard of neckin'?"

"No."

"Well, that's just another word for kissin'. We're

gonna kiss a little bit. Engaged people neck all the time. They're supposed to."

"They are?"

"Yeah. It's a way to get really good and acquainted. Now, I know you're a good girl, so I ain't gonna try anything funny. All you got to do is relax. I'll teach you how to neck."

He kissed her slowly and gently at first. Her heart was soon beating up a storm. He was so lovely, so incredibly tender, and after all the years she'd endured the aching puppy love for him, finally having him was just too glorious for words. She forgot everything as his kiss deepened. Waves of new tingles joined the first batch when he put his tongue in her mouth.

She was dizzy and shaky with need when he stopped kissing her long enough to say in a husky voice, "Let's lay down, okay, May?"

"Okay," she answered in a breathy whisper.

Actually, she didn't care if he wanted to hang upside down as long as he kept kissing her. His weight was surprising, solid but not crushing. He kissed her and kissed her as he settled himself just right and, in the process, positioned her legs around his waist. But she wasn't afraid. They were both fully clothed. Everything was all right as long as they were fully clothed. Wasn't it?

She felt her first twinge of concern when he stopped kissing her and said, "This is gonna be good, May. I'm gonna show you how engaged couples make love. It gets the girl ready for the wedding night."

"Claude!"

He was kissing the side of her neck. "This is just

23

practice love," he said in a tight voice. "It ain't gonna hurt you."

She tried to struggle away, but his hand went under her squirming bottom. He was kissing her mouth wildly as he lifted her hips, pressed her pelvic center against a hardened bulge she could feel beneath his fly buttons. He moaned in his throat as he kissed her harder, mercilessly rotating his hips against hers, holding her tightly against him. A light inside her skull suddenly blinded her, and she cried out. Claude buried his face in her neck and pushed his body harder, his hips pumping.

"Claude!"

"Go with it, baby," he rasped. "Make yourself real happy."

Her entire body arched as stars exploded inside her brain and an intense pleasure took command of all her senses. She cried again and he pumped harder and faster. She peaked, then began the rolling fall of thousands of feet back to earth.

Moments later, dazed, confused, and thoroughly exhausted, she felt Claude dragging her up into a sitting position. Their noses touching, he smiled into her face. "Pretty fun, huh?" She could only whimper as she stared at him with wide, disbelieving eyes. "And that was just practice. Once we're married an' it's legal for us to take all our clothes off, I'll show you what a good time really is. An' naturally, I'll get to have a good time too. But until then I'll just have to go without. But that's okay. It's what I'm supposed to do to get you ready for being married."

"It is?"

Claude propped her jelly-like body against the passenger door. On his side of the truck he rolled down the window to let in some cool air and then opened the glove compartment. Inside were tobacco and papers. Almost as if he had forgotten she was there, he rolled a cigarette.

"Heck, yeah. Only a real cold-blooded man would ever marry a girl without teaching her a little something first. But teaching is real special, real personal. It's something a guy only does for the woman he's going to marry. That's why I did it for you."

"And—and we're supposed to do that—a lot?" she asked weakly.

Claude struck a match and lit the cigarette, inhaled deeply. Through the smoke cloud he squinted at her. "Did I hurt ya?"

"N-no."

"Did it feel real nice?"

She blushed crimson.

Claude chuckled. "You don't have to tell me. I know it did. Your legs almost squeezed me in half."

Her chin bobbled as she tried not to cry. "But it—it felt like what we did was a sin."

"Muffin," he laughed, "as long as we're gettin' married, it's not a sin. Why, hell," he cried, waving his hand, the lighted cigarette coming dangerously close to her tousled hair, "you could even take your shirt off if you wanted to while we're neckin' an' it'd be okay. Lots of stuff like that's all right as long as people are engaged."

"Really?"

"Shit, yeah. An' I could take my shirt off too an' we could play 'belly to belly' an' nobody'd say a word. Except maybe your daddy. Seein's how he's Jesus road, he'd probably have a fit over us holdin' hands—so maybe you'd better not tell him about us necking, okay, May?"

She nodded mutely as he smoked the cigarette to a glowing nub and flipped the small remainder out the cab window. He had an awful ache in his groin. Making love unselfishly was not Claude's strong suit, but in this case it was worth the pain. He had awakened a hunger inside her. A hunger that made her his. Feeling completely good about that, he put the truck in gear and started the engine, the truck rumbling to life. He reversed, raising dust, put the gear in first, and headed out back toward the main road.

"Muffin, you'd better fix your hair a little bit. I can't be talkin' to your daddy about marryin' you while you're standin' there lookin' all torn up. He'll think I raped you."

I think you did, May Rose thought numbly. As he drove, she obediently finger-combed her hair.

Chapter Two

Claude had one hand on the steering wheel, the other between May's legs. She was quiet as she sat close beside him. Whenever they encountered vehicles coming in the opposite direction, she clearly saw the drivers gasp, mouths flying open in shocked surprise.

What the devil is May Rose Fallen Hawk doing with Claude Rainwater?

She could almost hear that question being asked as Claude casually waved to the passing cars and trucks. She kept telling herself not to be afraid, that being with Claude was something she had dreamed of for years. Yet as they were spotted together, blind fear caused her to lower her head and press her to hide on the floor of the cab. As Claude drove closer to the small town of Urainia, her heart pounded harder in her chest and nervous sweat dribbled into her eyes, blinding her to the wallowing landscape of Osage County.

Claude reassuringly patted the inside of her denim-covered thigh. "It's all right, sweetheart. Folks are only lookin' at us funny 'cause they don't know yet that we're practically married. Once they know the truth, it's them that'll be embarrassed for thinkin' dirty." .

"They—they're thinking dirty?" May Rose gulped. Shame flamed her cheeks.

"Hell, yeah," Claude chortled. "They're thinkin' I just had ya out on the plains pokin' fun at ya." He looked at her, a broad, knowing smile flashing across his sinfully handsome face. "But won't they go crazy when they find out that for once I was takin' it serious!"

She licked her lips nervously, trying to encourage saliva in a cotton ball-dry mouth. "You—you're still serious? You haven't changed your mind?"

"Hell, no!" Claude cried. "What made ya think that?"

May Rose looked at him quickly, then looked away, her teeth scraping her lower lip. "You—you can still change your mind."

"No, I can't!" he cried. Again he patted the inside of her leg possessively. "We've loved up on each other, girl. That means something. It means we belong to each other."

Claude clucked his tongue, turning his face away, looking out the side window as he spoke. "Been thinkin' about this talk I'm about to have with your daddy."

He turned, looking at her. She stared back, her face drained, eyes glassy. The hand on her leg felt her entire body trembling. She looked and felt like a bunched deer about to bolt. Purposefully he had driven straight for Urainia. He hadn't needed to. There was a back road that was not only semi-private but quicker by five miles. He'd chosen this very public route, with May Rose close beside him, with the sole intention of setting the gossiping tongues wagging. The more people knowing they had been together, the stronger and more confining the box to trap old Walt Fallen Hawk inside. With any luck, some of these gawkers would be dashing for a phone, telephoning the Fallen Hawks, preparing Walt for Claude's sudden appearance on his property and with his daughter.

"Your daddy hates me 'cause of who I am. He ain't gonna exactly throw his arms around me an' welcome me into your family. 'Specially since he's got Charlie Redlands all picked out for ya. I got to be sure in my mind you ain't gonna back out on me, May."

Claude looked straight out the grimy windshield, his jawline twitching, as he seemed to fix his thoughts. "I know you're scared. You got ever' right to be. I'm pretty scared too. But I don't mind takin' a beatin' for lovin' you. I can take whatever your father gives just so long as I know you're still set on being my wife."

May Rose swallowed noisily.

"You just let me handle your daddy," he continued. "Everything's gonna be okay. But you got to promise to stick with me, May. I can't fight him alone. You got to start thinking like my wife and stand right there beside me. Promise?"

"I promise," she answered softly. She sat back, closing her eyes, fighting the tears scalding her lids.

I do love him. I do. And I'm the one who pushed him into this. Then I let him make practice love to me. Oh, please God, don't let my daddy whip me. I'm sorry I was bad. If you help us, I promise I won't let Claude do that to me again until we're properly married.

Walt Fallen Hawk was waiting for them, all right. The wall-mounted telephone in the central hallway had started ringing five minutes ago, and as soon as one call was finished, another came through. It seemed everyone within a twenty-mile radius of Urainia had either seen May Rose in the truck with Claude Rainwater or heard about it from a concerned friend. No one could wait to break the disgrace to her parents. Then Walt made a few calls. The men he telephoned came running. Now they were standing with him on the deep, covered porch. His sons, his two brothers, and the aggrieved Charlie Redlands. And every man jack held a rifle. As soon as they knew May Rose was safe, Claude Rainwater was dead meat.

"Here comes his truck," Walt snarled. And as the truck pulled into the drive, stopping behind a collection of trucks, Walt led the family posse down the porch steps.

For the remainder of her life May Rose would always remember that extra bolt of fear that charged through her as she watched her father approach the truck. And she would always remember him cocking that rifle and the look of unadulterated hatred on his face. She had not only defied him, she had driven him to the edge of murder. As unthinking as she had been earlier in the day when beginning this sordid little escapade, May Rose scrambled out of the truck and ran.

"Daddy!" she screamed, flinging herself at him. "Daddy, don't do it! Don't kill him!"

Walt Fallen Hawk looked down at his daughter with utter loathing. "You been playin' whore to that trash, girl?"

"No, Daddy!"

Her father all but spat in her face as he flung her

away from him. May Rose collided with the ground, landing hard on the side of her hip. And lying there in the dusty drive, she saw her father raise his rifle. She scrambled like a hurrying crab away from him. A pair of hands grabbed hold of her arms and lifted her to her feet. Blinking madly, trying to clear her vision, which was partially blinded by dust and tears, she realized she was standing behind Claude. He raised his hands level with his shoulders as the muzzle of her father's rifle was planted against Claude's chest.

"May Rose ain't no whore," Claude said evenly. "I ain't even gonna let her daddy say that 'bout her."

"I'll blow you six ways from Sunday, you sonofabitch," Walt Fallen Hawk growled.

"Then go ahead on!" Claude dared. "Ain't nobody but God can stop you. But before you shoot, you're gonna have to know your daughter's a good girl. The only thing she's done wrong is love me. An' I love her back. The only way you're gonna stop me marryin' her is to shoot me down right in front of her."

"Then that's just what I'll do." To make his point, Walt cocked the hammer.

Claude barked a laugh. "Like I said, go ahead on. If I can't have May, I'm as good as dead anyhow."

Walt Fallen Hawk blinked. That was all the time Claude needed. He was the best fighter of a family of fighters. And he was twenty-five years younger than his present adversary.

May Rose heard someone scream, then realized the scream had come from her as in a flashing blur Claude took hold of the rifle barrel and flipped the gun and her father, who was still hanging onto the other end of it. In that heartbeat of time while Walt

31

Fallen Hawk sailed heels-over-head through the air, the rifle went off, the bullet nailing a tire in one of the parked trucks. The tire popped, the sound almost as loud as the rifle report. The truck crashed to the hub during the same seconds Walt Fallen Hawk landed at Claude Rainwater's feet. When the older man came to his senses, Claude was holding the business end of the rifle against Walt's chest.

"Please don't make me kill you," Claude said calmly. He didn't have to look up to know the others were closing in. "Tell 'em to stand down, Mr. Fallen Hawk. I didn't come here to hurt nobody. But that don't mean I'm gonna stand still and get shot up. I might feel a twinge about shooting you, but I wouldn't feel nothing shootin' any of them."

"Danny! Charlie!" Walt yelled. He lay, staring into the barrel pointed inches from his face. "Stay put. Don't do nothing. This boy's crazy."

"I ain't crazy."

Walt Fallen Hawk licked his dry lips. He'd had the wind knocked out of him. Not only had he felt it, he'd heard his lungs exploding air as he hit the hard ground with his back. Now he was having to pant like a dog in order to breathe. What really galled him was that the miscreant who had tossed him had done so without even raising a sweat line across his upper lip.

"What are ya, then?" Walt demanded.

Claude laughed lightly. "I thought you'd already figured that out. I'm the man who's marryin' your girl."

"Charlie Redlands's more man than you'll ever be," Walt growled.

"Not if I shoot his balls off, he ain't."

The new subject of the discussion, Charlie Redlands, blanched. In a shaking voice he stammered, "Walt, me marryin' May Rose ain't exactly been talked through." Glancing furtively from Claude to Walt, Charlie dropped his rifle and stuck his hands up in surrender.

Claude sounded a mirthless laugh. "Hell, I wouldn't waste a good load on you." He looked down at Walt Fallen Hawk. "He still the man you want to make you some grandchildren?"

Walt sat up, sent Charlie Redlands a withering look. Then he raised his left hand. Claude took it and helped his future father-in-law to his feet. As Walt stood next to Claude, dusting himself off, he said, "Best come on in the house. If you're serious about marryin' my daughter, there's a few things we gotta get straight right from the get-go."

"Want your gun back?"

Walt looked meaningfully at Charlie. "Not yet."

Claude took hold of May Rose's hand. As they walked behind her father and through the dispersing mob, Claude said close to her ear, "So, Muffin, how do you like this engagement stuff so far?"

A month and a half later, May Rose and Claude were married. She had never been in a hotel room in her entire life; now here she was, locked in the bathroom of the Sooner Hotel. Thankfully, it was a nice bathroom, part of the honeymoon suite, which was a suite because the room boasted its very own bathroom. The suite furnishings were all right, but not as nice as the furnishings in her bedroom. She couldn't help but worry about the many different people who had been in the hotel room, had slept in that same bed. This suite had to have known hundreds of people because the hotel was smack in the middle of downtown Tulsa. Three days and two nights in this hotel was considered an expensive honeymoon. Her father was footing the bill by way of apology for having pulled a gun on Claude. Brushing her hair, May Rose worried again about just how clean the bed mattress might be.

The wedding, which had been held at noon of this same day, had been small. There were a lot of people who had tried to wangle an invitation, but Walt knew it was because they wouldn't believe May Rose was really marrying Claude Rainwater until they saw her do it with their own eyes. Walt did not want his daughter's wedding turned into a spectacle.

Claude had especially forbidden any of his kin to attend. They didn't do well in public, and he didn't want to remember his wedding day as just another family brawl. So in the end it had just been the immediate families of the Fallen Hawks and Clear Creeks (Mona Fallen Hawk's relatives). The one non-family member had been Delbert Black Eagle, who had acted as Claude's best man.

The wedding had taken place forty-five days following the memorable moments in the front yard. And during that time Walt had gotten Claude on the payroll at the local oil company, working the "patch." He also had Claude move out of the Rainwaters' house and into the Fallen Hawk family home. It was a grand two-story with a deep, covered wraparound porch. The house was full of nice sofas and chairs Claude was afraid to sit on and the modern conveniences of indoor plumbing and electricity. The Fallen Hawks also had a cook named Annie. Claude slept out on the screened-in back service porch. Having Claude under his roof allowed Walt to keep a close eye on his soon-to-be son-in-law. Walt was waiting, almost praying, for Claude to revert to type, but Claude stayed away from alcohol and every day he went to work and came straight home right on time.

Claude didn't mind the restrictive lifestyle or that Walt was watching him so closely. He might be resigned to the porch because Walt wouldn't trust him in an upper-floor bedroom close to May Rose, but he had a clean bed to sleep in—and alone—for once in his life not having to share with a brother or an uncle flopping down next to him. He was also eating extremely well, as meal times at the Fallen Hawks' table were more on the order of banquets, and when he was at work, he looked forward to a full lunch bucket.

Before May Rose was sent off to her room and he to the porch, the two were allowed to take "walks." Unfortunately for May Rose, Claude's idea of a walk was to run her into the bushes. And in the bushes he would kiss her senseless and beg her to take her blouse off.

"No! I promised God that if we were still alive after tellin' my daddy we wanted to get married, I'd be a good girl."

"But, May!" Claude whined. "God won't care if you let me see just a little bit of booby."

"Claude Rainwater, don't you dare blaspheme."

Well, now they were married and Claude was waiting just beyond the bathroom door. She checked over the new nightgown her mother had made for her. She brushed her hair one last time. Taking a deep breath and steeling herself, she unlocked the door and stepped timidly out.

Claude was stripped off to his BVD's, sitting on the edge of the double bed, holding a beer bottle by its neck to his lips. His eyes rolled to the corners as May Rose stepped out. He stopped drinking and lowered the bottle.

The gown she wore stopped at the tops of her feet. It was made of a light white cotton material, and he could see the outline of her body through the fabric. Her hair hung about her like a black velvety curtain. She fidgeted as she stood there enduring his appraising gaze. She looked beautiful and very clean. Knowing that he would be the only man to ever touch her, Claude began to burn with an excited lust.

"Come here, May," he said in a ragged voice.

She didn't move except to lower her head. He heard her sniffle slightly.

"May Rose Rainwater. I said, come here."

With her head bowed she puttered along like a wooden doll on invisible casters, her steps so tiny she seemed to be rolling. When she stopped in front of him, he set the beer bottle on the bedside table and took her limp hands in his.

"I ain't gonna be rough with ya, May. I promise."

This was, in fact, the same promise he'd made to her father earlier in the day. An hour before the wedding, outside the Free Will Baptist Church, Walt and Claude had gone for a little walk, Walt seeking this very promise.

"I know how you been raised," Walt had said as they slowly roamed the outside edges of the church. "But I want you to know how I raised up my daughter. I've always taught her to respect herself. An' I want you to respect her too."

Walt paused, placing a hand on Claude's shoulder. Claude stood there obediently, aware of himself inside his new suit. He fervently wished that they were taking this little walk in the shade, not in the blaring sun. He was terrified he would soon be sopping wet from sweat. But Walt was taking his time and Claude was sweating.

"Son, I want you to remember how special it is for a woman to take a man. It means she accepts him into her own body. Now you just think about that. To take another person inside herself means that a woman must have confidence that the man she loves will do her no harm. So you, as her husband, must always be aware of this special trust and act accordingly."

Walt's little speech sure beat the fire out of advice Claude had received from his father many long years ago.

"Men," his father had said when Claude had been but fourteen years old, "go through life lookin' for one thing. A hole. That's 'cause when they're born, they come out of a hole. They spend the rest of their lives trying to get back into a hole. When they die, they finally get buried in a hole."

"What about girls?"

His father waved a dismissing hand. "Never worry about them. Girls already got holes."

"If you have a little swig of beer," he said earnestly, "you won't be so nervous."

"I'm a Baptist person," she murmured. "We don't drink beer."

37

"Muffin," he snapped. "It's your damn honey-moon. God ain't gonna strike you dead if you have a swig of beer!"

May Rose chewed the inside of her cheek as she thought it over. "Well, all right. But just because I'm so nervous."

Claude popped up like a jack-in-the-box. "Okay, honey," he said, placing his hands on her shoulders and forcing her to sit on the edge of the bed. "You just stay right here, and I'll get you a beer from the cooler."

It took about twenty minutes for the two beers May Rose chugged to hit, but when they did, oh Hannah! Claude had a wild woman on his hands, a giggling drunk he had to chase around the room be-cause she had taken her gown off and was wheeling it over her head like a lasso as she ran yelling, "Can't catch meeee! Can't catch meeeeeee!"

She had to be the cheapest drunk he had ever known in his entire life. And as it happened, because of the beer and its relieving her of every particle of timidity, she was also the best lay. For a virgin, she certainly knew how to move her tail. He didn't know if he should be shocked or wildly happy. The next morning when she was stone sober and sick with a headache, she was also nervous again, acting as if he'd never touched her.

"Muffin!" His tone was complaining as he kissed her neck and she lay as still as a two-by-four plank of wood. "Don't be like this. You were so much fun last night."

She stiffened replying waspishly, "I don't remem-ber a thing about last night!"

Claude groaned and rolled off her laying on his

back, one arm slung over his eyes. "Damn. And we're out of beer."

May Rose sat up, holding the sheet against her breasts. "If you think I'm going to become a drunk just to please you, think again, Claude Rainwater!"

Now Claude was angry. He sat up, but unlike his prudish wife, he made no attempt to conceal himself. "I'm gonna tell you something, girl. The Creator only gave Rainwater men one thing in life that's worth a fig—the knowledge of how to make women happy. And last night you were so happy I thought your screamin' would bring down the walls of the hotel." He grabbed her shoulders. "Admit it. You loved it, May. You loved every bit of it."

May Rose gulped noisily. "I-I screamed?"

"Like a harridan outta hell."

"I-I must have been in a lot of pain."

Claude barked a laugh. "Does"—his voice temporarily became a high falsetto—" 'Deeper, deeper' "—his voice returned to a sarcastic normality—"sound like someone in pain? Trust me, I couldn't give it to you fast enough. I thought you were going to kill me."

May Rose puckered her face. She was shocked and angry. "You're lying! You're just stone lying!"

"Would you care to make a bet?"

Her mouth dropped as she stared at him for a moment. Then in a small voice she asked, "Bet what?"

"Bet I can make you as happy sober as I made you while you were drunk. But if I can't, then I swear I'll never lay another hand on ya."

"You'd bet that?" she squeaked.

"Right now, *to-day*."

"W-what do I have to do?"

"Not a damn thing."

She considered at length, then flopped backward on the bed. Staring up at the ceiling she said, "All right. You have a bet."

Seconds later, May Rose was struggling to breathe. His hands were everywhere, spreading fire across her skin as his mouth devoured hers. Something was happening to her, something she couldn't control. She was only half conscious of opening her legs as he moved on top of her and groaned in his throat. Then he abruptly stopped kissing her and shifted his body. All she could see was his chest and feel something hard penetrating her. She braced herself for pain. There was none. Claude easily glided inside her, and the sensation was incredible.

"Oh, my!" she gasped. Claude began to move. May Rose gasped again. Then her body began to melt, merge with his. Loud cries escaped her throat, her legs curled tightly around his waist.

"Want more?" he panted against her ear.

"Yes!"

"Lot more?"

"Yes!"

"Get ready to come for me."

"Claudeeee!"

"Damn, Muffin. You're so hot."

She was drifting blissfully back to earth when he roughly flipped her over onto her stomach. Groggily she realized that she was staring at the wrought-iron railing as he entered her again. She turned her head, saw him standing on his knees. His hands gripped her hips, and the bed springs squeaked in a furious rhythm as he rapidly slammed into her. Then he cried out and she felt him stiffen and shudder. A strange warmth filled her. Seconds later, he did a slow fall and pinned her facedown on the mattress with his weight. He lay still for a very long time. She felt his hand brush tangled hair away from her face as he whispered in her ear.

"I told ya. I told ya it was good. And we can do this all the time, May. We can do this just as much as we want."

"Could you please get off me?" she said into the pillow. "You're heavy."

"Oh."

He pulled out of her and rolled off. When she lifted her head, all she could think was that now she felt strangely empty. Evidently their separation wasn't as disturbing for him. She looked to the side, saw him sitting with his long legs crossed at the ankles, his back against the bed frame. Ignoring her, he lit up a cigarette. She stared at the profile of his beautiful face before her gaze drifted down to his wonderfully male body. Claude took a long drag on the cigarette, playfully expelling the smoke in rings. She still couldn't move. Even her eyelids felt paralyzed. Then he sprang off the bed with all the energy in the world. She despised him for that, and for the fact that he'd won the bet.

"I hate you," she said in a tiny, strangled voice.

Claude gave her thigh a pat. "I know, Muff. Tell you what, I'll go run us a bath. That'll make you feel better before we make love again."

"You—you're gonna make me do that—again!"

Claude paused, looking back at her over his shoulder, the cigarette hanging from the corner of his mouth, one eye squinting against the smoke. "Yeah.

41

That's the whole idea of the honeymoon. And don't forget, when we leave here, we'll be living with your folks. Your dad won't like hearing you yelling in the middle of the night."

He took the cigarette out of his mouth and winked at her. "Don't be embarrassed, Muffin. Personally, I love it when you yell." He sauntered away as naked as a jay bird, into the bathroom. May Rose groaned, burying her flaming face in the pillow. From the bathroom she heard him whistling and turning on the spigots. As the tub filled he called for her.

"Hey, May? Come on in here. Let's play tubby."

The last morning in the hotel, Claude paid the bill. He had twenty-five dollars left. Money which had been slipped to him during the reception as he stood with Delbert.

"There's a few extra dollars in there," Walt whispered as he handed Claude an envelope. "Tulsa's a nice town. It's got a moving-picture house and real nice restaurants. You an' May Rose won't get bored just havin' to stay in the hotel." He nodded sagely, then moved off to mingle with other members of the family.

Claude looked at the fat envelope stuffed with ones and fives, then looked with a confused expression into Delbert's smirking face.

"Is he kidding?"

"No," Delbert chuckled. "He's a father. He don't want to think about his little baby girl being alone with you. It'll be easier for him to think of you two spending your honeymoon goin' to the movin' pictures. If you're smart, you'll let him believe that's just what you did."

Striving to be compliant, Claude appeared at the dining room breakfast table, where May Rose was already seated, looking over the menu. A newspaper was tucked under his arm.

"I guess I'll just have the toast and coffee," she said, sounding worried.

Claude sat down across from her and unfolded the newspaper to the entertainment section. He slowly read the announcements for the movies that had been playing during their stay in Tulsa. He wanted to be able to recite a few titles as Delbert had suggested.

"Have anything you want, sweetheart. I got money to feed ya with."

"Really?" She began to review the menu with a keener interest. "What do you think you'll have? They have just about everything in the world anyone could eat."

Claude continued the laborious task of reading, grunting, "Pick out what you want, then double up the order for me."

When the waitress appeared, May Rose ordered eggs, toast, grits, potatoes, melons, bacon and sausages, fruit juice, and coffee.

An hour later, as stuffed as a pair of turkeys, they drove out of Tulsa. During the long drive May Rose fell asleep, her head on Claude's lap. She woke sometime later as the truck came to a dusty stop. She sat up, blinking gummy eyes, vaguely realizing they were not in her father's drive.

"Where are we?"

"Our private place." Claude grinned.

"What are we doing here!" she cried.

"We're gonna see how well everything works in a truck."

"You mean—now?" May panicked. "In the middle of the day?"

"Yep."

"Claude Rainwater," she cried. "You're crazy."

"No, baby. I'm horny. An' you sleepin' with your face next to my fly didn't help. Now, you got a choice. You either give it to me here, or you give it to me the minute we get inside your daddy's house. But one place or the other, you're definitely gonna give it to me."

May Rose sighed wearily as she began unbuttoning her blouse, Claude watching her, grinning like a Cheshire cat. "Claude Rainwater, I don't know if I'm ever going to get used to you."

But in her heart she knew she was already used to him. Not only was she used to him, she found herself craving him with a physical ache.

They lived with her parents for six months while the house they would live in the rest of their lives was under construction. It was just five miles down the road from her parents. And during all of those months the young couple lived with them, Mona Fallen Hawk was heard to remark, "May Rose and Claude are so cute. They're just like a little old couple, always going for drives right after supper."

May Rose was pregnant with her first child when she and Claude moved out of her parents' house and into their neat little single-story house. As small as the house was, box-shaped and only four rooms, they were heavily in debt. Along with the building costs for their home, Claude had bought eighty-five acres of land. Debt made May Rose extremely nervous; the pregnancy made her extremely ill. Claude had a very laid-back attitude to both. When she tried to goad Claude into caring more, they began to bicker. Gradually, bickering turned into heated arguments. Then escalated into knock-down drag-out fights. May Rose had a quick mind and a fast, waspish tongue. He wasn't a match for her. The one and only time he raised his hand against her was on the occasion of an especially nasty argument caused by Claude driving home in a brand-new truck. Before he could say a word, May Rose flew at him, screaming abuse. Like the eighty-five acres, he bought the truck without mentioning a word to her, and because she was the designated bill payer, she was hysterical.

Claude raised his fist. His temper was formidable, and his hand shook as he battled hard not to strike. She was his wife, his four-months-pregnant wife. It took every fraction of willpower he owned not to hit her. As he struggled for control, May Rose looked from his shaking poised fist to his livid face. Suddenly terrified of him, she ran out of the house, jumped into the new vehicle, and in tears drove for her parents' home.

Her mother tried to console her, but her father grabbed her by the arm, frog-marched her out of his house, and stood with her on the porch.

"Little girl, you wanted that man. You defied me, you defied God in Heaven just so you could have him. Okey-dokey, you got him. An' now you got his baby inside you. So here's what you're going to do. You're going back to your own house, and you're going to make your marriage work because for better or for worse, it is your marriage."

Weeping, she drove home. When she pulled into the drive, she spotted Claude sitting on the front porch steps. He stood and walked into the drive. He stood quietly near the driver's window as she switched off the engine.

"I been real worried, Muffin."

She covered her eyes with her hand as she wept. "I can't go on like this anymore, Claude. You got to help me. I'm so worried about money, and I'm sick all the time because of the baby."

"I know, sweetheart."

"No, you don't!" she shouted. "If you did, you wouldn't have bought this truck when we already have a perfectly good truck. We don't need two trucks."

"Yes, we do! You expect me to walk all the way to Whizbang?"

She looked at him, her face bleached with shock, her eyes wide and blank. "Whizbang? What are you talking about?"

"That's what I've been trying to tell you, May. Come next week, I'm gonna be up in Whizbang. You're gonna need this truck because I gotta take the old one."

It took considerable effort to believe what she was hearing. The new oil boomtown of Whizbang was way over on the other side of Pawhuska, the capital of the Osage Nation and the county seat for Osage County. He would be almost a hundred miles away, which meant that she would be alone. Trembling with terror, May Rose scrambled out of the truck.

"You can't do this to me, Claude. You can't go off and leave me."

His hands gripped her shoulders. "I got to, sweetheart. If we want to keep paying for the house and land, I gotta go where the work is. But you're gonna be all right, you got your folks to look out for you."

For the next week, May Rose followed him around, nagging, pleading, crying. Again, Claude's temper snapped.

"Quit talkin' to me about headright money! We can't live on it, May. Not like other folks because we ain't other folks. Your daddy's got your money tied up with those stocks he's always buying, and my money's all but claimed by the debts my family keeps running up. You wanted a house, and I wanted land, so that means I gotta go to Whizbang."

Chapter Three

The spring day was very mild, and while her father and brothers noisily built the barn she needed for the cow and chickens she planned to buy, May Rose began her kitchen garden, applying the hoe to the ground still soggy from last night's thunderstorm. It had been a very bad storm, and May Rose had spent the night huddling in a closet, listening to the thunder booming over her head. When one boom shook the house, she massaged her swollen abdomen and sang hymns to comfort herself as well as the squirming child just beneath her skin.

It would do her no good to talk to her father. He was in a black mood because Claude had left her. His mood would be even blacker if he knew that Claude rarely called. When Claude did call, the sounds in the background were suspicious. He said he was telephoning from a café. She had no other choice but to believe him. She desperately wanted to share her fears and concerns with her parents, but on the second occasion she had tried, three weeks following Claude's departure, her father had firmly placed any and all discussion of her marriage out-of-bounds.

"I am not going to tell you again, little girl. You

chose him. I had Charlie Redlands all picked out for you. Maybe I was wrong about Charlie; then again, maybe I wasn't. We'll never know for sure. There's just no use talking about something that can't be changed."

Her parents and brothers were faithful about checking on her, seeing to it that any heavy work that needed doing was done. At no time, however, did they ask about Claude, how he was doing in Whizbang, or when he might be coming home. Wielding the hoe with force, she was deep in thought about her troubled marriage when her father came up behind her.

"Keep that up an' you're gonna chop yourself all the way to Oklahoma City."

May Rose stopped and, leaning tiredly on the hoe handle, she forced a hollow-sounding laugh.

"Your momma said for me to tell you that since your time is gettin' close, maybe she should come over an' live with you a bit. Told her I'd ask, so I'm asking."

May Rose studied her father for a moment. He was a very tall man and kept his hair in the traditional fashion, shaved down to skin on the sides, the middle portion swept back. His hairstyle was always at odds with the three-piece suit he wore to church on Sundays, even more at odds with the overalls and white shirt he was wearing now. From the hard glint in his dark eyes, May Rose knew the offer of her mother coming to stay with her was a type of test.

"Tell Momma thank you, but I'm all right." She wasn't, and both she and her father knew that very well, but declining the company of her mother invoked an approving grunt.

"I'll tell her." Squinting up at the cobalt sky, he said, "We brought you up good, May Rose. We loved you as best we knew how. You turned out to be a strong person. That's just about the best thing anybody can ever hope to be."

A month later and on a very hot summer night, she couldn't settle down to sleep. Every time she tried, her stomach tightened and remained in a hardened grip for what felt like an eternity, but by the tick of the clock on the nightstand she timed the discomfort as being a little over a minute. A half hour would pass when the discomfort again pulled her out of a light sleep. Then the half hour between the awful agony shortened to fifteen minutes. Believing that if she went to the toilet she would feel better, she stumbled into the bathroom. Before she sat down on the toilet, her water broke, flooding down her legs, splashing on the hardwood floor. Her heart in her throat, May Rose made it to the wall phone in the hallway and cranked the handle six times, her parents' number. Finally she heard her mother's tinny voice in the earpiece.

"Momma! Something's happening to me. I think it's the baby."

Following nine hours of excruciating labor and delivered by his maternal grandmother and a midwife, Matthew Kenneth Rainwater was born. He was a lusty eight-pounder, and he looked exactly like Claude. Shortly after the birth, Walt Fallen Hawk sent the absentee father a telegram, and a week later, Claude came home.

From her easy chair May Rose watched him,

watched the way he held the baby and paced the floor. Claude paused and sent her a dazzling smile.

"He's great, Muffin. He's got such cute little hands. I didn't know anything could be this little."

"He didn't feel little when he was coming out," she chuckled. "He felt like a pumpkin."

Claude slowly approached, carefully sat down on the ottoman near the chair. "You've done a real good job, May. Not just with the baby, but with everything. The house looks good. I like all the new furniture an' stuff. It feels real homey."

May Rose sighed and rested the side of her face against her hand. "It would be even more homey if you could be home."

Claude looked up from the baby and grinned. "That's just what I was gonna tell you. I'm gonna be over in the Dewy field. Almost right in our own backyard. Least ways, I'll be there for a while. New fields are opening all the time, so I can't say where they'll send me next."

She knew this to be absolutely true. The undulating bluestem grasslands were filling up fast with wooden derricks. Closer into Bartlesville, the horizon was a forest of derricks, and the once peaceful prairie air was disturbed by the constant sound of steam engines driving the well pumps. Even in the middle of the night she could hear the machinery, smell the oil being extracted. Like Delbert, May Rose was beginning to hate the oil business. Ironically, Claude seemed to love it. Love the dirt and the danger, love the camaraderie shared by the oil riggers. The only way she could explain her husband to herself was that he had found acceptance inside this completely male world. An acceptance he had been missing in his own, born-into, world.

Matt was a good baby. He slept through the night, especially when sleeping in the bed between his parents. He only cried when he desperately needed something, like food or a diaper change, and then his cries sounded apologetic. Claude was home all through the winter, and that first Christmas as a family was private and wonderful. May Rose was genuinely happy. Until she discovered she was pregnant again.

Following the examination in the doctor's small office, she yelled, "How can I be pregnant? I've still got a baby at the breast."

The doctor irritated the breath out of her when he chuckled and replied, "Miz May, a nursing cow penned in with a prime bull comes up with a new calf. Womenfolk ain't that different."

That evening May Rose remained at the living room window, watching for Claude, worrying about him driving home in the heavy snowfall. When the truck lights appeared in the drive, she was standing in the doorway.

"I'm going to have another baby," she wailed.

Claude shook off the snow like a dog shaking off water. "Well damn, May. Seems like you could have planned better. I just got the word that I gotta go all the way over to the Burbank site."

Her hands covering her mouth, she staggered several paces backward. *Burbank.* It was on the other side of the county. How could he do this to her? Again! But Claude wasn't thinking about her fears;

his concern was the inconvenience May Rose had suddenly caused.

"Burbank's a rough place. Everybody's living in tents right there on the site. You an' Matt maybe would have been all right, but I can't risk you comin' with me now that you're up the spout again. Damn it all, May. Now I gotta sleep alone and eat cold beans out of a can. I wish the hell you would have thought about me for a minute before you decided to surprise me with another kid."

While in Burbank, Claude telephoned only once a month, and when he did there was more distance in his tone than the actual miles between them. Once again May Rose did not bother running home to her parents with her fears for her marriage. Every day without Claude began and ended the same. She woke, took care of Matt, her cow, and half dozen chickens. In the late spring she filled the days with tending her vegetable garden and watching Matt crawl through the rows until he was black from the soil. She no longer went to church because even this social outlet had begun to prove a strain. The gushing kindness of the people said it all. Everyone felt sorry for her, saw her as being trapped in a futile marriage. Driving into town to do her meager shopping was a burden as well and for the same reason. All of her evenings were passed in the same wearisome way. Once Matt was asleep in bed, May Rose sat and knitted baby clothes, waiting for the telephone to ring, waiting for the relief of Claude's voice. While she waited and knitted, she told herself that her self-imposed isolation was not going to get her, that she would not lose her mind. All the while the telephone remained silent, and she was terrified she already had.

Once again Claude was absent when his child was born. His second son was again delivered by May Rose's mother and the midwife, this time in the middle of the afternoon during a record-setting heat wave for the month of September. Walt Fallen Hawk sent another telegram.

Born, son named Jacob Joseph—Stop—May Rose fine— Stop Walt had also wanted to add, *Wish you would come home, where you belong,* but he didn't. Claude Rainwater was his daughter's business. Walt's pride would not allow him to interfere.

Jacob, nicknamed Jake, was as different from Matt as two babies could ever hope to be. When Matt was born, he had been as round and as fat as a berry. When Jake was born, he looked like a long noodle. Matt had needed a slap to get him crying after he was born. Jake was born screaming, and he continued to scream night and day. He always wanted to be held, always wanted to be at the breast even when he wasn't hungry. May Rose simply did not have the time to comply with his many demands, and so Jake screamed. The only thing her sons seemed to have in common was the fact that both of them looked exactly like their father. Jake was three months old and screaming his lungs loose when Claude finally walked in the house.

Hearing the baby in the back bedroom, Claude didn't pause. He went straight there and rescued Jake. The instant the baby was in his arms, Jake stopped screaming. Old memories pressing hard, Claude looked coldly at May Rose.

"I thought you were a good mother. A woman I could trust with my children."

"I am a good mother!"

Claude's jawline worked, the muscle ticking furiously. "Now that I'm home for good, I better never hear this baby cry again."

The problem of Jake made for a continuing argument between his parents. Finally, at her wit's end, May Rose called the midwife who had delivered both of her children. Listening to the distraught young woman, Thelma Flower said tersely, "I'll be right there." When she appeared twenty minutes later, May Rose was staring agog at the thing in Thelma's hands.

"I know you don't hold much with old-timey ways," Thelma said, "but your modern ways are making you crazy. Give me that baby."

May Rose handed Jake over, and wringing her hands, she watched and worried the whole time Thelma strapped her baby inside the cradle board.

"Now, what you do," Thelma said as she tied up the many laces, "is you keep him on your back an' you sing to him. When you're working in the hot sun, you hang him from a tree limb so he can be in the shade but he can still see you an' hear you. May Rose, you do just what I'm tellin' you, an' he won't scream no more."

He didn't. When Claude came home that evening and found her in the kitchen, Jake on her back and Matt playing on the floor, he laughed. For a long time after that, peace ruled in the Rainwater household. And then Jake outgrew the cradle board, became old enough to crawl and climb. May Rose felt out of control again as she spent her days running to rescue her spidery son from one hazard after another. Matt took his job of watching Jake very seriously, but he was still too small to do anything more than toddle to his mother, pull on the hem of her dress, and make noises in his throat. That was all the signal May Rose needed to send her running to find Jake.

Complaining to Claude did nothing to relieve the situation. Besides, he was becoming discontent with being stuck in one place. The Osage Hills had become quiet. Men were now simply looking after producing wells. Claude missed the action of drilling. There was a lot of new action going on in Borger, Texas. Claude wanted to go to Borger. What stopped him was the fact that in Texas, Indians weren't all that welcome, hadn't been since 1858, when Texas legislature passed a law stating that Indians were not allowed to remain in Texas for any period longer than twenty-four hours. In 1925, this law was showing no favorable signs of a hasty repeal. Quietly furious that even though the Borger site was owned and operated by the Oklahoma company, as long as Borger was in Texas, Claude's experience as a driller would be partially judged on the fact that he was also an Indian. As more men left for the Borger site and Claude was left with the tedium of maintaining a field of producing wells, he started staying out late, hanging out at the infamous U-Know, a bar in Urainia that served whiskey and *"U-Know what else."*

During this last year Delbert had retired from farming and "messing with raising cattle." Suddenly finding himself a man of leisure, he began spending time in town, hanging out at the feed and grain store, listening to gossip. He wasn't pleased with what he heard. May Rose was pregnant again, and Claude was said to be running wild. Unlike Walt Fallen Hawk, Delbert decided that it was high time someone interfered in May Rose's marriage before it changed from shaky to shattered beyond repair.

He found her around the back of her neat little one-story house, working in her garden. Little Matthew had a stick and was pointing it like a lance as he chased a chicken out of the turnip rows. Jake was in a playpen set up in the shade of a cottonwood and screaming to be released. Solely fixed on her troubles, mindlessly chopping weeds, May Rose didn't hear her yelling son or Delbert's quiet approach. She started when Delbert placed his hand on the hoe. Then she was near to weeping as he pried the hoe out of her hands and led her to the bench under the same cottonwood shading Jake.

The little boy turned up a hopeful, tear-stained face to the strange man standing close by his little prison. As May Rose sat down on the bench, Delbert said, "How come you don't let this baby outta that thing? He don't like being caged up while his brother gets to run."

May Rose ran a hand over her pale and sweaty face. "Because when he's not in the pen, he runs around like he's crazy. Just like his father," she added bitterly.

Delbert leaned heavily against the hoe. "Yeah. I heard he's been givin' you grief."

Battling tears, she looked quickly away from Delbert. "It's my problem."

Delbert sighed, hefted the hoe, and walked toward the blast of sunshine that bored down on the verdant garden. While he hoed weeds, poking up around the cabbages, he talked, sounding as if he were speaking solely to himself.

"The one thing I never could abide was a naggin' woman. As soon as a woman commenced to nag me, I either took off or I packed up her bags an' sent her off. My last wife was a good 'un, though. Wish she hadn't died like she done 'cause she sure was a real good woman. Use to treat me like a dog."

May Rose's drooping head bobbed up. "A what?"

Delbert stopped hoeing, looked back at her, and grinned broadly. "Like a dog, May. She used to pet me all the time. I loved that. Most men do. Anyway, she was one of the few women I ever hooked up with who understood just how much a man loves being petted. But that woman could give with one hand an' take with the other, 'cause she sure kept me on a short leash. Whenever I got to actin' wild, she'd choke up on the leash. When I settled some, didn't pull against the leash so hard, why, she'd pet me just the way I liked her to, to show me I was a good boy. Worked every time."

"I-I don't understand."

"You don't?" He laughed. "Well, you just sit there an' you think about it, think about that old hound dog you got last year to watch the place. Now, when that hound gets to barkin' or diggin' up your flowers, do you stand over it and talk it half to death? No sir, I don't think you do, 'cause you know that hound dog would just look at you stupid. On the other hand, I bet when you say sit, that hound dog sits down pretty quick."

He leaned over and pulled loose a weed, tossed it out of the garden. "You know, May, womenfolk are always claimin' that men are dogs. I can't figure out why if they think that, they just don't follow on through. Why they still use forty words against their men when one word would do."

Delbert set aside the hoe and walked out of the garden, coming back into the shade. He sat down beside her on the bench. "May," he said softly as he watched a subdued Jake playing with a toy in the playpen, "how bad do you want Claude to quit ramblin'?"

She lowered her shamed face, snuffled a string of snot back up her nose.

"Now, don't go all weepy on me, girl. It was a pretty fair question. If you want him to go away and maybe after a while get yourself a new man, ain't nobody in town gonna blame you. Everybody already knows he's been cuttin' loose on ya. Truth to tell, folks around here have long been expecting you to do that very thing. It's a credit to you he didn't start running until just lately. Usually Rainwater men start into messing right after they say I do.

"I told you once that Claude was the pick of a real raw litter. Guess you weren't listening close. What I was trying to tell you was that even the best of something raw is still raw. Oh sure, you can hose down a wild critter an' bring it on into the house, but it's always gonna be wild. It ain't never gonna be a good house pet. What you got to get into your sweet little head is that Claude Rainwater was born an' raised wild. Being married to him is always going to be a whole lot of work. If you've got so tired that you just can't face any more, now, while you're young an' you still got your life all stretched out in front of you, would be a real good time to shuck him."

Her chin bobbling badly, a new tear rolling down her cheek, she said in a small voice, "I love him. I don't want to, Delbert, but I can't help it."

He grunted a sour laugh. "It's that pretty face of his, ain't it?"

She sniffed again, nodded.

Delbert slapped his hands against his thighs. "That's just what I figured. May? Do you know why the Devil gets away with so much evil?"

She shook a confused head.

"Well, it's 'cause the Devil's beautiful. Preachers all the time make out that the Devil's got horns and a tail, but he don't. He's beautiful. Bible says he was the most beautiful angel in Heaven. Mortal men an' women are real suckers when it comes to a pretty face. I've lived a long time, and I can tell you for a solid fact that a man or a woman will follow a beautiful devil straight into hell and on a dead run. And now you know why I never tried to stop you from runnin' after Claude. He's one of the prettiest devils ever to strut this earth. You had to have him. An' I knew then that fighting against a thing like that was just plain useless."

Pausing for breath, he took her hands in his. "But now you got to listen to me, May. You're not a little girl anymore, you're a grown woman with responsibilities, so you hear me good when I say that if you want to keep hold of Claude, you're gonna have to go about it a whole different way. You're gonna have to start lookin' at him like he's a big old dumb wild dog. You're gonna have to train him to the leash. You're gonna have to teach him to heel, and he's gonna have to know you mean what you say."

He let go of her hands and rose. With a curled

index finger under her chin, he lifted her head. Their eyes met and held. "Remember how to house-break a dog, May? First you rub his nose in his mess, an' then you throw him out of the house. There ain't no yellin' or fussin' needed. Just one good boot to the hind end and a night out in the cold oughta do the trick."

Delbert left her, went to the playpen and, reaching in, ruffled Jake's hair. "Please let this baby out of this cage."

"He'll hurt himself," she answered weakly.

Delbert looked at her over his shoulder. "That's not a bad thing, May. It'll teach him not to do whatever it was that hurt him. Boy babies have got to learn that early, or they stay boy babies all their lives."

Close to midnight of the same day Claude ambled home and was immediately stunned to find the door locked. Half drunk, he retaliated by kicking the door. When that didn't work, he pounded it with his fist.

"Maaaaay! Open the door!"

No answer. Crickets chirped and the house remained dark.

"Damn it, May! I mean it. Open this door or I'm bustin' it down."

A light came on inside the house. Fuming mad, Claude waited to hear the locking bolt turn. It didn't. He was thoroughly muddled when instead he heard May Rose's sleepy voice.

"Is that you, Claude?"

"Of course it's me. Open the door."

"No."

61

The one-word reply almost knocked him off his feet. "No! What the hell do you mean, no?"

"I mean, no."

Anger ripped through him, and he was instantly sober. Breathing steam in blasts from his nose, he growled, "You better explain yourself, woman. You keep foolin' around, an' God help you when I get ya."

"No."

Completely shocked, Claude jumped back. Then, flapping his arms like a goose, he walked in circles on the covered porch. After a minute, he was again standing in front of the locked door. "May Rose Rainwater! You got to the count of five to open this door."

"I think I should tell you, Claude, I have the gun."

In stone disbelief, his lower jaw became unhinged. Mouth agape, he stared wide-eyed at the barrier. When he could trust his voice he called hesitantly, "Honey babe?"

No answer.

"Love muffin? What are you doin' with the gun?"

"Protecting my door."

"From what?"

"From you. If you try breaking it in, I'll be real sorry but I will shoot you."

Claude ran his hands quickly over his face, pushed them over the temples and down the back of his neck as he licked his dry lips. "Muffin?" he tried. "You wouldn't shoot your lover man."

"Yes, I would. And I'll shoot right through the door if you beat on it again."

Claude jumped back. "For crying out loud, May! Have you lost your mind? You just can't go lockin' me out of my own house and then threatenin' to shoot me. Part of that's against the law."

"Protecting myself and my babies from a late-night prowler," she said calmly, "is not against the law."

"I'm not a prowler! I'm your husband."

"You're not my husband if you're not home by eight o'clock. From now on, that's when my door gets locked. If you can't come home before then, you should just stay wherever you are because I won't unlock the door to let you in."

"Then just where the hell am I supposed to sleep?"

"Well," she drawled, "you use to love the truck."

"Maaaaaay!"

The light went out and the house fell silent.

The next morning May Rose began her day as usual. After setting the coffeepot on the stove, she carried the milk pitcher out to the back porch, heading for the milk can. The instant she spotted Claude, sitting on the glider, swinging ever so slightly and glowering at her, she gasped. Her hand flew to the top of her robe, and fear lurched inside her. He stood and slowly approached, stopping just within arm's reach. His expression and his tone were tight as he placed his hands on his hips.

"That was quite a little trick you played on me, May. As you can see, I'm not laughing. I've been thinkin' pretty hard on it, and I think maybe after a trick like that, what we should do is just forget about being married."

"Fine."

For the second time in a span of six hours, Claude's mouth fell open. For a long moment all he could do was gape, his mouth opening and closing like a beached fish. Throwing his hands wide, he yelled, "Fine? Just like that? Our whole marriage is gone and you say, fine?"

"There's nothing more to say. Would you like a cup of coffee before you go?"

In a near coma, Claude stood rooted to the floor-boards as she breezed past him, filled the pitcher, noisily fitted the lid down on the standing milk can, went back into the kitchen. All through the night he had envisioned their confrontation remarkably differ-ent. In his mind, he had been strong and righteously angry, May Rose hysterically crying. Then when he threatened to leave her, she would become even more hysterical, getting down on her knees, begging him to stay. Anyway, that was the way their fighting used to be. Why was it suddenly different?

Then it came to him. *Damn! She wants me to leave. Well, I'll show her. I won't do it.* Claude stormed into the kitchen. She was at the stove, placing strips of bacon in the frying pan. She didn't turn around when he entered, so he stood behind her, yelling his head off.

"You can't throw me out of my own house. You're my wife and these babies are mine. I'm not going to clear off just because you say so."

"Suit yourself," she replied evenly. "Just remem-ber that supper is on the table at six and the front door is locked at eight."

He backed off, ready, waiting, hoping she would turn around and fight. She didn't. She fried up the bacon, placed it on a serving plate, set the plate on the table. Then she went off to take care of her wak-ing sons. Feeling alone and flustered, Claude poured himself a cup of coffee, ate a piece of bacon. When she came back, Jake was on her hip and Matt, holding her hand, was yawning. She settled the boys at the table, gave them each a cup of milk and a strip of bacon. Then she prepared Claude's lunch bucket. She had only one other thing to say to him as he left for work.

"Good-bye."

Claude cussed with every step he took. The sun was setting behind him as he strode down the middle of the dirt road. He wore oily jeans, a work shirt that was unbuttoned and fanning behind him as his boots angrily clogged the road. In his right hand he carried his lunch bucket. The empty bucket banged his leg as he stomped and muttered, stomped and muttered.

Delbert's one-horse wagon appeared on the rise. The wagon neared and Claude raised a hand in a slothful wave. Delbert pulled up on the reins.

"Hey boy, how come you're walking?"

Claude stopped, turning his head until his chin was aligned with his shoulder. He looked sheepishly at Delbert. "I ran outta gas."

After a brief moment, both men laughed.

Delbert turned the horse's head. When the wagon was redirected, Delbert patted the wooden seat. "Hop on up here, boy."

During the creaky ride, Delbert allowed Claude to do all of the talking.

"I knew I was suckin' near empty last night when I drove home. I was gonna fill the tank this morning, but the fight I had with May knocked me needing gas right out of my head. I had enough to get to work, but I didn't have enough to get home again.

You're not going to believe this, Del, but my truck is parked in the shade of three wells and there is not a drop of gas for miles."

"You had a fight with May Rose?"

Claude leaned back against the seat, looked without interest at the slowly passing terrain. "Sorta. I was all set for a fight, but she wouldn't fight. That's not like May at all. Usually she's a real good fighter. Today she wouldn't say hardly nothing. An' she was kinda cheerful too. It was real spooky."

"What were you wantin' to fight with her about?"

Agitated, Claude sat up, leaned forward, resting his arms on his knees. "About her locking me out of the house last night. That woman's gone plain crazy. When I said I'd leave her if she ever did that again, she said, fine. She even offered me a cup of coffee before I went. So then I got to thinkin' maybe she wanted me to go, so I said she couldn't make me, that it was my house. She said that was okay too as long as I remembered supper was at six and the doors were locked at eight. Can you believe that? I'm telling you, Del, she's gone crazy."

"No, she hasn't."

Claude sent Delbert a murderous look. Delbert merely smiled.

"Listen to me, boy," Delbert said mildly, "that little woman of yours has got a lot on her plate. She's chasing after two baby boys and building another baby inside her belly. What she doesn't need is to be hearing the tales goin' around town about you and a certain Miss Dixie. She certainly doesn't need to lay awake at night wonderin' when you're gonna decide to roll in. Seems to me that settin' down a few house rules is real reasonable."

Fuming, Claude scowled at Delbert. Delbert went on regardless.

"I'm gonna tell you something that you should take straight to your heart. There's a bunch of men around these parts just waitin' for May Rose to come to her senses and show you the gate. It don't matter to none of 'em that takin' on your babies will be part of the deal, because they all know that May Rose is worth the trouble. She's a fine woman, an' being married to a no-good like you, she's shown everybody what she's made of. During the whole time you've been runnin', May Rose has held her head high. A woman like that is more valuable than all the oil in the world, an' if you don't know it, then more fool you. Like I said, there's plenty who do know it, an' they're waitin'."

"May Rose would never take another man over me!"

Delbert snorted a laugh. "Yes, she would. If she's toed her last line in the sand, sounds to me like she's fixin' to do just that. You cross that line like you've crossed all the others, an' you're as good as gone. That's why she didn't fight with you this mornin', Claude. She must have figured out that you ain't worth the effort. So you just go ahead on an' be a fool if you wanna be. May Rose will divorce you, an' then pretty soon all your young'uns'll be callin' some other man Daddy. You can bet your boots whoever he might be, his feet will be right under her supper table come six on the dot 'cause he won't be stupid."

Claude began to gnaw the cuticle of his thumb. After a few minutes of stewing, horribly imagining *his* May Rose with another man, he yelped, "Delbert! Can't this old horse go any faster?"

May Rose was at the stove frying chicken in a skillet. Matt was underneath the kitchen table playing fort. There was no sign of Jake. The playpen in the corner was empty. When Claude entered, May Rose turned her head, looked at him briefly. Her heart was making a racket in her chest, and she could feel it thumping against her ribs as he set his lunch bucket on the work counter.

"I ran outta gas," he said lamely. "I ain't late, am I?"

"No," she said softly. "Supper won't be ready for another five minutes."

Claude ran his hand through his hair as he desperately thought of something else to say. "Uh, where's Jakey? How come he ain't in his pen?"

May Rose turned a piece of chicken in the bubbling cooking oil. "A wise person told me that little boys need to run."

"Yeah," Claude said. "I guess they do."

May Rose looked back at him. Claude offered her an embarrassed half smile.

"An' I guess grown men need to come home where they belong, right, May?"

"Yes, Claude. That's exactly right. You have just enough time to wash up before supper."

He quickly kissed her cheek and went to the sink.

Chapter Four

Having missed the final months of his wife's previous pregnancies, Claude was appalled by how huge she could grow and how this vast amount of weight slowed her down, made her tried and irritable. Making love was also out of the question. A firm believer in the myth that a man had to have sex at least once a day or he would become seriously ill, Claude suffered through May's ninth month certain that every disease known to God was about to strike him down. Then came the night she poked her finger rapidly into his bare shoulder, forcing him awake.

"Claude," she rasped. "Call my momma. Tell her it's time."

"May? It can't be more than three in the morning."

"I know what time it is, Claude. I've got the clock in my hand. Call my momma or you'll be delivering this baby right by yourself."

Completely awake, Claude scrambled out of the bed.

He was in a panic when the car pulled into the drive and three women crawled out. Within minutes of their arrival, every light in the house was on, and he was consigned to the porch. At first he was angry that his house had been taken over and that not one of those women was concerned about him, that maybe he needed a cup of coffee or something. Then he heard May Rose scream and his blood turned ice-cold.

"Call my husband," Mona Fallen Hawk said to the youngest woman. "Tell him to come and fetch the baby boys. This is going to be a long delivery. Matt and Jakey shouldn't be here."

"Should I say for him to take Claude too?"

"No," Mona answered sharply. "It's about time that man heard just what my daughter has to go through to give him children."

May Rose's screams were lifting the roof off the house by the time Walt Fallen Hawk drove up. Claude was so happy to see another male, even if it was his hateful father-in-law, that he was tempted to hug him. Walt did not give Claude a chance for any type of emotional display. When Walt was met at the door by the young woman, handing over the two very frightened little boys, Walt took them and left the porch, passing Claude as if his son-in-law did not exist. Then Walt drove off with his grandsons, leaving Claude choking in a cloud of brown dust and the sound of May Rose's screaming voice accusing him of being the sole cause of every vile act the male species has ever inflicted on womankind. When finally he heard a baby cry, he was so relieved he felt ready to faint. He would have, had not the sounds of May Rose's tortured screams begun all over again.

Mona held her daughter's shoulders while the midwife, Thelma, worked between May Rose's legs. "There's another one."

"Noooooo!"

"May Rose," Thelma said over her scream, "you got to bear down again."

"Nooo! I don't want another baby."

"Well, you got another one whether you want it or not, an' if you don't push for me, it's gonna tear you up gettin' itself out."

"Do what Thelma says, May." Mona wiped sweat from her laboring daughter's face. "An' you yell, honey. You yell good an' loud, 'cause this time that man of yours can hear you. He can hear every bit of what you're sufferin'."

May Rose yelled so loudly that Claude's trembling knees finally gave out, and he landed inelegantly on his backside.

By midafternoon Claude was summoned, and he entered the quiet house fearfully, slinking behind his mother-in-law like a whipped puppy. In their bedroom, the windows open to air out the musty, coppery smell of blood, May Rose was asleep in the freshly made bed. Mona led him to the dresser, and he saw two dark-haired little wads squirming inside a blanket-padded drawer.

"*Two* boys this time," Mona said with a frown. "Seems to me you could try givin' her a girl baby."

Claude nervously cleared his throat and spoke in a whisper. "Rainwaters only know how to make boy babies."

Mona made a disagreeable noise. "I wish you'd told her that before you married her. It might have got her to change her mind."

The first three weeks of his newly born sons' lives were bliss for their mother, an unqualified hell for

71

their father. The babies, named Walter and Wilber, were identical and a handful. Mona Fallen Hawk moved in to help out with the older boys while May Rose stayed in bed and nursed her babies. Other women were always coming in and going out of the house at all hours of the day and night. Claude was glad to go to work, but coming home in the evenings he felt displaced. He was even made to sleep on a pallet out on the back porch. One evening he came home to find his father-in-law and his brothers-in-law hauling lumber. He stopped his brother-in-law Danny.

"What's going on?"

"We're gonna build a new room for the twins."

Claude felt dismissed as Danny walked away and all of the men got on with the new construction. Now not only was he an intruder inside the house, he wasn't wanted on the outside either. Claude did what he did best. He ran to May Rose.

"Tell 'em to go home, May," he whined.

"No."

"But I can't live in this house with so many people tromping around."

May Rose looked at his crestfallen face, the face she loved, the face that always made her melt inside, caused her to yield to his overpowering physical attraction. Well, she couldn't this time; it was still too soon after a very hard birth. And for that she was grateful. During the course of making love, Claude had the ability to make her agree to most anything.

"Claude," she said firmly, "I need my family. You need them too. If Momma wasn't here, you wouldn't have any supper to eat. If Daddy and my brothers weren't here to build the extra room, you'd find yourself sleeping with me and the twins. You know you need to eat and you know you need almost the whole bed to sleep in, so you're going to have to put up with the inconvenience for a while. You can do it, Claude. I know deep down that you're a strong person."

"But I miss you, Muffin."

"I miss you too. Here, hold one of the twins."

Claude took one of the squirming babies. "Which one is it?"

May Rose settled the other baby at her engorged breast. Claude watched the nursing newborn with an expression of pure envy. "That's Wilber and this is Walt. I think."

Looking at the baby in his arms, Claude's mouth turned in a frown. "I think maybe we should brand them on the butt so we'll know for sure."

"No, Claude, that's not a good idea."

By the time the twins entered their second year of life and were toddling, May Rose lived to regret her words. The little boys looked so alike that even she had a terrible time knowing just who was who. The twins learned to answer to "Walt-Wil."

In the spring of 1928, Claude humored May Rose's father, even went along when Walt Fallen Hawk drove his oldest grandsons to the powwow in Pawhuska. As it was a three-day event, they lived in a tent. Jake ran helter-skelter all over the big field crowded with hundreds of people. He was perfectly safe, and neither his grandfather nor his father worried about him as he tagged after the dancers in full ceremonial dress. Matt wasn't as daring. He remained close to his father. Therefore, Matt was the only son to hear Claude say under his breath, "This old-timey stuff is gone. It's time these guys got wise and faced it."

That was the last good summer the Osage Nation would know for a very long time. With the advent of the Depression in 1929, the price of oil fell from ten dollars a barrel to thirty-five cents a barrel. The Osage Nation woke up one morning to find itself broke as working wells were capped and small oil companies disappeared, never to be heard from again. Within a few months company towns were deserted, became ghost towns. Somehow, Claude remained on the payroll but at a third less than what he previously earned. A few months later her father appeared on May's doorstep, tears like rain spilling down his face. He handed her a ream of documents.

"This ain't worth nothin', May," he said, tears nearly strangling his voice. "All these here stocks, all the money it took to buy 'em, none of it ain't worth nothing no more. I'm sorry. Please forgive me."

Six months later, her father, his pride and spirit completely broken, was dead. His passing left such an incredible emptiness inside her and numbed her so completely that for a month after his funeral she had to remind herself when to inhale, when to exhale. Her mother, unable to remain in the empty house, moved away, went to live with Aunt Bess in Wynona.

Urainia was a town that had grown up on the site of an Osage clan village of less than a dozen lodges. With the discovery of oil, Urainia exploded, became ostentatiously prosperous. During the first year and a half of the Depression, Urainia imploded. Only the businesses absolutely essential to everyday life and able to turn a skimpy profit survived. One by one, her brothers and their families left the area. When the last brother was gone, May Rose knew what it was to be truly alone. It was as if the early years of her marriage had prepared her for exactly what she now faced. Digging deep, she found the strength she needed to make Claude and their children her complete family.

The Depression worsened. Day after day her singular ambition was to keep good food, from her gardening and livestock management, on the table. Both endeavors required long hours of grueling labor. Playtime was effectively finished for Matt and Jake. May Rose had no choice but to induct them into the daily routine of farming chores and looking out for Walt and Wil. During the next two years she lulled herself into the belief that she and her family could cope, that nothing could possibly get worse. Then the strong nature of Oklahoma's incessant prairie winds proved her wrong. And Hell had a new name.

The Dust Bowl.

The dirt storms were called "Rollers" because that was exactly what the massive storms did. They rolled in unstoppable black waves of topsoil across the entire state, choking people to death, burying them in their homes. During the storms May Rose set her boys to soaking flour sacks, then hurrying the dripping sacks to her, where she hung the sacks over windows and pushed them into any and all cracks. Within minutes the sacks had to be replaced because the hanging sacks over the closed windows would fall from the weight of the blackness that seeped through. And all the time they worked in tandem, May Rose did not allow herself to think about

Claude, that he was out somewhere in the worst of it, either rescuing people trapped in their cars or homes or out trying to keep the few working well pumps going.

May Rose now had one burning ambition, to keep her sons and the untimely new life growing inside her alive. She couldn't think about anything else. She did not even allow herself to grieve for Delbert or think about the way he had been swamped by a roller while traveling in his old wagon. The bolting horse had flipped the wagon, and Delbert had been trapped underneath. He had been dead for almost a week when someone spotted the top rims of the wagon wheels in a mound of dirt. The mound was so high that it looked like a new hill had grown up in the road.

She missed Delbert, missed his friendship and his wise counsel, but she could not grieve for him. Not now. Not while she had to fight for clean air for her babies to breathe. Like an automaton, May Rose soaked and hung flour sacks over the windows, soaked and hung flour sacks over the windows. Day after day. Week after week. Month after month.

When her pregnancy progressed, Matt and Claude did the milking for her. Weak from near starvation and overwork and hampered as she was by her bulk, there was no way she could battle the weather to get to the shelter of the barn, where the cow and chickens had to remain shut inside. Claude had a guide rope tied from the back porch to the barn, and on some days when the dirt was too thick to see through, only by hanging onto the flapping rope could he get from one place to the other. He made certain that when Matt was with him, his son stayed a pace ahead so that he could grab him if Matt fell down. It was on such a day, as they battled to bring the milk can and the few eggs the hens had produced inside the house, that a frantic Jake met them at the back door.

"Daddy!" Jake shouted. Claude could barely hear him, Jake's terrified voice was being ripped away with the winds. "Daddy! Momma's hurtin' bad. She's bleeding!"

Kneeling by the side of the bed, holding her hand and stroking it, Claude stammered, "Oh, sweet Jesus, May. Muffin? Please don't do this now."

May Rose pulled herself up slightly. "Claude, you've got to help me. This baby is comin'."

"Could you tell it not to?"

"Claude!" she yelled. Then another contraction seized her. Only when it began to ease slightly could she speak again. Panting, her face shiny with sweat and dark from the dirt leaking into the room, she said as patiently as she could, "Honey, get some towels, the scissors, and some string. Tell the boys to keep soaking sacks and puttin' them over the windows. That'll keep them busy while me an' you deliver this baby."

"What?"

"Claude, if you don't help me, I swear to God I'll reach down your idiot throat an' pull your liver out with my bare hands!"

May Rose panted like a dog. "Look and tell me if you see the head."

This was the most horrible situation Claude could ever imagine. And it just kept getting worse. "May," he said, his voice a high vibrato, "you know I'm not one to go lookin' at womanly doo-dads. Please don't make me look at that stuff now."

Her bulbous body naked, she pushed herself up and sat in the middle of the bed with her arms braced behind her. Her legs were bent at the knees and widely spread. Her long hair was loose, washing over her shoulders and down her back, but mostly her hair shielded her face. Behind the hair, May Rose's expressions changed rapidly as she passed through several layers of agony.

"You gotta look, Claude!"

Claude was afraid to see a head. He moved cautiously from the side of the bed to the foot. He just knew that if he saw a little head and a pair of eyes looking at him from out of May Rose's uh-huh, he would scream and claw his way clean through the closed bedroom door. At the foot of the bed, after seeing only what he was, May Rose's sorta normal stuff, he put a hand to his heart and took a deep, relieved breath.

"Tell me what you see," she said, her tone strangled.

"All there is is a squished hairy thing."

"That's the head." She panted like a dog for a long moment. "Claude, get ready. I'm going to push again."

"Do you have to?"

Wishing she could get her hands on his throat, May Rose pushed with all the strength she had in her.

The baby wasn't breathing. The bloody little body lay limply in his hand. Claude quickly looked up into May Rose's anxious face. She began to cry. Hurt and frustration building inside him, Claude grabbed hold of the tiny ankles, held the baby upside down, and slapped it hard on the back. The baby coughed. Claude hit the back of the lungs again, and the baby howled. He wanted to laugh and cry all in the same moment. "May! It's another boy! I've got me another little boy."

Relieved that Claude had done it, that he had actually seen her through this crisis, she collapsed against the pillows.

The baby, Allen John, had to be watched over all the time. His brothers, Matt and Jake, took turns guarding him, keeping his cot covered with dampened blankets so that the dust couldn't get into his tiny lungs. Jake was also responsible for the face masks the twins wore to protect their lungs. Like little ducks, the twins bonded with Jake, following him around, always under his feet. Jake didn't mind. He was also the only one able to tell them apart. He absently corrected anyone he heard addressing the twins incorrectly.

"Wilbur!" May Rose scolded. "How many times—"

"Walt, Momma. That's Walt."

"Walt," she immediately amended, "how many times do I have to tell you . . ."

One bright morning May Rose woke up without dust on her face or grit covering the bed covers. Miraculously, the Dust Bowl was over. But the Depression was still with them and remained a firm way of life while May Rose, and the rest of the state of Oklahoma, struggled hopefully forward.

The "kid wagon" was the term used for the canvas-covered horse-drawn wagon that came by the

house to take Matt and Jake to Urainia elementary
school. Two years later, Walt and Wil were on the
wagon going to school too. It was a mixed school,
but the classrooms held more full-blood or mixed-
blood Osage children than white. Because of the Dust
Bowl, many of the white families had departed the
state. Matt and Jake grew up having no idea that in
other states in America, it wasn't such a good thing
to be an Indian. The fact that they were Indians was
never discussed. It was simply a thing they were,
the same way Matt's best friend, Mikey O'Brian, was
second-generation Irish. But the thing that fascinated
Jake about Mikey was his shock of orange-red hair.
Jake always wanted to touch it, and Mikey always
cut up rough whenever Jake did.

"Guys don't touch other guys' hair."

"Why not?"

" 'Cause, you dope, they just don't. If you want to
touch red hair, then you got to touch red *girl* hair."

"Oh."

Jake hoped that a red-haired girl would eventually
crop up, but one never did. All he saw in school
were plain old dark-haired and blond-haired girls.
Jake was never tempted to touch their hair. Nor was
he especially tempted to study hard the way his
brother Matt did. This lackluster attitude inevitably
found him out.

"An F!" May Rose cried. She looked at Jake's report card again, barely able to read the damning
grade swimming before her eyes. Mad as a wet hen,
May Rose grabbed her coat and drove to the school
to have words with Jake's teacher.

Mr. Lawson was an affable man. He sat quietly at
his desk and endured Mrs. Rainwater's ranting. He

didn't even blink when she thrust the report card in his face. When she eventually was quiet, he spoke.

"Miz Rainwater, I'm afraid your son Jake is never gonna be a genius. But, I'll tell you one thing about your son, he's got himself a million-dollar personality. Now, your son Matt is a good, serious student. He'll go far, but for all his hard work he'll never be able to buy his way out of a brown paper bag on the strength of his personality. What you got to realize is that your boys are completely different. You can't expect one to do just like the other. Having been the teacher for both boys, I can tell you for a fact that Matt can be counted on to work as hard as a Trojan, and Jake can be counted on to keep the classroom from gettin' bored. Even if I did have to fail him at math, he's been the most fun kid I've ever had in my career. With or without mathematical abilities, I can guarantee you your Jake is going to be all right. He'll make it through life slicker than goose grease because folks can't help but like him."

Allen was such a dour little boy. And he pitched fits. May Rose learned to ignore him. Then Allen changed tactics. He started holding his breath until he went blue in the face. This won him his mother's attention, and she was forced to hold him while he kicked, screamed, spat, and tried to bite. By the time he was five, she couldn't stand any more of his physical abuse. The next time he threw a fit and held his breath, she let him pass out. Then she threw water in his face to revive him. Allen sputtered back to life and screamed his hatred. When he realized how deeply that wounded her, and how much easier it had been that holding his breath, Allen screamed his hatred whenever the mood took him. May Rose came to dread being alone in the house with Allen. One fall morning he was in the process of working himself into another one of his famous fits when May Rose distracted him.

"Honey boy? Some chicks are hatching in the barn. Don't you want to see the baby chickens comin' out of their eggs?"

Allen stopped mid-scream, canting his head, his dark little eyes glittering with the tears that he could either let fall or draw back, according to his whim. He drew this crop back and accepted her hand. Bundled up against the chilly fall air, they trooped out to the barn.

Claude had installed an electric hatchery so that May Rose could enlarge the number of her flock. Under the bright warming light, eggs ready to hatch moved, appeared to be breathing. Allen watched intently the laborious process of an egg beginning to crack. It took a very long time for the chick to make its tiny way into the world, but Allen was patient. He didn't move a muscle. He waited. May Rose left him to this fascination as she milked the cow, poured the milk from the bucket into the protective can, turned the cow out of the barn to browse in the field. All of this took about a half hour. When she came back to Allen, he held out his hand. In his palm was a dead chick.

"Ooops," he giggled. "I broke the baby."

A coldness gripped her heart as she looked from the dead chick to her giggling son. She couldn't fathom which upset her more, that he had actually waited for that chick to hatch in order to pinch its neck hard enough to break it, or that he felt no re-morse for having killed a helpless creature.

None of her other sons actually said so, but the older Allen grew, the more they disliked him. Some-times, especially when she remembered his gleeful little face when showing her the dead chick, she didn't like him very much herself. And on these occa-sions she felt horribly guilty. Jake, secretly her favor-ite child, she no longer worried about. She had never worried about Matt. She couldn't even bring herself to worry about Walt and Wilber even though the twins at times were a law unto themselves. But she worried constantly about Allen. Especially after he started school and was home for bad behavior more school days than he attended. May Rose made ex-cuses for him, defended him to the teeth. But in her heart she knew that the teachers were right about Allen. She also knew that when they said he was a "disruptive influence," they were trying to be kind.

The years passed. May Rose's mother died. She and Claude drove to Wynona to escort Mona Fallen Hawk's body back to Urainia. She was buried next to her husband, Walt. Standing by the new grave, after everyone else had gone, May Rose felt like an orphan. It was the most awful feeling in the world. Then she felt a hand take hers. She looked to the side, and there was her tall, adolescent Jake. When their eyes met, she knew he sensed exactly what she was feeling.

"It's all right, Momma. I promise, I'll never go away."

She squeezed his hand and with tears in her voice said, "Thank you, Jakey."

* * *

The Depression was on the wane. President Roosevelt was elected for a third term. A minor prosperity began to emerge in Oklahoma as oil regained lost ground. The people protesting around the capitol building these days were folks determined that America not be drawn into the war in Europe. It was a time of America for Americans—period. And there were many a heated debate over at the feed and grain store on that very subject. The Isolationist folks wanted to know where the Europeans had been when America was going through all its rough times. The more worldly countered that if Hitler wasn't stopped in Europe, he'd come across the ocean. That sooner or later Hitler had to be stopped. Being Oklahomans, they voted Sooner.

Fistfights broke out at the feed and grain.

May Rose was scandalized by the way folks were beginning to behave, but she didn't have much time to dwell on the matter. Her sons were becoming young men. Their attitudes, along with their bodies, were changing. All of her sons were wonderfully good-looking, but teenage Jake was a wonderfully good-looking rascal. The telephone always rang for Jake, and when May Rose answered, she heard giggly girls on the end of the line. May Rose thought that was shameful, girls calling up a boy. But she said nothing. After all, she had been a girl once. A girl who had gone so far as to track down the boy she wanted and trap him in a barn. Nevertheless, she still disapproved of so many girls calling up her Jakey. And he had so many girlfriends that he had to write the name of his date on the palm of his hand so he wouldn't forget who he was with during the evening.

Matt was more settled, going around with a girl from just up the road. A nice girl called Irma Greybird. Irma never called Matt. She waited for Matt to call her. May Rose heartily approved of that. She approved even more that Irma's mother insisted that Matt and Irma take Irma's little sister Lucy along when they went to the movies. Matt said Lucy was a pushy brat, that he hated her. But as big and as lusty-looking as Matt was growing up to be, May Rose could well understand just why Irma's mother wanted little Lucy kept between the courting couple.

The twins as yet weren't interested in girls. They liked playing football and pounding other football players into the ground. Claude and May Rose always went to the games, although May Rose hid her eyes behind her hand during all of that tackling business. She was certain that when the dust cleared, either Walt or Wilber would be under the pile of young male bodies with a broken leg.

Allen was still giving her trouble because he was always *in* trouble. But he'd branched out, no longer content simply to be in trouble at school. He was now getting into trouble in town. Allen stole. Allen drank. Allen also tried to beat a woman at the U-Know. He'd swaggered into the bar, told a particular woman that he had five dollars. The woman laughed in his face, told him he was too young. To prove he wasn't, Allen knocked her down. The other men had to pull him off before he hurt her. Now it was said the woman slept with a loaded gun in case Allen tried to visit her again. Someone said that he was *all* Rainwater. He was. Even though Claude himself forbade it, Allen ran with his wild Rainwater cousins. Then came the day he was arrested for running moonshine with his cousins. Because they were older, the cousins went straight to jail. Being underage, Allen was sent off to do six months in the juvenile-offenders home. Those were the most peaceful six months his family had known since his birth. All hope that he had learned his lesson dwindled like dew on a hot morning when he arrived home and within minutes was sent to his room for cussing out his mother. Allen slithered out his bedroom window, stole his father's truck, and was gone for over a week. Claude wanted to report it, have him picked up again. May Rose simply couldn't face another disgrace. The family waited, and finally Allen showed up. Without a word of apology or an explanation, he went to bed and slept for the next three days. When he woke up, May Rose drove him to school and enrolled him. Surprisingly, he stayed out of serious trouble. As a reward for this better behavior, the family pretended he wasn't there. Which was exactly what he wanted.

In the spring of 1940, Claude bought May Rose a brand-new Packard. In that same year fists started flying between her sons. Matt habitually threw Jake out of their shared bedroom because he wanted to study and Jake wouldn't stop making noise. Jake retaliated, and of course the twins came in on Jake's side. When Allen jumped into the fray, everyone would stop fighting each other and take on Allen. They had to. Allen loved to fight, and he didn't seem to feel any pain. Added to this bliss was the over-abundance of male odors permeating the air, assaulting May Rose's sensitive female nose. Clearly, her growing boys needed more space in which to grow.

Claude hired a contractor to add two additional bedrooms and a much needed second bathroom to the house. The enlarged house was treated to an expanded back porch, which was fine with May Rose. She needed more shelves to accommodate her wealth of canning jars. When the new bedrooms were complete, Matt claimed the biggest room, and Jake happily helped him move into it. The twins voted Allen out of the bedroom the three had been sharing together. Allen gladly took over the smaller back room. May Rose was a bit grieved by this. She had nursed the vague hope that after all of these years she would finally have a quiet little sewing room, a womanly bolt hole, a place where she could hide and lock the door against the too many males demanding her attention.

A couple of weeks before Christmas in 1941, Claude surprised the family with a big new radio. He had been too happy about the surprise to wait for Christmas. The radio was delivered and set up in the living room. Claude did the honors of plugging it in and switching it on. The very first program the Rainwaters heard on the big floor-model, genuine mahogany case RCA radio was President Roosevelt's emotion wreaked voice.

"Yesterday, on December seventh, 1941, a date that will live in infamy, the United States was attacked by the Japanese at Pearl Harbor. . . . I now declare that a state of war exists between the United States and the country of Japan."

May Rose's legs went out from under her. She fell heavily into a wing-back chair, placed a hand on her

87

chest, and felt the rampant thudding of her heart. Blood whirled in her ears, partially drowning out the oaths of vengeance her husband and her sons shouted at the radio.

"Oh, dear Jesus," she whispered. The Isolationists had lost the battle to stay out of the world conflict. Now a needy nation would come for her boys.

Chapter Five

1942

May Rose had not seen Matt in ten months. But she couldn't cry about that now, not on Jake's last night home. Jake had come home on a two-week furlough from his training base in North Carolina. He was a qualified paratrooper now. A young soldier who jumped out of airplanes. The very idea of him doing something like that terrified the life out of her, for this form of combat combined both her worst fears. One, being in a flying airplane. Two, leaping out of a flying airplane.

Tomorrow, he would board the train for New Jersey, and there he'd board a ship for England. She glanced up from her continual knitting, her eyes tearing as she fixed on him. He sat near the radio on the other side of the living room next to Claude. Off to the side sat Walt and Wilber. May Rose was thankful that the twins were barely seventeen. Because they were still so young and had two brothers already in the military, they had been turned down when they'd tried to enlist. Feeling as though they still needed to contribute to the war effort, the twins had dropped out of school, had gone to work in the oil fields to help produce the badly needed fuel that would keep the airplanes flying, the tanks rolling. There was an ugly rumor that the day the twins quit school the faculty threw a party. May Rose knew that if this was true, the teachers weren't celebrating because the twins were bad boys, but because they were so identical. The twins tended to use this as a weapon when pulling harmless pranks. Allen, seated behind his twin brothers, tall and grown-up-looking though he was, was only fourteen, far too young for the draft, far too young to work in the fields. Neither he nor his teachers liked it very much that he had to remain in school.

She put her knitting aside, lowering her head, hiding her face behind a hand as she wept quietly. She missed Matt, worried about him. Now she would spend her nights on her knees praying for Jake the same way she prayed for Matt. If she only knew exactly where Matt was, it might help her nerves. Matt was a Marine. All the Marine Corps would tell them was that their son was doing his duty in the Pacific.

She was pulled from her thoughts by the sound of Jake's laughter. He was laughing at the jokes coming from the standing radio. Jokes being told on the George Burns and Gracie Allen show. May Rose couldn't find one thing funny about Gracie Allen. And she didn't understand George Burns at all. How could a man put up with such a stupid woman?

The show ended, all of the Rainwater men clapping their hands and laughing. Then there came a news brief concerning the war. Everyone, especially May Rose, leaned forward in their seats. The news was giving a report on the Pacific front.

Matt was in the Pacific.

May Rose twisted her hands as she listened to the sketchy update, this report more about the Navy— *Matt's a Marine. When are they going to talk about the Marines?*

As she listened she stared at Jake's profile. *He is so beautiful. He's the most beautiful boy you gave me,* May Rose mentally said to God. *Please, please don't let anything happen to my beautiful boy. Please bring him home to me, safe and whole.*

Jake turned on the ottoman, spoke to his mother. "Did Matt's last letter say the name of any nearby country the Navy ship he was on was maybe passing?"

"There was something," she said, clearing her voice of tears, "but it was under a lot of black lines. I couldn't read through the black."

Jake nodded, turned again to the radio, spoke lowly to his father. "All letters get screened by the censor department. Anything they think is too sensitive, they black it out."

Claude twisted his lips to the side. "So the Marines don't want us to know where they took our Matt."

"No."

"But he's my boy. Doesn't his own father have a right to know where he is?"

"No."

"Well, that's a hell of a way to run a war."

"It's modern warfare, Dad."

"Yeah? Well, it sucks eggs to me. My grandfather used to tell me about the old-timey wars he remembered. Osage warriors used to go right up to the village of an enemy and say, 'Come out and fight.'

Then the enemy would, and they would fight until the sun went down."

Very interested in what his father was saying, Jake asked, "Was that because they were afraid their spirits would get lost if they died in the dark?"

Claude chuckled. "Well, that sounds good, but actually they quit because they couldn't see. It was better to get a good night's sleep and wait for the sun to come up so a warrior could be sure he was fighting the right man." The younger generation of Rainwater men hooted in laughter. Claude looked askance at his group of sons. "You puppies got any better ideas on how it should have been done?"

The boys stopped laughing, each silently trying to puzzle out the trials of early combat.

"Nope," Walt finally said. "The way they did it in the old days sounds pretty good to me."

"Me too," Wilber immediately added.

"I'd have used the dark to sneak up on the enemy," Allen said with a leering smile. "Then I'd have killed them while *they* were sleeping."

Claude and his remaining three sons looked away. A heavy, uncomfortable silence ruled as everyone listened to the radio.

The Marines had doubled Matt's bulk. Boot camp had been hard, the drill sergeants screaming madmen. Matt could take the hard physical training, the men yelling profanities in his face. What he couldn't understand was why he and other non-whites were treated so differently, segregated off into separate Quonset huts. The white Marines were billeted on one side of the parade ground, the coloreds on the other. Only on the parade ground or during field

Rainwater on the White Road

training were the platoons mixed. At chow time, the whites ate first, then came the Indians and the Mexicans, then the Negroes. He and his childhood friend, Mikey O'Brian, had joined the Marines together and had promised to stay together no matter what. Five minutes after their arrival in South Carolina, they were separated. For the six weeks they were there, Matt rarely saw Mikey; then they were separated completely when Mikey's platoon was sent out first. Mikey never wrote to him.

The Marine Corps was Matt's first taste of prejudice, just as the Army was Jake's. Jake used to write to him all the time from his boot camp base, and from the tone of his letters, he was going through the same thing, except that in the Army there were more Indians and Jake had lots of friends. Matt wasn't very good at turning a stranger into a friend, he never had been. Matt retreated into himself, worked hard, hid his feelings. This was something he did very well.

Far away in the Rainwater living room, the radio began playing, "I've got a girl in Kalamazoo." This was the very same tune Matt hummed softly as he stalked the jungles of a far-flung island in the Pacific so small it wasn't even on the map.

Matt was a forward scout. It was another sunny day in paradise. With air so humid it was liquid. There wasn't a dry patch to be found anywhere on Matt's entire body. The jungle was a thick and dangerous lush green. And the Japanese were in the palm trees, squatting on platforms, aiming machine guns on the slowly advancing troop of Marines.

Now that the Japanese were the defenders of the islands instead of the invaders, their tactics had

93

changed dramatically. Every tree, every bush, was a potential booby trap. Not even the jungle floor could be trusted to be what it appeared. Too often Marine units had been gunned down when the ground suddenly opened up, trapdoors covered with dirt and living plants flinging back, the emerging Japanese firing steady streams of bullets, striking their marks.

The Japanese during World War II gave birth to what would be commonly known during the 1960s and 1970s as guerilla warfare. Early 1940s Marine basic training hadn't prepared the troops for this type of fighting. For the first two and a half years in the Pacific, the Marines were chewed up like raw meat.

If there are any fanciful notions about World War II, the Pacific theater held none of them. The Marines didn't have a pistol-packing Patton to follow into the bowels of war. And when George Patton was heard to declare of the world conflict, "I love this. God help me, I love this war," it was because he hadn't a clue about the Pacific. Chasing Rommel with a tank was a long chalk from crawling around on one's belly through a jungle alive with Japanese, mosquitoes, and leeches.

There was a corporal in Matt's unit that loved to call him "Indian." The entire time they had been on the troop ship, Corporal Bliss called him that. It was meant as an insult, and Matt was fully aware that Bliss was trying to lure him into a fight. It was pretty dull on the ship most days, and Bliss liked to fight when he was bored. Matt was close to Bliss's considerable size and weight. Bliss ached to fight Matt. Only after they had set down on their first island did Bliss suddenly reverse his opinion and put it around that Indians could "see things." In this case, the Japanese. Bliss became Matt's unwelcome companion, still calling him Indian, but staying close to Matt's side. On that first island the Marines had fought a hard battle, neutralized the enemy, secured the island for the Navy Seabees. Matt had led the forward assault, Bliss right behind him. A lot of good men died on that sand hill in the ocean, but Matt and Bliss walked way without a scratch. Bliss stopped calling Matt Indian. Matt's new name was "Lucky Ticket."

"We're going to be pals, Rainwater," Bliss said, a cigarette dangling from the corner of his mouth. "Yep, as long as I stick with my lucky ticket, I'll be home in no time, and showing a certain little number back in Saint Paul just how much muscle the Marines built between my legs. Man, when I ram into her, she'll do some real squealing."

Matt hated Corporal Bliss, and he felt intensely sorry for Bliss's certain little number. He needn't have bothered, for on this day, and on this island, Bliss's faith in his lucky ticket vanished without a trace. The Japanese in the trees hit Matt's unit without mercy. The treetops poured down death like heavy rain. Matt belly-flopped to the ground, but Bliss just stood there, looking scared out of his mind and too stupid to drop as he had been trained to do. Seven bullets struck him in quick succession in the face, turning his surprised features into a bloody mush. Matt quickly scrambled away as Bliss melted to his knees and then fell forward, as dead as a door knocker.

Bullets were still pouring down as the unit tried to take cover. But there was no cover from the Japanese in the trees. Marines were picked off, and the few to survive were pinned down. From his low-crawl vantage point, and daring to lift his head, Matt peered out from beneath his helmet and saw the radio man. He could hear him screaming incoherently for help, could see the blood pouring from the radio man's mouth all over the field mike. Then the radio man died, and white static sounded. Matt knew he had to get to that radio, give the following unit their detailed coordinates. Thinking only of that, Matt started crawling.

Halfway to his goal, Matt took six rounds in the left leg. He let go a piercing scream as his knee and shin were splintered. Trapped out in the open, all he could do was lie on his back and fire his rifle. And as the pain burned away everything except his sense of survival, he kept on firing.

Time had no meaning. He could have been out in the open and on his own for seconds, minutes, hours. The importance of actual time drifted away as Matt began to weaken from excessive blood loss. He vaguely remembered groping for a machine gun that fell out of the sky, missing his body by a few inches. The gun had been like manna from heaven. He remembered engaging the weapon, then there was no memory whatsoever.

He awoke to find himself on a stretcher. Two medics toted it, and a third walked beside him, carrying a bag of blood with a snaking tube secured into the bottom of it. Matt lifted his head, fuzzily looking around. He saw that the tube was connected to his arm, the needle in his vein hidden by cotton bandages. His leg throbbed with white-hot pain, making him even dizzier.

The Navy medic walking beside Matt wore a helmet, no shirt, Marine fatigues slung on narrow hips.

Dog tags hanging around the medic's neck reflected and winked shafts of sunlight. As Matt lay back down, the medic noticed the movement.

"Hey!" he half laughed, a cigarette bobbing in his mouth. "The hero's awake!"

The forward stretcher bearer looked back over his bare, sunburned shoulder, his head twisting inside the oversized helmet. "Hang in there, buddy." The bearer smiled. "You're homeward bound. And with that fat medal you're sure to get, back in stateside, you'll be up to your armpits in pussy. Them USO babes love men with medals. Yes, sir," the medic grunted, hefting the stretcher bars, getting a better grip, "you got yourself something to look forward to. Man oh man, if I could just trade places with you, would my pecker be happy."

Matt blacked out.

Navy medics might be a lot of things, but they weren't liars. It didn't take long before it was well known all over the medical ship that they had a "Congress-Med" aboard. World War II terminology for Congressional Medal of Honor candidate.

The only one unaware of this singular honor was Matt. He was in and out of consciousness erratically, his mind flying high on morphine. He remained doped and groggy during the week it took the ship to sail to Pearl Harbor. From the ship he was transported to the naval hospital.

In the hospital they cut the medication in half following the first series of operations. The doctors were doing everything humanly possible to save his leg, and the nurses were doing everything possible to care for Matt. He was in a private room and completely at the mercy of the special attentions the nurses offered. He was known among them as "the dream man." Not only was he a hero, he was also the finest specimen of manhood any of them had ever seen. They could not keep their hands off him. During daylight hours Matt had more sponge baths than any patient in history. The nights held a special terror, and with his leg in traction, he was helpless.

One nurse in particular made him squeamish. She always came in about one or two in the morning. Because the room was dark and he was half awake, he never got a clear look at her, but he always knew it was her. He had a horrible feeling that she was "mature." She had the coldest hands in the universe, and she always put them on his most vulnerable place.

"Hey, handsome," her husky smoker's voice crooned. "The chart said you've been restless. Let's see what we can do about that."

Her mouth was not cold.

Oral sex was something he had heard eagerly discussed among the white Marines, but it was something he didn't think he would ever care for. Anyway, he and Irma had never tried it, hadn't even thought about trying it. He supposed that was another startling difference between the cultures he hadn't considered. White men seemed to crave it, and white women seemed more than happy to oblige. At any rate, Miss Two o'Clock, as Matt thought of her, certainly seemed happy. But he was embarrassed. He much preferred Miss Nine o'Clock. When she opened the door, the hall lights revealed her outline. She was plump. She never said anything. She simply came in, sat by his bed, touched him softly now and then

98

while he drifted off into a deep sleep. After he got over feeling spooked, her visits were sort of pleasant. Anyway, he much preferred her over Miss Two o'Clock.

About a week after the nightly visits began, the novelty of his late-night callers had worn thin. He wanted to be left alone. He did not want to be watched or touched. Alone meant alone. And because he never knew which nurse to accuse or recoil from, he didn't smile back at the three nurses smiling at him while the orthopedic doctor removed the cast to examine his leg. And he made certain that his lower torso was covered as much as possible by the white cotton sheet while the doctor went about his business. The nurses giggled, and Matt's onyx eyes flitted from one female to the next, his bare chest glistening with a sheen of sweat. Their smiles were the absolute last insult he could endure.

"Doc?" Matt's voice broke and squeaked like a prepubescent boy's. "Could we talk? Privately, I mean?"

Dr. Parker, a lean, tall man in his late thirties, looked at the young hero blankly. "You have a problem, son?"

"Yes, sir, I have a big problem." Matt replied. He strenuously avoided looking at the nurses.

"All right," Parker returned tiredly. "Just let me get the new bandages on and this leg recast. Then I'll have a few minutes. But just a few."

After the retreat of the nurses, Dr. Parker pulled up a stool and sat beside Matt's bed. Parker's speciality was orthopedics, and with the war sending him mangled arms, legs, feet, and hands in the multitudes, he was overworked, understaffed, and exhausted. He admired the young man who was his patient, but then he admired all of his patients. Yet the thing that irritated him with all of them was their singular question:

"Doc, how is this gonna affect my sex life?"

Parker was fully prepared to hear the eternal question yet again as he made himself comfortable on the padded rolling stool. So prepared that he didn't see the need to await the inevitable. Waving off Matt's bashful hemming and hawing, Parker got right to it.

"Corporal Rainwater, you have a bad leg. You have more pins in you than the diapers on four sets of quintuplets. Your knee will never bend again. You're going to walk stiff in one leg for the rest of your life, but you will walk. Hell! You'll even do a mean waltz. The jitterbugging is over, but I never could stand that dance anyway, so I personally don't count that as any great loss. Otherwise, you are fully functional. The bullets got your leg, not your groin. You will—"

"Doc!" Matt yelped. "That's not what I want to talk about!"

Dr. Parker's thick brows shot up his forehead. "It isn't?"

"No, sir! Begging your pardon, sir, but I know that part works. It works just a little too good if you want to know the truth. I just wanted to ask if there ware any *male* nurses in this place. The females are always touching me!"

Dr. Parker, a full lieutenant in this man's navy, sat in stunned silence for several moments. Then his shoulders began to shake as he gave himself over to soundless laughter. One hand shielded his eyes as he struggled for control. Then he cleared his throat, turned his face away.

"Uh, son. How long has this been going on?"

"I'm not real sure, Doc," Matt whined nasally. "It's all sort of fuzzy. All I know is a lot of women have been in my life, and I don't even know their names. Don't get me wrong, I think it's mighty nice of 'em an' all, but it's a little . . ." He couldn't continue. "I'm just not gettin' a whole lot of sleep. If you could just do me a favor and put some guys around me, I'd be real grateful."

Enter Bud.

Robert "Bud" Foley, a nineteen-year-old sandy-haired swab, long of limb, quick of wit, mouth full of Juicy Fruit gum—a self-described "Real Zoot." In other words, a jitterbug fanatic. Dr. Parker relieved Bud of his command over the hospital mops and placed him as guard-companion to the recovering Marine in Room 5.

Matt awoke from a peaceful nap to find a pair of piercing blue eyes studying him. The owner of the eyes rested his chin on the side of the bed. Everything except the eyes and a crown of closely cropped blond hair was hidden behind by Matt's pillow.

"Hey, cat," a voice demanded. "Are you really a real live Indian?"

Matt shifted uneasily in his bed, his movements hampered by the leg brace and traction sling.

"Yes."

Bud bolted from the chair and did a small hop around the room. "Man, oh, man! That is solid Jackson!" Just as quickly Bud was back in the chair, both elbows propped on the edge of the bed as he further interrogated his prisoner.

"Do you like, live in a tepee an' shit? Are you like, a big chief? Hey! Are you the grandson of Crazy Horse or some cat like that? You must be!" Bud half shrilled. "You're a heap big hero an' all. Yeah! Crazy Horse! You're probably the grandson of Crazy Horse!"

"You're full of crap," Matt growled.

"Prove it, Jackson." Bud grinned. "Make me believe, brother."

"I'm not your brother! And my name's not Jackson, so don't call me that." Matt smoothed the bed sheets, his temper beginning to settle. In a steadier voice he said, "Crazy Horse was Lakota. I'm Osage. Crazy Horse didn't have any more children after his little daughter died. Satisfied?"

"Well, allllll ret!" Bud grinned, rapidly chewing the wad of gum. Then calming down, he asked, "You need to take a piss or something?"

Matt lost it. Normally he could keep a lid on his temper, but this kid pushed all the wrong buttons.

"Why the hell do you want to know?"

"It's my job, Jackson." The wad of gum clearly showed as Bud chewed frantically on his back molars. "You're my new duty. I'm here to tote that food tray an' lift that bed pan. Doc Parker says I'm never to leave your side. Hell! I even have to sleep in here. Ain't that a blip? I might even get to go stateside with ya. Cruise with ya all the way home. Maybe get to flap my peepers on a real Indian princess and get her gone on me. Now, that would be some solid action! I could really get in to that!"

Matt groaned and closed his eyes.

May Rose received a cablegram. She crumpled it next to her heart and wept. When Claude came home, she ran to show it to him. The telegram informed them that their son Matthew Rainwater's condition was improving, that he would be home to stay in six months.

"Have you called Irma?"

"Not yet," May Rose said quickly. "I wanted his father to know before I called his girlfriend."

Claude hugged his wife. They clung to each other for a long moment. Then Claude said in a raspy voice, "Better call Irma now. She's got a right to know."

May Rose called the Greybirds' number. Lucy Greybird answered.

"May I speak to Irma, please?"

Lucy recognized May Rose's voice. Having developed a crush on handsome Matt Rainwater since the day he started keeping company with her sister, Lucy couldn't contain herself.

"This is Lucy. Is Matt okay?"

"Yes," May Rose sighed happily. "He's still pretty bad off, but he's going to be all right. He'll be home soon for a visit before he goes to the military hospital in Oklahoma City. But he'll just be there for therapy." May Rose let go a tiny laugh. "*Now* may I please speak to Irma?"

Lucy yelled for Irma, then while Irma was on the phone, she hung back, absorbing every word of the one-sided conversation.

"Just how bad is his leg?" Irma listened, her expression becoming tight. "What does that mean, his knee is gone?" Irma listened some more. "I-I see. Yes, thank you for the call." Irma set the receiver down. Then she covered her face with her hands and wept.

Lucy couldn't stand the suspense. "What? What's wrong?"

Irma wheeled on her younger sister. "He's a cripple!" she screamed and cried. "He's a cripple and he'll be a cripple for the rest of his life. He should have died. He just should have died!" Irma ran to her room in a flood of tears.

Lucy's heart pounded hard as she stood stock still and willed herself to think. Unlike Irma, who could have Matt without having to do a lot of thinking about it, Lucy, who was not nearly as pretty as Irma, had to think and think hard. Her heart pounded harder as excitement built inside her. This was her chance, the chance she had been waiting and hoping for. But she would have to be very careful. Irma might be shallow and silly, but she wasn't stupid. The odds were high that Matt would receive some kind of medal for being shot in the war. Irma loved medals. If Irma paused long enough to really think beyond Matt's permanent injury, she would be waiting for Matt when he came home.

Lucy couldn't allow that.

"Go away!" Irma yelled in response to the soft knock on her bedroom door.

Lucy ignored this command, opening the door, slipping in, and going to the bed where Irma lay sprawled, crying into her pillow. "I'm so sorry," she said gently.

Irma raised her head and sniffed loudly. "What am I going to do, Lucy?" she wailed. "You know I've been faithful and true. I've stayed home night after night, even when Buck Hatchet has practically begged me to go out with him. But I haven't gone out. I've been saving myself for Matt. And for what?

104

So I can end up with a hopeless cripple? He'll never be able to get a decent job now. If we get married, I'll end up working to support him."

Lucy edged herself onto the bed, hugged her weeping sister. "Then maybe it would be best if you just went out with Buck. I'm sure Matt would understand. After all, it's not like you're engaged or anything."

"That's right!" Irma cried. "We're not engaged. Matt can't hold me to any promise I made about waiting for him."

"No," Lucy said. "That wouldn't be fair of him."

"Then I will go out with Buck. Matt will just have to understand."

"And I'm sure he will." She stroked Irma's wavy dark hair. "Why don't you dry your eyes and give Buck a call? Go on out tonight to cheer yourself up. Even if it works out that you don't like Buck all that much, at least you'll know for sure if waiting for Matt is what you really want. After all, Matt's going to be in hospitals for a long, long time. You'll need to be sure."

"In hospitals for a long, long time?"

"That's what his momma said. When they send him home, it will be to a hospital in Oklahoma City. He's going to have to learn to walk all over again. And with braces and a cane."

"Oh, my God," Irma whimpered.

Seconds later she was scrambling off the bed. Lucy stayed where she was, a slow smile creeping across her face as she heard Irma dial the phone and then say, "Hello, Buck? This is Irma. You still want to take me dancing? Okay. I can be ready at seven."

That evening while Irma was out with Buck, Lucy

penned a brief letter to Matt, using the overseas military address she found on one of the letters Matt had written to Irma.

> *Dear Matt,*
> *I am sorry you are in the hospital, but I'm glad you are going to be all right. I'm afraid Irma won't be writing to you anymore because she has started going around with Buck Hatchet. . . .*

When Matt received the letter and read it, anger turned his face to stone. He crumpled the letter into a ball and threw it across the room.

The Allies were pouring men and equipment into England. Jake's regiment of paratroopers were assigned to a prefab base in the county of Kent, just outside London. There wasn't a lot to do in the countryside, and the locals in the nearest village didn't exactly welcome Yanks into the one and only pub after a brawl the Yanks got into with some of the RAF boys. It was a funny old alliance: the British seemed to hate Americans, and the Americans quickly learned to hate them right back.

London was different. Londoners didn't seem to mind American soldiers all over the place. But in London a guy had to learn fast just where to go because the city was blacked out during the nights, and any city in a blackout, especially a blacked-out city being bombed, could be tricky. Jake's best friend, an Apache named Rex but called King, had London all lined out. In no time at all, which was amazing because there were never any signs posted, King found out just where the best brothels were and the best dance halls. On their second weekend pass, King and Jake took the train into London, Jake wanting to go to the brothel in Soho, King arguing in favor of a dance hall.

"I don't want to dance unless it's the naked tango," Jake complained.

Undaunted, Rex (King) Thompson threw an arm around Jake's unwilling shoulder. "Ya gotta see the dishes at the dance hall." King grinned. "We're talkin' prime filets. You can mambo with a whore anytime. These dance hall babes you can take home to Momma without her havin' a heart attack. Plus, you can feed these dolls all kinds of lines and they go for it. An' if ya get lucky, ya don't have to worry about no disease an' shit. This is strictly clean stuff."

"I don't know." Jake frowned. "I'm not lookin' for love, just a piece of tail."

"Ten minutes of your life, Boogie-Man," Rex said. "That's all I'm asking. If you don't see anything that turns ya on, you can cut out. Hell! You'll spend more time than that waitin' in line at the cathouse."

With logic that hard to fight, Jake allowed himself to be towed along through the narrow and dark streets of London.

It didn't look like a dance hall. It looked like a big ugly dark building. And old, really old. But he could hear music, so he trusted King and went inside.

Once they walked through the big door, the doorman quickly closed it after them so that the bright lights wouldn't give the Germans a visible target. The sudden change made Jake a trifle breathless. The music from the band was very loud, and the enormous dance hall was packed. There were a lot of girls standing on the sidelines anxious to dance, and they winked at Jake and King hopefully. King chose a pretty brunette, and she went willingly to the dance floor, where they were immediately swallowed up by the crowd. Jake hung back, ignoring the silent signals being sent to him by the remaining young women as he watched the dancing.

It was pretty clear that this dance hall was very popular with the GI's. Army uniforms were everywhere. What struck him immediately was that the soldiers were mixing, the whites and the coloreds all dancing and sweating together. Jake found that mildly amusing, seeing as how on the base they didn't eat or sleep together and they certainly didn't use the same latrines. Jake looked again at the girls still giving him the eye.

He still wasn't sure about this dancing thing. After a few minutes of wandering, he wanted to leave. Trouble was, he was having the devil's own time trying to find King inside the pressing mob. Then, on the dance floor, from the corner of his eye he saw a flash of red. Jake turned his head in that direction.

She was dressed in a plaid skirt, white sweater, bobby socks, and black loafers, dancing like mad, red frizzy hair flying. Her partner was a huge paratrooper. At least the enormous man *seemed* to be her partner. It wasn't easy to tell. The girl had both index fingers near her flame-red head as she did the dance known as Truckin'. Her little feet were a blur as she kept time to the music blasting from the live band. Jake grinned. He was still watching the little red-haired girl when an excited King suddenly appeared at his side.

"Man oh man," King shouted. "That little girl was sure a good dancer. But she had ugly teeth, so I ditched her. Have you ever noticed that a lot of English people have ugly teeth? And they smell funny too. Kinda fishy." King shuddered.

"That one," Jake said, nudging King. "I want that one."

King followed Jake's captured gaze. "That one?" he yelled over the music. "Oh man, dream on! You see that dude she Truckin' with? That's Homicide Hogan! The man's crazy! Talk around the base is he plans to collect the ears of dead Germans to take home to his momma. I wouldn't advise you trying to cut in on the homicide man. He might take your ear off."

"I'm going to dance with her."

"Your funeral."

Jake was craftier than those who had formerly attempted a frontal assault when trying to cut in on Homicide Hogan. Jake drifted around the dance hall until he found exactly what he was looking for.

The biggest, blackest soldier in the entire building.

Ever friendly, Jake eased himself within the group of Negro troopers.

"Say, young hoss," Jake's handpicked Goliath said with a wide, winning smile, "how come fine stuff like you ain't dancin'?"

"Can't," Jake shrugged.

"Sho' you can." The unsuspecting gladiator laughed. He clapped Jake solidly on the spine, bucking Jake forward. "These here girls'll dance with ya. If they'll dance with me, they'll dance with most any-thang."

"See that guy?" Jake pointed, standing on his toes to shout into the giant's ear. "He said if he saw any of us coloreds dancing with any of these girls, he would personally stab us in the heart with a burning cross."

"He say what?" The smile on the black man's face withered. Anger began to shine from his eyes.

Jake repeated the charge. "Hey!" Jake called as the herculean black man moved away from him. "Where you going?"

"I'm gonna eat me some peckerwood."

Hurriedly, Jake skirted the crowd, lining himself up with the dancing couple. When the otherwise Jolly Black Giant mauled his way through the dance floor and reached Hogan, Jake was ready for the rebound.

Hogan didn't know what hit him. There he was one minute, jerking to the beat of the "Pennsylvania 55000," and then hands grabbed him by the neck. Flailing, gasping for air, Hogan was lifted bodily, his feet dangling inches above the floor.

Hogan choked and thrashed. Frightened girls began screaming. Equally frightened GI's hauled the girls away from the fracas. Friends of Hogan (and there were many more than Jake had figured on) entered the melee. More blacks jumped in to help defend their man. The girl was caught in the middle of all of it. She was screaming hysterically when an arm encircled her waist and pulled her out. Before she could catch her breath, thank her rescuer, she realized she was being trundled out of the dance hall.

"My coat!" she cried.

Jake didn't pause, holding her hand firmly as he made a dash for the door.

"I'll buy you another!"

It was raining as they stumbled out the door. They stood in the partial cover of the stoop. Jake was still holding her hand. She was looking him over from head to toe when they heard the warble of police sirens.

"The doorman called the coppers!" she cried. "We have to get out of here."

Jake hauled her out onto the sidewalk and madly waved his arm over his head. A little black cab ducked through the eerily silhouetted traffic and braked by the side of the curb. Jake opened the door and shoved her inside, jumping in quickly behind her.

"Get out of here, now!" he yelled. As the cabbie pulled away, the pair looked out the rear window. Police cars were arriving fast. But they didn't go after the cab. The police bounded out of their cars and rushed into the dance hall. Still, Jake didn't draw an easy breath until the cab turned a corner and they were on a quiet street. Then he looked at the red-haired girl sitting next to him, her eyelashes blinking away raindrops as she stared at him.

"I hope you're not a sexual fiend," she said blandly.

"Nope," he laughed. "Just your typical asshole 'Murican.' "

"Oh, well," she shrugged. "That's all right, then. I've grown quite used to those."

Jake laughed. *Damn, she's cute.*

Not much was available in the way of nightlife considering the bombed condition of London. But the all-knowing cabbie suggested a little coffee house in Knightsbridge. The coffee shop was a trifle fancier than Jake had counted on, and pricy to boot. Yet, in for a penny, in for a bob, as they say in Jolly Ole.

Jake looped his Army cap through his belt as they

were led to a small corner table. Jake ordered two coffees.

When it arrived, the coffee looked like sludge and tasted worse, but to the English palate, man, that's java. After one sip Jake feverishly worked to lace the coffee with milk and sugar. His "date" watched him.

The coffee house had muted lighting, but even in its softness she could clearly see that he was unnervingly good-looking. His black hair was sheared down to his skull the way the American Army liked to keep its men sheared, but the bad haircut did not hinder his appearance in the least. His bone structure was incredible, high cheekbones, long curved nose, square-shaped jaw. His eyes were almost Oriental and black as pitch. His mouth was fabulous, wide, full, quick to smile.

"How tall are you?" she asked.

Jake didn't look up from pouring milk into his cup. He was hoping that sooner or later the stuff in his cup would turn a little whiter. "I'm between six foot three and six four. Depends on if I'm wearing shoes or not." He glanced at her, that smile she found so attractive in full display. "How tall are you?"

She blushed furiously. "Much shorter."

His tongue playfully toying at the corner of his lips, Jake grinned and nodded. "About five three? Four?"

She giggled. "Depends on if I'm wearing shoes."

Jake chuckled. "Oh, yeah," he said. "There's something else you might want to know. I'm a Native American."

Her mouth flew open, her eyes reacting with delight. "Do you mean you're a red-Indian?"

"Yeah, I guess so. Except that I'm kinda brown,

and there's no way in hell anyone's ever going to get me to eat curry." Jake pushed the awful coffee away. He folded his arms on the tabletop as he leaned toward her. "Look, kid, Columbus made a mistake. He was looking for India, but he found us, so calling us Indians was an even bigger mistake. If you want to be my friend, just think of me as Osage because that's *really* what I am. Got it?"

"Got it."

"Mind if I touch your hair?"

She looked at him suspiciously. "You don't have a scalping knife, do you?"

"Nope. I left it at the base."

The thought of him touching her sent a thrill all the way to her toes. "All right, then, you may touch my hair."

Rubbing a lock of her hair between his fingers, Jake laughed. "Man, this stuff feels like wire. How do you brush it?"

"Very carefully."

Jake let go of her hair and sat back, studying her freckled, heart-shaped face. "What's your name?"

"Georgina Marshall. What's your name?"

"Jake Rainwater."

Georgina pulled a face. "Ooooh. Jake. What kind of name is Jake?"

"It's short for Jacob."

"Oh. Well, here in England, Jack is short for Jacob. I'm going to call you Jack."

Jake shrugged. "Whatever makes your socks roll up and down."

"What?"

"Nothing. It's just an expression. It means whatever makes you happy."

Georgina primly sipped her coffee, returned the cup to the saucer. "Jack. Jack makes me happy."

Jake wiggled his eyebrows. "Baby, I haven't even started making you happy."

"Please don't call me baby. I happen to be a grown woman."

Jake looked her over again, then bent at the waist, lifted the tablecloth, and examined what he could see of her under the table. He sat up straight. "Mind telling me exactly where you're grown up? I can't find it."

"I like you," she laughed. "You're impossibly rude."

"You're cute too."

Outside, Jake hailed another cab and saw Georgina safely home. She lived very close to the East End, in a house centered in a row of connected houses. Jake immediately didn't like this dark street; it looked poor and overcrowded. Standing on the top stair, he continually glanced back over his shoulder to make certain the cab was still waiting. The last thing he wanted was to find himself lost and alone on this street. How could a girl like Georgina live in a dump like this? But never mind. She was still cute, and she was fun to talk to.

Jake hadn't had a girlfriend since joining the Army. Not because the girl he had left behind wasn't willing to wait, but because he didn't think it was fair because there was no way in hell he was going to wait. Especially not now that he'd found Georgina. Red-haired girls didn't just come along every day. He knew because he'd been wanting one, a *real* one, not a Bottle Betty, since puberty. If he was ever going to fulfil his fantasy of laying a red-haired girl, then he'd better lay this one.

"Can I see you again?"

"I think you'd better," she returned casually as she turned the key in the latch. "You owe me a coat, remember?"

"Hey, you better give me your telephone number."

She approached and stood very near. "Repeat after me, Central 8-349."

Jake repeated the number. Then she kissed him. "Central 8-349," she whispered against his lips.

"I've got it."

"Good. Good night, Jack."

"Good night, George."

Jake was back inside the cab and the dark vehicle gliding down the quiet street when a thoroughly happy Georgina slipped quietly into the house. Her father was waiting for her.

"Just who the bloody hell was that?"

Georgina almost jumped out of her socks. "He-he's an American."

"I can see that," her father ranted. "But just what kind of an American? He's not one of those Blackies, is he?"

"N-no. He, he's a red-Indian."

"Oh, my God. That's all we need. Your Aunt Patricia is running amock with a Blackie, and now you're steaming off with a bloody red-Indian. I know I can't stop you going out, but if you do something silly and get yourself 'in the club' the way the rest of the women in this country are turnin' up, don't expect me to help you raise any papoose. If you go off with"—he waved an angry hand—"*that*, then you'll bloody well be on your own."

* * *

Wartime England bred the need for young people to fall in love instantly. If, when a couple met, there wasn't that heated spark, each moved off rather quickly to find someone they could fall in love with instantly. This unconsciously calculating courting manner cannot be considered callous when one considers that fleeting moments were all anyone was guaranteed. The moment she met Jake, Georgina was certain she'd found the man for her. He fulfilled her every requirement. He was tall, stunningly attractive, funny. And because he was an American, he was also rich. She worried and waited all through the next day for his call. At five-thirty, with her nerves so fraught she felt too big for her skin, her father sent her into a new tailspin when he gave her a couple of shillings and commanded she run out to the chippie. Because her mother was working late and her father was about to set off to work at the same factory, someone had to see to it that hot food was in the house. That someone was Georgina, and she had no choice but to go.

She ran the full two blocks, rudely jumped the queue in the fish and chips shop, paid for the family supper, ran home again. She came crashing through the door just in time to hear her brother Tommy saying into the telephone, "Georgina isn't home, I'm afraid."

"Who is it?" she yelled.

Tommy held the receiver away from his ear. "Some American bloke."

Georgina pushed the steaming, greasy parcel into her brother's hands and snatched the telephone. "Jack?"

"Hey, George," she heard him say. "You sound out of breath."

"I-I had to pop out to the chippie. Where are you?"

"Still on the base. But I've got a pass. I can be at your house in a couple of hours."

"No," she said quickly. "I'll meet you at the station. Which one?"

"Victoria."

"I'll be there."

When the train pulled in, Georgina was on the platform, scanning the faces peering from the coach windows. When she saw his, she waved and kept on waving until she was sure he saw her as well.

Jake frowned. She was wearing the same clothes she had worn last night. He couldn't believe she was wearing the same clothing just so he would recognize her in the crowd. Her bright hair was like a beacon that went before her. The chances were high, with what he had seen of the abject poverty England had been suffering since the beginning of the war, that the clothing she was wearing again, as simple as it was, were the nicest things she owned. It made him feel guilty about losing her her coat. She waved again and then hugged herself. The poor little thing looked cold. As the train came to a rolling stop, Jake opened the carriage door and jumped out. Standing before her, he unbuttoned his Army-issue overcoat and draped it around her. His coat swallowed her whole, made her look like a shivering refugee.

"Come on, babe. We're getting you a new coat."

"But the shops are closed."

"They'll open up fast when I wave around some good old Yankee green."

The lady proprietor did indeed open the doors of

her shut-up shop, but she was stern-faced and disapproving, trying to appear as if she didn't need the custom of a pushy American. Jake knew it was a front and kept pushing, going through the clothing racks like a man in a hurry.

"You have coupons, of course."

"Nope," Jake airily replied. He kept on searching for things in Georgina's size while Georgina hung back, afraid of the fierce-looking woman.

"I'm afraid I cannot sell anything without the proper coupons."

Jake sent her a meaningful look. Both he and the woman knew that American money on the black market would earn her nearly four times the worth of anything she sold to him on the sly. Realizing he wouldn't buy anything if she said another word, the woman snapped her mouth shut. Jake went back to searching through the racks.

Outside, dressed in her new pure wool gray coat and carrying two of the five packed bundles of clothing, she held his hand and walked quickly beside him. "I-I'm afraid I can't accept all of this."

"Sure you can, babe."

"B-but, the dresses and skirts—"

"Are just presents for my girl."

A wonderful warmth swept through her. She tried, over the excitement she felt, to keep her voice light, her tone mocking. "Oh, I'm your girl, am I?"

Jake lowered his head, kissed her mouth. "Yes, you are."

"And I've nothing to say on the matter?"

"Nope. Not a word."

"Am I supposed to simply give up and fling myself into your strong arms?"

"Now you're gettin' the idea." He bent at the knees and grinned in her face. "Let's get something to eat. I'm starving." This was a lie. He had eaten on the base. But Georgina looked hungry. She looked very hungry.

"T-there's a little restaurant a few blocks away," she said meekly.

"Great. Let's go."

Georgina livened up over dinner. And she ate. Boy, did she eat. Because she was short and practically skin and bones, Jake could not imagine where she was packing it all away. He simply toyed with the food on his plate, doing his best to pretend he wasn't noticing as she gobbled hers. Through the meal he told her about Oklahoma, about his family. Georgina nodded and kept eating. Then they went to the cinema, and Georgina asked for popcorn. Jake bought himself a small bag too and promptly gagged on his first taste of British popcorn.

"Oh, man!" he shouted in a whisper. He spat the popcorn out. "They put sugar on my popcorn."

Georgina looked at him in the dim gray light. Her mouth was full and she muffled, "Of course they did. Sugared corn is a special treat."

"Not in my life," he muttered. He passed his bag of popcorn to Georgina. She ate every kernel.

The wide beam of light projecting the blatantly war morale-booster film, was hazy because of all the cigarette smoke. While Georgina popped popcorn into her mouth, Jake studied her profile. She had the cutest little upturned nose, and her hair, even in the dim black-and-white light, was pure Technicolor. Just looking at her made his heart skip a beat. He leaned in and kissed the side of her munching mouth.

119

As she felt his lips softly touch hers, butterflies kicked up a fuss in her wonderfully full stomach. Responding to his tender display of affection, she turned her head, and Jake put his arm around her and kissed her properly. Excitement ripped through her as the kiss deepened. This was Jack, beautiful, exotic Jack. Not only could she taste him, she inhaled his masculine scent each time she drew a ragged breath through her nose. The butterflies went crazy.

" 'Ere!" a male voice behind them whispered irritably. "Some of us would like to see the bleedin' film."

Reluctantly, their heads separated. Jake grinned at her as his hand slipped over hers and his long fingers entwined between her much smaller ones. He squeezed her hand and whispered, "Great kiss, babe."

Georgina watched the screen, but she was so happy she couldn't get a fix on what the film was actually about. She was in love. In love with a dishy American red-Indian. And he was in love with her too. He'd said so. He really had. This love at first sight thingy that she'd been hearing so much about actually worked!

Trains no longer ran after midnight, so on leaving the movie theater they had to proceed immediately to the train station. On the platform, waiting for the signal man to blow the boarding whistle, Jake kissed Georgina. He didn't care that they were in public or that she had to stand on a bench in order to kiss him comfortably. He simply couldn't get enough of her. Then he heard the first shrill warning whistle. He had to stop kissing her because he had to hurriedly talk to her.

"I can't get another pass into town tomorrow. But

if I give you some money, could you come down to see me?"

I'd battle my way through hell to see you, she thought. But what she said was, "Well, all right."

Jake fished in his back pocket for his wallet. He produced a ten-dollar bill. "Great! Now, you'll have to wait outside the gates, but don't worry, George, I'll be there." He thrust the bill at her. "This should be enough to get you a train ticket tomorrow and a cab home tonight."

"Oh, I can walk home."

"No, you can't. It's late and you've got all these packages. I want you to take a cab."

"Ooooh, you are a bossy boots."

"Yeah. Get used to it." The second warning whistle sounded. "Quick, give me a kiss. I gotta go."

George obediently kissed him again. The third and final whistle sounded. The separation of their mouths was like an excruciating ache.

Hanging recklessly out of the compartment door as the train picked up speed, he yelled. "Tomorrow, George. I'll see you tomorrow."

Temporarily abandoning the packages on the platform, she trotted after the train. "What time?"

"As early as you can!" he yelled back. "Just wait, I promise I'll be there."

She watched as the train pulled away and became smaller and smaller. When the train was gone and the platform was quiet, George retrieved the packages and left the station. She passed the taxi racks, saw the cabs waiting, the drivers watching her hopefully. She held on tightly to the money he had given her and, balancing the packages in her arms, she walked home.

Mardi Oakley Medawar

The next morning was a very cold, overcast day, the dark, slate gray clouds hanging low. On days such as these England breathed a collective sigh of relief. German planes would not be flying. Leaving her parents a cryptic note and wearing one of her new dresses and lovely warm coat, she left the house and made her way to the station. There she endured the baleful looks of the ticketing agent when she handed over American money and named her destination. The train she boarded was already crowded with women, of remarkably varying types. Every last one of them was heading for the American base. Even dressed in her new clothing, George felt immature beside the more seasoned women, outclassed by their sophistication. During the long trip, when a lipstick was passed around George quickly asked to borrow a bit.

"Here you go, lovey," one of the seasoned women said, handing the tube over. "You're new, ain't ya? First time, then?"

Applying the lipstick, George made an agreeing noise.

"Well, nothing to be afraid of. Just follow this here crowd. Got a fella waitin'?"

George handed back the lipstick. "Yes. His name is Jack."

The woman laughed. "They're all named Jack. Or John. Don't matter, though. They'll be gone quick enough an' then there'll be a new batch of Jacks an' Johns."

One of the sophisticated women turned in her seat, looked back and down her nose at the laughing woman. When the woman then arched a well-groomed brow and looked at her, seemed to examine her, George shriveled. After the train came into the village station, next came the awful walk through the village to the base. George straggled behind, trying to pretend she wasn't with this migratory herd of women. At the gates, the vain pretense ended.

The M.P.'s were surly and rude, going about with clipboards, taking the names of the women. She glanced to the side and recognized the woman from the train who'd shared the lipstick. When she smiled, George felt a bit better. Not quite so alone. Craning to see over the heads of the feminine crowd, she saw the more sophisticated women form the train being loaded into jeeps and then driven through the opening gates.

"Officers' women," the woman near her said. "They get the best of everything. They even get fed in there. Just fancy, eh? We get treated like whores while the real whores are treated like bloody ladies."

"They're—they're prostitutes?"

" 'Course they are. That's why we stay clear of 'em in the trains. Us, we got honest fellas. That lot, they don't even know their fellas, do they? Not till the last minute, they don't. But cor, don't they live grand?"

King had commandeered a troop truck. With Jake hiding in the back, and the M.P's waving the truck through, King drove out of the gates, scattering the separate groups of waiting women. Then King slammed on the brakes, and Jake threw back the dull green canvas flap. Hearing her name, Georgina turned her head, her face registering surprise. Jake called for her again, and she felt hands on her back shoving her forward.

"Crikey! He's bloody gorgeous. Run, lovey!" the

woman yelled in her ear. "Before all these women set out after him!"

George ran, her arm extended. Jake grabbed her hand and hauled her up. When she was safely inside, Jake shouted, "Go!" The truck took off, and Jake and George were knocked down by the sudden burst of speed.

Their bodies tangled, George cried, "What are you doing?"

"It's called kidnap. You're the kid and I'm napping you."

"Jack!" she screamed, trying to wriggle away. "You'll get into trouble."

"Yeah," he laughed, hanging on to her. "But not for five hours, so just take it easy and enjoy the ride. Hey? Are you hungry?"

"Yes."

"Great. I stole some Spam." His brows furrowed over his nose as he looked at her. "What's that red crap on your mouth?"

"Lipstick."

Jake fished out a crumpled white handkerchief and handed it to her. "Wipe it off. It makes you look like one of those cheapies hanging outside the gates."

As agreed, King drove the troop truck to the canal, parked inside the cover of trees, grabbed his make-shift fishing pole, and went off to do a spot of fishing. In the back of the troop carrier, Jake and George sat cross-legged on a brown wool blanket. Jake made a stack of Spam sandwiches while she drank real American coffee from a thermos. Then he gave her a sandwich.

Chewing the first bite, she moaned, "Oh, this is

lovely." She ate three more sandwiches without pausing for a breath.

Watching her eat, Jake felt impatient. "Swallow!" he barked. "I have to kiss you."

"Life or death, is it?"

"Yes."

Chapter Six

Kissing George was just about the nicest thing he had ever done. She was so responsive, so ardent. He loved the feel and the taste of her, even if her breath did taste of Spam and coffee. Holding her little face in his hands, he adored the sight. He loved every freckle dotting the pale skin, loved the green eyes staring back at him, even her red eyelashes. He knew he had to have her. Right now.

"George, let's grab the blanket and take a walk."

"Why?"

"Because this troop truck smells like a bunch of sweaty guys. It's a little tough to be romantic around all this B.O."

If they had been back home, he would have gone slowly, courted her properly before ever daring to make the kind of serious move he was planning now. But this was wartime England. Time was at a premium. If he was ever going to have her, it would have to be now. Jake helped her out of the troop carrier and, holding her hand and with the blankets under his arm, he walked her to a secluded spot along the canal.

Georgina sat down on the spread blankets and hugged herself inside her coat. "It's cold out here."

Jake put his arms around her. "Just give me a couple of minutes and I'll have you real warm."

She loved kissing him, and the way he kissed her now, his head twisting back and forth as his tongue explored her mouth, made her very warm indeed. She didn't fight him when he lay her back and moved himself on top of her.

"Babe," he gasped. "Are you my girl?"

"Oh yes, Jack."

He kissed her again, more ardently, then his mouth moved to her neck. "George," he said raggedly. "Let's be together. Okay?"

A new thrill rushed through her. She closed her eyes as Jake mouthed her neck, her ear. "Oh, yes."

It is absolutely true that England and America will forever remain divided by a common language. Jake was talking about sex. Georgina believed he was proposing marriage. Utterly smitten, over the moon with happiness that he wanted to marry her, she kissed him with renewed passion as he unbuttoned her coat. But when she felt the hand inside her knickers, she gasped and broke off the kiss.

"Jack! What are you doing?"

"I'm just lovin' you. I can't help loving you, George."

"Oh," she said, her tone uncertain.

He was kissing her again, his hand going between her legs, rubbing her in a place that . . . Her head went back and she gasped raggedly. He kissed her along her arching throat.

"You're such a hot little baby."

"Jack—" Then she couldn't say anything. She was trembling from head to toe as his hand did incredible things that made her see stars. She was in a dazed state when he unbuttoned the fly of his fatigues.

"This is going to be good, sweetheart," she heard his husky voice say. "This is going to be so good." His mouth traced the thin skin covering her upper breast bones. Georgina arched and shuttered. "Oh," she dimly heard him say, "you are so ready."

Still lost in a fog of sensations, she obscurely felt her limp body being shifted, her hips being raised, her legs being separated by his hips. She crashed back into the present when a hardened mass bumped into her, and she cried out against the burning, tearing pain.

"Oh, jeez," he gasped. "You are so damn tight." Jake lost whatever was left of his reason. He forgot, as he lost himself to the most incredible sensation of his life, to put on the rubber he'd happily packed inside his wallet just after he'd stolen the Spam and bread from the mess hall the night before. When she struggled to get away from him, he held on to her and slammed all the way in. While his hips pumped, Georgina wiggled, made a lot of mewling noises against his chest. Her tiny cries, her movements, the fact that she was so small inside, made him so excited that, too soon, he spilled himself inside her.

George was crying when he looked down at her. "I'm sorry, babe. It went too fast. I couldn't help—"

Her hand slapped his face. Stunned, Jake looked stupidly at her. "Get off of me," she yelled. "Now."

"But, George, I said—"

"Now!"

At the station, King discreetly waited in the truck. Jake paced, ran his hand through the burr of dark hair on the side of his head. Then he stopped in front of her. "George," he yelped. "What the hell is wrong? Why won't you talk to me?"

She turned and looked at him coldly.

Completely dumbfounded by her attitude, he yelled, "Oh, for Christ's sake, George! I said I was sorry. I couldn't help it that it went so fast. But you don't have to be so pissed off."

She refused to look at him again, and Jake was fuming so much he couldn't speak. When the train arrived at the station, he gallantly helped her aboard. Before the door closed, he managed to say, "I'll call you tonight."

"Please don't trouble yourself."

Standing at attention next to King in their C.O.'s office, he didn't hear the lengthy lecture delivered by Colonel T'Hart. His mind dwelled instead on George.

". . . and Private Rainwater." The sound of his name brought him back to the moment. "For your part in this truck-stealing fiasco, you're going to get down on your hands and knees and clean one end of the billet to the other with a toothbrush. Now, the both of you, get out of my office."

Jake and King saluted, did an about-face, and marched out. Steaming mad, Colonel Dutch T'Hart sat down behind his desk, opened a drawer, fished out a cigar, angrily bit off the butt end, and lit up, smoke puffing in furious clouds. He hated being the commander of the Indian troop. And he hated it when his fellow officers called him Custer. Being Pennsylvania Dutch, he'd never been around Indians in his life. Since the first day of command, he'd had no idea what to expect from his platoon. What he hated most about his troops were the times they reverted to their separate languages. He just knew that they were talking about him to his face, but he had no way to prove it. The second thing he didn't especially care for was how they always retaliated when one of their own was punished for an infraction of Army rules. Lately, this retaliation had taken the form of pounding on a thrown-together drum and singing the whole time a member of the company was being punished. Beating that drum and chanting was meant to be a punishment for their colonel.

It was.

But neither could he put a stop to their noise. On the one occasion he had tried, he was duly informed that the caterwauling was their right of religious preference. If he couldn't order a trooper to stop being a Methodist, he certainly couldn't order a trooper to stop being a member of the Native American church. It was just unfortunate for him that in the Native American church, beating a drum and singing in very loud, very piercing voices were part of the religious practice.

Two minutes after King and Rainwater left his office, the drumming started. "Oh, here it comes." Five minutes later, when the drumming and singing had him galloping hard toward the edge of insanity, he went to the door, opened it, peeked around. Rainwater was in his T-shirt and BVD's, scrubbing the concrete floor with a toothbrush, a pail of sudsy water in tow. Glancing across the narrow hall, he spotted King in the communal toilets, scrubbing the crappers. Dutch sighed, wishing they would both finish their punishment quickly. The pounding drum and high, shrill singing were giving him a migraine.

He closed the door, returned to his desk, and checked his watch. He had two more hours before his duty for the day ended and he could escape his Indians.

One of the singers quickly hand-signed to Jake. The colonel had made his obligatory check, now the coast was clear. Jake dashed away from his punishment duty, and another Indian, a Navaho, took Jake's place. But because he looked nothing like Jake, he aimed his BVD-covered rear end to the hallway. That would be all the colonel would see should he check again. Jake quickly dressed, slithered out of the window. Then he dashed for the PX and the only available telephone.

A little boy answered, the same one Jake had spoken to before. "Please, may I speak to Georgina?"

"She says she doesn't want to talk to you."

"Tell her it's very, very important." Just as he finished saying this, Georgina was on the line, whispering so rapidly her words sounded hissed.

"You are never to ring this number again."

"George, how many times do I have to say I'm sorry? I promise, if you just give me another chance, next time will be better."

"There will never be a next time. I have decided to seek legal advice. Raping a virgin happens to be against the law. Even for Americans."

She slammed the phone down.

Damn. A virgin, he thought numbly. *No wonder she was so tight.*

The long walk back to his billet gave Jake time to think. The more he thought, the more worried he became. George sounded as if she really meant it about charging him with rape. And if she did, he was going to be in a lot of trouble. He had to talk to his C.O.

Seeing Private Rainwater fully dressed and entering without bothering to knock set Dutch back in his chair. Then he jumped up and ran to the door, looking out. An Indian was scrubbing the floor, all right, but it wasn't the right Indian. He rounded on Jake.

"What the hell's going on, Private?"

"I'm in a lot of trouble, sir."

"You've got that just about as right as you'll ever be in your whole miserable life."

Undaunted by his furiously red-faced colonel, Jake said, his voice shaky, "A British girl is going to charge me with rape."

Every last trace of color drained from Dutch's face. He looked out the opened door again and yelled down the hall. "Shut the fuck up!" The drumming and singing ended abruptly. Dutch closed the door. "Sit down, Private. You're going to tell me everything, and you're not going to leave out a single dirty detail."

The small office was a smog of blue cigar smoke as Jake talked and Dutch smoked and listened. Narrowing down the details, Jake blubbered, "I didn't know. I didn't know she was a virgin. And she said she wanted me. Is it my fault I believed her?"

Dutch kept puffing. For any soldier, raping a white woman was a serious charge. For a colored, it was an automatic death penalty. Not only would facing the rope be dire for Rainwater, it would be a permanent blot on Dutch's military career as a commander. If he couldn't be trusted to keep the fly zipped on a lowly trooper's pants, no one would trust him with serious responsibility when he was finally on the field. There was no way around it. The British girl would have to be silenced before she put forward her charge and damned them both.

"Give me her phone number," he snapped.

"She won't talk to me," Jake stammered. "I just tried and—"

"Give me the goddamn number!"

Jake quickly babbled the number. As Dutch went through the base exchange, he angrily waved Jake out of the office. In the corridor Jake paced, his buddies quickly surrounding him, their worried voices low as they tried to worm information out of him. Jake signaled for silence as he strained to hear the one-sided conversation trickling through the closed door.

Little Tommy answered. Georgina, wringing her hands nervously, stood right behind him. "I'll just get him," Tommy said.

"Who?" Georgina quizzed. "Who is it?"

"Just some bloke for Dad." Tommy scampered away.

Disappointed that it wasn't Jake, that he wasn't calling again to beg her forgiveness so that she could have the pleasure of threatening him, listening to him squirm, Georgina made her way up the stairs for a good long weep in her bedroom.

"Mr. Marshall," Dutch wearily began. "My name is Colonel T'Hart. I'm calling on behalf of one of my troopers. It appears that my Private Rainwater and your daughter have become acquainted in the biblical sense, and now Private Rainwater insists on doing the honorable thing."

Joe Marshall became livid as he listened. As more minutes passed and his fury trebled, he agreed fully with the American colonel's recommendations. Then he put the phone down and barreled up the stairs.

Georgina was startled from her crying as her father stormed into her room. "Pack up your kit, slut. You're leaving this house."

"What?"

"You heard. You're to take the train back to the Americans. They've agreed to have you, with my good riddance."

"Married?" Jake's voice cracked just saying the word.

"That's the deal, Private," Dutch said flatly. "You either marry the girl or you face the gallows."

Jake lost all ability to stand. He puddled into a chair. Dutch rose from behind his desk, walked around it, sat down on the edge. "Listen, it won't be as bad as it seems. You'll get a quick wedding. I'll fix it with the base chaplain. Then, in a month, maybe less, you're out of here. If you survive the war, you'll only pass through England on your way home. Once you're home, you get a divorce. Because you'll be out of reach and out of the Army, there won't be a damn thing she can do."

Jake thought long and hard. He knew he liked Georgina a lot, but she was a stranger. How the hell did anyone marry a stranger? Even temporarily? Then he thought about not marrying her, about maybe being hung. Suddenly, being temporarily married didn't seem all that bad. "I-I'll marry her, sir."

Relieved, Dutch clapped his shoulder. "Good man. Now, I'm giving you permission to meet her train because her father's agreed she should come straight back. The minute she arrives, you take her to the village pub. The landlord will rent you a room. After that, you're to stay the hell away from her while I get this wedding all fixed up. Should only take a few days. Once it's done and you're safe, you can do whatever the hell you want. Take my word for it, wives cannot cry rape. Especially not to the military."

Outside his C.O.'s office, Jake filled in his worried friends.

"Oh, man," King said. "That's the oldest trick in the book, and you fell for it."

"What?"

"What do you mean, *what*? Are you completely dumb? Haven't I always told you to pick your lays with great care? Well, this is why, boogie man. You lay down with the wrong girl, she screams rape and you've got to marry her. And why does she want to marry you? Well, it ain't love, pal. She wants the allotment check. For five minutes of wiggling around on her back, she gets half your pay check for the rest of the time you're in the Army. Oh, man, you have been so had."

Jake became so furious he couldn't breathe.

Georgina was crying as she struggled to board the train with her two heavy cases. Her father had had her pack everything, leaving not a trace of herself in her bedroom.

"I told you what would happen if you lay down with that scum. You wouldn't listen, now you'll have to learn. And God help you."

She had no money except for what was left out of the ten-dollar bill Jake had given her. Her pride was still deeply wounded, salved only by the knowledge that Jake still wanted to marry her. That he wanted to marry her so much he had gone to extraordinary means to make certain they were married. But during the lengthy trip she worried what she would do if he changed his mind and wasn't there to meet her at the station. When the train pulled in and she saw him standing on the platform, she almost swooned with relief. Her beautiful Jack loved her. He truly did. The least she could do was forgive him his earlier impetuousness. Nevertheless, she was very nervous about getting married in such a rush. Georgina always talked rapidly when she was nervous. Her mouth was going like a machine gun as Jake helped her with her cases, piled them into a jeep, helped her in, and drove her to the pub.

Jake didn't say a word.

Once he checked her in, made certain she was comfortable in the little room, he left. She didn't see him again for two days. On the morning of the third day she was summoned by the pub's landlady. Georgina hurried down the stairs to speak to Jake on the phone.

"Wear something real nice, George. I'll be there in an hour."

"Where are we going?"

"To the base chapel. We're kinda getting married."

"Oh."

Jake hung up.

She wore her new powder blue dress and, because she didn't have any stockings, a pair of white socks with her white shoes. She brushed her wiry red hair into a semblance of control, and because Jake didn't like lipstick, she didn't use any, even though the landlady kindly tried to press some on her.

"But it's your wedding day, dearie."

"He-he doesn't like me in lipstick."

When he arrived, she was ready and waiting, her coat on and buttoned up to her chin. He wasn't alone. Three other Indians were with him, and none of them spoke to her or looked at her as she climbed into the jeep.

The base was a series of metal Quonset huts, and the base chapel could be identified only by a large wooden cross stuck into a tiny patch of lawn. Georgina, now as solemn as Jake and his friends, wordlessly clambered out of the jeep. Jake did not even offer her his hand. She walked behind him, and his three friends followed behind her as they all went inside the chapel.

At the first sight of the bride, Dutch rocked back on his heels. *Sweet Jesus, she's only a kid!* Then he realized just how right he was to push this marriage escape route. If she had pressed her charge, Dutch could well imagine the grievance review board's reaction when the top brass got a look at her. This was no cheapie hanging outside the gates, hoping to snag an American GI. This was a little, innocent girl. Had she been given the opportunity to open her mouth and cry rape, Private Rainwater could have kissed his sorry ass good-bye. And Dutch, any hope of furthering his military career. As she removed her coat and smoothed her simple dress over her waif-like form, Dutch decided it was paramount this ceremony be cut to the bare bone. He leaned in and whispered into the chaplain's ear.

"Forget the hearts and flowers. Just get straight to the skinny. Have 'em say I do and then you do."

Sadly, the chaplain took his place before the strained young couple.

Her wedding was over before she was able to draw a full breath. Jake slipped a plain band on her finger. The ring was too big. She had to keep her hand in a fist so that it wouldn't fall off as she signed the registry. After Jake signed, he took her hand and led her out of the chapel. No one wished them well. In the jeep again, this time without his friends, they drove back to the pub. Jake paused at the bar, bought a bottle of gin, followed her up the stairs.

Georgina was struggling not to cry as Jake closed the door with the heel of his foot, removed his hat, tossed it on the bed, uncapped the bottle of gin, and poured himself a stiff drink. She removed her coat and waited for him to speak. He loosened his tie, sat down, and drained the glass of gin. Then he set the glass down on the small table and glared at her.

"Well, I hope you're happy."

"Excuse me?"

"Happy, George. You know, because you got what you wanted. A dumb American. A big fat allotment check."

"What's an allotment check?"

Jake sneered. "Cut the crap, George. Every broad in England knows what an allotment check is. It's legal payment for services rendered. Well, babe, you're gonna earn yours. You're gonna earn every damn dime."

George was prepared for the worst. What she wasn't prepared for was that he drank more gin, took off all of his clothing, and went to sleep on the bed. Wearing only her slip, she curled up beside him and watched him sleep. He was beautiful again now that his features were finally relaxed, the deep scowl smoothed away. She couldn't help but inspect his long body. Heat rose inside her, flaming her cheeks. She had never seen a completely naked man before. She couldn't believe another man could possibly be as wonderfully made as he.

Despite herself she remembered him laughing, remembered every little scrap of their whirlwind courtship. She hadn't really planned to go to the law, report him for rape. All she'd wanted was for him to grovel. A lot. Then propose marriage to her properly. And give her a ring that actually fit. He hadn't done any of those things; he'd only married her. And now he was being completely awful. If this was the way their marriage would always be, she didn't want him. As much as she still cared for him, she decided it would be best to leave while she could. She began to ease herself off the bed. A hand caught her wrist.

"Where do you think you're going?"

"If you will kindly release me, I will take myself as far away from you as humanly possible."

"Not yet, you won't. I have a four-day pass." She let go a startled squawk as he pulled her back down on the bed. His mouth covered hers and his hands were everywhere.

He wanted to hate her, he really did. But the sight of her, the feel of her, excited him. He pulled her slip off, then her panties. She whimpered, but she didn't fight him. When he ran his hands the length of her slender body and she arched herself, her little breasts going flat against her ribs, only the rosy, hardened peaks of her nipples distended, Jake could feel himself losing control.

Money, he reminded himself. *She's only doing this for the money. Don't let her fool you again.* This time he remembered the rubber before he entered her. George twitched and squirmed beneath him. As he pounded his hips against hers, he stared at the printed wallpaper and thought about other things, anything but how good she felt, how nicely she fit around him. He definitely didn't think about the way she had grabbed onto his rear end and wrapped her legs around his. But when he felt her release, heard her cry out, he couldn't take it anymore.

"Damn you, George!" he roared as he spent himself.

For four days and nights they ate together, slept together, and made love whenever the mood took them. George was deeply in love. She had Jack, the way he was when they'd first met, again. Only now everything was so much better because they were married. He was hers, completely hers. And although he laughed a lot, he lay still while she explored every delicious inch of him.

Howling laughter, Jake curled up defensively. "Cut it out, George! That tickles."

"You promised," she said as she kissed him along the rib cage. "You promised I could."

"Yeah! But I can't stand it."

He rolled away from her, lay huddled on his side. George crawled over him, her upside-down face peering into his. He was still breathing hard, his laughter beginning to fade.

"You're weird, George."

Rainwater on the White Road

"Ah, but can you resist me? Now, there's the question."

Jake thought the question through. She was right. He couldn't resist her. The more he had her, the more he wanted her. He craved her the way an alcoholic craved the bottle. And she was his temporary wife, so what the hell?

On the morning of their fifth day of married life, George woke to find him gone. There wasn't a note, there wasn't anything but a blank emptiness in the room they'd shared. He did not call her that day, or the next. She drifted around in a hurting daze as more days passed. Finally, needing something to do, she went into a little stitchery shop and, using some of the money she found on the dresser, she bought a cross-stitch pattern book, material, needles, and colored threads. Staying shut up in their room and concentrating on her stitchery, she waited for her husband to reappear.

Trying to forget her, trying to hold on to what he knew, that she'd played him for a sucker, Jake rigorously applied himself to further training, physically exhausting himself as he set new goals for himself on the obstacle course. Then, when he couldn't stand the thought of George being just down the road, that she was legally his to take whenever he wanted, he went to his company sergeant, a mildly understanding man and a member of the Delaware Nation. He asked for, and received, the rare privilege of sleeping off base.

"But you better be back here every morning at 0530, Rainwater."

"Yes, sir, Sergeant, sir."

George started in surprise when the door banged open. "Baby," he said, yanking his tie, "get your clothes off. It's time to make Daddy a real happy bunny."

The new adventure of Jake tearing in, wanting her so badly that it took her breath away, went on for weeks. Then one afternoon when he came crashing in, George was sick in bed.

"What's the matter?"

"I don't know," she sobbed. "I just feel so ill."

"Well, damn, George! Maybe you're sick from all those kippers you eat."

The mention of kippers had her leaping off the bed and running for the wash sink, heaving into the basin. The force and volume of her vomiting scared him to death.

"Oh, man, I'm taking you to the doctor."

The base doctor was hardly a gynecologist, but he knew the textbook signs of an early pregnancy when he saw them. He left Georgina to dress and went out to have a talk with Jake.

"She's what?"

"With child," the doctor drawled, "in the family way."

"She can't be! I've been using rubbers since the day we got married."

"And was there perhaps an unprotected occasion prior to the happy event?"

Jake's mouth dropped, and his eyes flew wide. "Oh, my God." He quickly looked at the doctor. "There was only one time. One measly time. A woman can't get pregnant from just one time!"

"Ooooooh, yes, she can. And she did."

Rainwater on the White Road

*   *   *

"Oh, not again!" Colonel T'Hart cried. "Rainwater, I'm getting really tired of bailing you out."

"I'm sorry, Colonel. But the situation has kinda changed on me. Now that my wife is having my baby, I need to get her out of England. Fast."

"No, you don't. Nothing has changed if you don't want it to be changed. All you've got to do is stay with Plan A. Hundreds of British broads come up pregnant, but trust me, there's nothing they can do once the would-be fathers are long gone. Rest assured, your little nipper will never know that the next guy in bed with Mommy is not his real daddy."

But I'll know, Jake thought. He did not bother saying this to his commander. This child was half Osage. He couldn't stand the thought of a half–Osage child being raised on the mean street where George's parents lived. If he abandoned his baby, his child would grow up never knowing who or what he or she really was. His firstborn would be just one more little bastard resulting from the war and would be raised to feel ashamed. Just the thought of English people taunting his helpless little half-caste child drove Jake crazy. And too, the knowledge that there was a child made him strangely happy. He already loved his baby. Loved his baby so much he would do anything for it. Even if the anything meant keeping its mother.

"I formally request that my wife be sent home to my parents. Please. Sir."

His colonel eyed Jake as he stood at ramrod attention. Since Jake had formally requested his wife's expatriation and this request was seen as reasonable by the Army, especially in view of the fact that she would have somewhere in the States to go and her pregnancy was a valid reason for evacuation, he couldn't turn his trooper down. But this was hardly a love match. It had been a marriage by entrapment. Now it was being used as a way to leave the country. That little girl might look innocent, but she had to be the most scheming bitch since Jezebel. And once again she was getting exactly what she wanted.

"Rainwater," Dutch snarled. "You have got to be the dumbest fuckin' Indian in a whole garrison of dumb fuckin' Indians."

"Thank you. Sir."

He returned Jake's salute. "Dismissed."

George was sobbing as Jake helped her with her cases, placing them on the waiting train. When that was done, he made certain the E-Vac badge dangling from a chain around her neck was placed just right over her buttoned-up coat.

"Now, remember what I told you, George. Always keep your papers with you. Don't let anybody walk away with them. You only get off the train at Portsmouth. And remember to eat right. Drink lots of milk."

"I don't like milk."

"It's for the baby, George. You have to drink lots of milk for the baby. Promise me."

"Oh, all right."

"As soon as the boat gets to America, you call my folks. You got the number?"

She meekly nodded.

"My mom will take good care of you. You do everything she says. Everything, George."

She looked up at him, her green-blue eyes brimming with new tears. "Will you write to me?"

Rainwater on the White Road

"Sure, kid. No sweat. Now, you'd better get on the train." He pecked her cheek and helped load her aboard. Then he waved and walked off, leaving long before the train pulled away.

Chapter Seven

Reading the telegram, May Rose had to sit down, read it again to make certain that her eyes weren't playing tricks on her.

Am Married—Stop—Sending Wife Home to You—Stop—Her name Is Georgina—Stop

Jake.

May Rose immediately fired off a letter to her son, but it wasn't answered. The date it arrived in England was June 6, 1944. Jake was in a troop plane over France. George was in Portsmouth. She remained in Portsmouth for nearly two months.

The American Navy was very organized. American Navy women processed the British war brides with indifferent efficiency. The war brides were always to wear their identity badges. They were reprimanded sharply whenever a bride happened to forget. At night they were crammed together in a barracks, sleeping on cots. Their meals were mess-hall style. Georgina remembered to drink milk. After the interminable wait, she and her group of women were finally shuffled onto a ship. She had never been on a ship before, and thanks to rough seas, being pregnant, terrified of leaving the only home she knew, and feeling as if she had stepped off a cliff into the great unknown, she was as sick as a dog throughout the crossing of the Atlantic.

Her eventual arrival in America would be a memory she would spend the rest of her life trying to blot out.

After docking, the women carried their luggage into a waiting area where their papers were examined at length. Then they were shown into a huge building and told to strip down. Stern-faced military police stood at the only doorway leading out, and more police stood along the walls should trouble arise. In front of all of these strange men, the women shyly removed their clothing. Then teams of doctors took turns shining lights in their eyes, their ears, and down their throats. The hair on their heads was examined for lice. Pubic hair was combed for crabs. After yielding to the blood and urine tests, they were made to shower in one great shower stall. While they showered, someone had very heavy-handedly gone through their luggage. It required patience and remarkable control of mutual fury to sort out which clothing belonged to whom and repack their cases. Then they were loaded onto a bus and taken to a hotel for women. They were not allowed to leave the hotel for any reason until the time came for them to depart for their final destinations. And again they would be taken under watchful escort to bus depots or train stations.

Welcome to the land of the free.

George waited in the long line snaking its way to the two desks set up in what should have been the hotel's reception. Since this was a special hotel,

known as the "War Bride Hilton," no real reception
was needed. The desks were staffed by two busy
women thumbing through massive travel books,
magically helping each bride plot her best route to
wherever her soldier husband wanted her to go.
While Georgina waited her turn in line, she tried to
recall her soldier husband's face. All she could remember clearly was his bare chest because that was
what she'd seen days before their separation. Jake
had been determined to have just as much sex as he
could before she left, and as he had forsaken the use
of those rubber thingies, he had been rather zealous.
It would have helped a great deal if she'd had a
picture of him. At this juncture a visual aid to remind
herself just why she was doing all of this was badly
needed. But she didn't. All she had of him was the
wedding ring, held firmly in place thanks to a wad
of taped-over paper, a copy of his dog tags on the
chain bearing her identity badge, and his baby sleeping inside her womb. She was very homesick, but
her home was solidly closed against her. Her father
had made that more than clear. On her last day in
Portsmouth, she'd plucked up her courage to ring
home to say good-bye. Hearing her voice, her father
had hung up.

Georgina shuffled forward. The line divided at the
two desks. Relieved to be off her feet, she sat down
on the metal chair facing the second desk.

The woman didn't even look up at her. "Destination, please."

Georgina handed over the mauled scrap of paper.
"I'm afraid I can't pronounce it."

The woman snatched the paper and read it. "Bartlesville, Oklahoma," she said nasally. "This phone number is the number I call to confirm?"

"Yes."

The woman picked up the receiver, dialed the long-distance operator.

May Rose was doing the supper dishes when the hallway telephone rang. She heard Claude answer, heard him speak in an odd manner.

"Yes. My son is Jacob Rainwater. Yes, this is his home number. What's the matter with my son?"

May Rose ran.

Holding the receiver away from his ear, Claude looked back at her. "Jakey's wife is in America. You want to talk to her?"

May Rose grabbed the phone. "Hello? Georgina?"

As soon as she heard the female voice, Georgina's throat seized shut.

"Georgina? Can you hear me?"

"Y-yes," she answered, her tone strangled.

On her end of the line, May Rose's brows shot up. *The poor little thing sounds scared to death!* Instantly, her mothering instincts leapt ahead of her. "Are they treating you all right, Georgina? Those Army people?"

George swiped her hand under her nose. *No. They're not treating me all right. They're hateful.* But to her stranger mother-in-law she said, "Everyone's been very . . . kind."

"But you're feelin' all alone, ain't ya?"

"Yes. Rather."

"Well, you just come on home." She had more to say, but a new voice came on the line, and May Rose did not like this woman's tone.

149

"We can have your daughter-in-law shipped to you on tonight's train."

Shipped to me? What do you think she is? A basket of fruit?

"The train will arrive tomorrow afternoon, six p.m. Oklahoma time. You of course will be expected to meet her and sign the proper release forms."

Now May Rose definitely knew she didn't like this woman's tone. "Of course I'll meet her. Let me talk to my daughter, please."

"Sorry, that isn't possible. This line is for official use only." The woman hung up. May Rose was so infuriated she slammed the phone down.

"What's the matter?" Claude asked.

"They're treatin' our son's wife bad, that's what's the matter."

"Now, Momma—"

"Don't you now Momma me! That poor little girl is all by herself, and she's scared. The least folks could be is pleasant to her. If Jakey was standin' in front of me right now, I'd slap him bowlegged for puttin' his own wife through something like I just heard." Then she remembered the early horrible first years of her own marriage. Angrily she pushed past Claude. "Get out of my way."

"What are you gonna do?"

"I'm gonna clean out that squirrel's nest Jakey calls a bedroom."

May Rose kept the house awake all through the night as she furiously cleaned and vacuumed. Then she redecorated, adding as a finishing touch a framed photograph of Jake on the brightly polished bedside table. When the room was neat and cleaned to her high standards, to the relief of her family of men, she collapsed in her own bed. She slept only three hours. She then occupied herself with ripping the rest of the house apart, cleaning every nook and cranny, putting it all back together again. Then she cooked Jake's favorite meal. Ham, candied yams, cornbread, black-eyed peas. All of it was left to warm in the oven while the Rainwaters drove into Bartlesville to meet the train.

A lot of people came off that train. May Rose searched the faces, believing she would know her foreigner daughter-in-law on sight. She believed this because she remembered vividly the type of girls Jake went around with. She was confident that his wife would be the very same type, tall, willowy, and with long dark hair.

Claude looked at the little girl lost inside a long buttoned-up coat and a square-shaped badge hanging down the center of the coat. A man with a clipboard stood beside her. The little girl looked worried. Claude nudged May Rose.

"I'll bet that's her."

May Rose looked in the direction Claude indicated with a lift of his chin. Her eyes flared. The little girl he meant had a white-white face and a zillion freckles. Her wild red hair was easily the eighth wonder of the world. Even with that too big coat on, if that very short girl weighed more than a hundred pounds, she'd be lucky.

"Oh, for pete's sake, Claude. That's not her. That's somebody's child."

"Yeah," he agreed. "An' I think she's ours."

May Rose was about to protest again when Wilber

spoke up. "Hey? Does everybody remember Matt's friend? Mikey O'Brian?"

"Well, of course we remember Mikey," May Rose snapped. "What's Mikey got to do with anything?"

"He had red hair," Wil laughed. "And Jake was always driving him nuts wanting to touch it. Mikey said Jake was only supposed to touch red *girl* hair. Guess that's what he finally did."

May Rose felt her blood draining to her ankles as her men exploded in life-threatening laughter.

She still couldn't believe that this child, staring at them with wide-eyed terror, was really Jake's wife, even though the man with the clipboard showed them the girl's identity badge and made Claude sign for her. The twins each picked up a suitcase, indicating that they were fully prepared to take their brother's wife home. Without realizing what she was doing, May Rose took the girl by the hand, and Georgina obediently toddled after her brand-new American-Indian mother.

In the car, huge by British standards, Georgina sat in the front seat between May Rose and Claude. Nervously she glanced over her shoulder at Jake's three brothers in the backseat. It was unnerving, but they looked so much like her vague memory of Jake. The twins were identical and seemed friendly. The youngest brother smirked and then turned his face away, looked out the window. The twins tried to break the uncomfortable silence in the car.

"I'm Walt."

"I'm Wilber."

"No, you're not. I'm Wilber."

"No way. My underwear says I'm Wilber."

"You're wearing my underwear."

Rainwater on the White Road

"I am?"

"Yeah. Give it back."

"Right here?"

"Yeah!"

"Boys!" May Rose cried. "Stop it right now." She patted Georgina's cold white hand. "They do that all the time. Mostly we ignore it."

Georgina fought against her instincts to leap out and run screaming from the car, far, far away from this totally alien life she had agreed to accept when she'd said I do.

The road was so dippy that the speeding car felt like a carnival ride. The countryside felt even more open and vast than it had from her small view of it through the train windows. Because it was almost spring, the hundreds of miles of rolling grasslands were changing from winter brown to a blueish-green. There were very few trees. And no other cars on the wide and rolling road.

"Does anyone else live in Oklahoma?" she asked timidly.

"Yeah!" a voice called from the backseat. "Indians. Thousands of Indians. And they're all gonna want your freaky hair."

"Allen!" Claude frowned darkly through the rearview mirror at his son. "One more word an' you'll be walkin' home."

Again, May Rose patted her frightened daughter-in-law's bloodless hand.

To Georgina, the Rainwater home was extremely large. There were no neighbors for miles. A series of six steps led up to the deep, covered front porch that ran the width of the front of the house and contained several rocking chairs. In the middle of her new family, George climbed the stairs, walked across the porch, and entered the house through the door her father-in-law held open for her. As she passed him, he spoke softly to her.

"Welcome home, little one."

Georgina ground her back teeth, fighting hard against the sudden urge to cry.

From what she saw of it, the front living room looked very clean, very lived in. There were two settees and several overstuffed chairs, standing lamps, an enormous radio. Framed photographs of stern-faced Indian men and women, as well as photographs of boy children of various ages, littered the walls, stared blankly at her as she followed her mother-in-law. "Momma-May, you just call me Momma-May," she said as she led the way to Jake's bedroom.

Her nerves, held together with spit and string, snapped when she saw the photograph of Jake on the bedside table. As she looked at that face she now remembered with startling clarity, the face she'd fallen so madly for practically the first second she saw him, her nerves snapped. Her hands covering her mouth and nose, she stared at Jake's smiling face and began to sob, her body shaking uncontrollably.

"Oh, my poor little soul," May Rose crooned, wrapping her arms around Georgina's trembling form. "Oh, bless your little heart." She stroked Georgina's wiry red hair and held onto her, making shushing noises. When Claude appeared in the doorway with the two suitcases, May Rose quickly shook her head, sending him away. "You just go ahead and cry, sweetheart. This is a real hard time for you. I know just how alone you feel. I really do. But you're safe now. You're safe."

"I-I need him," Georgina blubbered. "I need him so much."

"I know," May Rose whispered. "I know how that feels too."

When Georgina came shyly into the kitchen, May Rose looked askance at her baggy green woollen dress. That had to be just about the ugliest dress she had ever seen. Besides being ugly, it looked miles too big for her. Just like her coat was too big for her. English people sure didn't know how to dress.

"This is Jakey's favorite supper," she said as a slightly calmer Georgina sat down at the family table. She eyed the food Momma-May was piling onto the plate before her. "I know this has gotta be strange from what you're used to eatin', but you'll like it. I'm gonna have to teach you just how to cook for Jakey."

Her father-in-law, Daddy-Claude, was stuffing the corner of his napkin in the top of his shirt. "Jakey's pretty fussy. When he used to sleep over at a friend's house, if they weren't having food just like his momma cooked, he'd come home. So, you wanna keep him home, you better learn to cook just like your Momma-May."

Georgina did not like "Jakey's" favorite food. It was too salty, and the yellowy bread fell apart when she tried to butter it. She ate the food anyway, washing each mouthful down with glass after glass of milk.

"It's a good thing we got a cow," May Rose joked. "You sure do love milk."

"No," she answered. "Actually, I don't like milk

at all. I'm only drinking it because Jack—Jake," she quickly amended, "made me promise that I would."

May Rose's brows knit together. "Why would he make you promise that?"

"Because of the baby. He said milk is good for the baby."

All around her cutlery clattered against china.

"Baby!" May Rose whooped.

"Well, that little sonofagun," Claude cackled.

"Way to go, Jakey!" one of the twins yelped.

"One of us is gonna be an uncle," the other twin cried.

The first twin turned in his chair. "It's gonna be me. I was born first."

"Oh, yeah? Prove it. Even Momma doesn't know which one of us was born first."

"My birth certificate says me, Walt. I was born first, so I get to be an uncle first. You can have the next baby."

"I want this baby."

"Tough."

"Boys!" May Rose banged the table with her fist. Georgina was the only person seated around the oval table who jumped in her chair. May Rose didn't notice. She was looking at each male face meaningfully. She turned to Georgina. "Sweet girl, eat all of your supper. Then I want you to go straight to bed. You need your rest."

During her first week in residence, the hot weather was awful. Momma-May was equally awful. She treated Georgina like a fragile doll, always making her take naps at noon under an oscillating fan, eat every scrap of food she presented her. The one food Georgina actually liked were the odd little crackers

Momma-May called Saltines. They were like British cream crackers but with salt baked in. And then she discovered a wonderful treat. Marshmallows. She discovered these quite by accident when helping Momma-May put away the bags of groceries. When she inquired about the marshmallows, Momma-May allowed her to try one. Georgina actually hummed while the marshmallow melted in her mouth. Momma-May laughed.

To combat the weather and to accommodate her growing bulge, George cut off the legs of a pair of Jake's jeans. Then she took off the sleeves of one of his shirts. Seeing her in this odd attire, Momma-May laughed. But not as merrily as she had about the marshmallows. When Momma-May concerned herself with other things in the kitchen, George stole the bag of marshmallows and the box of saltines. Then she scooted out to the front porch and sat cross-legged on the floor, basking in the sun and eating sandwiches made of crackers and marshmallows. Her mouth was full when Walt and Wil came bounding up the steps. In those seconds George learned just how hard it was for a person to swallow marshmallows and crackers in one big gulp. She was almost choking to death when her twin brothers-in-law reached her.

Wil whacked her solidly on the back. When she coughed and choked even more, he cried, "What is she eating?"

Walt held up the incriminating box and bag. "Can you believe *this*?"

"Oh, man! Get her some water."

Walt rushed into the house. George's coughing came under a modicum of control. Wil stopped slapping and began to rub her back in circles. "George, if you're gonna eat junk, at least eat good junk. I'll buy you some Baby Ruth's or something."

"What's that?"

"You've never heard of a Baby Ruth?"

"No."

She coughed again, and Wil rubbed some more. Wil noticed her little legs sticking out of the cutoff jeans. On top of everything else, she was getting a sunburn. Wil stood and drew George up with him, taking her to a rocking chair in the shade.

"A Baby Ruth is a candy bar. I'll get you a bunch if you promise you'll do something for me."

"What?"

"Go easy on the sunning stuff. You don't have the skin for it. You're gonna have to take being in the sun in stages until your skin toughens up."

"Okay."

Walt came out with a glass of water, handing it to her.

"Thank you, Walt."

Wil and Walt's eyes slewed to the corners. They stared at each other, sharing the same thought. No names had been mentioned. How did she know it had been Walt who had gone for water? Suddenly needing to test her, both squatted down in front of the rocking chair. Their faces stared up at her while George drank the water.

"Who am I?" Wil asked.

"You're Wil," Georgina replied.

"How do you know?"

She looked from one to the other. It would be a long time before she herself actually understood. All she knew in this particular moment was that she could quite easily identify each twin.

"I-I just do. You're Wil." She turned to Walt. "You're Walt."

The twins looked at each other. Walt said, "It's gotta be because we're wearing different stuff."

"Yeah, you're right." Wil looked quickly at George. "Wait right here. Don't move."

Five minutes later, they were back on the porch in identical clothing, jeans, plaid short-sleeve shirts. The game of Who Am I? started again.

"Walt," Georgina giggled, pointing at the correct twin.

"Shit! She's right. I think I am Walt."

"Let's make this *really* hard." Wil dragged his brother back into the house. Seconds later, a twin emerged, solo.

"Hello, Wil," George laughed.

Wil flapped his arms and sailed back toward the screened door.

"How did she do that?" Walt's voice from inside the house bayed.

Wil pulled open the door. "Damned if I know!" Minutes later, Wil drove into Urainia and bought George a box of Baby Ruth's. He also brought back a pack of playing cards, and in the softer light of the setting sun, he sat with George on the floor of the front porch, teaching her to play poker. Three days later, Wil took his mother off to the side and let loose his temper.

"Momma, you got to stop pushing George around."

"I'm not pushing her around. I'm taking care of her."

"Momma," he said, trying to remain patient, "you're

159

treating her like she's five years old. Jake's not going to like that."

"Now, how do you know—"

"I *know*, Momma!" Wil shouted. "Because if she was my wife, I wouldn't like it. I wouldn't like it one bit. And you know something else I wouldn't like? I wouldn't like it that my wife has to run around in rags because she's too pregnant to fit in her regular clothes."

The next morning, Momma-May woke George up by bringing in a cup of coffee. Georgina sipped the coffee, heavily loaded with milk and sugar, while May Rose opened the drapes to let the sunshine into the room.

"We got a busy day today, George. We've got to go to town."

"Why?"

"Well, I want to show you off is why. And you need yourself some pregnancy clothes. Now, stir yourself, sweet girl. Breakfast is waiting."

"Doesn't she talk cute?" the woman in the store cried. "I swear, she sounds just like in the movies. And she's so little. I didn't know English people was little."

May Rose was both proud and proprietary about her daughter-in-law. May rose took full charge of the shopping expedition. "We're gonna have to dress her from the skin out. Because of the war, English people don't have much to wear, and what with her being pregnant an' all—"

"Jakey's gonna be a daddy?"

May rose beamed. "He sure is. That's why he sent

his wife home to his momma. He didn't want his baby gettin' bombed."

"Well, of course he didn't." The woman led May Rose to the counter. "Let's start with underwear. Do English girls wear underwear?"

"In my house they do."

Looking at Georgina, the woman edged her glasses down her narrow nose. "Is she wearing *socks* with those low heels?"

Georgina vainly tried to hide one foot.

"She likes to wear socks," May Rose said defensively. "Guess we better try her on a pair of penny loafers."

Outside the store, as May Rose bundled the packages into the backseat of the car, a slender Indian girl approached her.

"Miz Rainwater?"

May Rose turned. "Well, hello, Lucy. How are you, girl?" Then quickly, "Lucy, I want you to meet Jake's wife. Her name is Georgina, but it's okay to call her George."

The young woman, about Georgina's age, offered her hand for a shake. As they shook, Lucy looked her over. "Are you from out of town?"

"Oh, yes," May Rose answered for George. "She's all the way from England. She just got here, really, and she doesn't have any friends yet. Maybe you should come over."

Knowing an opportunity when it was handed to her, Lucy beamed. "Thank you, Miz May. I'd love to."

Lucy came over that very afternoon. Wil and George were playing cards, and George was eating another Baby Ruth. Wil didn't particularly care for Lucy, and he didn't care for the way she was muscling in on George. Wil badly wanted Lucy to go away.

She didn't.

Chapter Eight

May Rose stood at the kitchen sink looking out of the window, seeing absolutely nothing. She hadn't been feeling all that well lately. Just a little wrung out and troubled now and then by bouts of heartburn. It had been easy to put these minor discomforts out of her mind, believe they were simply caused by the excitement of getting to know Jake's wife, getting her settled in. When she'd taken George in for a checkup at the doctor's (which was only smart—God only knew what George had been exposed to in England), she decided she might as well have a checkup too.

Never in a thousand years had she expected what the doctor told her. "Mrs. Rainwater, you don't have indigestion. What you have here is a pregnancy. Almost three months worth. Which makes you about two and a half months behind your daughter-in-law."

Oh, dear Lord, she wept. *What am I going to do?*

"No!" she said out loud. "I can't be pregnant. I'm about to be a grandmother. If I have a baby younger than my own grandchild, I'll be a laughingstock."

Bud was all right once Matt got used to him. That took a number of weeks. Bud was very prompt with the beck-and-call bit, but even better, he kept the nurses at bay. Yet he was torture when it came to rehab.

Bud forced Matt to work the stiffened leg until sweat poured out of every pore in his body. The way Bud worked this minor miracle was his ability to piss the hell out of Matt.

"What you wanna be the rest of your life, Jackson? Some kinda pity-me crip?"

And then when Matt didn't think he had another ounce of strength to carry on, Bud would shrug and say, "Well, so much for Indians being able to take a lot of pain without whinin'."

Hate blazing from his dark eyes, Matt would hoist himself between the parallel bars and force himself to walk another few feet, trying to get to Bud, who waited smugly at the other end. And with each forced step Matt would threaten, "I'm going to kill you."

Bud, his arms crossed over his chest, chewed his ever present wad of gum, smirking. "Gotta catch me first—Jackson."

"Stop calling me Jackson!"

"You just walk over here and make me—Jackson."

Bud loved Matt's wheelchair. With Bud in control, Matt found himself loving it as well. Bud ran it at top speed, Matt hanging on for dear life as they made a riot of hospital corridors. But outside the hospital walls, Bud had come up with his own form of physical therapy. He took Matt to the beach, propelling him in the wheelchair. And on the beach he walked Matt in the shallows of the ocean, using himself as a crutch for Matt to lean on. Working against the sand and the pull of the ocean woke up muscles in Matt's atrophied leg.

"I saw this in a movie once," Bud explained. "It was about a racehorse that blew some tendons and was said to be all washed up. Well, the jockey—I think it was Mickey Rooney—started working the horse in the ocean, and what do ya know? The nag bounces back and wins the mother load of races. You ain't a horse, Jackson, but you're pretty close."

"You know, of course, one day I will kill you for all the Jackson shit you keep dishing out, don't ya?" A wave caught them and knocked them down.

Bud rescued a nearly drowned Matt. "You can't kill me until you pay off the ten grand you owe me from poker. Besides, I just saved your life."

"Thanks, Pud," Matt wheezed.

"It's Bud!" the swabby yelped.

"When I stop being Jackson," Matt smiled, "you stop being Pud."

"Well, allllll ret, all ret!" Bud grinned. "My main cat's gettn' hep to that jive!"

"You're hopeless."

May Rose watched Claude stop the truck in the drive. She watched him climb out, amble toward the screened-in back porch, lunch bucket dangling from his left hand. She was there to open the screened door for him as he climbed the set of six steps.

"I got something to tell ya, Claude."

Standing in front of her, he bent at the waist and kissed her frowning mouth. "What's the problem, love muffin?"

"I'm gonna have another baby."

The left corner of Claude's mouth began to lift.

"Don't you dare grin!"

"I ain't grinnin'."

"Yes, you are," she growled. "You're standing there grinning like a fool. An' this ain't funny, Claude. What's everybody gonna say when I have a baby just about the same time my daughter-in-law has a baby?"

Claude lifted his shoulders in a shrug. "Guess they're gonna say what they've always said. That you can't keep your hands off me."

May Rose slapped his arm. "They don't say that!"

"Okay," he laughed. "I guess I'm the one who always says that. But it's still true. You're the horniest damn woman I ever met in my whole life. It's a wonder we don't have twenty kids."

May Rose puckered up her face to cry. "But I'm so embarrassed about this baby," she squalled. "Everybody's gonna laugh at me because I'm too old to have a baby."

Claude wrapped an arm around her as she cried against his chest. "It's gonna be all right, Muffin. I think maybe this late baby means God's got something real special in mind."

A tear spilled down her cheek as she looked up at him. "Do you really think so, Claude?"

"Well, I sure hope so. Startin' us all over again at our age, He'd better have one hell of a reason."

In Hawaii, it was hard to tell one season from another. It felt like summer as Matt sat in the wheelchair on the lawn of the hospital grounds, his eyes straight ahead, not seeing the view of Diamond Head. Actually, it was coming hard up on autumn. A letter from Lucy dangled from his hand. Bud lay on the grass, popping his gum as he read a book, a western by Zane Grey. Lucy's letters were coming almost daily, filled with news about home and Jake's wife—a girl everyone called George. Irma's letters were nonexistent. If not for Lucy sitting with George and writing letters every day, Matt would have very little mail. His father never wrote, and his mother, he knew, was deeply ashamed of her small abilities. When she did write, her letters were only a few lines. Lucy stood the breech, and though her face was blurry in his mind, he was grateful to her for taking up the slack. Though why she bothered was a mystery. He had never liked her. Couldn't even remember being nice to her.

Bud looked up from his novel toward the contemplating Matt. "Bad news from home?"

"No," Matt grunted.

"Gettin' antsy about gettin' the big one pinned on ya tomorrow?"

Matt turned and gazed at Bud. Here was another mystery Matt had yet to fathom. Why was he getting the Medal of Honor? He had wanted to ask many times but hadn't out of embarrassment. He was afraid if he showed his ignorance, the preferential treatment he received would end. If they thought he was a fool, he might lose the meals of thick steaks. The private room would suddenly be a bed on a ward. Then too, there was the real prospect of being laughed at for not knowing.

Matt chewed the corner of his mouth as he studied Bud. He decided to ask the question which had been nagging him. He could tolerate Bud laughing at him. Hell! When didn't Bud laugh at him?

"Pud," Matt began softly. "If I were to ask you

something, but before I asked, swore you to keep the question secret, would you do it?"

Bud rose and sat cross-legged. "Solid, Jackson. Depend on me. You want a broad or something?"

"No," Matt snapped irritably. "Just the answer to a question."

"Shoot," Bud said, his face devoid of its normal grin. "If I know it, you got it."

Matt inhaled deeply, his large chest expanding and contracting. "Before anybody puts a medal on me, I gotta know"—his eyes were pleading as he looked at Bud—"just what did I do to deserve it?"

Bud's jaw dropped and the gum fell out, plopping onto the grassy spot between his crossed legs. He worked his gaping mouth several times before he found his voice.

"You mean, you don't know?"

Matt further amazed him, shaking his head silently. Bud jumped to his feet, waving his arms like a goony bird flapping for a takeoff. "Man, oh man!" Bud shouted to the cobalt heavens. "Ain't that a pip! An' all this time I thought you were pulling the modesty routine."

He squatted down in front of Matt. "You know the score, quiet guy who saves his whole regiment but's too shy and too manly to talk about it. You sure fit that bill. But not knowing, hey, cat, that's too heavy-duty even for me. You absolutely, positively sure you don't know? This just ain't some lame-o way of talkin' about it without lookin' like you're really talkin' about it, is it? I mean, 'cause if it is, hey, I can dig it."

"Do you know or don't you?" Matt shouted.

"Hey! I know, all right," Bud replied excitedly. "I mean, everyone *knows*!"

"Then would you mind very much telling *me*?" Matt leaned forward in his chair. "Now?"

"Steady, Jackson," Bud returned. His hands pushed against Matt's shoulders, settling him back in the chair. "This is a long story. Might as well stay cool and comfy for this one."

And so began Bud's action-packed tale of Matt the hero. He even acted it out. It was rather thrilling and highly entertaining, this story of the lone Marine, busted from hip to foot in one leg, lying on his back, a machine gun in each hand defending the shreds of his unit. Then Bud/Matt heroically took out Jap snipers in the trees, and taking the pins out of the grenades with his teeth, Bud/Matt blew up the Japs holed up in ground tunnels.

Matt applauded, then he laughed. "What a load of bull!"

Bud came to stand before him, his expression solemn. "No, it ain't, man. The E-Vacs got the dope from the guys you saved. They told the whole story while you were out cold. But before you flaked out, you almost blew a hole through a jarhead second louie, thinkin' he was a Jap too. It wasn't until you knew for sure the Marines had landed that you finally laid your guns down. That louie almost crapped his pants comin' that close to the Big D. But word is he did crap 'em after the gook body count. A couple of the slants had broken necks from where you just shot the tree out from under 'em an' they hit the ground headfirst."

"Really?" Matt's voice broke like a pubescent boy soprano's.

"Straight skinny, blood brother."

Desperately trying to remember, Matt rested his chin in the palm of his hand. "I sound like one hell of a guy."

"Just don't let it go to your head," Bud warned. "I liked you better thinkin' you were modest. If you go all arrogant, you can just find some other sucker to push your chair."

Grudgingly, Matt laughed. "I would hate to lose you now, Pud. I mean, we've become so close."

Bud stood and grabbed the back handles of the wheelchair. "Can't get no closer than one guy wipin' another guy's ass. But don't try jackin' me around, Jackson. I'm sensitive."

The award ceremony was so full of pomp it reeked of circumstance. A stage had been constructed out on the hospital's lawn that fronted the huge gray-painted flat-board building. There were so many brass present one couldn't help wondering who was left to run the war.

Matt was dressed in Marine dress blues, one pant leg altered to fit over the thigh-to-ankle metal leg brace. He was lifted onto the stage since he couldn't manage the steps. The press on hand to photograph the event had the decency not to shoot pictures of Matt being hoisted onto the stage. There were speeches, which Matt had to stand through, long bouts of applause, and finally the commandant of the Marine Corps draped America's most coveted medal around Matt's neck.

The press boys went wild. Another American Indian had scored for the United States. The second, also a Marine, was a Pima. This second Indian Marine had helped to hoist the flag over Iwo Jima. There was now talk of making a national monument depicting the historic moment. One could almost picture generals Sherman, Sheridan, and Custer rolling in their respective graves.

Flashbulbs popped all around Matt. The only thing he was able to see were blue spots and Bud's grinning face as Bud stood in front of the cheering throng. There was a celebration dinner slated, but Matt got out of it claiming fatigue. Bud played it up, taking charge of Matt, daring even to slap away the hands of an admiral who had tried to commandeer Matt's chair. Back in the safety of Matt's room the pair hooted and laughed.

Big trays loaded with food were trollied in. The two toasted one another with cold beer. For Matt, this private meal with a real friend was the best part of the day. The celebration was made even better by another letter from Lucy.

He took long pulls on his beer as he sat comfortably on his bed, reading her familiar scrawl. In this letter she had included a Kodak snap of herself hugging and grinning with the image of Jake's wife, George. Now, happily, Lucy's face was very clear in Matt's mind. But she was no longer the little skinny girl he vaguely remembered. She was, as Bud would say, a real looker.

Bud spotted the photograph and made a rude grab for it. Before Matt could stop him, Bud was whistling as he held it for inspection.

"Now, this is something!" Bud said, impressed with what he saw. "You been holding out, Jackson. I thought you said you didn't know any Indian princesses. If this ain't one, then man, I'm dyin'. Who's the white babe?''

Matt snatched the snapshot back, frowning, "Don't talk about her like that. She's my brother's wife." Matt studied the photograph for a long time without saying any more. When he finished his beer, he startled Bud by asking, "Have we got any paper in this hole? I feel like writin' a letter."

Wil was working extra shifts of overtime. George missed him. He was a lot of fun. After slowly getting her skin used to sun, she surprised even herself with the light tan she'd developed. And more freckles. Wil called her Pinto.

"Why do you call me, Pinto?"

"Well, I guess 'cause I know you'd get teed off if I called you Appaloosa."

On his days off, Wil always took her for drives, showing her the many aspects of Oklahoma. George fell in love with her new home. But the days when Wil and Walt weren't around, she was so bored she wanted to scream. Slowly, she became dependent on Lucy for company. Lucy was a very self-assured person. They had absolutely nothing in common, but Lucy seemed strangely eager to be her friend. Lucy came over almost daily, and they spent their time together sitting out under a tree writing letters, Lucy to Matt and George to Jake. But it was as if all of their letters to each brother were swallowed up in a black hole. Neither of them ever received a reply. George at times despaired, but Lucy was certain that the fault lay with the mail service.

"What we do is we just keep writing. We'll get an answer when we least expect it."

Rainwater on the White Road

"How long have you been in love with Matt?"

Lucy looked up, practically glared at her. Then she seemed to relax. "Almost all of my life. Ever since he started going around with my sister Irma. But she's going steady with another guy now. They're going to get married. So, I've decided to see if Matt might like me. Anyway, I hope he does."

"I'm sure he will."

"George," Lucy drawled. "Let's keep this a secret from Miz May."

"Why?"

"Well, she can be a little . . . possessive about her sons. Especially Matt because he's her oldest son and she's still just getting used to Jake being married. Maybe knowing how I feel about Matt would, well, make her want to warn him that I was out to get him or something."

"I don't think that's true."

"But promise me anyway."

"All right, Lucy."

George found Matt's letter in the yard mailbox during her everyday hunt for a letter from Jake. She ran as fast as she could back to the house, where she put in a call to Lucy. All George had time to say was, "You got a letter," when the line went dead. Lucy ran the two and a half miles separating her parents' house from the Rainwaters'. George met her in the front drive, the precious letter hot in her hand.

Dear Lucy,

Sorry about not writing before. The truth is, I didn't know what to say. I still saw you as a little girl, I guess. Your last letter with the picture ended that. But I have to ask you, what is a pretty girl like you doing writing to a banged-up old man like me? It's awful nice of you and I really hope you don't stop, but I hope you're, dating other guys and not making me into something I'm not, the way the newspapers are doing. I'd hate for you to wait around for something that might disappoint you.

My leg is healing up, but in all honesty it won't ever be the same. I can walk now, thanks to my pal Bud, but I'm still as slow as a turtle. I told all this to Irma, and I figure that's why she doesn't write me much anymore. Maybe she didn't tell you. Anyway, that's the size of it. If your letters stop coming, I'll understand with no hard feelings. I'll just count myself lucky that a beautiful girl like you wasted as much time as she did.

Best regards, Matt

Lucy promptly answered. She made certain that her letters neither flooded nor did they trickle. They were a constant flow that Matt learned to count on and look forward to. Slowly, his replies became more consistent. "Best regards" changed to "thinking of you." In the final days Matt was in Hawaii, "thinking of you" changed to "love." Then his letters stopped. Lucy was frantic, almost at the point of tearing out her hair. After an especially bad night spent dreaming of Matt writing to tell her that he was in love with a nurse, she woke to hear her mother shouting into the phone. "Matt? You want to talk to Lucy? Not Irma?"

Lucy was out of her bed and running to the phone like a shot. Like a wild woman she grappled with her confused parent for the receiver. Matt's voice came over the wire, filling Lucy's savagely pounding heart.

"Hey, Luce. Guess where I am?"

"I'll bite," she laughed. "Where are you?"

"Frisco. You know, California. I'm out of the war, Luce. I'm coming home."

"Oh," Lucy sobbed. "Oh, Matt. This is the best Christmas present."

"We kinda missed Christmas," he chuckled. "And we're still too early for Valentine's Day."

"I don't care!"

There was a long pause before Matt said, "I was kinda hopin' "—a lengthy pause—"you would maybe meet my train? I'd really like to see you."

"Just tell me when and I'll be there."

Matt gave her the needed information and cradled the telephone. Then he sat quietly staring at it. Bud walked over to him, handed him a bottle of beer.

"Everything okay?"

"I guess so," Matt said softly. Looking up at Bud, he sighed. "She said she'd meet the train."

Bud clapped Matt's shoulder. "Way to go, Jackson."

Matt took a long swig of beer. "I don't know, Pud. I'm gettin' kind of scared about this."

"Why?" Bud yelped. "You got this eye-poppin' babe meetin' you at the station an'—"

"And I'll come gimping off like some old man with braces on his leg," Matt shouted.

"Yeah, an' with a big fat medal around his neck."

Matt slammed the beer bottle down on the bedside table. It foamed over in retaliation. Neither Bud nor Matt worried about the spillage.

"Any girl that beautiful isn't going to have her head turned by a medal," Matt snapped. "She's going to want a man. A whole man. Face it, Pud. I'm a wash-out.''

"Oh, pity me, pity me!" Bud mocked. "Save it, Jackson, for somebody who doesn't know better. I'm in on the whole deal, remember? I'm the one who sat and listened to every letter that little dish wrote to ya. When I tell ya that little gal is gone on ya, brother, I ain't sayin' it just to blow smoke up your ass. If there's any cold feet around, they're all yours.''

Matt looked sheepishly at his friend. "Thanks, Pud."

"What for, Jackson?"

"For everything."

"Do me a favor." Bud grimaced. "Save the thank-you's till the end of the line."

"Alllll ret," Matt laughed.

It was a very cold but clear day when the town of Bartlesville, as well as the president and ruling council of the Osage Nation, turned out with the Rainwaters to welcome home their local hero. As the crowd waited for the train, snow crunched beneath feet and breath came out in foggy puffs. When at last the train was spotted and its whistle cut through the stillness, the crowd let go a cheer.

Lucy was as nervous as a cat in heat. Everything she had worked for, planned for, was about to happen. George mistook Lucy's mood, thought that she was becoming apprehensive. She wrapped an arm around Lucy's shoulders and whispered, "Head up. He's home. Put a smile on your face."

Lucy's head immediately popped up, and a smile spread and froze.

Meanwhile, on the train Matt was receiving similar instructions.

"Jackson," Bud said as he straightened Matt's tie. "Remember what I said. Hang onto the side rails and take the stairs like you would if you were still on crutches. Both legs swingin' at once. Don't think about nothing else except getting down those stairs. An' don't let the porters try an' help you. They'll just make you look like an asshole while they're gettin' in your way. Just do it the way we practiced back in Pearl."

Matt panicked. "What if I fall down in the snow?"

"Ya ain't gonna fall." Bud frowned. " 'Cause if you do, I'll just leave you there kickin'. It'll serve you right for embarrassing me."

"Thanks, Pud."

"No problem, Jackson."

Matt's heart lurched right along with the train as it came to a wobbly halt. He swallowed hard and turned the doorknob. He glanced briefly back at Bud, standing right behind him, duffel bags strapped to each shoulder.

"Don't make me kick a hero in the ass," Bud warned. "It'll look bad in the newspapers."

Matt opened the door, braced his courage, placed his gloved hands on the side rails, and took the stairs exactly the way he and Bud had practiced, letter perfect, coming to stand on the platform, trembling badly as the crowd roared its approval. Matt barely heard them over Bud's voice hissing like a snake in his ear.

"Jackson. You're forgetting the part where you sidestep enough for *me*, so's I can get off the effin' train too!"

"Sorry, Pud." Matt made two small sliding steps to the left. He breathed a huge sigh of relief when Bud was there, standing shoulder to shoulder with him.

A band was playing as two members of the state militia tried to escort Matt toward a raised platform. Bud quickly intervened.

"He don't do stairs. He's gotta stand *in front* of the stage."

"Uh-oh," a militia man worried. "The governor wants him on the stage. He's gonna be real mad if we don't get him up on the stage."

"Oh, yeah? Well, if the governor had a ten-pound brace on his leg, he wouldn't be able to climb up those steps either! You're governor is an idiot, and you can tell him Seaman First Class Robert J. Foley said so."

Other arrangements were quickly made. Matt was escorted, laboriously, to the front of the stage, and the governor and the mayor stood on either side of him. The cheering crowd hushed as the president of the Osage Nation, on the stage, gave a speech. Then he, and all of the members of the council, descended the ill-planned steps and shook Matt's hand.

May Rose couldn't stand another second of the ceremony. She ran from her designated spot to her son, flinging her arms around him. Holding her, Matt laughed.

"Ma? You got fat!"

May Rose thumped his solid chest as she clung more tightly against him, all to the grand benediction of the mob. Matt's eyes lifted and he scanned the faces. Lucy waggled her fingers in a shy wave.

Lucy had a new dress suit for the occasion, and

her hair was tied back into a thick bun at the nape of her neck. She had paid a lot of attention to her makeup. A little pillbox hat was pinned just above it, the fine black netting crossing her brows. She was nothing like the little, bratty girl who used to sit between Matt and Irma at the movies. Matt was awestruck as she raced toward him. May Rose was surprised when Matt pushed her away, opened up his arms to Lucy. He staggered as Lucy impacted with him, but the ever watchful Bud blocked any danger that the embracing pair might fall over like Humpty-Dumpty and friend.

Flashbulbs exploded as Matt kissed Lucy. "Returning Hero Gets Warm Welcome," the next morning newspaper headlines read.

May Rose had outdone herself preparing the welcome-home feast. Everything was on the table including the fatted calf. Her home overflowed with family and friends. George was as uncomfortable as hell. She didn't know all of these people, and she felt severely out of place. From having to stand for so long at the welcoming ceremony and now staying on her feet to carry around trays, serve drinks, pick up and wash out abandoned glasses, her legs felt swollen. And there was a pressure in her pelvis that made her eyes water. Somehow, believing she was fooling everyone, she managed to smile and get through the evening. Wil noticed George's strained expression. He was relieved when his mother began tossing people out because Matt looked tired.

Matt was tired. Tired of people slapping him on the back and shaking his hand. All he wanted was a little peace and a few moments alone with Lucy. Bud had deserted him. Thankfully, Lucy remained by his side. The whole time Bud worked the party like a hunting ferret searching out his princess. And it seemed he'd found her. Little Tammy Bates, Matt's third cousin. Only she wasn't little anymore. She was seventeen and stunning. Bud seemed to be having some success because Tammy was laughing at just about everything he said. The Bates clan were saying their good-byes, but Bud clung onto Tammy's hand.

"Give me your phone number!" Bud was heard shouting over the voices in the room. "Your home address. Your shoe!"

Tammy was laughing so hard she was almost in tears. The rest of the room joined in. Bud was one funny guy, but in this moment of time he wasn't trying to be. He was in dead earnest, frantic this girl would get away from him. Dragging Tammy by the hand, he made a beeline for Matt.

"Ya gotta help me, Jackson," he panted.

"How?" Matt asked, his brows knitting.

Like a man fighting for his life Bud hurriedly suggested, "We can all go for a ride or something. You an' Luce, me and Tammy. Come on, buddy. Do this for me!"

Matt puffed a long stream of air through his mouth. "P-P-P-P-Bud." Matt blushed as he caught himself just in the nick of time. "You know I can't drive!"

"I'll drive!" Bud screamed.

"All right, all right." Matt puffed his cheeks. "Go get the keys to the car from my dad." He turned to Lucy, "Would you mind a lot if we went—?"

Lucy ran to get her coat.

* * *

180

Rainwater on the White Road

Getting Matt into the car was no easy task. His braced leg could not bend. The ride to the Rainwater stronghold hadn't been much of a problem, for he and Lucy had been given the privilege of riding in the governor's car. The limousine had had miles of leg room in the backseat. The Ford coupe owned by the Rainwaters wasn't as accommodating. Like a frenzied demon, Bud pushed Matt around like an oversize bag of oats, finally securing Matt in the front seat.

As Bud sat behind the wheel of the auto, their eyes slid and met. The girls, in the backseat, tittered softly as Bud said, "Jackson. I think there's something wrong with this plan."

"And just what would that be?" Matt deadpanned.

From the backseat, Lucy tapped Bud's peacoat shoulder. "Bud, I can drive."

Bud popped open the front door and hauled back the folding seat, allowing Lucy to wriggle through. Then he made a dash to be in the back with Tammy. Lucy settled in behind the wheel and then realized with some dismay that she could barely reach the pedals. And because of Matt's leg, moving the seat forward was out of the question. She cast Matt a worried look. Realizing her plight, Matt laughed.

"Just aim for the barn, Luce, and pull around behind it. Nobody wanted to go for a long ride anyway."

Lucy put the car in first and tippy-toed the gas pedal, and they set off with all the breakneck speed of a pregnant slug. After steering the car around behind the barn, Lucy killed the car lights but left the motor running. The snow had turned to sleet, and

181

the car heater was barely able to keep up with the cold of the night.

Not that Bud or Tammy noticed. Neither of them were visible through the rearview mirror. Lucy slid next to Matt, her hands busy bundling his long coat around his leg to make certain the metal brace didn't attract any more cold air.

"You're a little worry wart," Matt chuckled.

"You're uncomfortable enough without being cold." Lucy felt her face heating under his intent gaze.

His curled fingers caressed her cheek. "There's a better way to keep me warm."

Lucy sat transfixed as his face neared hers and their mouths touched. His kiss was so gentle and soft. And this was Matt, the man she wanted. How odd that she did not feel the fire she had been expecting. The fire that George went on about when she talked about kissing Jake. Lucy moved closer, thinking that if she kissed him enough, the fire would start. It didn't. Not even when Matt's arm encircled her, pulled her tightly against him. She felt his tongue slowly invade her parted lips, and she heard a muffled moan emitted from his chest as his kiss grew more ardent, more demanding. She yielded herself to it and moaned too. Mainly because that's what everyone else in the car was doing, and because it seemed to please Matt.

George helped May Rose shuffle the last of the dishes from the living room buffet table to the kitchen. May Rose was still on cloud nine, chatting her head off as George dottered behind her.

"I am so surprised about Matt and Lucy." She took the dishes from George and added them to the stack near the sink. "It worries me that he's taking up with Irma's own sister. I think maybe I should have a talk with Matt an—"

"Mom!" Wil's voice bellowed behind her. Turning, she saw Wil holding George by the shoulders and George holding on to the kitchen counter with both hands. George's face was very pale, and her zillion freckles looked almost black against her snow white skin.

"Oh, my! Wil! Get her to the bedroom."

Wil half carried her as May Rose hurried alongside, talking to George.

"Is it the baby?"

"I-I don't know," George sobbed. "I just keep feeling the urge to—"

"Move your bowels?"

Biting hard on her lower lip, George nodded.

"Little girl? Didn't anyone ever tell you that having a baby is like tryin' to poop a pumpkin?"

"Mom? Should I be hearing this stuff?" Wil hollered.

May Rose slapped her son on the back of his head. "Just get her in the bed and then call the doctor."

Wil paced the living room rug down to bare fiber as the doctor examined George in the back bedroom. Walt and Claude watched Wil. Allen, his expression thoroughly bored, skimmed through a magazine. Wil stopped pacing long enough to yell at his father.

"What's going on in there?"

"Well," Claude drawled, "she ain't yellin' so can't be much happenin'."

"Yelling?" Wil visibly paled. "Women . . . yell?"

"Scream their lungs loose," Claude cackled. "It's

the most awfulest sound you'll ever hear in your whole life."

Suddenly Wil had to sit down.

"Jake's real lucky he's missing this," Walt said with a huge sigh.

Wil shot his twin a filthy look.

"Braxton-Hicks," the doctor said lightly. He folded away his stethoscope. May Rose held her hand as Georgina lay on the bed and looked at him in utter confusion. He smiled. "That's just a fancy name for practice contractions. You've only got a few weeks left, so your uterus is practicing being in labor."

"But," she said hesitantly, "if this is only practice, how will I know when it's the real thing?"

"Oh, you'll know. Believe me, you'll know."

Matt was out on yet another date with Lucy. Now that his sailor friend was gone, Matt was spending a lot of time with Lucy, and that worried May Rose. It wasn't simply because Lucy was Irma's sister; there was something else, something she couldn't put her finger on. But she never had the time to talk to Matt properly because Lucy was always hovering over him, eating up every second of his time. And now that Matt was home, Lucy didn't have time to be friends with George anymore. George was hurt by Lucy's indifferent attitude, and she was miserable having to stay in bed so much. On top of that, Jake wasn't writing to her again. In all the months George had been here, the letters from Jake could be counted on one hand. Of course, he was in the middle of a war, but May Rose knew other women with men in the war, and those men always managed to write.

Thank heavens for Wil. He played cards with

Rainwater on the White Road

George and brought her books from the library. And candy bars. May Rose told him no on the candy bars, but Wil sneaked them in to George anyway. Wil was a good brother to his new sister. May Rose was proud of him. Now if she could only figure out Jake, life would be bliss. Here he had his sweet little wife who was as big as a house with his baby, and he wasn't even writing to her. May Rose realized that she was mad at both of her sons. Mad at Matt for always needing to be with Lucy, mad at Jake for not writing to George during the time she most needed him. Then she remembered her own bitter loneliness when she had carried Jake.

She threw her hands in the air and lamented, "What goes around comes around. I'm sorry, George. It's just the way our men are."

The war in Europe was in its final throes. The Germans were putting up a valiant effort to save Berlin, but the steady march of Americans was consuming them like a prairie fire intent on burning out its chosen course. Jake's company were finally given three days of rest in a captured German village twenty kilometers from the German high command. They would be twenty of the war's bloodiest "klicks."

Jake was filthy from having fought, marched, and slept in his fatigues for three weeks. He was afraid to unlace his boots. Afraid his skin would come away with his rotting socks. But the "Dutch-Man" had ordered everyone to bathe and eat hot food. Jake didn't have the strength for either. He slumped against a shell- and bullet-battered wall. He rested his head on arms that were folded atop bent knees. He knew

185

from somewhere he would have to find the strength to obey Dutch's orders.

As if he were thinking of the devil, Dutch approached, squatting down beside Jake. "You smell, Corporal."

Not bothering to raise his head, Jake replied, "You're no calla lily, sir."

Dutch grunted a laugh. "Yeah, but you're still gonna want to kiss me smack on the mouth because of the news I've got for you."

Jake raised his head just enough to peer at his C.O. Dutch was grinning from ear to ear and wriggling his heavy eyebrows. "You're a daddy."

"W-what?"

Dutch slapped Jake on the shoulder. "What's the matter, Corporal? Shell shocked? Am I gonna have to play like Patton and slap you around a little?"

Still grinning, Dutch tossed his helmeted head in the direction of the temporary command building. "Just got the news. It's a couple of weeks old, but we've been kind of hard to keep up with. You've got a little girl. Mama and child doing just fine."

"A baby girl?" Jake breathed as if unable to grasp the idea.

"Yep!" Dutch cackled. "And I hope for the world's sake she looks like her mother. The last thing anybody needs is one more pug-ugly. Now, hit the showers and get some food. I'll go and sort out the mail and get yours to you as fast as I can."

Suddenly Jake had the energy of ten men. (Well, maybe two men and one sturdy boy.) He jumped to his feet and ran toward the abandoned building that had been turned into a communal shower.

It seemed Dutch had already spread the good

news. As Jake peeled off his clothing, making ready to stand in line with all the other buck-nakeds, both of his hands were pumped and his back clapped.

Scrubbed down and in cleaner clothing, Jake joined the chow line. By way of celebration, the cooks (their hearts were in the right place) piled on extra portions of hot Spam and reconstituted mashed potatoes. He was sitting in a crowd of men wolfing the food when he spied Dutch walking toward him with a pile of letters in his hand. Jake dropped his metal plate and leaped over the heads of his buddies as he raced toward his colonel. He grabbed his mail, furiously shook Dutch's hand, and then scooted off to find a relatively private corner.

His excited fingers leafed through the letters as his eyes scanned all the postmarks, trying to find the latest date. He found the latest, dated February 23, 1945, and ripped it open.

Dearest Jack,

I've had the baby. It's a little girl. Your mother said she's a miracle. Not only because she's a girl but because she's the prettiest baby she has ever seen. I have named her Sally Nora. Don't ask me why, but she looks like a Sally and your mother liked Nora. I hope to be sending you pictures of her soon. Stay well. I miss you. I do wish you had more time to write.

Love, George

Jake folded the letter neatly and stuffed it into his breast pocket. He forgot about George's other letters. He left them lying on the ground as he stood and walked out of the little corner. He'd gone less than a dozen yards into the glaring sunshine when he heard a voice scream, "heads up! In-coming!"

Behind him a mortar shell exploded, somersaulting him into the air. A second later he came thudding back down to earth. King watched, horrified. Forgetting himself, he broke cover and raced for Jake, grabbing him, dragging him to safety. The whole time he dragged him, he said over and over, "don't be dead, Jake. Don't be dead." Then, when they were under cover, King tore open Jake's field shirt, looking for wounds. There weren't any. Jake came groggily around.

"Man! Are my ears ringin'."

"Boogie man! You are the luckiest sonofabitch I've ever met in my whole life."

Jake cupped a hand around an ear. "What?"

Laughing, King curled up like a doodle bug.

When the time came for Matt to go to the V.A. Hospital in Oklahoma City for further therapy, he blandly announced that Lucy would be going with him. May Rose was so livid she couldn't speak. But during the time it took him to go to his bedroom to pack his bags, she found her tongue and went after him.

"It's too soon for this, Matthew. You need to get yourself up on your own feet before you start thinking seriously about Lucy, or any other girl."

Matt felt guilty. His guilt wouldn't let him listen to his mother. There was something she didn't know, and he certainly couldn't tell her. He had taken away Lucy's virginity. Well, not actually taken it. It was more like . . . Hell, he didn't know what it was like. There was nothing he could compare it to. The loss of Lucy's virginity had been very, very strange. Even stranger than the nurses in Hawaii, and he never believed anything could ever be stranger than that. So while his mother stood there lecturing her biggest and her shyest boy, Matt refused to meet her eye. The shame of remembering what had happened just four evenings ago wouldn't allow him to look his mother in the eye. He kept his head bowed, mentally accepting the full responsibility for what happened with Lucy. Never once did he entertain the notion that she might possibly have planned the entire thing, or that in planning it she had used his inability to run away to her advantage.

From the first day he had appeared at the door to start going out with Irma, Lucy had wanted him. She had seen him nearly all of her life, but it was only when he first started going about with Irma that Lucy was of the age to be appreciative of Matt's blatant physical attraction. All of the Rainwater boys practically had the same face, but their bodies were different. Jake was weedy, the twins were built like blocks. Lucy never looked twice at the twins because they were just kids. All right, they were her age and in her same class at school, but they were never of any interest to her. They still weren't. Allen was the town demon child, and the less said about him the better. Matt, on the other hand, was built like a wall of solid granite, and his shyness added mightily to his sex appeal. Pity he couldn't kiss worth a fig, but never mind. Matt had other qualities his brothers, particularly Jake, lacked. Matt had ambition. He had been an A student. He wanted to go to college. She just knew that he had it in him to be an important person. Dear God, he already *was* an important per-

189

son. And ha-ha, Irma the dope was married to that fool Buck Hatchet.

All of her years of waiting with the patience of Job was about to pay off. But he still hadn't mentioned marriage, and he wasn't making any serious moves to consummate the relationship. Now that he was practically hers, she had to do something radical to accomplish her goal. Knowing his serious and responsible nature as well as she did, she knew how committed he would feel if he took her virginity. It was a paltry thing to give if it afforded her a lifetime of being his wife. As being out with him never went beyond a few passionate kisses, it was up to her to give him her virginity and make it *seem* as if he'd taken it. And the time was now, while he was still confused about where he was, about what he was going to do with the rest of his life. If she waited, his thinking would clear. She knew she couldn't afford that to happen.

She drove the car to "their" spot, a dead-end road, and parked the car. Typically, their parking meant only that they would kiss a little bit and then Matt would boringly bare his soul. When he turned his head, opened his mouth to speak, she stopped him with hers.

Getting excited during the necking sessions was a hard thing to do. Kissing him was like kissing cement. But she adored his body. As long as she didn't have to think about his leg. Or see it. The trouble was, Matt habitually kept his body under wraps. While she necked with him on this occasion, she was forced to literally peel him like an onion.

"Luce," Matt choked. He tried to push her away as she unbuttoned his shirt. "What are you doing?"

Her tone was husky and her fingers kept unbuttoning his shirt. "I just want to kiss your neck and your chest. Please let me."

"Well, okay. If you're sure you really want to—"

His breath caught sharply in his throat as her mouth began to devour his exposed neck, work downward. "Oh God, Luce. That feels so good." Matt went into a stupor as Lucy moaned, touched and kissed him all over, her hand reaching into his unzipped trousers. He cried raggedly as her hand closed around his hardened bulge, and then she began to stroke him.

Matt was nearly cataleptic when events escalated. He couldn't remember when Lucy lost her blouse and her bra, but at some point she had because her naked breasts were in his face. Taking this as permission to kiss her there, he did, paying no attention to the fact that she was straddling him, or that her skirt was hiked up to her waist and her panties were gone. He only realized these things when her hand gripped him more tightly, held him steady while she used him like a battering ram against her stubborn hymen. It had to have been painful for her because she made sobbing sounds. This had to be the worst way possible for a girl to lose her virginity. Matt tried to stop her before she did herself a serious injury. But Lucy was running on stubborn; she wouldn't listen, nor would she stop pressing herself down on him. A second later, her hymen ruptured and she let out a shriek when he suddenly went deep inside her. He felt her blood, definitely heard her tears. Then she stopped.

Panting, looking him in the eyes, she said, her voice trembly. "Oh, Matt, you're so forceful."

I am?

"Oh, Matt, you've broken me. Is this all we're supposed to do?"

He couldn't believe it. She knew he was supposed to be inside her, but she didn't have a clue as to what was expected next.

"Uhm, well," he stammered. "You're supposed to, uhm, you kinda have to keep moving and then I—" He couldn't say it. This was simply too bizarre. He wanted her off him. He wanted to go home.

Lucy could feel him withering inside her. She knew instinctively that she was losing him. Lucy did not like to lose. He'd hinted that she was supposed to move. Fine, then that's what she would do. She began to move up and down until she felt him getting bigger inside her again. She watched his face; he looked like he was being tortured. She heard him groan and pant, his hands going to her hips, moving her even faster. Then he lay his head back against the car seat as her hips rose and sank all the way down the shaft. "Oh, God," he moaned. "Oh, yeah. Oh, damn. Oh, damn." Then everything became a blur as he forcibly lifted her and tossed her away from him.

Lucy watched in complete fascination as the colossal Matthew Rainwater was suddenly reduced to a weakened, shivering hulk. And she felt enormously powerful. She had managed to do something a thousand armed Japanese couldn't do. She had made the powerful Medal of Honor–winning Marine cry. He kept his back turned to her as he shuddered and tiny sounds, like whimpers, escaped his throat. Now she felt disgusted and impatient. Especially when he sniffled. "Luce? I-I can't go home like this. My-my pants are a mess."

She repaired the minor damage to herself and drove to her house. She slipped inside, thankful that her mother was asleep, as she retrieved a towel and a warm, sudsy washcloth. Back in the car, she cleaned a thoroughly embarrassed Matt.

"Does this happen all the time?"

"Yeah. That's why it's better to have rubbers. Then—then there isn't this . . ." His voice faded as his embarrassment increased.

He is such a baby. "Where do I buy rubbers?"

Appalled, Matt shouted, "For pete's sake, Luce. Women just can't buy a guy some rubbers!"

"Don't be silly, Matt. There isn't anything I wouldn't do for you."

The very next day she went to the drugstore in Bartlesville, where she wasn't known, posed as a newly married woman, and had a private talk with the discomfited druggist, who became even more discomfited when she graphically described Matt's length and width. Now that Matt was absolutely hers, it was her responsibility to make certain he always had everything he needed. That evening when they parked, Matt taught her how to put the rubber on him, and he was duly rewarded. Lucy bounced on him until he exploded. But this time he hung on to her, and she felt every burst. He was still exploding when she forced his head back and kissed him. Then against his mouth she whispered, "I'm so happy we're getting married."

As if a bucket of cold water had splashed his face, his eyes flared. Lucy was kissing him again as his mind reeled. Of course he would have to marry her.

193

And maybe getting married would be a good thing. Lucy was smart. Lucy had direction. Matt badly needed direction. He was floundering, uncertain of what his family, even the people outside his family, expected of a big-shot war hero. He didn't feel like a hero, he felt like a total fraud. Which is why he had needed Lucy. In the past weeks she had kept him straight. Anticipated his needs and filled every one of them. Lucy loved him. Maybe he loved her too. He just didn't know. But any girl who had the guts to buy a guy some rubbers had to be the kind of girl who would stand by him no matter what.

The next morning Lucy took him to the car dealer, and Matt bought a new car. Then he bought her an engagement ring and matching wedding band. Matt didn't tell his mother about either ring as he waved to his family and Lucy drove them both away to Oklahoma City.

Watching the car disappear, May Rose felt her heart break in half. Her boy, her sweetest son, was making a terrible mistake, but he wouldn't listen to her. He had even turned his back on her when she had tried one last time to make him see reason. There was only one saving grace for that wretched morning. A letter had arrived from Jake. Judging by the feel of it, it was a nice fat letter. Flinging tears from her face, May Rose hurried to take the letter to George.

Wil was in the bedroom burping the baby when she entered. She momentarily forgot about Matt as she yelled at her other son.

"You weren't in here while George nursed her baby, were you?"

"Heck, no. But I did change Sally's diaper."

Rainwater on the White Road

"He's going to be a good father someday," George beamed.

May Rose shook her head. "Then he'll be the first Rainwater male ever to be called that." She held out the letter. George's face lit up like a Christmas tree. She grabbed the letter and excitedly tore open the envelope.

Hi, Kid!
I am so happy. I'm a daddy. I can't believe it . . .

After that, his letter was a two-page questionnaire about his daughter. As Sally slept in her little bed, George dutifully answered each question. Then she slipped in a photograph taken of her holding Sally. She had sent him dozens of photographs over the past months. She was afraid that by now his wallet would be too full.

It wasn't. Jake didn't have a single photo because up until Sally's birth he had never opened her letters. What was the point? He would be divorcing her as soon as he made it home. But this next letter he opened. The photo fell out. He picked it up and stared at it. The baby was beautiful. And so was George. Funny how he had forgotten that. Looking at her face, her very healthy, happy face, he remembered making love to her. Remembered rolling around on the bed while she tortured him with tickly kisses. Shoving those memories firmly out of his mind, Jake folded the photo in half so that only Sally was visible and put the photo in his empty wallet. Then he answered her letter. His letter arrived just two weeks after she'd answered his. And then another letter came the next day and the next. Suddenly George had to write day and night to keep up with the replies.

Two months later, the Germans formally surrendered. Victory in Europe, or VE Day, was a celebration the allied forces kicked off with a bang and champagne. In the Rainwater household May Rose listened to the radio, crying tears of relief that the war in Europe was over. She kissed and cuddled her infant daughter. And in honor of the world's celebration, she named the little girl she had waited for all of her marriage—Victoria.

In Jake's most recent letter there was a photograph of him in his Army clothes, boots, and helmet. He looked very warrior-like and handsome. And because he needed to talk to someone, he told George all about the fact that his best friend had been killed.

"King. I know you remember my pal, King . . ."

King died eight days before the cease-fire. Jake took King's death very badly. Colonel T'Hart allowed his mixed bag of Native Americans to see out their dead in their own fashion; King their last, "Down Warrior."

Dutch watched as his men beat something close to a drum and sang their songs of prayer and praise, honoring the spirits of lost warriors. Over the time served with his Redskin Brigade, their singing no longer got on his nerves. So when a Shaved Tail second lieutenant, with the brigade a hot whole month, asked if what their troopers were doing was against military code, Dutch, cigar stuck in his mouth, squinted hard at the younger officer.

"The regs weren't written for the 'Skins. In this outfit we ignore 'em. You got any more questions, Lieutenant?"

"No, sir."

"Then stand at attention and show some respect!"

Chapter Nine

The two babies made the house seem too full. They were always crying, always smelly. Allen hated both babies. He also hated it that Walt and Wilber watched him like a pair of steely-eyed buzzards, blatantly guarding Jake's baby. May Rose was always with the baby girl she had wanted so badly. Allen would have never gotten past her to do something vile to little Toya (Victoria). But without the twins Georgina was vulnerable. She was afraid of Allen, and liking that, Allen made it his business to secretly torment her every chance he got. George never told anyone, not even Wil. Then one day she let go a long-held breath. Allen started going back to school on a regular basis. When he was home, it was only to eat and sleep. It was if he either forgot about George, about her baby, or he was too bored with the game of terror to continue playing. Something or someone else much more interesting now had all of his attention.

Her name was Tara Ravenwing, and she had long legs, a beautiful smile, and jet black hair that billowed behind her when she walked along with her friends. Allen tried everything he could think of to gain her attention. Wisely, Tara would have none of him. Allen was a known bully and a miserable student. But because he didn't want to go to work or join the military, he was cagey enough to make certain the bullying could never be proved, and he did just enough class work to prevent him from being expelled. Because Tara rebuffed him daily, she was making him crazy. Allen could be especially unpleasant when people made him crazy. His chance to humble her came when he saw her walking alone toward the edge of the campus to join the line of young people already waiting for the school bus. Allen went after her.

"I wanna talk to you, girl," he said. To stop her, he pulled her arm brutally.

She clutched her books tightly against her breasts as he jerked her around to face him. "I don't want to talk to you, Allen Rainwater. Leave me alone! You'll make me miss my bus."

"So miss it! I don't give a damn."

"You're not supposed to swear on school grounds."

"Look," he said, trying to curb his mounting temper. "All I want to do is ask ya to step out with me. Maybe go to a movie or something."

"No. I don't ever want to go out with you."

Allen's hooded eyes smoldered. His fist clenched and unclenched. "You better watch out. You just better remember who you're talkin' to. I'll come for you Saturday night. You be ready."

"If you come near my house," she warned, "I'll tell my daddy to shoot you."

Allen laughed. The sound was not pleasant. "Your daddy wouldn't shoot another Osage."

Tara nervously adjusted the books in her arms.

"You're not an Osage. I don't know what you are, but you're not one of us."

Allen's fist connected with her mouth, and she staggered back, dropping her books. Tara was crying, holding her hands against her mouth as Allen calmly picked up her books and carried them while he escorted her to the bus stop. The other kids, having seen what had happened, were careful to stand away, pretend they hadn't seen. No one looked at them because no one wanted to attract "Crazy Allen's" attention. When the bus arrived and opened its doors, Allen gallantly helped Tara up the steel steps. When the bus driver's eyes rounded at the sight of the young girl bleeding from her mouth, Allen merely smiled.

"She tripped." Then he spoke to Tara. "Here's your books, sweetheart. I'll see you tomorrow. Don't' forget to ask your dad about coming to the movies on Saturday."

She didn't ask her father. She didn't tell him anything about Allen taking her to the movies because she knew her father would never agree to her dating Allen Rainwater. But she had to go out with him, at least once, so that maybe he would become bored with her, leave her alone, pick on some other poor girl. On Saturday she told her parents she was walking down to her girlfriend's house, that she would be home by eleven. Her parents never questioned her. Tara had never lied to them, and it didn't enter their minds that she might be lying now.

On Saturday nights Walt and Wilber preferred going into Bartlesville because it was more like a city. Urainia had become a mud hole with only a few standing buildings. The girls of Bartlesville seemed prettier too. At first they were a little shocked that Allen's date would be standing in the road waiting for their car, but Allen explained it away by saying Tara's father was too strict. That Tara always had to sneak and lie if she wanted to have any fun. Well, any girl dumb enough to want to go out with Allen would have to sneak and lie.

The twins put it out of their minds after four Saturdays passed, and picking up Tara from the road became an annoying routine. Then they would drive over into B'ville, the twins going to their favorite pool hall, Allen and his stony date going to the movies. No one, Walt, Wilber, or Tara, suspected that Allen had grown weary of simply going to the movies and holding her stiff hand. He wanted more now, and after all the money he'd paid out to keep her entertained, he felt he was due.

On this, their fourth, and according to his promise to Tara, their very last date, he didn't make any moves to get out of the car when his brother parked at the curb. Wilber looked questioningly over his shoulder at Allen.

"We want to talk for a while," Allen said.

"You'll be late for the pictures."

"We'll only miss the newsreel and the cartoon."

Walt looked at Wilber. Both shrugged and left the car. As soon as they disappeared inside the pool hall, Allen jumped into the front seat and hot-wired the ignition. Tara climbed into the front seat too. With an animal's instinct for impending danger, she knew that this was not to be a normal night out. While Allen played with some wires under the dashboard, Tara tried to escape out the car door.

Allen grabbed her by the hair and slammed her

against the seat and growled into her frightened face. "You're making me mad, Tara."

He drove to the outskirts of town, Tara sobbing and pleading with him. To shut her up, Allen back-handed her across the mouth. Blood poured from her split lips. Shaking like a leaf in a gale, Tara tried to keep her tears from further disturbing Allen. He turned off the main road onto a gravel farm road. He drove another mile or two, then pulled the car into a small copse of cottonwoods, killed the head-lights, but left the dashboard lights on when he switched off the engine.

"Allen," Tara cried. "Please take me back. Please let's just go to the movies."

Allen reclined against he door and looked at her. "Tell you what I'll do. You show me your tits, and I'll take you back to town."

"W-what?"

"I said," he repeated in a maddeningly calm tone, "take off your blouse and bra."

Both of her hands flew protectively to her chest. Her blouse was bloody from her recent injury, and the material was sticky to the touch.

Allen pulled out a pack of Camels from his shirt pocket, tapped a cigarette from the pack, stuck it into his mouth, and lit it. This casual attitude frightened her more than his notable temper.

"Baby, how long we been going steady? About five weeks, right? That's a pretty long time for a steady boyfriend not to even know what his girlfriend's tits look like. If you want me to keep my promise about this being our last date, you better show me some tit. Otherwise, I'll see you next Saturday, and then next Saturday and more Saturdays after that."

Rainwater on the White Road

Tara could hear her heart thumping in her chest. She absolutely needed this to be their last date. Her parents were becoming suspicious, and she hated lying to them. She had held herself together during tonight's lies by telling herself over and over that this would be the very last time, that after tonight her life would return to normal, that she would never have to go out with Allen Rainwater again.

Not that Allen was ugly. He was anything but. Any girl not knowing his true nature would have done a back flip if he asked her out. He was an extremely good-looking boy. One day he would be a devastatingly handsome man. But he was mean. And his meanness corrupted the outward appearance. Frankly, Tara couldn't wait to be rid of him. She was tired of being afraid, tired of being hit, and more than tired of the way her girlfriends avoided her now that she was going out with Allen. In the past five weeks he'd managed to strip her of everything, her pride, her confidence, even her family and friends. If showing him her breasts was what it would take to have him out of her life, then she would show her breasts. When she got to the very last button, she pulled her blouse open, reached behind her, unhooked her bra, and it fell to her lap. Allen flipped the cigarette out of the car window. He slid over to her and cupped one breast in his hand.

"Oh, baby. Just look what I've been missing."

Tara closed her eyes and gritted her teeth as his mouth went to her nipple. He sucked at her like a greedy infant. Then he bit her. When she muffled a complaint, Allen's mouth went to the other breast and the process began again. When she could stand no more of this treatment she mewled, "Please stop."

Allen's voice was husky and trembling. "Just let me put my hand in your panties." When she tried to squirm away, his mouth came crashing down on hers. His tongue filled her mouth. When she tried to twist her head away, he grabbed her by the hair and his fist broke her nose. Tara screamed, her nose bled profusely. And because of his rough kissing, her lips were bleeding again too. Allen didn't seem to mind because his hand pushed inside her skirt, pulled at her panties. His probing fingers were hurting her, and his heat was suffocating. She was fighting for breath, and because her nose was fully blocked, she raggedly drew a much needed lungful of air through her mouth.

"You really like this finger stuff, don't you, Tara?"

"No—!" Her screams were quickly stifled as Allen's mouth covered hers again. His fingers brutally probed and pushed. He kept it up, his hand going faster and faster. The pain of his kiss combined with the torture of his hand were unbearable. Revulsion and fear caused her to lose grip on reality, and when she was at her weakest, in one blinding move Allen pulled her down on the seat and pinned her under his weight.

His hips pumped against her as he rasped in her ear, "If you like my finger, you're gonna love my dick."

"Please stop, Allen!"

It was a nightmare. He sat on top of her, unbuckling his belt, unbuttoning the fly of his jeans. All the time she screamed and begged, he smiled. Smiled just like a beautiful devil. That smile chilled her to the bone and gave her renewed strength. Thrashing wildly, she nearly threw him off. His face in the dim light was a repellent mask of rage as he roared and lunged for her. Tara's knee caught him in the optimum area. His breath flew out of his mouth, and he doubled over, crumpled to the floorboard. Tara lost no time scrambling out of the car. Blindly, in the pitch blackness of the prairie night, she ran along the road.

"TARRRRRAAA!"

Hearing him bellowing her name moved her to greater speed. She heard the car rumble to life, heard it driving away. She prayed very hard that he would simply abandon her, punish her by leaving her lost and alone. He didn't. He turned the car and then the headlights came on. The sudden brightness washed around her running form. She was about to duck off the road when the car picked up speed and hit her, throwing her to the side. She felt every bump and pebble of the hardpan road as she fell and slid on the side of her body to a stop. She lay panting, disoriented, too weak to move. All she could manage was a hopeful prayer that she would black out. She didn't. She was fully conscious when Allen got out of the car, stood in the center of the lights.

"You really love pissing me off, don't you?" he yelled. "Well, now you're going to find out just how pissed off you made me."

Allen thoroughly punished Tara.

At ten-thirty, right on their usual time, Walt and Wilber came out of the pool hall laughing and slapping. They jumped into the car parked at the curb just where they'd left it. Walt turned to say something to Allen. Then his mouth fell open.

Allen wasn't there.

205

Tara was.

Wilber drove at high speed to the hospital. While the doctors sedated the injured girl, Wilber telephoned Tara's parents.

"Mr. Ravenwing," Wilber said shakily. "This is Wilber Rainwater. You've got to come to Bartlesville, Mr. Ravenwing. Your daughter Tara's been hurt. Me and my brother Walt, we brought her here to the hospital. The doctors say she's hurt real bad."

Walt stood beside his brother as Wilber spoke on the pay telephone in the booth off to the side of hospital reception. While Wilber spoke, Walt bit the corner of his bottom lip and sweated.

"Well, she was with our younger brother, Allen," Wilber said. Then he paused and listened. "She's been going out with Allen for a few weeks now."

Walt could hear Mr. Ravenwing's yelling all the way through Wilber's head.

"Look, Mr. Ravenwing, if me an' Walt had known that Allen would—"

More yelling.

"Yes, sir. We're pretty sure it was Allen who hurt her, but— Yes, sir. We'll wait right here." Wilber hung up, looked worriedly at Walt. "We've got to find him, find him and kill him. That little puke's disgraced this family for the last time."

Walt ran a hand through his thick hair and sighed heavily. "We can't go after him now. We've got to call Dad and wait for him and Mr. Ravenwing. And it's kinda important we be here for that little girl. Damn, she's busted up so bad. The doctors say she could die. We can't just go after Allen an' leave her to die all alone."

Walter was about to say more when he was cut

off by the sight of a team of nurses and two doctors wheeling a gurney out of the emergency treatment room. Tara lay on it, her face a swollen mass, her eyes staring vacantly and two separate IV's plugged into her contused arms. The twins followed the moving gurney down the hallway. Walt took Tara's cold hand and held it. The procession came to a stop at the door of a private room, and a hefty nurse wrenched Walt's hand away.

"Go to the waiting area," she barked. "The police want to talk to you."

Walt and Wilber retreated under her hateful stare. Walking the long corridor with their heads bowed, Wilber muttered, "They think we did it."

"I know," Walt agreed. "Everybody's gonna think we did it until Tara can talk and tell them different."

Wilber was seething. "I'm gonna stomp Allen. I swear to God I'm gonna stomp him until his guts are spread all over the ground."

After ditching Tara, Allen roamed the streets of Bartlesville. He could have left her on the road to die the way she deserved to die, but he didn't want to get hung just because of some prick-tease. Anyway, a couple of Band-Aids and she'd be all right. And she'd never tease another guy again. So in a way, he'd done her a real favor. He'd taught her what guys would put up with and what they wouldn't. She really should thank him. Hell, her father should thank him. But he knew that neither would.

Typical. That's just so typical. Well, to hell with all of them. I'm sick of Oklahoma anyway. I'll go west. Yeah, to Hollywood. I bet I could be a movie star or something. I'm sure a lot better-lookin' than that old guy Clark Gable.

I could be in the Western movies. I could be the handsome Indian chief that all the white girls go for. Ha. That would be really great.

Utterly remorseless, Allen searched the streets for a likely car to make good his escape. He found a parked Oldsmobile 88. He pulled off his hot-wiring trick, and within minutes, and with a Benny Goodman tune blasting from the radio, he drove out of town.

Elmer Ravenwing stood by his daughter's bed. Her lovely face was beaten so badly he barely recognized her. Elmer dismissed the hovering nurse, waving her tersely out of the room. After the door closed behind her, Elmer Ravenwing wept.

"He'll pay, sweet girl," he said softly through trembling lips. "Whichever Rainwater boy that did this to you, I swear on my life, he's gonna pay."

In a sequestered waiting room a policeman stood behind Claude Rainwater as he questioned his sons.

"Dad!" Wilber bayed, "I swear it wasn't me an' Walt. You can ask anybody over at the White Horse 'cause that's were we were, shooting pool just like always. We thought Allen took Tara to the movies. When we came out, the car was parked just where we left it. But when we got in, there was only Tara. An' when we saw her, we drove like crazy straight here."

"You mean to tell me," Claude growled, "that Allen abused that girl on a public street and no one heard her screaming?"

Walter stepped forward. "Dad, we don't know any more about it than you do. If she had been screaming outside the White Horse, we would have heard her. Best we can figure, Allen took her somewhere. How, we don't know because Wilber had the keys to the car in his pocket."

Another policeman entered the private waiting room. Everyone shifted their attention to him. He ignored the Rainwater men, speaking only to the other policeman.

"There's blood smeared all over that car, front and back." He looked coldly at the twins. "You boys care to turn around?" When the twins complied, the two policemen inspected Walt and Wilber's blue-jeaned behinds.

"What do you think?" one policeman said.

"Looks like they sat in it, all right. But it seems they sat in it after the blood in the front was almost dry. The blood in the backseat is still wet from where the girl was when they brought her in. Anyway, we're checking out their alibi at the White Horse."

"It wasn't us!" Wil shouted. "How many times do we have to say it?"

A snarling policeman jerked Wilber around and pushed his face into Wil's. "You'll need to say it as many times as we think we need to hear it, punk."

Claude quickly intervened. "There's no call for you pushing around my boy. If he said he didn't do it, he didn't do it."

The policeman was about to say something else when a third officer rushed in. "Hey, Murph! We just got a call on a stolen car. It belongs to Councilman Peters, and he's hoppin' mad. It's his brand-new Olds 88. He's at the station now fillin' out a death warrant on whoever boosted it."

"Allen," Walt sighed wearily.

Officer Murphy gave Walt a hard look. "Maybe your kid brother took it, an' maybe he didn't. But until we find the kid and the car, I don't want you two leavin' town. I want you right where I can get my hands on you fast."

"Yes, sir," Walt said. "We'll stay right here at the hospital."

"An' I'll leave one of my officers to make sure you do," Murphy jeered.

When Murphy and the third policeman left, Claude looked at the remaining cop. "Would it be all right for me to go out to the lobby and telephone my wife? She's pretty worried."

"You can go," the surly cop answered. "But these two stay right here."

May Rose held her hand against her forehead, listening to Claude speaking to her over the line. When she heard a baby cry, turned and saw George huddling close, both babies in her arms, she snapped at her daughter-in-law.

"Take the babies to the back room, and please keep them quiet. I can't hear myself think!"

Momma-May had never raised her voice to her before. That she raised her voice now could only mean that what she was hearing over the phone was bad. Extremely bad. George hustled away, closed the door to the bedroom. Sally was asleep. She laid Sally in the middle of the bed. Because Toya was crying and because George had no other means of pacifying the infant, George offered the baby her breast. And as Toya nursed, George rocked and hummed softly. A bond she would feel toward Toya throughout the remainder of their lives developed out of her panicky need to keep the baby quiet. George never told any-one about the emergency feed. It was her secret and firmly remained her secret.

May Rose sobbed as she listened to Claude. She knew the twins were innocent, knew just who the guilty son was. And she felt guilty, guilty for having given Allen birth, guilty for not taking a strap to him on the day he'd broken the neck of the hatched chick. Maybe if she'd done it, he would have known that harming something helpless and innocent was wrong and he wouldn't have harmed that little girl. Maybe, but with Allen one could ever be sure. He just didn't seem to care about what was right, or what was wrong. He didn't think the way normal people did, never had. She couldn't think about Allen now. Her twins were in trouble.

"I'm coming to the hospital."

"No, May. I'll take care of this."

"I'm coming, Claude!"

On the other end of the line, Claude found himself becoming well and truly angry with his wife.

"May Rose!" he shouted. "This is man's business. I'm the man, I'm the father. For once you're gonna let me take care of my boys all by myself." He slammed the phone down.

Under the close scrutiny of the officer assigned to watch them all, Claude sat with his twin sons. Each of them sipped hot black coffee from cardboard cups.

"This is the most terrible thing that has ever hap-pened in the history of our family," Claude said. "I don't know how we can ever right this wrong, this offense done against the Ravenwing people."

"I do," Walt said softly. He stared down at the

211

paper cup of tepid coffee in his hands. His father and brother turned toward him, neither saying anything as they waited. Walt's eyes were bloodshot, his young face haggard. Feeling an early hangover developing from the beers he'd drunk, he took a deep cleansing breath. "Dad, the old-timey ways say a man's got to give a son for a son."

Claude sat back. "What are you talking about?"

Walt sadly shook his head. "Listen to me, Dad. Mr. Ravenwing is traditional. I know a lot about traditional. Both me an' Walt do. We kinda been studying up on it when you weren't looking. You've got to let us talk to him."

"He's right," Wil said through gritted teeth. "We need to talk to Mr. Ravenwing."

"I said, me!" Walt half shouted.

Wilber shouted back. "But I'm another son. I'm just as good as you."

"No, you're not. I'm older."

"Two hours!" Wil flared.

"Two hours, two years," Walt cried. "Older is older. Custom says the next oldest. Jake's married. Matt's almost married. Then comes me."

"What are you two talkin' about?" Claude demanded.

"He's talking about standing for punishment," Wil said flatly. "Standing in Allen's place and taking whatever Mr. Ravenwing decides is the best punishment."

"Well, you will do no such thing," Claude scoffed. "The police will find Allen."

"That takes care of the law side," Walt nodded. "But we still got the traditional side. You're gonna have to let me talk to Mr. Ravenwing. If you don't, the whole family's gonna suffer for this."

Walt and Wilber shifted uneasily on their feet. At the end of the hallway, just outside Tara's room, their father conferred with Elmer Ravenwing. After a muted discussion that seemed to drag on for hours, Elmer looked down the hall toward the waiting young men. He motioned for them to approach.

"This is it," Walt whispered to Wilber.

"Let me take your place," Wil pleaded.

"No."

Coming to stand before the careworn Elmer Ravenwing, Walt stood to his full six-foot-three height. The older man regarded him and then finally said, "Your father told me your wish to remain faithful to the old ways. But before I decide this matter, you and I will talk in private."

Elmer turned on his heel and walked farther down the hallway, Walt following a respectful pace behind. When they were a good distance, Elmer stopped and leaned against the cold hospital wall. He didn't look at Walt. He couldn't bring himself to.

"My little girl," Elmer began with a shaky voice, "is still a child. I wanted many things for her life. Many things." He bowed his graying head and steeled himself to go on. "The thing I wanted most was a husband who would honor her and love her. All fathers want that for their daughters, but I wanted it more for my Tara. The doctors say she wasn't violated. But you tell me how many folks are going to believe that. It don't matter no more if she was raped or if she wasn't; everybody's gonna believe she was. The real trouble about all this is that she was sneaking out to be with him, so folks are just gonna naturally blame her for what happened. An honorable man wants an honorable woman. My Tara's honor has been stolen." He paused only because his voice broke.

Walt's own voice was less than trustworthy. He cleared his throat twice, then said, "Mr. Ravenwing, I'd be proud to marry Tara. An' I won't let anybody ever hurt her again. You have my word."

Elmer Ravenwing nodded mutely, placed a hand to his eyes, and wept.

By noon of the next day the Tulsa police had Allen in custody. A brand-new Olds 88 with an Indian kid driving it was a hard thing to miss. The police spotted Allen as he cruised Sheridan Street. Allen had found some money in the glove compartment, and feeling peckish, went looking for a restaurant. He'd pulled into a likely little greasy spoon and was just getting out of the car when a patrol car pulled in right behind him. Because the girl in Bartlesville had also named him as her assailant, Allen was arrested for more than just grand theft auto. He was eating soup and cornbread in the slammer around the same time Walt and Wilber were given their freedom to leave the hospital.

Allen cooled his heels in juvenile detention for three days. On the morning of the fourth day, the charges of assault and battery were suddenly dropped. Walt's standing in Allen's place on that matter had wiped Allen's slate clean with the Osage. Now there was only the charge of grand theft to own up to. And for that charge, since he was a minor, he was released on bail into the custody of his parents.

"You're gettin' let out, kid," the guard informed him as he handed over Allen's normal street wear. "Change into your duds quick before somebody gets smart and changes their mind."

Allen was grinning as he walked into the reception room of the juvenile hall and saw Wilber. Wilber wasn't smiling. His face was as dark as a thunder head.

"Dad signed you out," Wilber said. "You're to come with me."

Allen knew a trickle of fear as he followed his older brother outside. Claude sat in the car parked at the curb, and Allen aimed for it. Wilber grabbed his arm and pulled him back.

"You ain't ridin', kid. Dad don't want to breathe the same air with you no more. You just follow me, and no funny stuff or I'll pop your face right off your skull."

Allen followed doggedly after Wilber's long form as they walked for miles. Finally Wilber opened the door of the Greyhound Bus depot and held it for Allen to pass through. Standing together in line for the ticket window, Wil asked, "Kid, if you could go any place outside Oklahoma, where would it be?"

Without a second's hesitation Allen replied, "Hollywood."

When their turn came at the window, Wilber pulled out his billfold and bought Allen a ticket.

One-way.

Billfold still in hand, Wilber counted out a series of twenties. "Ya got your ticket an' a hundred an' sixty bucks. It was all we could spare out of Ma's stash. Just get it in your head that there ain't no more where this came from."

He handed the money over to Allen, stuffing it in to his hands. With another cold look Wilber said, "Now, come out back with me. I got a few questions to ask ya before you get on the bus."

Allen was feeling pretty cocky. He had his ticket to ride, plus a pocket full of loot. Life was good. Willingly he followed Wilber outside into the bus depot's back alley. Allen had all sorts of things to say to Wilber. Things beginning with *Tara's just a big tease. She teased me too much.*

The second he opened his mouth, Wilber's fist stopped the first syllable cold. Wilber beat Allen to a messy pulp, and as Allen slid down the bus depot wall into the gutter, Wilber stood over him.

"That was for Tara."

He delivered a kick to Allen's midsection, air and blood exploding from Allen's mouth in a *Oooooph.*

"That was for Walt. Now, you crawl outta here, you piece of shit, and don't you ever come back. 'Cause if you do, every man with a drop of Osage blood in him will be waitin'. An' Dad says for you to change your name once you get where you're going. He says you ain't his son no more, so you can't have his name. An' you ain't my brother. If I ever see you again, count on it, Allen, I will put a bullet in your heart."

Wilber walked out of the alleyway, wiping Allen's blood from his hands against his jeans.

Good news invariably follows bad. The Rainwaters' spirits were lifted when they received a telegram about Jake. He would be coming home in about six or seven months. May Rose telephoned the hospital in Oklahoma City to tell Matt about Jake, but she wasn't able to speak to him. He was in therapy.

Matt had to use two canes after the removal of the brace. Searing hot pain tortured him every time he put a portion of his weight on his bad leg. While he'd had the heavy brace he'd cursed it. Now that it was gone, he realized just how valuable it had been. The same could be said of Bud. As Matt winced, tried to relearn the art of walking, his mind went back to the days when Bud had half carried him as they plowed through the warm ocean breakers. Matt hadn't had the brace on those times either, but he'd had Bud. Bud to lean on, Bud to goad him, Bud to make him laugh, and Bud to set even larger goals.

"See those rocks over there, Jackson? Get them in your mind. We're going all the way to those rocks."

"Don't let go of me."

"Never happen, Jackson."

But Bud had let go when the Navy ordered him back to Pearl Harbor. Now Matt was alone in the V.A. Hospital, and it was a big place. A big, indifferent place. And filled with guys worse off than he. Never mind that he was a big medal-winning war hero, the nurses concentrated on those who needed them most. None of them tried to get too friendly, so he no longer needed a Bud to guard him while he slept. Besides, he wasn't in a private room like the big shot he'd been in Hawaii. Now he was on a ward and had to wait his turn to be noticed.

The only bright spot in his day was when Lucy came during visiting hours. She was always tired when she came and it showed, no matter how she tried to conceal her fatigue. She had a job as a telephone operator-trainee. The trainee part meant that

she had to work longer hours than the regular opera-
tors. Lucy was skipping sleep to visit Matt. Once he
felt really badly about her being so exhausted and
told her not to come the next day.

She didn't.

It was the most miserable day of Matt's life. He
never asked her to do that again. Today, she didn't
come in all tired-out looking. Today, she was bouncy
and excited when she joined him in the visitors day
room, plunked down in the overstuffed chair next
to his.

"I have so much news," she said, "that I don't
know where to begin. First, your application to college has been accepted. And that's not all. I can get
a transfer to Norman. Of course, I'll have to go down
there and find us an apartment or a bungalow. Don't
worry about any of that, I'll take care of it. But here's
the best news. The government will be paying for
you to go to college. And because of your high school
grades and your outstanding service to your country,
not only will you have a full scholarship, you'll get
living expenses."

Matt lay back and smiled. This was the best news
she could have brought him. "I can be a lawyer."

Lucy's eyes flared. Of course, she remembered
hearing him talking to Irma about being a lawyer,
but his being a lawyer was out of the question. Who
on earth would ever hire a crippled lawyer? To get
him through this pipe dream, he would have to be
properly and firmly led.

"Matthew, be reasonable. Lawyers have a hard
time starting out. Now that you've been crippled,
being a lawyer would be ten times harder. Not only
that, but you would have to go to college and then

to law school on what *I* earn. But if you agree to do an engineering course, not only will you go to school for free, you'll be able to get a good job right away. And we'll have a future, a real future. Matt, for both our sakes, please see good sense."

Matt thought about it for a couple of days. Then, when Lucy brought in the forms, all of them already neatly filled out, he signed where she pointed. Of the other bit of news she had for him, the news about his brother Walt getting married, she breathed not a word. Matt couldn't possibly be expected to interrupt his therapy to attend a wedding! It would put him off schedule for starting school in September. But if he knew about Walt getting married, of course he would insist on attending. Which is why Lucy didn't tell him and why she told May Rose a whopper. Said that Matt had had a relapse, that he was too despondent to speak to anyone, but that she would certainly keep May Rose appraised of Matt's progress.

The wedding of Walt and Tara took place months later. Almost as soon as Tara was healed enough to manage to walk down the aisle on her father's arm. Mr. Ravenwing had been right about the gossip that would fly around town. Even though Allen was a thoroughly disagreeable character, the local opinion was that Tara had brought the trauma down on herself by going out with him in the first place. Poor Walt was having to pick up his brother's leavings just to keep peace in the Osage community. What was really shocking was that the bride had the gall to wear a white dress.

Walt and Wilber were a month and a half away from turning twenty. Tara was four months away

219

from turning sixteen. Only immediate families of the bride and groom were present in the Baptist church. Walt said his vows to love and honor in a loud, clear voice. Elmer Ravenwing gave over his daughter as bride with a renewed sense of pride. He even found that he could smile at the dinner party following the ceremony. It was the first smile to crescent his lips since that terrible night.

The newly married couple were to live in the Rainwater household. Wilber moved out of the bedroom he had, all of his life, shared with Walt. His new bedroom was Allen's old room. May Rose and George redecorated the twins' room, ripping down the girlie pictures scavenged from hotsy calendars. In tandem and on their knees, they waxed and buffed the floor. Throwing open the windows, they relieved the room of its strong male scent. Next, they sewed frilly curtains and a matching bedspread. The day of the wedding the room was finally suitable for a female inhabitant.

But the bride and groom wouldn't see it for the first three days of their marriage. Walt had already paid for the honeymoon suite at the Bartlesville Hotel.

Walt was nervous as he looked about the spacious hotel suite. Along with a big bed, dresser, and freestanding wardrobe, it had a couch and two easy chairs and a private bathroom. Floor-to-ceiling windows had drapes that exactly matched the bedspread, and these were color-coordinated with the couch and chairs.

"This is a real nice place," he said softly.

Tara only nodded as she unpacked her small case. Although it was hidden, buried in the bottom of the case, Walt saw one eye and the nose of a teddy bear. That plastic eye staring sightlessly at him wrenched his heart. Wrenched it so hard that for the first year of their marriage, Walt never saw Tara. He only saw the teddy bear belonging to a frightened girl bride.

Walt's teeth scraped the corner of his lip as he stared anxiously at the lone bed. He was supposed to consummate the marriage on that neatly made double bed, but in his heart he knew he couldn't go through with it.

"Tara," he said, "I'm gonna go down to the lobby and get us some cold drinks."

"Okay." She didn't bother saying good-bye as he left.

Walt came back twenty minutes later carrying a Coke for her, a beer for him. She was wearing a pretty nightdress and sitting uncomfortably on the side of the bed, her fingers shredding one of the ribbons decorating the bodice. Walt sat down next to her, handing her the Coke. She took it, but continued sitting with her head down, her hair effectively shielding her little face.

Walt took a long pull of beer, swallowed it with difficulty and then said, "Look, Tara. I know we're married an' all, but jeez, kid, it don't have to be too bad. I mean, I been thinkin' . . ."

Tara raised her head a fraction. Through strands of her hanging hair she furtively studied his profile. He looked like Allen. An older Allen. Tara shuddered and dropped her head again.

"What if," Walt proposed, "what if we acted married in front of everybody but we were just brother and sister in private?"

Tara's head shot up. This sounded like a reprieve!

221

But Allen had offered reprieves, only to go back again on his word. She probably couldn't believe his brother either. Innocent hope had been beaten out of her.

Walt looked down. He touched her hair with one hand, pulling it back, looping it behind an ear. He saw a tear sliding down the curve of her cheek. "I mean it, Tara," he said softly. "We could just be brother and sister. When we go to bed, we don't have to do anything except sleep. Who's to know except us?"

Tara worried her lower lip, turning her head and looking at him intently. After a quiet moment she ventured, "Are you trying to fool me—like Allen did?"

"Naw, Kid," Walt returned sadly, shaking his head. "Forget Allen. He's gone forever. It's just me here, an' I ain't nothing like him. You can breathe easy on that score. I like older women. I don't mean to hurt your feelings, but you're way too young for me. That's what got me to thinkin'." He turned on the bed to face her. "How about you an' me makin' a deal?"

"What kind of deal?" she asked warily.

"A good one." He grinned. "One I know we'll both like. See, I don't reckon our lives have to change all that much if we don't want 'em to. I'll still go to work an' shoot pool with Wil on Saturday nights, an' you can still go off to school an' hang out with your friends."

"Really?"

Walt's smile widened. "Sure! Why not? You like school, don't ya?"

Tara turned on the bed to face him. "Yes."

"Then you'll go to school. After a while you'll see that the only thing that's changed is your name and where you live." He was glad that she appeared more relaxed. "Think maybe if we had this little deal that you could handle this marriage stuff?"

"Yes."

"Good. Then we got a deal. My life won't change. Your life won't change. An' we'll just keep our brother and sister nightlife to ourselves. Okay?"

"Okay." Tara was so relieved she didn't spare a thought that perhaps a few months down the road she might regret this little bargain. Might regret it very much.

After three days of playing cards and games of checkers on the set Walt bought for the honeymoon occasion, the bride and groom came home. Tara was very timid about the reception she would receive among the Rainwaters. Knowing she was apprehensive, Walt was very protective of her. He was even more protective when on her first day back in school she tearfully called him from the principal's office. The principal had told her to go home. She needed Walt to pick her up.

"Why did your principal say you can't go to school?"

Tara snuffled loudly. "She says married women don't go to school. Married women are supposed to stay home when they're having babies."

"She thinks you're having a baby?"

"Yes," Tara said softly. "Everyone does. They think I'm having Allen's baby. And that's why you married me."

Filled with rage, Walt drove to the school. Tara

223

had to wait in the outer office while Walt had strong words with her principal.

"Mr. Rainwater," the principal began firmly. A fiftyish matron with a severe bun secured to the top of her head and Chinese chopsticks sticking out of it, she glowered at him. "Even if, as you say, Tara isn't expecting, it still isn't natural for a married woman to attend school."

"Why not!" Walt quizzed. "My wife's a nice girl, and she's always got high marks here."

"Yes, but that was prior to her change in status."

"What's that got to do with anything?"

The principal, Mrs. Ashley, eyed Walt speculatively as she returned to the chair behind her desk. She motioned for Walt to take a chair, and he complied.

"Mr. Rainwater," she began in her "reasonable" voice. She sat with her fingers entwined, hands resting on the desktop. "Let's speak frankly. The other girls in this school are vir—" She quickly bit that back. ". . . are impressionable. Tara is simply no longer their peer."

Walt's burning fury was a dark shadow forming on his features. "Are you sayin' my wife ain't good enough to go to this school no more?"

"No." the principal licked her lips nervously. "I mean she's now more . . . advanced than the other girls."

Walt's cheeks flamed and his nostrils flared. He squirmed angrily in the chair. "Lady, you best start talkin' a little bit plainer."

"I'm trying to spare your feelings, Mr. Rainwater."

"You're not doing a good job, so just cut the fancy footwork and get straight to it."

"Oh, very well," she sighed. "Mr. Rainwater, a married girl has a certain knowledge about . . . life that she might inadvertently share with the other girls."

"Sex, right?"

The principal's eyes flared, and she blushed crimson. She turned her face to the side, scratching her cheek with one hand, her eyes decidedly averted away from the virile young man scowling at her. "Yes, that's—that's right."

"You're married, ain't ya?"

"I am, but I don't see what—"

"You talk sex with the girls?"

Mrs. Ashley's mouth flew open in astonishment. "Good heavens, no!"

"Tara won't neither," he said flatly. "She'll be just like any other girl in this school. The only difference in the way she was before and the way she is now is that she's got a new last name. She won't put Mrs. on her homework papers or nothin'. She wants to go to school and she's gonna go to school, or me an' my family, plus her daddy's family, is gonna raise holy hell. This is *Osage* County, and in *Osage* County your outside rules about who gets into school don't work. Especially since Mrs. Eleanor Roosevelt's runnin' all over the country worryin' about colored folks not knowing how to read. You keep messin' with my Tara, an' you'll get yourself a letter from Mrs. E. herself. You can count on it."

And that, as they say, was that. Walt walked Tara back to her classroom. Standing just outside the closed door, he sighed and said, "Muffin, everything's going to be all right."

At the sound of this endearment, Tara's head swiveled on her neck. Daddy-Claude called Momma-May muffin. In just the brief time she had been in the household, she had observed enough to know that Daddy-Claude loved the very breath out of Momma-May. Walt's use of this very same pet name could only mean that he cared for her. Narrowing her eyes, she closely examined Walt while he continued to speak.

"Things might be a little touchy for the first few weeks, but you just ride it out. If anybody tries to give you serious grief, you come straight to me. I'll take care of it. Okay?"

"Okay."

She knew he was only trying to cheer her up when he kissed her forehead, but his lips were very soft, very warm. The sweet sensation remained as she watched his tall form walk away.

Matt and Lucy were married in the hospital chapel the day before he was discharged. Matt wanted to be married at home, but Lucy explained for the umpteenth time that they couldn't afford something like that. My goodness, they couldn't even afford a wedding band for Matt. Besides which, Lucy had to start work in Norman right away, and she had to help him learn his way around the university campus. The latter proved to be a most humiliating adventure. Lucy led him around like an overgrown, hobbling baby. Matt had always been shy, and faced with this new dilemma of going to college in a strange city scared the snot out of him. His fears were made worse by Lucy insisting on staying with him for days, wouldn't leave him alone until she was absolutely certain that he felt comfortable with the layout of the campus. In the afternoons she always picked him up. Back at home, she fed him and then left for work on the evening shift at the phone company while he sat at the kitchen table doing his studies. The minute she was gone, Matt got himself a fresh cup of coffee and enjoyed a cigarette. But he had to blow the smoke out of the window because Lucy hated the smell of stale smoke in her clean bungalow.

All of this hyperactivity might have exhausted a normal human, but Lucy was far above such ordinary weaknesses. Nothing was going to interfere with her plans for the future. Absolutely nothing. When Matt began to complain about having sex with rubbers, Lucy went to the doctor and had herself fitted for a diaphragm. Matt didn't know about the diaphragm. He was too happy to be having sex the way a man expected to have sex with his wife to notice that she always went to the bathroom before joining him in bed. When he talked about having children, Lucy made all the right agreeing sounds. But children were out of the question. She already had a needy, dependent child.

She had Matt.

The Rainwater household settled into a new routine. George waited for the telegram that would tell her just when Jake would be home. Walt and Wil resumed playing pool on Saturday nights, Walt leaving Tara to do whatever it was a sixteen-year-old girl wanted to do. May Rose had been opposed to the marriage, not because she held any ill feeling toward Tara or felt that what had happened to her was in any way Tara's fault. May Rose knew Allen too well to blame Tara for anything. Her opposition to the marriage was based solely on the fact that she could

227

not be convinced that Walt was under any moral obligation to Tara. But now that there was a marriage, she was determined to make the best of it, be as loving toward Tara as a mother-in-law ought to be. After all, it was traditional for the older woman to raise up and train the younger women. This attitude had worked very well with George, and George wasn't even Osage. What worked with a white girl would most definitely work with a full Osage girl. Now that Tara was beginning to loose some of her nervousness about living among them, she was proving herself to be a pleasant girl and she was a wonderfully handy baby-sitter. With the advent of Tara, May Rose and George could go out, baby free. As May Rose and George frequently enjoyed doing. So, all was well on the mother-in-law, daughter-in-law front. The person May Rose could not understand was Walt. He still went out rambling with Wil, and when he was home he spoke to his wife as if she were nothing more than a kid sister. How could a man treat the woman he shared the same bed with like his sister?

Tara walked out of the school with her best friend, Emma, both of them bundled up against the snowy day of December 23, 1946. It was the last day of school until January 5. Shouting to their departing friends, "See you next year!" they carried their books in satchels as they minded the icy pathway. Clearing the edge of the school building, Tara saw the old Ford. Walt and Wil stood in front of it, wearing their identical heavy overcoats and black cowboy hats.

Emma nudged closer to Tara and confided, "You

know, those two do look like Cary Grant. How do you tell them apart?"

Tara's proud gaze was firmly fixed on Walt. "My Walt looks *more* like Cary Grant."

The two girls were shoulder to shoulder as they giggled and scooted along down the path.

"Think you can fix me up with Wil?"

"Sure."

"When?" Emma insisted.

"How about now?"

Emma grinned and nodded rapidly.

"Hi ya, kid." Walt smiled as Tara stood before him. His hands were deep in his pockets, and the coat collar was turned up against the bitting winds. "Study hard today?"

"I got an A plus in math on a really hard test."

"Way to go, muffin."

"This is Emma Hawk," Tara said. "Can we give her a ride home? Please, please, please? It's so cold on the bus."

Walt shrugged. "Sure. I guess it'll be okay."

Normally when the brothers picked up Tara after school, and those days numbered in the rare, Walt and Wilber sat in front while Tara and her load of books filled the backseat. Today, they had a guest. A guest who believed Tara and Walt were man and wife. Walt climbed into the back with Tara, and Emma hit the front seat next to Wilber. Tara snuggled in close to her husband. When Walt looked down at her in slight surprise, Tara hugged herself and shivered.

"It's cold." She made a burring sound for effect.

Walt passed off the snuggling at face value. He

229

was dense to the fact that his young wife had developed a hard crush on him.

"Walt, help me," Tara whined. "I can't get warm."

Walt obliged by wrapping an arm around her, and Tara snuggled against his side.

Emma took up the same cry and edged next to Wilber. He steered the moving car as he looked askance.

"Your heater doesn't put out a lot of heat, does it?" Emma complained.

"This ain't the Ritz, sweetheart."

"Then your body heat will have to do."

"Well, jeez, honey," Wil cried. "Try not be so shy!"

"I vote for cocoa!" Tara called.

"Cocoa?" Walt puzzled. "You see any café's around here?"

"We've got cocoa at the house," Tara replied. She looked intently into his face. "Let's have cocoa before we take Emma home."

Walt's gloved hand scratched his temple. "Well, me an' Wil sorta had—"

"What?" She knew perfectly well what. It meant that Walt had plans that did not include having cocoa with her.

Walt avoided her eyes. "Nothing. Never mind."

May Rose was more than a little stunned when the four young people trooped into her kitchen. Walt and Tara were holding hands. Walt's expression held a hint of embarrassment, but Tara was beaming.

"Hi, Ma!" Tara sang. "We're home!" She paused long enough while removing her coat to kiss May Rose's cheek. Tara's eyes slid toward their visitor.

"This is my best friend. Emma Hawk. Emma, this is Momma-May."

"Pleased to meet you," May Rose said.

Walt looked sheepishly at his mother. "Uh, Ma, these girls are wantin' cocoa."

May Rose bit the inside corner of her mouth to prevent herself from smiling. "Your wife"—she lightly stressed the word—"knows where everything is. I'll just leave you young folks to it."

Wil cheerfully drove Emma home. During the drinking of cocoa in the kitchen, the pair had hit it off like a house on fire. Now that they were all in the car again to drive Emma home, she was even less shy about cuddling against Wil.

"You know," he said with a laugh, "you're not half bad for a little snot-nosed kid."

"And for a real old guy, you might pass in the dark with a kick and a shove."

Wil gripped the steering wheel as he gave Emma another long glance. "You got a mouth on ya."

"I won't take your guff, if that's what you mean."

"Hey? Are you old enough to date?"

"Depends on who's asking."

Walt's regular Saturday night was fried. Wil was in the bathroom dousing himself with Old Spice, getting ready for his date with Emma. Wil had promised Emma's father that they would be chaperoned at all times, so that meant Walt and Tara were going along too. Walt didn't mind taking Tara to the movies, but tonight's feature was a Cary Grant movie, which guaranteed the movie would be a romantic tearjerking romp. Walt couldn't stand that stuff. He was a Bogart man. Old Bogie didn't go in for mush. He couldn't. He didn't have much of a face for it.

Walt and Tara were in their room, dressing for the big evening of movies and burgers. As usual, they dressed with their backs turned to each other. Walt was shirtless as he stood in stockinged feet, zipping the fly of his good trousers.

"I just don't know what to wear!" he heard Tara complain. "Walt! I need your help."

Walt turned slightly and looked over his left shoulder. Tara stood in a gray skirt that struck the middle of her kneecaps and was topped off by a green sweater.

"Which looks better?" she demanded. "This sweater? Or maybe . . ." An instant later she pulled the sweater over her head, her breasts plainly visible inside the sheer bra.

"Hey!" Walt shouted, whirling away from her.

"What's the matter?"

"Don't do that," he growled. His shaking hand fumbled with his waist button. The more comfortable he was becoming with Tara, the harder it was to sleep with her like a brother. The last thing he needed was to see her half naked.

"Walt," Tara sighed. "I need your opinion about this other sweater."

"Well, put it on and I'll tell ya!" Irritably, he grabbed up his own sweater off the bed, tugged it over his head.

"You can turn around now," he heard her say. He turned but only slightly. When he saw that she was fully clothed, he turned completely. She was wearing the pink fuzzy sweater he, on impulse, had bought for her when he had been shopping around for her

Christmas present. He ended up buying her two sweaters. The pink one for now, a bright red one for Christmas. The pink sweater made her look like a delicious piece of candy. But he didn't say that.

"Yeah, that one looks okay."

He quickly turned away again, sat down on the bed, and fished out his shoes from underneath. He threw her a furtive glance as he tied his shoe laces. While she had been in the hospital, a doctor had reset her nose. Being a white doctor, instead of curving the tip downward, he had tipped it slightly up. It was funny but at the same time kind of cute. And then there was her eyes, her hair. Walt would not allow himself to think about her body. *Damn, she's pretty.*

After tying the laces, he stood behind her at the lone mirror. Tara brushed out her long hair while Walt ran a brush through his shoulder-length mane. Tara watched him in the mirror as he pulled it back into a ponytail, securing his hair with a rubber band.

"Why do you and Wil wear your hair long?"

Walt tossed the brush onto the dresser top and shrugged as he walked away from her. "We're old-fashioned. About lots of stuff. You 'bout ready?"

"Yes."

"Good." Taking a deep breath, he placed his hand on the doorknob. "Let's get this over with."

The evening was far more horrible than Walt had allowed himself to imagine. They pulled up to the Hawks' house and trooped inside, where Mrs. Hawk served coffee and cake. Then she whipped out an old Kodak camera and took an entire roll of pictures. With Mr. Hawk standing right behind them, the four young people were required to lock arms and say, Cheese.

Then there was the damn movie.

Cary Grant played a college professor who married a young student because she was pregnant with another man's baby and he didn't want her to be disgraced. Walt put a hand over his face and peeked at the thing through spread fingers. Except for the fact that Tara definitely wasn't pregnant, this movie hit too close to home. Walt squirmed in his seat while Tara stuffed popcorn in her mouth, eyes wide and glued to the ghostly images on the distant screen. At the end of the movie, good ole Cary got the girl and claimed the baby as his and they all lived happily ever after. Cary, the broad, the bastard baby, and some weird old butler. Walt wanted to puke. And of the four seated together viewing the monstrosity, he seemed the only one bothered by the plot! When the house lights went up, the two girls were bawling their heads off.

"Wasn't that beautiful?" Emma wept.

"Oh, it was!" Tara blubbered.

The brothers steered the weeping girls out and walked them down to the diner, where they ordered fat hamburgers and Cokes.

"You know," Emma said to Tara as she leaned on the table, burger in both hands, "they really do look like Cary Grant."

The two girls turned to the young men beside them, studying their faces.

"We look like *who*?" Wil barked.

"Cary Grant," Emma replied.

Wil tossed the soiled paper napkin onto his plate. "Girl, you're crazy."

Emma shrugged and took a large bite of her

burger. "I'm going out with you," she muffled, "so I guess you're right."

Playfully Wil wrapped his hands around her neck, pretending to strangle her. "Did you take the onions out of that thing before you bit into it?"

Emma put a hand to her mouth and nodded yes as she tried to giggle and swallow at the same time.

"Good," he breathed, letting go of her. "Now I'll kiss ya."

"Not in here!"

" 'Course not in here," Wil frowned. "I'm the Redman's answer to Cary Grant, remember? You ever see Cary Grant kiss a girl with her mouth full of burger and fries?"

Walt and Tara had the front seat, Walt the driver as they drove back toward Emma's house. Halfway down the road Wil stopped kissing Emma long enough to put in a request for Walt to kill the headlights and park the car. Walt complied and then sat stonily quiet. Both he and Tara tried to shut their ears to the kissing sounds and low moans of pleasure emitting from the backseat.

"Some movie, huh, muffin?" Walt threw out as a conversational ice breaker.

"It was wonderful."

"Oh, Wil," Emma's voice panted.

"Oh, baby," Wil responded.

Walt pulled the collar of his sweater as he watched a steamy fog roll in, steadily reduce visibility through the windows. Feeling the heat radiating from the backseat, Walt wormed around, his mind struggling for another topic of conversation. He couldn't think of a thing. Well, actually he could, but it didn't involve talking. Feeling frayed around the edges, he hurriedly suggested he and Tara get out of the car for a breath of fresh air.

Leaning against the car door with Tara beside him, he felt her shiver.

"It's cold, Walt. Let's get back in the car before we freeze."

Walt, still battling the hot blood coursing through his veins, pleaded, "Just one more minute. Okay, muffin?"

"No!" she cried, stamping her foot. "I'm cold. I don't want to catch pneumonia just because you can't stand to be around a little harmless kissing."

"Who can't stand it?"

"You can't!" she cried. "If I was a girl from the White Horse, you wouldn't be out here. But since I'm only your wife, well then, it's the cold winds and the—"

"Hey, look!" Walt angrily pushed himself away from the car and, grabbing her arm, dragged her out of earshot. In a lower voice he said, "We got a deal, remember? You're supposed to go to school and I'm supposed to keep my hands off. It's what we both agreed. I'm sorry if it bothers you that I go around with a few girls from the White Horse, but I'm a man. Believe me, if I didn't go with other girls, which I do as a favor to you, I'd be on my knees chewing our damn bedroom rug."

Tara stood mute, blinking away the tears that filled her eyes. Walt slapped his thighs and stomped away from her. He hated it when she cried. Primarily because he never knew *why* she cried or how to make her stop. And lately she was getting worse about it. Walt could not puzzle out what he was doing that was making her so upset.

He shoved his hands deep into his coat pockets and walked back, planting himself in front of her. He had to bend at the knees in order to look at her tear-stained face.

"You don't want me going around with other women, is that it?"

He really couldn't believe that was it, and he was stunned stupid when she nodded yes.

"Tara!" he thundered. "Do you know what you're askin'?"

"Yes!"

Walt slapped his thighs again, and kept slapping them as he walked around in circles. It was the movie, he reasoned as he paced like a circus horse in the center ring. It had to be that stupid movie. All that happy-ever-after guano had eaten up her brains. She had swallowed that made-up story like a big mouth bass swallowing a minnow. Enraged, Walt parked himself in front of her once more.

"Just what the hell do you want from me!"

Tara was crying so hard her answer came out in jerking blasts.

"I want you to start looking at me as a person," she wailed. "I'm tired of you feeling sorry for me!"

Tara spun on her heels, dashing back to the car. She flung open the door and jumped inside, slamming the door hard. His lower jaw, hanging almost to his chest, the bitterly cold wind slapped his face like an invisible hand.

Wil and Emma bobbed to the surface when Walt finally climbed into the car. Walt and Tara glared hatefully at each other before snapping their heads forward.

"You two having a fight?" Wil asked.

"Shut up, Wil!" Walt started the car.

*　*　*

Dressing for bed was done on the rota system. Tonight had been her turn to change in the bathroom. When she padded into the bedroom wearing a flannel nightgown, Walt was already in bed, one arm hooked behind his head as he stared up at the ceiling. Tara crawled into bed and clicked off the bedside lamp. Her back was to him as she curled up in the fetal position.

"Tara," he said in the darkness, "I just want you to know that I have always seen you as a person. I don't feel sorry for you. I'm—I'm proud of you."

She rolled onto her back. "You are?"

"Yes, I am. You're a real nice kid, and you're no trouble to have around. My folks like you a lot. This marriage thing will work if we just don't fight anymore. Okay? Can we have a truce and just go on as normal?"

Silence.

"Tara?"

Nothing.

"Muffin?"

"NO."

"Sonofabitch!" Walt roared. He bolted up in bed, and Tara sat up along with him. "What the hell do you want from me?"

"How about a good-night kiss?"

"Have you lost your mind?"

"Oh, I see," she said huffily. "You can kiss other girls, but I have to be crazy to expect you to kiss me just because I happen to be your wife?"

Walt expelled a long stream of air through his nose. "You want a kiss, huh? Okay, I'll kiss you." He grabbed her by the shoulders and pulled her to him, kissing her so hard she saw stars. Then he shoved her away, flopped down, and clung desperately to his side of the bed.

Gloating, Tara calmly fluffed her pillow and lay down.

The long-awaited telegram finally arrived. According to the telegram, Jake was due to arrive in Tulsa December 27, and he would call from Tulsa. May Rose put Christmas on hold. At six a.m. on the twenty-seventh, Jake called. Having not slept one wink, George was sitting by the telephone and answered on the first ring. And when she heard his voice, she couldn't speak through the tears choking her. Putting on her bathrobe, May Rose came out of her bedroom into the hallway. Immediately she saw the distress George was in and took the receiver out of her hand.

"Ma?"

"Jakey!" she cried.

"I'll be on the next train to Bartlesville. I'll be there around ten."

"We'll be right there to meet you."

"Great. I can't wait to see everybody. Make sure Sally's dressed real warm. It's colder than a well digger's ass out here."

"Jakey," May Rose chuckled. "You are so funny."

"See you soon, Mom." Jake hung up.

A bit baffled that he didn't ask to speak to George again, May Rose cradled the receiver. "He—he had to rush to catch the train. I'll get the coffee going. You wake up the rest of the family. We'll have to hurry if we're going to get to the station on time."

Chapter Ten

The last few months had been hell. He had seen things that had made him very angry. And frustrated. The frustration stemming from the fact that there was nothing he could do. He was powerless to punish those responsible for their crimes against the innocent. That power lay in the hands of those in higher positions. As a common sergeant, all he could do was walk away, try to put the war and Germany out of his mind. But during the extensive travel home his anger festered, and he focused it on George. During the crossing of the Atlantic, he went to his colonel's cabin, and Colonel Dutch advised him on just how to handle his first weeks home before hitting George with a divorce.

"Do not go in with guns blazing. Your whole family will think you've gone nutty. To keep your kid, you'll have to be as nice as hell while you're quietly seeing a lawyer. Doing this right is going to take time, and it's going to take patience. And something else.

"What?"

"Abstinence."

Jake blanched. "Are you serious?"

"Do you want a divorce?"

Jake hesitated. "Yeah."

"Then you can't play in the ball park."

"Damn."

After that his anger turned to depression. Then, in the Army processing center at Fort Dix, Jake said good-bye forever to his friends, his colonel. His depression deepened, stole the joy of being on the train, seeing the countryside whip by the windows. It was only when he arrived in Tulsa and called home that happiness at being so very close to home began to take root in his heart. During the last miles of the journey, he stared at the picture of his baby. Very soon he would be holding his very own daughter. She was his Sally. His.

As the train began to slow, Jake wiped the condensation from the window. His heart missed several vital beats when he saw his family. As if drawn against his will, his eyes went straight to George, and his breath caught in his throat. She was even prettier than he remembered. And her hair was longer, looked more tamed. She even looked a bit taller. Jake experienced second thoughts. Especially about abstinence. Then his eyes went to the baby in her arms. His heart stopped. Second thoughts faded.

Jake wouldn't wait for the train to stop. He grabbed his heavy duffel bag and made his way to the door. The train was slowing when the porter yelled at him because he had opened the door and was leaning dangerously out.

Seeing him, George began to wave frantically. Then she pointed at him and spoke to Sally. "That's Daddy. See Daddy." George felt so excited, she was ready to leap out of her skin. She waved again, her face split in half by a smile.

Sally rolled her green-brown eyes in the direction her mother pointed. But since she was barely a year old, her attention span was limited. When the other members of the family started shouting, Sally commenced to wail. Her crying set off Toya. Both babies were in full voice when Jake was met first by his father. Claude very nearly lifted Jake off his feet in a crushing bear hug. As soon as his father let go of him, Jake rushed for his crying daughter.

He quickly kissed George's mouth as he pried Sally out of her arms. Finally in possession of his very own baby, he held her at arm's length and laughed while Sally howled. She was dressed very warmly in a little blue coat (*how do they make coats this small?*) and matching hat. Her chubby little legs were covered in white woolly stockings. White ankle-high shoes were on her dangling little feet. Her rosebud mouth was turned downward as she cried. Fat silvery tears ran down chubby, rosy cheeks. She was the prettiest baby in the whole world. He wanted to inspect every inch of her. But his mother had him by the neck, raining kisses on the side of his face, and the rest of the family crowded in. Thoroughly inspecting his baby would have to wait.

The family had driven two cars to the station. Claude drove the lead car with May Rose and Toya beside him in the front seat. In the back were Jake, George, and Sally. The twins and Tara followed in the second car. Claude looked at the couple in the back through the rearview mirror. George was staring at Jake as if she couldn't get enough of the sight of him while Jake held Sally and talked baby-talk to her. Sally wasn't interested. She was reaching hard for her mother and making *Uhhhing* noises. Jake ignored the obvious, that his baby didn't want any part of him. Undaunted by her squirming to get away from him, he untied the ribbon beneath her chubby chin and removed her bonnet. The minute he saw her hair, Jake laughed like a loon.

"Look at this!"

Startled, Sally turned rounded eyes at this stranger who wouldn't let her go.

"My God! No one has hair like this."

"It's auburn," George said with a giggle. "A lot of people have auburn hair."

Jake scowled at George. "No, they don't. Just my Sally has this kind of hair." He pulled Sally close to him, touched his nose against hers, and cooed. "Just my pumpkin. Just my little baby pumpkin has pretty dark red hair."

Feeling just a tad more friendly, Sally slobbered on Jake's nose. Exhilarated by this small show of acceptance, Jake covered her round little face with kisses.

George didn't know what to do. It was as if he had forgotten she was in the car. She had missed him so much and for so long. She'd imagined a lot of things happening after he came off the train. Cutting her to the quick with a frown and then ignoring her wasn't among those things. An uncomfortable silence lingered as the car traveled on and Jake played with Sally.

May Rose glanced back at her son. She couldn't imagine what was wrong with him. He wasn't holding his wife's hand, wasn't stealing any kisses from her. He was only kissing Sally. Feeling the need to do something, she raised the sleeping Toya from her shoulder.

"What do you think of your baby sister?"

Jake glanced up, looked at Toya, quickly looked back at Sally. The comparison between the two babies only reaffirmed what he already knew. His baby was the prettiest. But he couldn't say this to his mother. "She's really cute, Mom." Finally, he spoke to George. "How many toys did Sally get from Santa Claus?"

"She hasn't got any yet. Santa Claus has been waiting to visit her after her daddy came home."

"Really?" Jake said excitedly. "Then I didn't miss Christmas?"

"No." George ventured another giggle. "We're having Christmas and New Year's on the same day."

"That's great. Now I can do some shopping for my girl."

Still holding his daughter, Jake ran through the house like a ferret. "Nothing's changed," he cried. "Everything's still the same. Man, you don't know how much I've dreamed of being home. When do we eat? I've got to have some home cooking, fast."

The men sat in the living room, Jake and Claude on the couch, their baby daughters sleeping on their shoulders. The three women worked in the kitchen to get the meal on the table. In muted voices the Rainwater men filled Jake in about Allen, about Matt. In deference to Walt, Matt was the dominant subject.

"We weren't even invited to the wedding," Claude said sadly. "That broke up your mother pretty bad. And you know something, every time we try to call him, you know, to find out how he's getting along, we end up talking just to Lucy. Your momma says Lucy's bound and determined to cut everyone else out of Matt's life. I gotta tell you, I think she's right. What beats me is why Matt's lettin' her do it. I mean, we're his family. The only thing we've ever done is love him, try to do the best we could for him. Just like we've done for all our kids. It hurts that he can just toss that away an' never look back."

"You won't catch me doing that," Jake snorted. "I'm home and this is where I'm staying."

Claude chuckled. "You gonna live with your momma for the rest of your life?"

"Yep."

"Gonna get kinda crowded when you have more kids."

Jake looked down at his sleeping baby. "I don't want any more kids. I just want Sally."

Uneasy glances flickered between Claude and the twins. Claude cleared his throat. "You know, there's a nice piece of land up on the hill just behind the house. Me an' your momma thought it would be pretty good piece of land to put a house on. That land's all yours if you want it."

Jake looked eagerly at his father. "Really? Thanks, Dad. Just let me get settled, get myself a job, and then I'll start building." He kissed the back of Sally's head and whispered, "Daddy's going to build his princess a big castle on a hill."

"George likes it up there too," Claude ventured.

"Oh, yeah?"

"It's the war," May Rose said. At the stove, George only nodded and kept stirring the bubbling gravy. May Rose could feel the hurt pouring out of her. Setting the table, Tara caught May Rose's eye. Apparently even across the kitchen Tara could feel George's

245

pain too. May Rose tried again. "Being home has got to be very strange for him. Like he's walking in a dream. It's probably going to take him a while to get used to it. We're all going to have to be patient."

George couldn't take it anymore. She dropped the spoon, covered her face with her hands as she buckled under the weight of her sorrow. May Rose flew to her, wrapped her arms around her, led her out of the kitchen onto the back porch, and closed the door. Holding her daughter-in-law, who felt like a trembling, wounded bird, May Rose stroked her wiry hair.

"Shoooo, sweet girl. It's going to be all right. Everything is going to be all right."

"Oh, Momma-May!" George sobbed. "Do you really think so?"

Well, actually no. Jake was not behaving the way a husband newly reunited with his wife was expected to behave. But George's expression was so desperately hopeful. "Of course I think so. That man just needs to calm down a little, get things in the right order. After being away for so long, it's only natural he would feel a little . . . awkward."

Wiping tears from her face, George did not remind Momma-May that she had been away from her real home, her real family, for just as long as Jake had been away from his. Or that because of Jake, her real home was closed to her. She wondered now if perhaps she had gone a trifle overboard with this trying to blend in thing. Perhaps if she hadn't worked so hard at being a member of the household, Momma-May wouldn't toss her concerns off so lightly.

"You just go in and wash your face and come out for dinner wearing a sunny smile," May Rose continued. "You still got the night time coming up. A bit later on, Jake will start feeling *very* romantic."

"T-thank you, Momma-May."

May Rose kissed the side of George's head, sent her off. Alone on the porch, May Rose couldn't help but wonder if what she'd said was true. Then she thought about Walt. During the whole time he had been married to Tara, Walt had been about as romantic as a tree stump. Now here was Jake acting the very same way. How the devil had Walt and Jake turned out to be so cold-blooded? They certainly hadn't gotten their frigid natures from Claude.

Or from her.

The afternoon meal was lingered over, Jake dominating the table talk, remembering stories of the old days, telling jokes. Tara was bored out of her skull. She didn't think she liked Jake all that much, and compared to Walt (and Wil ever in tow), Jake was only good-looking in a rangy sort of way. His body ran to thin, his facial features, angular. Tara liked a man with some meat on him. Walt (and yes! Wil) were beefy. But not as beefy as Matt. Which was good because if Matt didn't watch it, one morning he would wake up really, really fat.

Tara was worried about her quiet sister-in-law. George had always been so nice to her. But then, that was George. She would do anything to please. And she was so earnest about it, as if pleasing people was a mission from God or something. Now that Jake was home, George was noticeably edgy, not just at odds and ends as Momma-May said. George seemed afraid as she sat beside Jake. Terror is an isolating emotion. The whole time Allen menaced her, Tara had been terrified and alone. Now here was George displaying the same signs, Tara recognized every one of them. She could almost hear George's thumping heart, feel her stomach twisting. And that George worked so hard to appear normal caused Tara to worry all the more.

When the meal was over, Tara stayed with George as much as possible, doing the dishes with her, offering her silent support while the rest of the family laughed it up in the living room. Then they both heard Momma-May say, "I just don't know how I survived before my daughters came to live with me. For years I worked like a mule keeping up with you men. Life has been a lot nicer since I got me my helper girls."

And then there was Jake's low voice. "George really pitched in, did she?"

"Yes. She's a real credit to you, Jakey."

"Jakey" didn't offer any comment. Tara pressed her shoulder against George's. George glanced at her with watery eyes. Tara wanted to say something, but what was there to say?

The dishes were finished, the kitchen neat as a pin. Tara and George couldn't stall any longer. Each had to return to their separate game of pretense at happy families. Hearing Sally fussing in the bedroom, George rushed to her while Tara went to the couch and sat down beside Walt. The instant their bodies touched, she felt him tense. He had been this way ever since she'd forced him to kiss her good night. He made her feel as if she should examine herself for cooties. She never asked for any more kisses, and Walt didn't offer. He couldn't. He wasn't around to offer. He was always gone, either working overtime or just—gone. And when he finally dragged in, he was always very careful not to wake her. She knew because she wasn't asleep when he crept into bed, smelling strongly of beer.

George was changing Sally's diaper when Jake came up behind her, startling her with his presence. She gasped when she felt the pressure of his hand coming to rest on her shoulder. George steeled her flurry of emotions, concentrated on cleaning Sally.

"Thanks, George."

"For what?"

"For the baby. For being so nice to my folks."

"I couldn't help the one," she laughed brittlely. "The other was never an issue. Your parents are lovely. Your mother especially. I'm quite fond of Momma-May."

This was not turning out the way he'd hoped or the way King had predicted.

Listen, Boogie-man, that little dame is gonna be ready to walk back to England after she spends a few months living with Indians. She's just not gonna cut it.

Well, she had. She moved in and made herself right at home. In *his* home!"

Becoming livid, he left the room. Walking down the hallway, he shoved his hands deeply into his trouser pockets. Now more than ever he wanted her to go back to England. He knew he should concentrate on all of Dutch's good advice, but Dutch wasn't here. He wasn't able to see George, see how even more sexy she'd turned out to be. And she hadn't been lost at all among Indians. Damn! She'd thrived like some kind of fungus feeding off everything that belonged to him. Then again, he returned to how sexy she was. Having a baby had really agreed with

249

her. The last time he had been with her, she had been little more than a stringy girl. Now she had boobs . . . and hips.

Jake stopped, leaned wearily against the wall. Coming up on her in the bedroom, being close enough to touch her, had done him in. Even over Sally's poopy stink he could smell George's subtle womanly fragrance. And touching her, he'd felt the too familiar current of physical attraction rush through him. He closed his eyes to the ache he felt all the way to his teeth.

He pushed away from the wall. He needed air. Cold air. He rushed into the living room and suggested to his brothers they go for a ride to see the old hometown.

"But it's dark!" Wil replied. "An' Urainia rolls up the sidewalks at five o'clock. There's nothing to see out there except maybe a few blackjack trees."

"I'd like to go for a ride anyway."

"Let's go to the Horse," Walt promptly suggested.

Tara rose from the couch, said her good-nights. If the three brothers were heading for the White Horse, that meant family night was well and truly over.

Jake and Wil held their cue sticks while Walt leaned across the pool table, carefully taking aim. He hit the white cue ball, which smacked against the colored balls and scattered them across the green surface. Two balls promptly disappeared into side pockets. Wil looked forlornly at Jake.

"We might as well sit down. Our brother's a real hustler. He'll have the table for the whole game. He always does."

Jake and Wil sat down away from the table Walt

dominated. Wil couldn't stand the suspense any longer. Turning his face toward Jake, he said angrily, "What the hell are you doing here?"

"What?"

"Don't what me, Jakey. You know what I'm asking. What are you doing playing pool when you should be home with George?"

Jake ran his tongue over his teeth. "It's a long story."

"Most stories are," Wil snorted. "But hey, ain't you in luck. I just happen to have plenty of time to listen."

Jake thought for a moment, then said, "I'll tell you, but only if you promise not to tell Ma. If she knows any of this, she'll ruin everything and then maybe I'll lose Sally."

"What the hell are you talkin' about?"

"Just promise me."

"Okay, okay, okay. I promise. Now spill it."

Having absolutely no idea that he was talking to the wrong brother, Jake told Wil everything, left no gory detail out. Wil was stunned to the core. Then he felt himself becoming angry, then incensed. He couldn't believe that Jake couldn't appreciate the obvious. That when George had first arrived she had been little more than a half-starved waif and wearing clothes that were no better than rags. Just for Jake she had crossed an ocean all by herself, trusting that a whole mess of strangers wouldn't be mean to her.

Wil smoldered as Jake talked on, and vividly recalling how eagerly George had tried to adapt and how Mom had bossed her and the way George had just taken it. God knows how long that would have gone on if he hadn't stepped in and set Mom straight. Even then, it was only after Matt came home that Mom had eased up, really started to appreciate George. And she had really appreciated the hell out of George once she ran the house, did all the cooking and cleaning after Mom had had such a hard time having Toya that she had to stay in bed for three weeks.

Then with the thing about Allen and then Walt and Tara getting married, Mom would have gone crazy if George hadn't been there. Now here was Jake putting the bad mouth on George, saying everything was just an act. Well, if it was an act, it had to be just about the strongest act in history. But it wasn't an act. Never had been. Jake didn't know George at all. He was as blind as a bat. What difference did it make *why* they got married? Jake should go down on his knees and thank God that a girl like George had married him. Wil knew that if he had been the one who married George, that was exactly what he would do. Feeling the urgent need to get away from Jake before he busted him right in the mouth, he jumped up, hurried to the pool table. Walt was lining up another shot. Wil bumped him on purpose, causing Walt to miss.

"Hey!" Walt shouted. "I get to do that shot over."

"No, you don't," Wil growled. He leaned across the table and hit the cue ball so hard it bounced over to the next table and clicked loudly against the balls on that table. The players at this table didn't care for that very much, and a verbal war ensued. Wil took out the boiling anger he felt against his brother on innocent bystanders.

At midnight they drove home. Wil sat in the back, still too livid to speak. Once they were in the house, the brothers dispersed. In his bedroom, Jake slipped quietly into bed without disturbing George. Down the hall in his room, Walt was doing the very same thing. Walt was always terrified about waking Tara. Afraid that if he woke her, she might ask for a good-night kiss. He did not want to kiss Tara. Kissing her made him feel hot. If she only knew how hard it was for him to keep his hands off her, she would be too afraid to ask for kisses.

All alone in his bedroom, Wil was free to make all the noise he wanted and he did, throwing his clothing off and stomping on the floor. He couldn't stand remembering the garbage Jake had said. And now that he knew Jake didn't love George, he couldn't stand thinking about Jake crawling into her bed. If Jake was really going to divorce her, then he should do the decent thing and sleep somewhere else. He should definitely not cuddle up with . . . Pinto. Wil sat down on the edge of his bed. Pinto, that's who she really was. That's who she had been from the first moment he caught her sitting on the porch eating crackers and marshmallows. If Jake didn't want her, then Wil did. He wanted her more than he had ever wanted anything. Finally admitting this to himself, he suddenly couldn't bear it that Jake was with her.

"You better not touch her," Wil warned as he stared at the wall. "You touch her, and I swear to God I'll hurt you."

Wil lay in bed, unable to sleep a wink. He might have had he known that Jake had lifted Sally from her cot and placed the baby between himself and George. The next morning, Jake and George woke to find that the bed was soaked an so were they.

"Oh, no," George gasped. "I must have forgotten to put on her rubbers."

Jake helped her strip the bed. While he helped, he couldn't dismiss the thought that had he remembered a rubber, he and George wouldn't be sharing this slightly amusing moment, that there would be no Sally. The thought made him feel empty. Her back was toward him as she leaned over the crib changing Sally. He was in a slight daze, his hand reaching out to touch her, when he came back to himself, realized what he was doing. Jake promptly left the room.

In the bathroom he washed and changed into a pair of jeans and a shirt. It was the first pair of jeans he'd had on since boot camp, and they felt wonderful. Next he went into the kitchen and crept up on his mother, grabbing her around the waist as she stood at the stove.

Nuzzling her neck, he murmured, "How's the coffee?"

"It's ready," she laughed.

"Great. I'll take a cup in to George."

"Oh, you don't need to. Wil's taken her a cup."

Remembering Wil's look of hatred the night before and realizing Wil felt this because he felt deeply about George, Jake experienced a rip of jealousy. "Does Wil always take her coffee?"

May Rose turned a piece of frying bacon. "Yes, I suppose he does. Wil and George are good buddies."

"Oh? How good?"

"Well, Wil has always fussed over George. He'd take her out a lot too. Took her up to Woolaroc once to a big powwow. George really had a good time. When she got so big she couldn't go out so much, he stayed home and taught her to play poker and checkers. Like I said, they're real good buddies."

The rip became a tear.

Wil knocked, and when he heard her say come in, he did. George was a mess. Her wild hair was more wild than usual, and she was wearing a sodden nightdress. Smelly sheets were bundled up on the floor, and George was struggling to turn the mattress. Wil quickly set the cup of coffee on the dresser and went to her aid.

"What happened?"

"Jake brought Sally to bed. I stupidly forgot to put rubber pants over her night diapers. We both got a good soak."

Taking over the heavy job, Wil said tersely, "You're not stupid, Pinto. Jake's stupid."

Confused by his anger, she stood back while Wil turned the mattress. Then Jake came crashing in. The next thing she knew, she was standing between them as the two brothers glared at each other over her tangled head.

"Go get cleaned up, George," Jake ordered.

"Don't talk to her like that."

"Don't tell me how to talk to my wife."

"You're really asking for it."

"So are you."

Feeling the need to escape—and quickly—George stammered, "I-I'll just take Sally-"

"No. Just get the hell out."

Before she broke down sobbing, she ran out of the room.

When she was gone, Wil said in a menacing whisper, "You better stop talking to her like that, Jake. I mean it."

"And you better stop sucking after my wife."

"Try and make me."

The brothers were lunging for each other when their mother walked in. They backed off, but they weren't quick enough. May Rose saw the way they had gone for each other, and the tension in the room was so bulky it held the presence of an invisible fourth person.

"What is going on in here?" she demanded.

"Nothing, Ma," Jake answered.

She looked from Jake to Wil. Neither would look her in the eye. Finally she said, "Wil, your father and your brother are waiting in the truck. If you don't hurry, you'll all be late for work."

Wil brushed past her as she continued to stare holes through Jake. After long years of being the lone woman in a house of men, she had learned the hard way that it was best to let them sort out their man business on their own, especially when the testosterone filled the atmosphere so badly she choked on it. But there was something very wrong here.

"Jake, do you have something to say to me?"

Jake was tempted. Really tempted. But mistakenly he'd confided in Wil, and it had cost him a brother. He didn't want his mother turning against him too. Damn George. It was all her fault. She had to go. Forget about the waiting game. She had to go now before he lost his whole family.

"No, Ma," he said quietly. "Everything's fine. Me and Wil were just . . . playing."

May Rose wondered just how much money she'd have if she'd been given a nickel every time she'd heard that in her life. Sally ended the moment when she pulled herself up in the crib and squealed for their attention. May Rose turned to the baby bed and lifted her out, handing her over to her father. "Take Sally into the bathroom. She can have a bath with George."

George had just washed her hair. It lay flattened against her skull as she soaped herself in the tub. A stormy-expressioned Jake came in, carrying a naked Sally on his narrow hip. Seeing George, his heart stopped on a dime. Her breasts *had* filled out. Finally seeing just how much, his tongue became stuck to the roof of his mouth. Despite his resolve to remain abstinent, he broke out in a lusting sweat.

"Uh, Sally kind of, stinks." As he lowered her into the tub, Sally cooed and kicked her legs excitedly. Jake managed a hollow laugh.

"She must really like baths."

"Yes, she does." She settled Sally in her lap, and Sally began splashing the water with her hands. "Toya likes being in the tub too." Jake sat down on the closed toilet, his gaze wandering all over George as he pretended to watch Sally being bathed and George chattered nervously. "Usually I have both babies with me."

"Isn't that kind of hard?"

"Sometimes. They're like little eels. Very slippery. But they're fun."

She was genuinely smiling when she looked at him. Jake felt a new tightening in his groin. *Oh, damn.* His head still wanted her to go, but his body was screaming. To avoid what would most certainly happen if they slept together one more night, he had to

257

make the cut now or by tomorrow he would be suicidal. After all, he reminded himself, their marriage had been nothing more than a farce. Merely a means to keep his neck out of a rope. Now there was nothing more to be gained. A quick and clean end would be kinder for them both.

He turned his face away, took a deep breath. "George, I've been thinking. Our marriage was too quick. It was a mistake. I-I want a divorce."

All the blood drained from her face. She swallowed the painful lump in her throat, concentrated on taking even breaths to calm her rampant heart. She stared at the back of Sally's little head as she thought at length. The first thoughts that came to her was a little lecture Momma-May had delivered long ago.

"I had a real good friend once who told me that living with a man is just like training a dog."

Next her thoughts were about how strangely relieved she felt now that the fear she had harbored since Jake had gotten off the train had been realized. Being divorced would be hard, but not half as hard as trying to make a happy life with a man who didn't want her. Released from that burden, no longer having to worry about anything else except taking care of herself and her baby, she knew she would survive. She was very grateful they had not made love. It made the pain she felt bearable.

"All right," she said softly. "If you want a divorce, you may have a divorce."

He couldn't believe she was taking it so calmly. Wasn't she supposed to cry or something? He waited for tears, but they didn't fall. After a long moment, he said, "I suppose you'll go back to England."

George continued to bathe Sally. "No, I won't be going back to England."

Jake's eyes flared. She was supposed to say yes. Then he could get tough about Sally, get custody like Colonel Dutch said. But what the hell would happen if she stayed in Oklahoma?

"What do you want to hang around here for?" he yelled.

George didn't flicker so much as a red eyelash. "Oklahoma is my home. More important, this is Sally's home." Then she looked at him. Her green eyes were clear. There still wasn't a sign of tears. "Sally and I will be fine, Jake. And of course, you can visit Sally whenever you wish."

"What do you mean, visit? My kid's not leaving this house."

"Yes, she is."

From the firm tone in her voice, Jake knew she meant it. He also knew something else. George wasn't afraid of him. And damn her, damn her, damn her, he wanted her more than ever. Before he yielded to the strong temptation of jumping into the tub with her, taking back what he'd said about divorce, he stormed out of the bathroom.

May Rose could not believe the day she was having. Jake hadn't even been home twenty-four hours, and already hell was breaking loose all around her. First had been that alarming scene between Jake and Wil she'd walked in on. Second, and only minutes apart, Jake had come tearing into the kitchen, where she and Tara were planning just what kind of pie to bake for supper, yelling about a divorce. Then Tara pushed him aside, ran for the bathroom, and Jake went after Tara. But he wasn't fast enough. Tara slammed the bathroom door in his face and locked it. May Rose was steps behind her son as Jake beat on the door and Tara yelled at him:

"You're not coming in here!"

"The hell I'm not!"

Sally started to cry. From the back bedroom Toya began to cry. Claude and the twins were at work. There was no one else to sort out this mess, and May Rose felt woefully inadequate to the task as she grabbed Jake's arm.

"Stop this! Stop this right now."

"She's not taking my baby, Ma."

"That's her baby!"

"No, Sally's mine. She can't have Sally. I'll beat her stupid before I'll let her take Sally."

May Rose slapped her son's face. Jake instantly sobered, but May Rose was huffing and puffing with fury. "Don't you ever," she said in a measured tone, "say that. I've cut one son out of my heart. I won't hesitate to cut you out too."

"But, Ma—"

"Don't you Ma me. Any man who can raise his fist to a woman is too low-down to ever call himself *my* son. Take the car and drive around until you cool off."

"I'm sorry, Ma."

"Get away from me, Jake."

She watched from the window until the car was gone. Then she went to the bathroom and knocked the all-clear. The instant Tara unlocked the door, May Rose barreled in. George was out of the tub and wrapped in a towel, holding and crooning to Sally. May Rose marched right up to her. "What started all this?" she demanded.

"I-I suppose, while I pack, I should tell you the entire story."

"Yes," May Rose agreed. "I think you'd better."

Jake drove all over the place, not even knowing where he was half the time. A lot of the roads were new, and many of them dead-ended at a new oil patch. While he drove aimlessly, he did a lot of thinking. At the end of three hours, he decided it would be best if he just went home, had a long talk with George. Maybe they could work it out somehow, forget about how and why they got married and simply concentrate on the fact that they were married, that they had a child. A child who needed both a mother and a father. He'd convinced himself that all of this was still possible when he pulled into the drive. Then he noticed that the old banger the twins owned was gone. His blood turned ice-cold. He bolted from the car and ran to the house. The minute he stepped through the door, he knew she was gone. He felt her absence like a physical assault, but needing confirmation, he ran to his bedroom. Sally's crib was gone, and the door to the closet was open. George's clothing was missing. Hearing a noise in the kitchen, he went there.

Tara looked up from the pie dough she was rolling. The ashen look on his face pleased her all the way to the bone. And she especially loved it that she held the power to rub additional salt into his wounds.

"She's gone."

Jake struggled to find his voice. "W-where did she go?"

Tara snorted derisively. "I'm not telling you."

Delbert's house had been empty for about a thousand years. As he'd had no one else to leave it to, he'd left it to May Rose. That and the five acres surrounding the house. The rest of his lands had reverted back to the Osage Nation. Just after he died, May Rose had been shocked when she was told of Delbert's final gift to her. She hadn't set foot in the house since the day she'd inspected it with the lawyer, placed protective sheets over all the furniture. Over the years, Claude suggested she sell the place. Trouble was, there was no one with any money to buy it for what it was worth. She'd had a couple of inquiries about renting it, and she'd been tempted, since she could certainly have done with the extra income. But strangers living in Delbert's house just didn't sit right with her. May Rose declined both offers, and the house remained empty. She felt no hesitation in taking George to Delbert's house. George wasn't a stranger. George was family. Divorce or no divorce, George would always be family.

Driving up to the house, she could see that after so many years of neglect it was in sad condition, but that it was still sound. Delbert had built his little house to last. All it really needed was a good cleaning to make it livable, and the work would give George something to do. She would be all right for money because she had been like a squirrel, putting her allotment checks straight into the bank, then working at any task assigned to her to pay her way while she waited patiently for Jake to come home.

"Why didn't you tell me?" May Rose asked again for what had to be the hundredth time.

"I didn't think you would ever need to know," George answered softly. "The last time I saw Jake, when he was putting me on the train for Portsmouth, I thought we had a marriage. Now that he's home and he's made it abundantly clear he doesn't hold the same opinion, there's no longer any need to keep pesky secrets."

May Rose swallowed back tears. "I-I'll telephone the phone company. I'll get them to put in a new phone line. I called the electric people just before we left. Maybe they've switched it on by now. If they haven't, I know there are oil lamps in the house." She looked at her daughter-in-law's set profile. "George, if you need anything, anything at all, you call me. And just in case, I'll send Claude and the twins around regular to see that you're all right."

"Thank you. I appreciate your kindness." She turned a tear-stained face to May Rose. "I always have."

Both women wept, the gravel drive becoming blurry as the car approached the house.

Jake was freezing, but he ignored the cold as he waited for his mother on the back porch. The second she opened the screened door, he was on her like a starving rooster after a grain of corn.

"Where is she?"

"She's safe," May Rose said flatly. "So's Sally. That's all you need to know."

"Mom?"

May Rose kept walking.

*   *   *

It took him a couple of weeks to find out where she was. In that time he had started work, beginning at the bottom of the heap as a roustabout. Things were still fairly tense on the home front. The only person who really talked to him was his father. Walt acted as if he didn't know what to say half the time, Tara curled her lip in disgust whenever he happened to look at her, Wil left the room whenever he entered, but worst of all, his mother spoke to him in choppy sentences.

"Jake? You want more cornbread?"

"Jake, take your feet off the coffee table."

She probably wouldn't have said even that much if he hadn't sat her down, explained just as carefully as he could the full story of why he had married George.

"Everything would have been all right if she hadn't turned out pregnant. I could have just come home and divorced her while she was still in England."

She remembered George's version of the story, how Jake had forced himself on her, then by calling her father and telling him all about it, George had been thrown out of her parents' home. George had said she believed Jake had done this because he really loved her and didn't know what else to do when she wouldn't talk to him. Still making excuses for him, she said his getting her tossed out onto the street was his way of forcing her to come to him so that he could marry her. The events George tearfully described were just too close in detail to the day she herself had become engaged to Claude. History had blindly repeated itself. And Jake had proven that he *was* his father's son. Now he was trying to weasel out of the mess he had made and blame George into the bargain. May Rose got away from him quickly before she slapped him again.

During this second week Jake couldn't take it anymore. He had to see George, see for himself that she and Sally were all right, because his mother wasn't telling him anything. He had no idea if that old house was warm enough or if George had enough food to eat. And damn it! She was still his wife, still his responsibility. He had a right to know how she was doing. And if he saw for himself that that house was too cold or if she looked even slightly hungry, he would bring her straight back home.

Driving the new Chevrolet he'd bought just after starting work, he went to the old house that his mother owned for some obscure reason. The house she had just signed over to George, free and clear. The weather was very cold, even for January, the land blanketed with snow. Jake actually prayed that the old house had a lot of cracks in the walls, that snow blew in through the cracks. Thanks to the hubbub, the Rainwaters hadn't had Christmas or New Year. Santa Claus hadn't visited Sally. Jake was armed with a viable excuse to visit. Beside him on the car seat were wrapped presents for George and Sally.

When he stopped the car, George appeared at a window, looking out. The house didn't look too bad; in fact, it looked kind of homey the way it was lit up and smoke curled from the chimney. Any hope that he would find her freezing to death, died. It seemed that by leaving him, George had really landed on her feet. Then he became angry that he had worried (and hoped) that she wouldn't. It was just like King had said. For five minutes of wiggling on her back, George was getting everything she wanted. She had a legal right to be in America, and once they hit the divorce court, he could look forward to paying out alimony and child support. Tasting bitterness in his mouth, Jake scooped up the presents and slogged his way to the front porch.

George met him at the door. She didn't say a word as he knocked snow off his feet and entered. Bitterness evaporated the second he saw Sally sitting on a blanket in the middle of the neat living room. If he hadn't gone to the dance hall, if he hadn't met and married George, his precious child wouldn't exist. His heart wrenching painfully, he glanced at George. She looked great. She was dressed in a pleated skirt, plain sweater, and her hair was pulled back in a fat ponytail. He wanted to tell her she looked great, but he was lost for words. Then Sally made her happy crowing sound, and Jake went to his daughter, dropped the packages, lifted her up and hugged her. When he finally worked out just what he wanted to say and turned to speak, George wasn't there. Playing with Sally, helping her unwrap her presents, he looked around the tidy living room. George had turned this old place into a home. And she'd done it all by herself. Proof positive that she didn't need him. But he needed her. He needed her so badly he was choking on the need. When he knew he had to leave he called out good-bye, hoping she would pop back into the room.

She didn't. She only called out, "Thank you for coming," and remained wherever she was in the house. Feeling completely miserable, Jake left. He drove the long distance in a trance, and by the time he reached his parents' house, he knew he no longer wanted a divorce. He mentally kicked himself for not waiting to catch his breath after he came home before opening his big fat mouth. All he wanted now was to have his little family back. But how the hell was he supposed to get them back? If George no longer needed him or wanted him, what could he do? Then a more horrible thought occurred. What would he do if George started going around with another man? And she could. It would be real easy for her. She was pretty, she was smart, she had that cute accent, that red hair, and those zillion freckles. In practically no time at all, hundreds of guys would be beating down her door.

"Oh, shit!"

Jake drove faster for home.

Jake had no idea that his own brother would be first in the rush for George. From practically the same night Jake had spilled his guts, Wil had stopped phoning up his steady girlfriend, Emma. And during the weeks George and Jake had been separated, Wil spent a lot of time secretly with George. The only one who knew was Walt, and Walt could be trusted not to say a word. Besides which, Walt had problems of his own.

The more Walt tried to figure her out, the more he couldn't understand Tara at all. She was ignoring him, practically ignoring everybody in the family like she had a brand-new corncob up her butt. Then there was the rest of the family. Mom looked like she'd aged ten years. Jake was a real joy, always acting as if he was about ready to hit someone. Meanwhile

Dad had his head stuck down in the sand. It was as if he believed that if he just kept his ass in the air, all of this trouble would just blow over it. Well, it wasn't going to. In fact, everything would get quickly worse if Jake found out about Wil sneaking around after George. To prevent that from happening, Walt was telling lies to cover Wil's frequent absences.

Tonight, Wil was supposed to be with Emma, but of course he wasn't. He'd gone to George, and Walt was half out of his mind because while Wil had been in the bathroom, Jake had come in, grabbed a load of presents, and announced that he was going over to George's. Walt had managed to waylay Wil only by a few minutes.

Wil panicked. "He might hurt her. I'm not hanging around here while Jake hurts George."

Wil left and Jake was still gone. Walt paced in his bedroom, imagining the huge old fight that was probably taking place right now. When the door to the bedroom opened, Walt jumped three feet in the air.

"What's the matter?" Tara asked. "You look awful."

Walt rushed to her, hurriedly shutting the door. "Muffin, I need to talk to somebody."

"Gosh," she said with a sour laugh, "I hope I'll do."

He took her by the hand and led her to the bed. "Cut the pouty crap. This is serious. *Really* serious."

Walt started talking, and Tara listened. "I know," she said when he'd finished. "I've known all along."

"You did?"

"Walt Rainwater, sometimes you're as thick as a post. Emma happens to be my best friend, remember? For two weeks she's been crying on my shoulder that Wil hasn't bothered to phone her, and in the meantime I'm hearing Wil say like some kind of moron, 'Whelp, guess I'll go over to Emma's.' "

Walt couldn't help the laugh. Her impersonation of Wil had been too perfect. She slapped his thigh. "Stop laughing! This isn't funny. A new door to hell is going to swing open the second Jake finds out that Wil is after George."

"Yeah," Walt said soberly. "And it's probably swingin' now."

"Why?"

"Well, you know how Jake went over to see George tonight?"

"Uh-huh."

"Wil went after him."

Tara's eyes doubled in size. "Oh, my God." Then her eyes narrowed, pinning him with an accusing look. "Why didn't you stop him?"

"I tried, muffin. But it was kind of like trying to stop a charging bull. And I couldn't exactly fight him about it. Mom would hear."

"Shit."

Walt looked at her with total surprise. "Hey! When did you start cussin'?"

"Just now."

"Oh." He went quiet. Then he looked at her from beneath furrowed brows. "Well, don't do it anymore."

"You can't tell me what to do."

"The hell I can't."

Her tone mocking, Tara let fly with, "Hell, hell, hell, shit, shit, shit, damn, damn, damn, damn."

"Moooooom! Tara's cuss—"

Her hand flew to his mouth, and holding him

tightly by the face, she yelled in a whisper, "Shut up. I think I just heard someone come in the house."

Like a pair of sneak thieves, Walt and Tara cracked open their bedroom door and strained to listen. They heard Jake say, "Mom, could we have a talk, please?"

"About what, Jake?"

There was a long silence. "I need to talk about how to get George to come back to me."

Chapter Eleven

Walt closed the door, looking relieved. He whispered to Tara, who was looking at him with an odd glint in her eyes.

"Jake and Wil must have just missed each other. If Jake really wants George back like he says, and maybe Momma can help him, Wil'll back off, start seeing Emma again. I hope so. I want all of this trouble to be over." That little gleam in Tara's eyes grew brighter. Walt frowned at her. "Whatcha thinkin', muffin?"

That I've made up my mind. I'm going to get you, Walt Rainwater. I don't know how, but I just am.

But with a highly innocent tone she answered, "I'm not thinking anything."

May Rose and Jake were in the kitchen, sitting at the table.

"I really want her back, Mom."

May Rose shook her head in utter dismay. "I wish you had thought about what you were throwing away while you were throwing it. You weren't even off the train for five minutes when you told her you wanted a divorce. Now here you are saying you want her back."

"But I do, Mom—"

May Rose raised a silencing hand. "I believe you, but will George believe you? I don't think so. You embarrassed her and then you hurt her. If it was me, I wouldn't be real quick to forgive. And I know I wouldn't trust a man who can change his mind as fast as you can change yours."

"Mom, I know I made a mistake. To be honest, I didn't think I would miss her this much. But I do, and I want her back so bad I can't eat or sleep."

May Rose felt so happy she wanted to whoop. Instead she said hurriedly, "Then what you're gonna have to do is court her. Tomorrow you call on the phone and ask her out on a date. You're not in the middle of a war anymore. You've got time to take the courtship nice and slow. And *this* time, Jacob, you better be a gentleman."

Wil watched her as she prepared coffee. He had passed Jake on the road, and Jake had looked straight, but vacantly, at him, recognizing him only as another driver. Jake's vacuous expression, clearly visible when the two cars passed, had scared Wilber half to death. Jake looked as if he had seen something horrible and was now in a state of shock. Wil put on more speed, not caring when the car fishtailed on icy patches. Then he'd scared George half to death when he pounded on her door. When she peeked out the window and he saw that she was fine, he exhaled pure relief. He couldn't help but hug her when she opened the door. He had wanted to kiss her, but she wiggled out of his arms too quickly.

She and Sally had been in bed when Wil arrived. Not that it was late. It wasn't. It was just a bit after eight. But George didn't have a radio, so when she put Sally down to sleep, she went to bed with a novel. George had a stack of novels. She borrowed them from the lending library in Urainia. She had been going to the library since her first weeks in Oklahoma. Every Saturday after she and May Rose did the family shopping, George went to the little library, which stood close to Urainia Elementary School. The librarian, Mrs. Housego, loved George because George was one of the few avid readers in town. The two of them loved to discuss books and authors. Mrs. Housego began saving any brand-new novels that were sent for George to read first. Now, as George poured boiling water into the top portion of the drip-style coffeepot, she talked to Wil about the town librarian.

"Mrs. Housego has offered me a job as her assistant," George was saying.

Wil, with effort, clicked back into the moment. It was tough to do because George was wearing a shorty bathrobe, the hem struck about a couple of inches above her knees. George had great knees, the caps almost shaped like hearts, not bony or anything, just neat and sweet. Her legs, what there were of them, were great too. And freckled. Even her feet were freckled. The freckles on her arms, legs, and feet had really bloomed during the previous summer. Too hot to wear dresses, George had gone around in a pair of very short cotton shorts and sleeveless midriff blouses. The second she stepped into the sun, freckles bloomed on her body while he watched. Her ability to freckle fast was practically an entertainment. Mom wanted her to stay out of the sun, but Dad always said, *Let her go ahead on. If she gets enough*

273

brown spots, they'll maybe blend in and she'll look Osage. Well, that hadn't happened, but now George had a lot more freckles on her face. She even had them on her lips and eyelids. The funny thing about it was that the more she freckled, the prettier she looked. Just like a pretty pinto filly. He felt himself becoming lost in that prettiness when she sat down at the table across from him. Wil cleared his throat, tried to think about something else.

"So, you gonna take the job?"

George took a deep breath, expelled it slowly. "I want to. It's not just the money, it's—it's something to do. The trouble is, accepting the job means having to get into town every day and then home again."

"What about Sally?"

George left the table. The coffee was ready, and she poured two cups, brought them back, set one before Wil, and then sat down, thoughtfully sipping her cup of coffee.

"Sally really isn't that much of a problem. There are a lot of reliable women in town who would baby-sit on a steady basis if I asked."

"Really?"

George nodded. "My current situation is hardly a secret. You know how quickly word gets around Urainia. Momma-May has countered the gossip by saying that it's just temporary, until Jake readjusts to being home."

Wil chuckled. "She said almost the same thing about Matt going around with Lucy. Then he married her. Now here she is flapping her mouth about Jake. I really think Mom ought to stop talking before she has the whole town thinking our family's screaming nuts."

George sputtered a laugh.

Wil laughed. Sipping her coffee again, George watched him. She now knew just how she was able to tell the twins apart. Both frowned when they were thoughtful, both had tiny lines at the bridge of their nose where their brows met and furrowed, but Walt pursed his lips when he frowned in thought whereas Wil always pressed his lips together in a tight smile. Wil had tiny lines around the curve of his mouth. Walt didn't.

Wil was thinking and his features shouted his thoughtful state—brows furrowing, lips pressing. "What you need," he said after a moment, "is a car. I'll bet I could find you a good car for about fifty bucks."

"I don't know how to drive."

Wil grinned, wiggled his brows. "I can teach you."

George sat back as excitement began to build. If she had her own car and job, she would be independent. Everyone in the family, most especially Wil, had been extraordinarily kind. But how long could she count on this kindness once she and Jake were divorced? Then too, once he was free and actively involved with another woman, the family would quite naturally shift, and gradually they would begin to cut her out of their lives. She couldn't afford to still be dependent once that began to happen.

"I have fifty dollars."

"Forget about it, George," Wil said flatly. "I don't need fifty bucks from you. Jake can cough it up. He owes you that and a hell of a lot more."

"You'll tell him, then, what the money is for?"

"No. What he doesn't know won't kill him." Besides, he thought as he drained the cup, asked for

275

another as an excuse to hang around a few minutes longer, if Jake knew, he'd probably insist on teaching George to drive. Wil didn't want Jake teaching George anything.

The next morning, George telephoned the library, told Mrs. Housego she would be pleased to accept the offered job. Mrs. Housego agreed that George could begin in two weeks' time. This was the time George said she needed to get her car, learn how to drive it, and line Sally up with a responsible sitter. In the afternoon, when the telephone rang, George rushed to answer. For a second or two, she thought the male voice on the line was Wilber. Then she realized it was Jake.

"Uh, George? I was wondering, well, you know this Saturday night? I was wondering if maybe you'd like to go to the movies. Mom says she'll watch Sally."

"You mean, go with you?"

Jake's voice turned irritable. "Yeah, with me! What did you think, that I was calling to say Mom would baby-sit if you wanted to go to the movies all by yourself?"

"That was a rather safe assumption."

Jake was about to fire off when he remembered his mother's instruction to be nice. He took a deep breath, held it, then exhaled it slowly.

"Look, George, I'd really like to take you to the movies. Then maybe afterward we could get something to eat."

"This is beginning to sound as if you're asking me out on a date."

"That's because I am."

George was speechless.

"George? Are you still there?"

"Yes, Jake. I'm still on the line."

"Well, yes or no. Do you want to go out with me?"

"No."

George quickly hung up. Almost immediately the telephone rang again. She stood there staring at it, dry-washing her hands as the telephone trembled with each ring. She didn't pick up.

Jake was persistent, especially when he was angry. He telephoned her four more times, spacing the calls over the remainder of the afternoon. After he left work and walked into the house, he called her again.

George still wasn't answering. She was walking the floor, praying he would stop calling.

Jake slammed the receiver down. Wil was behind him.

"What are you doing?"

"None of your damn business!"

"Are you calling and hanging up on George?"

Jake lost his temper all over Wil. "Get away from me! Just leave me alone."

"Give me fifty bucks and I'm gone."

Out of his mind with fury, Jake pulled out his wallet and handed over the money. Then he stomped off to his bedroom and slammed the door. Wil was counting the money when he heard his mother knocking on Jake's door.

"Jakey, let me in."

"Go away, Mom."

"No, I won't."

A second later, Wil heard the lock turn, and his mother opened the door, went inside, closed it. Being careful not to make the floorboards creak, Wil went to the door and shamelessly eavesdropped.

"Did you ask her out like I said?"

"Yes."

"And?"

"She hung up on me. I've been calling her all day, and she won't pick up the phone. How can I date her if she won't even talk to me?"

Oh, no! He's trying to get George back.

"What you're going to do now," Momma was saying, "is write her a letter."

Wil ran out of the house. He knew Walt would be thoroughly pissed that he was taking the car again, abandoning Walt to suffer another night in, but Wil didn't care. He had to act quickly, help set George firmly up on her feet. Only then would she realize that she didn't need Jake for squat. Then, once he helped her get through the divorce, he would make his move. Wil thought with the precision of a tightly wound clock, taking life one tick at a time. At present he didn't allow himself to think beyond George's immediate needs. He didn't venture on to think about the commotion his courting his brother's ex-wife would cause in the family. Nor did he pause to consider that George might feel uncomfortable about him declaring himself. Those thoughts would be too many ticks sounding at once, and Wil wasn't mentally equipped to handle the racket. Keeping first things positively first, he drove to the filling station-cum-garage and used-car lot in Urainia. There was an old Ford he had his eye on. The owner of the garage had a cardboard sign in the back window of the car.

$75. It Runs.

Wil had sixty-five dollars and a glib tongue. Thirty minutes later and with a handshake, Wil left his own car at the garage while he drove the newly purchased car to George.

She was so excited, she bounced like a puppy. Then Wil helped her bundle up Sally to go out and have a closer look at her very own car. Excitement evaporated when Wil told her to get in, that her driving lessons began now.

"You mean, drive when there's snow on the ground?"

"The roads are clear. Besides, we have to go to town so I can get my car."

"But," she sputtered, "that means I'll have to drive it back all by myself."

"George, I'll be right behind you. And just so you won't get nervous, I'll keep Sally with me."

Wil could not remember the last time he'd laughed so hard. George was a terrible driver; she couldn't keep the pedals straight in her mind, and shifting gears seemed beyond her. The car died more often than it hucked and bucked along the road, and when another vehicle approached from behind, Wil stuck his arm out the window and waved the other motorist around. When encroaching darkness became solid black, George was in an all-out panic. Wil switched the car lights on, and the instant the dual beams illuminated the road, George squealed as if this perfectly ordinary event was a major miracle.

"George! You've been in cars at night thousands of times."

"Not with me driving them, I haven't. What gear am I in now?"

"Third. You're in third."

"Is that good?"

"For fifteen miles an hour, it's almost good. Thirty miles an hour would be very good."

"I'm not ready for great speeds."

Wil looked at her while she held onto the steering wheel with a two-fisted grip and peeked at the road *through* the steering wheel. George needed a booster cushion. She also needed a good kissing, but Wil shoved that out of his mind.

"From what I hear around the house, Jake's going to try to start dating you."

"I know," she said grimly. "He rang today. He's been ringing all day. It's been driving me mad."

"You don't want to date him?"

"No. He told me he didn't want our marriage. I see no point in our going out together. It would only prolong an agony I wish to put behind me."

"That's smart, George. Besides, he only wants to see you because of Sally. If he keeps you friendly, he'll get to see her a lot more."

That hurt. She didn't say anything, but he could tell she was hurt because her mouth twitched. Wil pressed the advantage. "Jake isn't too stupid. He knows a woman as good-looking as you could get married again real fast. Then Sally would have two fathers. Jake only wants her to have one father. Believe me, George, he's only interested in staying close to Sally. He doesn't care that his being around all the time will mean that you don't have a life. But you deserve a life. You deserve a man who's going to love you. Really love you. Take my advice, let him see Sally all he wants, but only see her through Mom. Don't let him near you or your house anymore. Don't let him know what you're doing or who you're seeing, because he'll run your friends off and boss you around while he's living his own life exactly the way he wants."

"Thank you, Wil," she said in a low, tight voice. "That's very good advice."

Wil twisted in the seat, settled Sally on his lap. "Tell you what. About this calling thing, when I call, I'll ring twice, hang up, and call right back. That way you'll always know when it's me."

"That's a good idea."

"Since you're not answering the phone, he may try writing to you. If I were you, I wouldn't even open the letters. If he has something really important to say, just let him tell you through Mom the way he has been doing."

"Yes," she said firmly. "That way is best."

Following closely behind as George laboriously drove ahead, Wil glanced at Sally sitting closely next to him. "Hey, little baby. How would you like it if I was your daddy?"

Sally looked up at him and cooed.

"I promise, I'll take good care of you and your mommy." Then, watching the car ahead, he said, "Heck, I was doing a good job taking care of both of you before *he* ever showed his face. The two of you have always been more mine than his. He doesn't deserve you. And he'll never deserve Pinto. Never in a thousand years."

Jake spent the next two weeks working and anxiously checking the mail. Through his mother he knew George was working full-time at the library, that she had her own car and didn't need May Rose to drive her to town on Saturdays anymore. When he saw Sally, it was always when he came home from work to find Sally already there. He had no idea that on these happy occasions when he was spending the evening with his daughter that George was in Bartlesville with Wil, seeing a movie, having supper. He was so caught up in his frustration at trying to win George back, he failed to notice that Walt was staying home a lot, playing cards or listening to the radio with Tara. It also failed to trigger a brain cell that around ten o'clock when George hooted the car horn for his mother to bring Sally out, about ten minutes later, Wil came in. He didn't notice because while Wil was saying his good-nights, Jake was locked in his room, writing yet another pleading letter.

Early Saturday morning, Jake was already standing at the mailbox at the top of the drive when the postman's truck rattled up the road. The man said hello, tried to pass the time with polite banter about the weather, how spring sure felt early for this time of year, as he sorted through the stack of letters. The second the postman handed the letters out, Jake snatched them, plowing through the envelopes looking for an envelope bearing George's well-remembered scrawl.

There wasn't one.

Slapping the mail against his leg as he walked back toward the house, Jake was steaming. Calling hadn't worked, and now letters weren't working. This left him with only one option. A face-to-face showdown. After throwing the mail down on the kitchen table, Jake left the house, his mother calling after him.

May Rose sensed trouble. She didn't like the look of dark fury on her son's face. As he strode out of the kitchen, she ran after him. "Jake! Jake! What are you going to do?"

He didn't answer. He slapped open the back porch screen door. It banged loudly shut behind him as he descended the steps. Standing at the door, May Rose worriedly watched him start up his car, gun the engine, and speed up the drive in reverse.

George's job mainly consisted of wheeling the trolley loaded with returned books up and down the aisles of standing shelves, replacing the books in the proper places. She was doing just that when she felt someone standing behind her. She turned and was instantly startled.

"I want to talk to you."

"Please be kind enough to whisper."

"I want to talk to you," Jake whispered.

"We have nothing to say to each other."

Jake moved closer, close enough to feel her body heat, smell the faint trace of her perfume, definitely close enough to see that she was wearing makeup. Powder subdued her freckles, mascara darkened her red eyelashes, and pale pink lipstick tinted her trembling mouth.

"What did I tell you about putting crap on your face?" he yelled.

Infuriated that he would come to the place she worked to yell at her at the top of his voice, George threw a book at him.

Jake ducked. And while he was slightly off guard, George began to whisper so rapidly she sounded like a snake:

"How dare you! If I want to wear makeup, I'll wear makeup. You don't own me, Jake Rainwater."

Jake straightened to his full height, frowning down at her. George backed away. "I'm not trying to own you. I'm just trying to be your husband again."

"You are too twisted to live."

"Just tell me why you won't talk to me. Why you won't answer my letters."

"Because I don't want to talk to you, and I never read your letters."

"What's the matter, George?" he mocked. "Are you afraid?"

She turned to the side, pointed her little nose toward the ceiling. "Absolutely not."

He moved to stand in front of her. Again, she turned her face away from him. "You're scared to death. You're so scared, you can't even look at me."

Her arms folded beneath her breasts, she tapped a foot impatiently. "And just why am I afraid, do you suppose?"

"You're afraid because the second you look at me, you're going to remember a lot of things."

"Such as?"

"Such as the way it felt when we used to kiss. The way it felt when we used to make love. And you're scared you're gonna want that again just as much as I do."

"What a load of twaddle."

Jake threw his arms out as he spoke to the high ceiling. "Well, Mom, I tried it your way. Now we're doing it my way."

Before George had time to ask just what way he had in mind, he had her by the shoulders, and his mouth crashed down on hers. She struggled and kicked, but Jake hung on, kissing her with every speck of passion he'd been hoarding since the moment he'd stepped off the train. He no longer cared for the opinions of his long-dead friend or his vaguely remembered colonel. No longer did he fret about the marriage trap George had set for him in England. Now all he wanted was to trap her and never let her get away again.

The second he stopped kissing her, she slapped him. Jake didn't flinch when her open hand connected with the side of his face.

"Do it again," he dared. "Go ahead. Slap the crap out of me. I won't budge. And I'll tell you this for free, I'm not going anywhere until you agree to come out with me tonight."

Her chin began to bobble, tears formed in her eyes. "Y-you only want me because of Sally. You can't have her without me. She's the only reason you're here."

"I want you *both*."

"Oh, I'm not going to stand here and listen to this, and I'm certainly never going out with you."

Jake tightened his hold on her shoulders and pushed his face close to hers. "Okay, then you can just forget about a friendly divorce."

George gasped sharply.

"As of now, you have a choice. You can either go out with me and listen to what I have to say, or you can get ready for a long fight. A fight that will drag on for years and years."

She gasped again.

"I really mean it, George."

"That's blackmail."

"Ain't it just." He made a face as he released her shoulders and his thumb wiped a mascara-stained tear from her cheek. "Do me a favor. When we go out tonight, don't wear this goop." His curled fingers lifted her chin. "Where's Sally."

"She's at the sitter's."

"I'll pick her up and take her home to Mom. I'll be waiting at your house when you get off work. When is that, by the way? About five?"

Her heart was banging, her blood racing. The attraction she felt for Jake, had always felt for Jake, was tearing her apart. In the end, this attraction won out over good sense and all of Wilber's solid advice. "I-I'm home by five-thirty."

"Okay, give me the sitter's address."

Her shaking hand wrote out the address on a scrap of notepaper. "I-I'm still not sure—"

"Look, George, I'm only going to say this one more time. We either talk things over while we're having a nice dinner, or we waste a lot of our lives talking through lawyers."

Sulkily she handed him the address. "I do not like being blackmailed. In fact, I'm quite certain I despise it."

"Great. Now you know how I feel about you wearing makeup." He turned on his heel and left.

May Rose gladly accepted Sally, stripping off her coat and hat, setting her inside the playpen with Toya. Claude clapped his son on the back.

"She's really going out with you?"

"Yeah," Jake laughed. "She really is. I got tired of waiting, so I tracked her down and dazzled her with my smile."

There was no blood in Wilber's face. Walt watched his twin as Jake kept talking.

"Damn, she's pretty. She's little an' mean as a

snake, but she's as pretty as a flower. Dad, I'm building that house up on the hill. I'm gonna start building it right away."

"Well, praise God," May Rose sighed. "At last this family's gonna be normal again." She leaned over the playpen and tickled Sally under the chin. "And maybe this little one will get herself a new brother or sister in a year or so."

Feeling sick, Wil left the kitchen. Walt bolted after him.

In the yard, Wil tried to shake Walt off. Walt would not be shaken. Still holding Wilber's arm, he spun him around.

"I can't believe it," Wil shouted. "I can't believe after all he's done that she'd take him back."

"Shut up!" Walt cried. "Everybody's gonna hear you."

"Let 'em! I don't care." He stuck his hand out. "Give me the keys to the car."

"Why? So you can go pester George?"

"I'm not pestering her. I'm being her friend."

"Bullshit!"

"Give me the keys, Walt."

"No."

"Goddamn it! I said, give me the keys."

"No. I'm through helping you chase after your own brother's wife. It isn't right and you know it. George is your sister. Even if she goes through with the divorce, she'll still be your sister. You can't have her!"

With a roar of rage Wil lunged for Walt, knocking him to the muddy ground. Like a pair of otters they rolled in the mud until they were filthy with it, both of them punching their identical face until blood mixed with mud. Finally, Walt had Wil pinned and straddled his chest, his hands holding Wil's arms down at the wrists as he yelled into Wil's face.

"It's over, damn it! I'm not going to let you throw yourself away on something you can't change. I'm not going to let you be stupid and get thrown out of the family. Like Allen. I can't lose you, Wil. You're part of me. Goddamn it, you're part of me. I need you. I need you more than she'll ever need you."

Wil's head went back, sinking in the soft mud. "Oh, God," he wept. "What the hell am I going to do?"

Walt moved off him and pulled him up. Holding him while Wil wept, Walt said soberly, "You're gonna love her enough to be the bother she's always believed you were."

Their mother's voice screeched at them from the porch. "What do you boys think you're doing rollin' around in that mud?"

In unison they tonelessly replied, "Playing, Mom."

Walt whispered urgently to Wil, "Tell me you're gonna stay. Promise me. Make a forever promise. The kind we used to make when we were kids."

"All right. I promise forever I'll never leave you. But I'm only promising because you asked so nice."

"And maybe because if you didn't, I'd kick your ass."

"That did occur to me."

Walt helped Wilber to his feet.

The twins stood at the bottom of the back porch steps, looking like a pair of mud urchins. May Rose was yelling her head off about them not setting one foot on her clean porch, where Jake and Claude stood behind her laughing like fools. Tara stood to the side, her hand over her mouth. She was the only one, it seemed, who noticed the blood. She knew the brothers had been fighting and why they'd been fighting. Before anyone else became wise, she had to do something. She shot forward, passing her mother-in-law as she raced down the porch steps. She went to the outside spigot and turned it on. Water began to gush down the garden hose. Tara grabbed the hose.

"Shit!" Walt hollered. His arms crossed in front of his face defensively as the spray of cold water pummeled his body. Feeling slightly better, Wil laughed as Walt tried to escape Tara's aim. Then the water hit him, and he hollered.

"Walt! Your wife's nuts!"

While the others laughed, Tara flicked the spray back and forth, hitting both of them, washing away the mud and the blood, saving them, albeit by torturous means, from the hard explaining they would have faced with May Rose.

"Muffin!" Walt shouted. "Cut it out."

"Say please."

Walt turned, his mouth open to yell again. Tara treated him to a throatful of water.

Jake was waiting in his car when her rattletrap car pulled in. When she got out and walked past him, Jake climbed out and followed her to the small porch.

"I want you to know," she said crisply, fumbling for her door key, "that I am going out with you under protest."

"And I want you to know that I don't care."

George made a disagreeable noise in the back of her throat and unlocked the door. But before opening the door, she turned and looked up at him. "No funny business, Jake. No more grabbing, no more kissing. We're only going to have a meal and talk."

Jake raised a hand. "Word of honor. I won't grab you. I won't kiss you." As she opened the door he quickly added. "But if you grab me, or kiss me, I won't mind."

George refused to be drawn. Ignoring him completely, she walked through the living room to the bedroom and closed the door.

It was cold in the house. Needing something to do, and eager to be helpful, Jake turned on the lamps and then went to the oil heater. Crouching down in front of it, he opened the valve and then struck a match, tossing it inside the belly of the heater. Standing up, he closed the hatch and went into the kitchen. After turning on the overhead light, he puttered around making coffee. While measuring coffee from the can, he felt a presence. Out of the corner of his eye, he saw a shadow. When the shadow moved, then disappeared, he almost jumped out of his skin. In the process he spilled coffee grounds all over the floor.

"Geooooorge!"

Hearing him shout, she ran out of the bedroom clad only in a slip. Jake was standing in the middle of a mess, his face ashy gray.

"What's the matter?"

His widened eyes turned toward her. "George?" he rasped. "Is this place . . . haunted?"

George lightly laughed. "Yes."

"And you can live here?"

"Of course I can." She went to the sink, dampened a dishcloth under the tap. She used the cloth to clean the coffee grounds from around a still-as-a-statue Jake.

"I-I saw it."

"Yes," she murmured. "I presumed you had."

Once the floor was cleaned, George relieved him of the coffee canister and led him out, taking him into the living room, sitting him down. Jake's eyes were still round, still staring at nothing, as she sat down beside him and scrambled to sit on her knees. Feeling motherly, she wrapped her arms around his neck.

"There's nothing to be afraid of. He's a friendly ghost."

Jake turned his face toward hers. "George, ghosts are ghosts. They're not friends."

"And as an Osage, you don't like being around ghosts very much."

"No. And I don't want you around them either. You might get ghost stuff on you."

"Ghost stuff!" George hooted.

"This isn't funny. This is serious. You've gotta come home. Now."

She tried to pull away, but Jake, forgetting his promise, grabbed her arms. "I mean it. I'm not letting you stay in this place one more minute."

"You can't make me do anything."

"Yes, I can."

"No, you can't."

She was struggling against him as he began to feel the presence come into the room. The presence became a dark shape and seemed to breathe. George didn't act as if she saw what he was seeing because she was still overly concerned about his hands on her, fighting against his hold on her, calling him names. Jake wasn't concerned because his eyes remained on the shadow that was doubling in size and breathing so much that it seemed to be trying to suck up all the air. Within seconds Jake couldn't breathe, and he wasn't about to waste his strangled breath arguing with George. He sprang from the couch, taking her with him. She called him something profoundly awful as he threw her over his shoulder. She beat his spine with her fists as he ran out of the house.

Before she knew what was happening, he dumped her unceremoniously into his car. Then he jumped in and sat on top of her to keep her still while he backed out of the drive. The tires squealed and left a pound of rubber on tarmac when he speed-shifted into first. He left even more rubber behind him as he went through the remaining gears as the car sped away.

"Do you realize I'm only wearing a slip?"

"It's okay, babe. I've got you covered."

"I know. And you're very heavy."

May Rose answered the telephone and went into a screaming fit. Claude raced to her. "What's wrong?"

"It's the fire department. George's house is on fire! Jake and George—"

"They're here, Mom," Walt shouted from the kitchen. "Jake's car is coming down the drive."

May Rose slammed the phone down, and the entire family ran to the back door and out onto the porch. They were just in time to see Jake getting out of the car, taking his coat off and handing it inside the car. A half minute later, George emerged wearing the coat. And yelling at Jake. He yelled right back. May Rose felt faint, steadying herself against Claude. They were fine. Her children were fine. Jake picked up George to spare her bare feet from the cold mud. Her arms were around his neck as he carried her. They were still bickering as he mounted the steps. The family backed away en masse as Jake opened the screen door and carried George inside, setting her down. He immediately began yelling at his mother.

"Mom! That house is haunted. I saw the thing myself. *Twice.* It scared the living hell out of me. How could you put my wife in a haunted house? And not just my wife. My baby was in there. Mom, I am *really* mad at you."

"Jakey, the fire department called. That house is burning down."

Jake looked stunned, but George flew into a tizzy. "My house! My sweet little house! And all of my things? What about my car? Did they say about my car?"

Jake pulled her into his arms, and she sobbed wretchedly against him. "It's okay, sweetheart. Everything's going to be okay."

He lifted the distraught George into his arms and carried her off to their bedroom. Claude and the twins went in the opposite direction, to the yard, jumping into the truck to drive to the fire. As they left, May Rose felt Tara slip her arm through hers.

"Did Jake really see a ghost?"

May Rose considered the question at length. And she remembered her old friend. Jake and George were now where they belonged, and because there wasn't a spare house for George to run to, they would be forced to make their marriage work. Just the way Delbert had forced her to make her marriage work.

Tears choking her voice, she said, "Oh, yes, Jake saw a ghost."

Chapter Twelve

George was sobbing as Jake laid her on the bed. "I can't believe it. My house. My sweet little house."

Jake stretched out beside her, held her against him. "I'll build you a new house, sweetheart."

"And my car!" she wailed.

"Honey," he said with a chuckle. "No offense, but that car was a rolling junk pile. If it burned, God did you a favor."

"I don't care what you think," she snuffled. "It was mine."

"I'll buy you another."

Georgina stopped crying. Tilting her head back, she looked at him. "I've heard that before. And in those very same words."

Jake gently pushed hair away from her teary face. "Yep. I remember. There I was, rushing the cutest girl I'd ever seen out of the door of a dance hall, and she was worrying about her coat."

Her chin bobbed as she screwed up her face for another weep. "I thought you were so handsome. That's why I left my coat. And in the end, why I left . . . everything."

"George," he said, his voice tight. "I'm sorry. I really am. Please believe me, I don't want a divorce."

She sniffed noisily. "Are you sure?"

"Yes, I am."

"Because of Sally?"

"She's a big part of it," he admitted. "But you're the biggest part. I guess when I wasn't lookin', I kinda fell in love with you. I don't care anymore that you tricked me into marrying you—"

George bolted upright. "I tricked *you*! Excuse me, but who was the one who rang up my father and had me chucked out on the street?"

Jake sat up beside her. "I didn't call your dad. That was my C.O. He said if you pressed charges, the Army would hang me for rape. That the only way to stop you doing that was to marry you fast."

George placed her hands over her mouth. She looked at him with astonished eyes.

Jake pried her hands away. "Come on, George, cut the act. You knew before we even said I do that I didn't want to get married."

Anger charged every corpuscle in her body. "Of course I knew you weren't the happiest groom I'd ever seen. And the first night of our honeymoon certainly isn't a memory I fondly recall. But if you'd said a word about the hanging business, I would have—"

"Left."

"Yes."

"And where would you have gone?"

"I've no idea."

"Then I'm glad I kept my mouth shut."

"Why?"

"Well, damn it, George. It's like I said, sometime between then and now, I sort of fell in love with you. And I'm glad your house burned down."

Scowling, George said, "You wouldn't have done anything to *cause* my house to burn down, would you?"

In a guilty flash, Jake remembered lighting up the oil heater. "No! I didn't touch a thing."

George remained skeptical. "I'm keeping my job."

"What for?"

"In case you change your mind again. You're a bit prone to the habit."

"Okay, okay, okay. Keep your job. I'll even buy you a good car and a bunch of new clothes so you can work." He placed a hand against her breast. "Now can we make love?"

"Jake! You are the most—"

"Jack," he corrected. "You used to call me Jack."

George blinked at the fresh tears forming in her eyes. "I-I didn't think you remembered."

"Oh, muffin—"

"Don't."

"Don't what?"

"Don't call me muffin. Every woman in this house is called muffin."

Jake was puzzled for a moment. "Okay. How about I call you sausage?"

George collapsed with laughter, and Jake jumped full press on top of her, kissing her face and her neck while she laughed. George stopped laughing when his mouth sought hers. Within seconds, still kissing him, she helped him rid themselves of unnecessary clothing. Then, her head trapped between his trembling arms, he said huskily, "It's been too long, George. I've been wanting you for too damn long."

"And I've been wanting you."

297

"Yeah, but if I go too fast—"
"I won't mind."

Wanting to know how George was coping with the shock of losing everything she owned, May Rose bustled to the bedroom door. She raised her hand to knock. It remained poised when she heard the sound of squeaking bedsprings. Realizing that Jake, in his own way, had everything under control, she turned and tiptoed away.

During the next weeks Jake and George were nauseatingly besotted with one another, acting as if the other members of the family existed only on the periphery. Jake bought George a new car, and she continued to go to work, May Rose taking care of Sally and Toya. As spring brightened, Jake and George were always up on the hill, pacing off the foundation of their new home and squabbling about just how big it should be. George wanted a small, neat house. Jake was determined to build her a palace. He hired a contractor, and like it or not, George was to have a two-story palace.

May Rose was quietly glad to have charge of both baby girls. They filled the creeping emptiness developing in her life. Walt and Wil were gone more than they were home, Claude was content simply to read the evening newspaper and listen to the radio before he went off to bed. Tara was gone quite a bit too. When May Rose quizzed her about her absences, Tara fobbed her off with excuses about studying with friends. She never said who these friends were, and May Rose wasn't given the opportunity to see them because when Tara came home, she walked down the drive. The car dropping her off remained on the road and took off before May Rose got a clear look out of the window. An uneasiness grew. Finally, she buttonholed Walt and put a good-sized flea in his ear.

"Something's going on over at that school. If you had any sense in your thick head, you'd go over there and find out just what's keeping your wife from comin' home on time and just who is giving her all these late-night rides."

During Jake and George's separation, Tara had enjoyed Walt's company. She had even begun to hope that he was paying attention to her because he wanted to, that he wasn't simply being with her to give Wil an alibi. But the second Jake and George were back together again, Walt was gone. At first Tara didn't get angry because she knew Walt needed to console Wilber. Then, when it was obvious that Wilber was making a remarkable recovery from his heartbreak, even calling up and seeing Emma again, her excuses for Walt were no longer valid. Walt was staying out because he *wanted* to stay out. Tara decided that if running around was all right for Walt, then it was all right for her too.

There was a boy in her class named Nathan Clearground. Never mind that she was married, Nathan liked her. Tara began dating Nathan. They had to sneak because Nathan's folks would be horrified if they knew he was dating a married woman, and Nathan was certain Walt wouldn't care very much for the idea either. Tara explained that her marriage was a sham and that she would be leaving her husband in June just after graduation. Nathan still insisted on keeping everything secret until then.

During school hours they never spoke, never gave

anyone any indication that they were going out together. After school they waited until the school was
empty, then they met and went out in Nathan's car,
going into Bartlesville for Cokes and burgers at a
little café. Tara had said that there would be no parking, definitely no necking until she was free. Nathan
respected that. Her strict rule made him feel better
about the planned talk he would give his parents in
a month's time when Tara filed for an annulment.
She said she would file for an annulment instead
of a divorce because her marriage had never been
consummated. That knowledge made Nathan feel
even better. He believed Tara because he needed to.
She was the most beautiful girl in the whole school,
and he worshiped the ground she trod. But after a
few weeks he couldn't put it out of his mind that he
wasn't even getting a kiss while her husband might
be getting all the action. It was early one school
morning when Nathan decided it was time for Tara
to prove just how much she cared for him. From
everything he'd read on the subject in girlie maga-
zines, he was certain he would know immediately if
she had been telling him the truth. He slipped a note
into her locker.

Meet me today. Same time. Need to be with you.
Nathan

At work, Walt tried to concentrate on the dangerous task of capping a well. Since it was in the nine-
ties, he was stripped down to his jeans and boots,
work gloves and hard hat. Waving one gloved hand,
signaling instructions to the crane operator lowering

the heavy well cap. And in his brain, his mother's voice was buzzing around like a hornet.

Mom's wrong, he thought. *Tara's just studying like she says she is. She's got tests and stuff.*

Yet if his mother was suspicious . . .

Tara wouldn't go out on me! She's my wife!

A new voice came alive inside his overheated brain. *Just how long will she be your wife after June? The deal you made on your honeymoon about living with her like a brother was only supposed to last until she was old enough to decide all by herself if she wanted to be a real wife. She's old enough now.*

Walt didn't like this new voice, and he knew he didn't like the mental road the voice was leading him down. But the voice was relentless, dragging him kicking and screaming down that road regardless.

Think about it. Think about all the times you could have had her the way you want to have her and nobody would have said a word. But like a sap on two legs, you never laid a finger on her. So now, what if she has a boyfriend? A boyfriend that's getting all the loving she never gave you while she shared your bed.

That absolutely did it. The well cap was still dangling by heavy chain when Walt turned and stomped away. Men yelled at him, the crane operator cussed the air blue, but Walt kept walking. Yards away from the well site, he jumped into his truck and roared off.

He sat outside the school, smoking cigarette after cigarette, waiting for school to be over. Finally, bells began to ring and high school kids came screaming out, the majority running for the cars in the lot where he was parked. The remainder headed for waiting busses. Tara was with neither the car crowd nor the bus crowd. After all of the cars were gone and the last of the busses pulled away, the school was eerily quiet. Walt lit another cigarette and watched the double glass doors of the two-story brick building. When the cigarette had been smoked down to his fingers, he saw Tara walking shoulder to shoulder with a lanky boy. They were heading for the only car left in the lot. Walt flipped the cigarette out the truck window and opened the door.

Tara and Nathan were so involved in their rather touchy conversation that they did not see Walt. Tara did not like this conversation, and as memories of being trapped in a car with Allen blossomed, she stopped walking.

"I don't have to prove *anything* to you."

"But if you love me you'll—"

The sound of running feet made Nathan lift his head, and seeing Walt charging straight for him, Nathan's knees turned to jelly.

Turning her head, seeing Walt, she felt relieved. When she saw the fury on his face, relief rapidly turned to fear. Before she could gather her wits, Walt was there, and with one well-aimed punch Nathan was flat on his back. Tara dropped her books and grabbed Walt's arm as he stood over Nathan, ready to hit him again if Nathan was dense enough to stand up and fight.

"Stop it!" she screamed.

Walt didn't hear her or notice her as she clung to his strong arm. Raising his arm to deliver another blow, he lifted Tara off the ground. He didn't notice that either. He was too busy yelling at the boy on the ground.

"What are you doing with my wife, you damn punk!"

"Wait!" Tara shrieked. "Stop it!"

He didn't hear that either. Tara continued to dangle as Walt continued to menace Nathan. "You better talk, you little bastard, or I'll beat the hell out of you."

Nathan commenced to jabber like a magpie. "She said she wasn't your wife. T-t-that it was okay for us to g-g-go together."

Walt finally realized Tara was hanging on to him. With one wave of his arm, he shook her off and she landed on her butt. Then he grabbed Nathan by the front of his shirt and lifted him. Pressing his nose against the frightened boy's, he growled, "And what else did she say?"

"S-s-she said, you weren't really m-m-married."

Walt tossed Nathan away like a broken toy. Then he rounded on Tara. Seeing his face, she started yelling. "Walt! You better not hurt me. I mean it. You hurt me and I promise I'll stab you in the heart while you're sleeping."

Tara's next sound was a high-pitched squawk as he took her by the arm and yanked her to her feet and then held her against his waist. Ignoring her kicking legs, he glared at the completely humbled Nathan.

"All you little boys better get something straight. This is *my* wife. The next boy I catch walking with her better know how to pray."

Walt carried the screaming Tara to the truck. Nathan picked himself up as the truck drove away, Tara's voice yelling and Walt's voice booming, "Shut up!"

* * *

Walt had to avoid Tara's flying fists as she hit and screamed at him. In pure self-defense his arm slapped against her chest, knocking her back against the seat. All of her breath left her, and for a space of minutes she couldn't move. Walt used that time to speed up and swerve onto a back road. She was beginning to rally when he pulled the truck over to the shoulder shaded by trees and stopped, killing the engine. Then he turned on her.

"Just what were you doing with that pimply-faced kid?"

"I—"

"You're supposed to be in that school to study! When we made our deal, I don't *ever* remember giving you permission to have boyfriends."

"Our deal!" Tara screamed. "It's always our deal. I'm sick to death of our deal. And it's a pretty one-sided deal, if you ask me. It's all right for you to go out, but I'm supposed to just sit around. Well, screw you, Walt Rainwater. If you can go out, I can go out. I'll go out as much as I please."

"The hell you will."

"The hell I won't."

"Stop your fuckin' swearing, Tara."

"Goddamn it, I'll swear if I want to."

"Tara! You're my wife and—"

Tara stopped him cold with a shrill, bitter laugh. "You're my *what*? My husband?" She laughed again. "You're not my husband. You're just my warden."

"Oh! I get it. Being married to me is like being in prison, huh?"

"Yes, it is. But the difference between being married to you and being in prison is that prison has to be a lot nicer."

"I'm not that bad."

"Yes, you are, and I'm starting to hate you."

Tears began to flow, and Walt remained dumbfounded as she rambled on.

"I hate you for being the good guy who married the little kid your brother beat up. I hate you for not wanting to be alone with me for more than five minutes. And I will hate you forever for making me feel that because of my funny nose and the scars on my face that I'm too ugly to love." ˙

She hid her face in her hands and wept.

"Tara," he rasped. "Muffin, don't." He moved close to her, tried to pull her hands away. Tara resisted with all of her might. "Come on, Tara. Please—"

"Let go of me!" she screamed.

He instantly let go of her wrists, but he wrapped his arms around her, holding her against him. She continued to cry, her tears bathing his bare chest. He rested the side of his face against her crown.

"Tara, I don't think like that. I think you're just about the prettiest girl in the whole county. And I'm real proud of you."

She was hiccupping and sobbing. "Y-you a-a-are?"

"Yes. But, I gotta ask you something. Did you and that guy—"

"No!"

Walt released a relieved breath. He held her more tightly. "I got to ask you something else. Are you saying that, well, maybe you wouldn't mind being my, you know, real wife?"

"Walt Rainwater," she yelled against his skin,

"you are such a thick-headed jackass." She wept even more violently.

Walt's eyebrows shot up. Well, that certainly seemed clear enough, even for Walt. His Adam's apple bobbed painfully in his sand dry throat. "Muffin, if-if you're real sure about this—"

"I am."

He expelled another breath through his mouth. He held onto her as hard as he could. "Okay. Then here's what we do. We'll start off nice and slow so you won't get scared or nothin' an'—"

Tara was fed up to her back teeth with Walt's deals. She didn't have the strength or the willpower to live through another one. And now that she was in his arms, could feel his heat, inhale his male musk, she wanted him. And she told him so.

"You mean right here, right now?" he yelped.

She wormed in his arms, looked him straight in the face with a challenging expression. "What's wrong with here and now?" she angrily cried.

"We're in an old truck."

"Momma-May said that she and Daddy-Claude use to go spooning in his old truck. She said it was very romantic."

Walt shuddered. "Muffin, there are some things a guy just does *not* want to know."

Tara sniffed back her tears. "Walt, do you really mean it about us being married?"

"Yeah!"

"Fine. I'd like to be married now, please."

"Awww, muffin."

"Now, Walt."

Defeated, he dug around in his back pocket and

produced an oily red bandanna. "Would you do me a favor and blow your nose first?"

Finally kissing Tara the way he had wanted to kiss Tara made him nervous. And when he looked at her, even with the tiny white scars here and there on her face, she was so beautiful he had to remind himself to breathe. Her long dark hair framed her face and fell behind her shoulders. Her breasts were proud and perfect. He wanted her so much he hurt. But he did not want her like this. He drew her to him and held her. Kissing the top of her head, he said, "It can't be this way because you're too special. So here's the deal . . ."

Walt and Tara breezed in, Walt informing his mother that they would not be staying for supper. Then he headed off for the bathroom. When she heard him in the shower, May Rose went to his bedroom and found Tara packing a bag.

"Are you leaving?"

Tara paused. "We're, uhm, going to a hotel." Hiding her blushing face behind her hair, she said softly, "We're going on our honeymoon."

They were given the very same room they'd had two years before. This time there wasn't a teddy bear or a set of checkers in the room with them. Lying naked and on their sides, they gently touched one another.

"You are so beautiful," he whispered.

"So are you."

Walt laughed. "Muff, men aren't beautiful."

"You are. To me."

He pulled her close and kissed her mouth. "I love you, Tara."

Walt knew, from jaded experience, just how great sex was. But he had never before experienced the incredible intensity of making love. This new knowledge shattered his mind. He lay on his back, staring off in a daze as Tara cuddled against him, kissing his chest.

"How long are we going to stay in the hotel, Walt?"

He answered in a croak. "Till I can feel my legs again. Forever, maybe."

Giggling, she moved on top of him. "Let's play being married some more."

"Oh jeez, muff!"

She silenced him with her mouth.

Lucy desperately needed motherly advice. She didn't think of calling her own mother, and her pride wouldn't allow her to call Mamma-May. Matt had settled well into university life. A little too well. Lucy felt threatened. Never mind that he walked with a pronounced stiff-legged gait; he was still handsome and when she picked him up in the afternoons, almost from day one, Lucy noticed the way the university women looked at him. During his first weeks when she picked him up, he would be waiting at the curb all by himself, looking forlorn. Now that he was in his second year, she found him talking with other students. Mostly female students.

Weeks ago he'd mentioned (Matt had no idea how to be sneaky, so she knew he believed that what he said was merely table talk conversation) a law student named April Wilson. When he never mentioned the name again, Lucy knew she should be worried. Especially since this April Wilson was studying the very same thing Matt had always wanted to study. Therefore, Matt most certainly had more in common with this April Wilson person than he'd ever had with her. Plus, to be a law student April Wilson had to be really smart. Certainly smarter than a telephone operator. Lately Matt had begun claiming that he was too exhausted to have sex. That set alarm bells ringing. Matt always had to have sex. Why wasn't he wanting it now?

April Wilson.

Matt fell in love the second he saw her. Never able to stay away from the law classes he longed to be a part of, he audited the three o'clock law lecture held in the amphitheater and sat at the top, in the last row. The only times he ever saw anything more than the foreshortened view of the back of the other students' heads were on the occasions of practice court sessions. The day he fell in love with April Wilson was the day he arrived, late as usual, and one such court was already in session.

It was a wildly funny case, but the class lecturer purposely assigned funny cases because his was the theory that lawyers read more hilarious cases than they read death-penalty cases. This being a fact of lawyerly life, it was in everyone's best interest to get over the giggles in a controlled classroom environment.

The case that day involved a wife charging her husband with threatening her with an incendiary device. Namely, a lit torch. Matt sat down in his usual seat, his game leg stuck out to the side, his elbow resting on the arm of the seat, his chin in his hand, watching a well-tailored young Indian woman state the case for the prosecution.

"The State charges the defendant, one Mr. Dew Lalley, with threatening his wife, Mrs. Malley Lalley, with grievous bodily harm. The State will prove that Mr. Lalley, on the afternoon of March third, approached the house belonging to the claimant's mother, Mrs. Fatamouth, with a burning torch. Mr. Lalley ordered his wife to come out of her mother's house. He said, in a tone loud enough to be heard by the entire neighborhood, that if she did not come out, he would burn her out."

A young man behind a desk jumped to his feet. "Objection, Your Honor! My client had a bucket of water with him to extinguish the torch."

The prosecutor turned. Matt's interest was piqued as he studied her profile and listened to her silken voice.

"And can my learned friend explain why his client would be carrying a torch if it wasn't for the purpose of harming his wife?"

"Your Honor, my client had a torch because it was dark."

"Your Honor," the little prosecutor laughed, "it was three in the afternoon."

"There was an eclipse!" the lawyer for the defense shouted.

Everyone, including the student judge, cracked up. And when the laughing prosecutor turned completely, allowing Matt a clear look at her face, he sat up quickly in his seat. His heart began to thump with such force that he felt each beat reverberate through him. He knew, in that moment, that he was looking at the woman he had always dreamed of but never for one moment believed existed. And because he'd believed instead that she was something that could only be found in his daydreams, he'd settled. First for silly Irma, then for faceless women, and finally for Lucy. Lucy, who had become his brace once Bud left him and his metal brace had been removed. He no longer wanted a mere brace. He wanted someone to love. Someone wonderful. Now she was here. She was real. And she had a name.

"April Wilson, prosecution for the State, rests, Your Honor."

He assured himself that getting to know her would not be a huge problem. All he would have to do would be hang around outside the lecture theater, and eventually she would notice him. When he didn't have to move, he was able to hang around with elan. Therefore, he didn't move. Day after day and reading a thick textbook, he stood where she would be certain to notice him.

April noticed him. She would have been blind not to notice him. He was almost six foot five and incredibly handsome. But she wouldn't talk to him because he was too perfect. In her twenty-two-year-old experience, perfect men were perfect assholes. She preferred men who were ruggedly ugly. Not only were ruggedly uglies extremely masculine, in the main, they were intensely loyal. April passed the tall, handsome young man standing in the corridor with her nose firmly in the air. This cutting attitude ended the day she turned to look back over her shoulder. She saw him close his book, walk off in the opposite direction. Her lower jaw dropped. Mr. Perfect wasn't perfect. He was severely lame. Then she felt her heart begin to flutter. The following day she made a point of speaking to him.

Matt could barely believe it when she stopped and began to chat. He'd gotten used to her walking on by. And as crazy as he was about this five-foot-two-inch young woman, he'd convinced himself that momentarily breathing the same air was enough. But now she was inviting him for coffee. Matt panicked. Going for coffee meant that he would have to walk, and then she would realize that he was Pegleg Pete. And she would regret the invitation. Worse, she would be embarrassed.

Matt hemmed and hawed with his usual adroitness. April was even more impressed. Not only was he gorgeous (but flawed), he was deliciously shy. She refused to take "Uh, I don't—" for an answer. She took the book out of his hand and stuffed it inside her book bag.

"That—that's my book."

"I know. I'm holding it for ransom. Either you have coffee with me or the book dies."

Matt ran a hand through his hair and looked away from her. "Walking is kind of—"

"I know," she said. "It takes you awhile. But that's all right. I don't have another class for two hours. What about you?"

Matt released a held breath. "I-I'm free too."

They found a table in the back of the common room, and over dozens of cups of coffee they talked.

"What nation are you with?" she asked.

"Osage."

April began to laugh. "Oh, say it ain't so! That makes us traditional enemies."

"Why?"

"I'm Cherokee."

"No wonder you're so short."

"I prefer 'laterally hindered,' thank you."

Matt barked a laugh. "What?"

"It's something I made up. It sounds so much better than short."

Matt lowered his head and chuckled.

"What are we going to do about our problem?"

He instantly thought of Lucy. "O-our problem?"

April leaned across the table. "Excuse me. Did you just mentally leave the room? We were discussing our traditional enemy problem, remember?"

"Oh. Well, I won't tell if you won't."

April extended her hand. "We have a bargain."

Walking her to her next class, Matt knew he was hopelessly in love. Then he thought of Lucy again, and his stomach, loaded with coffee, began to churn. He knew he should tell April he was married. He wanted to, but the words wouldn't come. And he was afraid to let the words come. Afraid that if he told her, she would never speak to him again. He knew he wouldn't be able to stand that. No, he decided as they walked along and April chattered, he would wait. Wait until he was positive about how April felt and then he would tell her. Just after he asked Lucy for a divorce.

Mom was right. I married Lucy too fast. I should have waited. Damn, why didn't I wait?

Hearing April voice a complaint brought him back to the moment.

"Oh, I can't stand this," she cried. "I'm going to break my neck looking up at you. I need to carry around a portable stool. Oh, wait a minute. This will work."

She hopped up onto a low brick wall and stood on it, looking him straight in the eye. Matt exploded with laughter. When he dared to look at her again she smiled and waved her hand near his face. He pealed with more laughter and cried, "Damn it, April!"

She put her hands on her hips and leaned forward so that he would be able to hear her over his din. "Swearing, are we? I suppose that means someone forgot to bring Mr. Dictionary today."

He was still laughing when he met Lucy waiting in the car just off campus.

"What's so funny?" she asked sourly.

"Nothing. Just something I heard in class."

"Something you want to share?"

Matt waved a dismissive hand. "You wouldn't understand."

Lucy felt that cut like a sharp knife. Matt was pulling away from her. She could feel it happening even as she drove for home. That night she worked even harder to prove to him just how much he needed her. Almost as if in retaliation, Matt declined her offer of sex, rolled over, and went to sleep.

It was the next night that he mentioned April Wilson and Lucy knew she'd heard the name of a potential enemy. An enemy with the power to make Matt laugh, put a new lightness in his crippled walk. April Wilson had to be stopped. Had to be crushed beyond repair, otherwise, she would have Matt. She would have the secure life Matt would be able to provide once he graduated from university. Vividly, Lucy recalled all the horrors of the Depression, all of the awful meals consisting only of cornbread and clabber because there had been nothing else to eat. Lucy hated being poor. She wanted a nice house, nice things, pots of money in the bank. Hardworking, seriously studious Matt could give her those things. She wasn't about to let him go, meekly step aside for some April Wilson.

As the days passed Matt zealously courted April. Then came the happy occasion of their first tremulous kiss. Matt was thoroughly tremulous. April stood on a huge stone so that they were approximately the same height and brought her mouth close to his. She kissed him. Then she laughed. Matt's eyes popped open in surprise.

"What?"

She was still laughing. "Matt, you don't have to unhinge your lower jaw. This is kissing, not oral surgery." Her hand went to his mouth, and she forced his lips into a stiff pucker. "Relax your lips, please."

Matt worked very hard at relaxing his lips while April held his face. Then, under these guided conditions, she kissed him. With his forcefully puckered lips parted only slightly, he felt the tip of her tongue glide into his mouth and lightly touch him just behind his upper teeth. It was like being struck by a bolt of lightning.

He looked completely muddled when she pulled back.

"April?" he wheezed. "W-would you please do that again?"

"Sure!"

She did and Matt was struck a second time. He had books and her book bag in his arms. While she kissed him, he threw all of that away and grabbed her. His lips no longer felt like newly set cement. For someone who'd had to be shown the simple basics of kissing, he learned fast. Then again, he was finally kissing the right woman.

Matt had been walking around in a dream state for days. Lucy could quite naturally go to the dean of women at the university and file a complaint, but how seriously would the dean take her complaint if her only charge was that April Wilson had the ability to make her husband walk around looking ga-ga?

No, she needed something much more serious, and that could only be a charge of immoral conduct. But she couldn't let them have an affair. That was out of the question. But if they weren't having an affair, it was impossible for her to go to the dean. She would have to begin to probe her enemy's weakness the way she had probed her own sister for a weakness. And once she found it, like Irma, April Wilson would be a memory.

As usual, Matt was waiting for her to come out of class. She came out looking drained.

"Honey? Are you all right?" he asked anxiously.

"I-I don't feel well," she muttered.

Then she swooned. He caught her, lifting her up in his arms. She weighed about as much as his jacket. When she came around, concerned students surrounded them asking if she was okay. April merely looked at them as she wrapped her arms around his neck and laid her head against his chest.

"You'd better get her over to the infirmary," someone said.

When he realized that April trusted him to carry

her, Matt felt more powerful than he had in ages. He carried her and her heavy book bag without the slightest mishap.

"When was the last time you ate, young lady?" the nurse asked unpleasantly.

April sat on the treatment cot, Matt standing close to her side, holding and stroking her hand. "Uhmmm, yesterday. I think."

The nurse scowled at Matt. "All she needs is food. And at regular intervals."

"She'll get it," Matt said. "I'll make sure she eats from now on."

"See that you do. I'm holding you personally responsible."

Outside the infirmary, Matt carried her book bag and held her hand as he guided April toward the cafeteria. April was almost skipping as she walked beside him.

"You're personally responsible for me from now on," she teased.

"I know. And I love it."

For weeks Matt was responsible for April, and in those weeks his confidence soared. He became positive that he would always be able to take care of April, even more positive that she cared for him. Now was the time to ask Lucy for a divorce. But he would need somewhere to live before he confronted her. That was only right. He couldn't expect her to put him up while they were divorcing. He made a late afternoon appointment with the housing department. It took another week before his appointment came through. On the morning of the day of his appointment when Lucy dropped him off, he blithely informed her that she needn't bother picking him up in the afternoon, that he would be studying late in the library.

"And just how do you think you'll get home?"

"I'll take the bus."

Lucy was fuming because she knew he was up to something. And whatever he was planning, she could feel that it was serious. Her time was running out. She had to strike. When he was out of sight, she parked the car in visitors parking and walked to the admissions office. There she used a pay phone and called in to work, saying she would be late because her poor crippled husband had had a bad night but that she would be in later and make up the lost time. Then she went to the admissions desk, dug out her assistant supervisor badge for the telephone company, and lied the underpants off the young woman at the main desk.

Fortunately, the young woman was a student on a work scholarship. Being a working student, she fell for Lucy's con job about another student desperate to make financial ends meet hook, line, and proverbial sinker.

"You have a law student by the name of April Wilson who has applied for part-time work with us," Lucy said, showing the badge. "As working for the phone company, even part-time, is such a trustworthy position, it's standard practice to screen each applicant carefully. Miss Wilson has given the university as a reference."

The young woman looked hesitant. "Uhm, I don't personally know a Miss Wilson. It's a big school."

"Yes, I'm well aware of that. At any rate, personal references simply won't do. I've come to see her records."

"I don't know if I can show you her records."

"This is the *phooone company* you're talking to," Lucy stressed. "We see *everyone's* records."

Well, that scared the whey out of that girl. Lucy felt smug as she watched her scamper off to the file cabinets. Moments later, she came back with a thick manila file. Lucy took the file and stood at the counter, thumbing through every sheet of paper. There was a small student photo of April Wilson. Now the enemy had a face. A tiny heart-shaped face with big eyes. She could just imagine April Wilson looking at Matt with those dopey, doggy eyes and Matt dissolving into a puddle of runny mush.

Lucy zeroed in on the personal sheet and found exactly what she needed. She made several notes in her pocket notebook, handed the file back to the young woman.

"Is—is she going to get the job?"

"Oh, yes," Lucy purred. "She's going to get it. I'll happily tell her myself if you'd be kind enough to direct me to"—she glanced first at her wristwatch and then at her notes—"L-Wing, Room 8L."

Lucy was waiting outside Room 8L when the scheduled class ended and April came out, walking in the middle of the flow of students. The face from the photo indelibly etched in her mind, Lucy knew her at once. Like a salmon sounding the upstream headwaters, Lucy aimed for April.

"Excuse me," she said, firmly placing her hand on the narrow shoulder. "Miss Wilson?"

April turned her head and looked up at the attractive but rather forbidding, taller woman. "Yes?"

The mob coursed around them. "I'd like to have a word with you, if you don't mind."

319

"I'm sorry, but I'll be late. My boyfriend is waiting for me."

"What a pity you'll be late."

April immediately did not like this woman. "I have no intention of being late." April turned away, began to walk off. Then she had the life startled out of her when the woman ran and planted herself in the way. "What do you think you're doing?"

"Stopping you from meeting my husband."

Completely enraged, April shouted, "Look, *lady*, I don't know who you are but—"

"Rainwater," Lucy snapped. "Mrs. Matthew Rainwater."

April was struck dumb. Trying to recover, she shook her head as she backed away. "No. No, you're not."

Lucy kept pace with April's retreat. She held up her left hand. There on her third finger was the diamond ring and wedding band. "Yes, I am. And I intend to *stay* Mrs. Matthew Rainwater. You go near my husband again, and I'll telephone your parents in Tahlequah. You might want to think about how they would feel hearing that their daughter is going around with a married man. And then there's your religion. From what I understand, your church has very strict rules about marriage."

She turned, walking briskly away. The sound of her high heels clicking against the marble flooring echoed throughout the corridor. After the formidable woman was gone, April, wrapped in a blanket of pain, began to slowly make her way to the cafeteria. She saw no one, heard no one. Her mind was churning too rapidly for ordinary life to register.

We never dated at night. We both have too much work. Besides, Matt can't drive. I didn't want to hurt his feelings.

Rainwater on the White Road

That's how he got away with being with me all day and going home to his wife. I should have hurt his feelings. How could he do this to me? And her! How could he be in love with me and then go to her? Oh, God, Matt, I hate you.

But she felt horrified too. Horrified that her sweet, bashful Matt was married to that—that Gorgon. Reaching the cafeteria, she stood outside the double glass doors watching him inside, carefully memorizing his every detail. She loved him. There was nothing she could do to change that now. It was much too late. She would always love him. And want him.

A very happy Matt was already seated at their table. Taking his job of making certain she ate when she was supposed to very seriously, he'd already ordered her a double cheeseburger and fries. The food was waiting when she finally appeared. She looked pasty, and when she sat down, she pushed the plate of food away.

"Honey? Are you okay?"

She couldn't look at him. She turned her face away as she said, "No. No, I'm not okay. I-I just met your . . . wife."

Matt had to steady himself. He grabbed onto the table to prevent himself from falling out of his chair. "You met who?"

She heard the truth. It had just shown itself in his tone. Matt really was married. She could look at him now. She did. "Your wife. I've been talking with your wife."

Neither spoke for a very long moment. They only stared at each other. Finally, Matt made a futile attempt to fight off the doom he felt.

"I'm divorcing her. I'm doing it right away. I'm moving into the dorms and—"

"No."

Another long, torturous moment followed.

"First," she said in a maddeningly calm voice, "you should have told me you were married. Not telling me was lying by omission. Second, I happen to be Catholic. Your wife, in few but very neatly chosen words, reminded me of that."

Matt tried to take her hand. April quickly pulled away.

"Don't touch me. And please, never come near me, or speak to me again." She rose shakily. "Goodbye, Matt."

He didn't move. He couldn't. Life trickled out of him with every step she took away from him. And as he saw each fatal step in slow motion, the dying process was lengthy and grisly. He had no idea how long he sat there. The waitress came to the table, spoke to him. Her words sounded strange, little better than incomprehensible babble. When he made no attempt to reply, she shrugged, took April's uneaten cheeseburger away, refilled his coffee cup. He didn't drink the coffee. It became cold and remained untouched as the faces in the cafeteria changed, noise of voices fading in, fading out as the crowd shifted, and at some point vanished, leaving him all alone in a great sea of empty tables.

"It's eight o'clock!" he heard a woman's voice say. He looked up at the frowning face of the waitress. "Eight o'clock," she impatiently repeated.

Oh, he thought dimly. *I've missed my appointment.*

"The cafeteria's shutting for the day. You gotta go."

Matt rose, and when he walked, his limp was as pronounced as when, encased in the heavy brace, he'd had to swing his leg in an arch.

Chapter Thirteen

"Would you just look at that thing?" George ranted. She followed May Rose around in the kitchen, waving her arms as she yelled. May Rose continually bit her lower lip to prevent her laughter. "Momma, just take a look out that window and tell me what you honestly think. You have my permission to be brutal."

May Rose paused, looked out the window, up to the hilltop where the skeleton of the house Jake was supervising was growing larger and in odd proportions. May Rose stifled another urge to laugh.

"It's a very . . . interesting house."

"Interesting?" George shrieked. "Your son has gone completely bonkers. That house is a monstrosity. The contractor is threatening to quit. But that's not stopping my Jack-o. Noooo, he keeps adding more rooms. His latest brain wave is a pool room. Off *my* kitchen. He says it has to be that way because he and his brothers will need easy access to the beer in the refrigerator. Well, silly me, I don't want them playing pool where I can see and hear them, and I certainly don't want them in and out of my kitchen." She grabbed May Rose by the shoulders and pleaded with her. "Momma-May, you have to do something. You have to stop him. Please!"

May Rose couldn't hold back another second. She laughed.

No one could stop Jake. He wasn't interested in outside form. The building progressed, the lower floor of the two-story house angling out in eccentric directions. From the outside the flat board and brick construction squatted on top of the hill like an hallucination. But when it was finished, even May Rose was impressed with the interior. The house was lovely and roomy. Plate-glass windows in practically every wall bathed the rooms on the lower floor with natural light. And because the house was on a hill, the view of the surrounding prairies from these windows was breathtaking. With virtually no furniture to speak of, Jake moved his little family into their rambling new home.

And so began a new form of family entertainment. During that summer Claude and May Rose didn't need to spend their evenings sitting in front of the radio. Instead, they sat on the back porch sipping iced tea, listening to Jake and George. Because it was an especially hot summer and the house on the hill suffered the worst of the heat, their windows were always wide open. It was very easy to hear Jake and George yelling the night away.

"Where are you?"

"Upstairs!"

"Where upstairs?"

"Follow the bread crumbs."

"I don't see any bread crumbs."

"That was sarcasm, Jack."

"Just keep screaming. I think I'm homing in on you."

Claude chuckled. "Kinda feels like they never moved out, don't it, Momma?"

Smiling, May Rose rattled the ice in the glass she held. Within a few minutes, her smile began to fade, for she was thinking about Walt and Tara. They were moving out too. But they were moving ten miles away.

The Finney house, she thought. *Why on earth did Walt buy that old place?*

Had she been one to pry, she would have learned that the Finney house had been Tara's idea. When Walt was snuggling with her in bed, asking her what she wanted for a present for graduating high school, Tara didn't hesitate. Like his mother, Walt had been flabbergasted.

"That old dump!"

"It's not a dump. It's a character house."

"Character, my ass. It's spooky. I bet the ghost of old Widow Finney is rattling around in there."

"No, she isn't."

Tara knew because she had already been inside the house. She and Emma had, just for a laugh, stopped the car in front of the old house, daring one another to have a closer look. The yard was a tangled jungle captured behind a sagging wire fence. Just outside the fence was a cement post with an iron loop. Horses used to be tethered to the post whenever visitors came to call at the house. Long ago, the Finney house had been the most glorious home in Urainia.

Built before the turn of the century, the house was antebellum in design, the colonnades of the front porch supporting an upper terrace. Mr. Finney, the town banker, had built the house for his Virginia bride, Maxine Finney. Wanting his refined wife to feel at home on the wild prairie, he'd copied her parents' Virginia home to the last detail. It was a shotgun house, meaning that the front door and the rear door were connected by a long hallway. Downstairs rooms were on either side of the hall, and a sweeping staircase led up to the second floor. Tara remembered her mother saying that when Mr. Finney was alive, that house was painted every year. In the blaze of summer, the house was blindingly white and all of the trim a soft grey.

After Mr. Finney died, Mrs. Finney became a recluse, the house becoming sadder with each passing year. Following her death ten years ago, the once proud house had been boarded up and abandoned to the elements. They had not been kind.

But standing on the deep porch, Tara felt the love and laughter that had once filled the home. She could almost hear the voices of the children that had been raised inside the house. Wanting to be inside, she pulled the boards nailed over the front double doors. Emma hadn't wanted to help, but in the end Tara had bullied her into it. They'd only managed to pull away two, make just enough space to reach through and try the doorknob. When it turned and the door swung open to the hall, Tara wriggled through. Emma flatly refused to follow. The interior was murky, but surprisingly, there wasn't even a hint of dust in the gloomy air. Instead, there was the soft fragrance of . . . honeysuckle. The floorboards creaked beneath her feet as she wandered, took a quick peek in the spacious rooms off the hall. Finally, she trusted the stairs and followed the sweeping curve to the upper floor. There was another long hallway, closed doors on either side. At the end of the hall was a large stained-glass window. There were no boards on the window, and the sun streaked through. The hall was a brilliant display of wonderful colors. Tara walked into this marvelous multicolored light, reached its source. She raised a hand, lovingly touched each section of color as if trying to catch the light, hold it tightly. That was when she knew she had to have the house. No other house would ever do.

Convincing Walt would not be easy, which is why she chose her moment carefully, when they were in bed and Walt in a state of dire need. When he wanted to make love, he would agree to anything. Which is how she finally got her own car and hours of driving lessons from a scared witless Walt. But the minute she mentioned the Finney house, Walt's interest in making love withered like a sun-dried prune.

He sat up, shaking his stubborn head. "No. No way. Forget about that old wreck. I'll build you something nice. A house like Jake built for George."

"I don't want a house like that!" she cried. "I want the Finney house."

"Are you nuts? It's falling down."

"No, it isn't. All it needs is a little restoration."

"Restoration! It probably needs indoor plumbing. Do you have any idea how much stuff like that costs? It would cost a damn fortune, that's what it would cost. Muffin, I hate to disappoint you, but you didn't marry a millionaire."

She placed her hand on his groin, slowly massaged him. "We can do most of the work ourselves," she crooned. "We can take our time. We can take years and years, and it would be so much fun, Walt."

Feeling himself harden, his voice broke. "B-but what about college? I thought you wanted to go to college."

"Not anymore. I just want to be with you."

His dark eyes clicked to the corners. "Really?"

She kissed the side of his mouth, and that was all the encouragement he needed. The next thing she knew, she was flat on her back and Walt's hips were pumping between her legs. When he was lost to the activity, Tara pressed her case.

"Can I have the house?"

"Oh damn, muffin!" he cried hoarsely.

Knowing just how much he loved it, she raked her nails from his groin to his abdomen. His locked arms trembled.

"Please, Walt?"

She raked him again.

"Yes!" he shouted as he exploded. "Oh baby, yes!"

But the next morning she had to drag him by his ankles to the bank to inquire about the Finney house. Then he almost fell through the cracks in the floor of the bank when the manager said yes, it was for sale. And for eight thousand dollars, an almost unheard-of price for a house, especially an old house that needed additional thousands in restoration. Tara had a thousand dollars in her college account. While she signed away her savings as earnest money on the Finney house, Walt made one last-ditch effort to talk her out of it. Speaking rapidly, he pointed out that Jake's huge, brand-new house had a mortgage of nine thousand dollars, needed no restoration at all, and that Jake would be paying on that house for the next ten years. Whereas they were taking on a debt which, even if they did do most of the refurbishing work themselves, would probably run for twenty years.

"Were you planning to leave me?"

"No!"

"Then we have twenty years." Tara signed the papers, and the bank manager grabbed them before she could change her mind.

They were now the proud owners of the Finney house.

Tara wore jeans and a T-shirt under her cap and gown when she graduated, and after the lengthy ceremony, instead of attending the senior class of '47's final bash, she and Walt were in their house stripping old wallpaper off the walls. They were joined a bit later by Jake, George, Wil, and Emma, who, to make the work party complete, had brought along a cooler of beer and a hamper of sandwiches. May Rose and Claude had been invited, but May Rose declined. She would only help out—"Walt's taking leave of his senses"—by baby-sitting Sally. Yet she might have felt differently had she seen the old house all lit up, heard the laughter. In response, the outline of the old house seemed to straighten, hold itself with a renewed pride against the full moonlight. The Finney house, which it would forever be called, had waited over a decade for just the right couple. A year later, the house was still in the awkward stages and Tara was pregnant. When Chad Raymond was eventually born and brought home from the hospital, the Finney house, even though some of the rooms were still waiting to be done, came fully alive. Chad was nearing his first birthday by the time May Rose was finally at peace with the fact that Walt and his family would always live on the other side of town. Besides, she had a different son to be mad at.

Matt.

Matt was buying a house all the way over in Bartlesville, and that just fried her liver every time she paused to think about it. Not only that, but Matt had robbed the family of the second biggest event in his life. Not only had they not been invited to his wedding, not one word had been mentioned about his graduating from the university until after the fact, when he and Lucy were back in the area and staying in the Bartlesville Hotel, of all places, while Lucy scoured the area in a crazed hunt for the perfect house. They finally consented to come to supper, which the entire family and Wil's girlfriend, Emma, included, planned as a family reunion. While May Rose baked for two days in the run-up to the supper, she planned a lot of things she would say to her eldest son. A son she hadn't even seen for nearly five years, thank you very much, and a son who couldn't even pause long enough from his new job and house-hunting expeditions to come see her. *Oh, yes*, she thought grimly as she took her anger out on hapless pie dough, *that young man is going to get a good tongue-lashing.*

Her fury dwindled the second Matt shuffled into the house behind Lucy. The rest of the assembled family cheered as Matt entered. May Rose couldn't utter a sound. Matt, her big strong handsome Matt, looked like the walking dead. Everything about him, the way he smiled, the way he moved, seemed forced. And when he spoke, even though he said all the right things, his voice was hollow, as if there wasn't a soul anywhere inside that big body. It was all May Rose could do not to scream at Lucy, *What have you done to my precious boy!*

Somehow she got through the awful evening, managed to grit her teeth and say nothing while Lucy prattled on, did most of the talking on Matt's behalf. Sheer willpower prevented her from lunging across the table and snatching Lucy bald-headed when she announced that, *finally*, they had the perfect house. In Bartlesville.

"Now perhaps we can start our family," Lucy said with a wink.

May Rose remained in the doldrums throughout the next weeks. She was relieved, only vaguely, by the shopping trip she took with George to Pawhuska to shop for dresses for Sally and Toya. September was quickly approaching, and they had to get both little girls ready for kindergarten. The Osage capital city had a big department store. George had fallen into a hard lust for this department store during her furniture-shopping days. Since then any excuse to drive all the way to Pawhuska would send George scampering to the car. And George had found something else too. A store in Pawhuska that sold hand-made crafts. May Rose felt embarrassed about all of these hand-made crafts littering George's house, especially the pair of war lances hung in an X on the wall of Jake's pool room.

"George, you're English," she'd said when viewing her daughter-in-law's decorating efforts.

George merely looked at her blankly. The lances remained, as did the woven rugs on the hardwood floors, the various pottery pieces, and the many bronzed statuettes of warriors on charging horses.

*   *   *

Sally and Toya started kindergarten in September. In October, Wil married Emma. It was a lovely wedding, and May Rose enjoyed herself with this much needed good excuse for weeping buckets of tears. Everyone believed she wept because her last son was flying the nest, because she was happy that he was marrying himself such a fine girl (even though Emma possessed a rather strong personality and had an opinion on every topic under heaven). But she was really crying because Matt still looked a papery facsimile of himself and she had not one clue how to help him.

Another year staggered past. Sally and Toya advanced to the first grade. Sally was a boisterous child, Toya very shy. In an effort to drain off a portion of Sally's lively spirit, George enrolled her daughter in tap-dancing classes. She tried to enroll Toya too, but at the dance school Toya hung back, would not let go of George's hand. To keep Toya slightly amused while Sally learned to do the Check-Ball-Change, George sat Toya down at a little table with a scrap piece of paper and a pencil. Toya drew a picture of Sally dancing. The sketch looked exactly like Sally, not simply a stick person any normal six-year-old would draw. Looking at the sketch, George realized her little sister-in-law had serious talent. George encouraged this talent, keeping Toya fully stocked with huge boxes of crayons, thick pads of drawing paper. Toya's remarkable art soon began to decorate the kitchens of all the women in the family. May Rose had always been especially fond of George, but seeing the way she mothered Toya, was always there for her when Toya's real siblings barely noticed she was alive while she wandered the forest of adult legs, May Rose began to love George. Love her deeply.

Wil and Emma lived five miles away in a newly built house on two acres of land neatly situated between his parents and his twin brother. George discovered she was pregnant, and Jake was so happy he was dancing on air. That Christmas Eve, when the family gathered to exchange gifts, Matt no longer looked like the walking dead. He looked worse. Far worse. So terrible that this time everyone noticed. Even Claude. He took his son to the side and tried to talk to him.

"Everything's fine, Dad," he said tightly. "Everything's just . . . fine."

But it wasn't and hadn't been since the day the new paralegal had come to Bartlesville to work for the company. The new paralegal was named April Wilson.

On October fourth, Matt came off the elevator so angry he was chewing nails. In his hand was a procurement contract that had been amended so many times and initialed ASW that the contract was unreadable. He stormed into the legal department, determined to find this ASW and chew some serious ass.

The legal department was open-planned for the ten paralegals, the offices for the company attorneys boxing in the open area. The doors to these offices were closed against the constant ringing of phones. Matt stopped at one desk, waved the contract under the nose of a harried female paralegal as she talked rapidly on the phone. She spared the contract a glance, saw the initials, then, still talking into the phone, rapidly pointed at a desk four desks away from hers. That desk was empty of a human life form, but it was piled high with stacks of paperwork indicating human activity. Matt shuffled off to that desk, sat down in the chair beside it, and listened to the chaos of the legal department while he waited. And waited.

Briskly walking out of her assigned attorney's office and toward her desk, April stopped in mid-stride. He was sitting with his back to her, but she knew exactly who he was. She would have recognized the back of that head and those broad shoulders anywhere. Then too, there was the outstretched leg. Her heart tried to knock its way out of her chest, and it took several seconds to calm herself before bearding this dreaded lion.

She hadn't wanted to take the job with the oil company in Bartlesville, even though the company was one of the few responding favorably to a female member of the Oklahoma bar. The company did not offer her a position as an attorney. She turned them down. Then, months later when her pride had been sufficiently pummeled and she desperately needed money to pay off loans and indulge in frivolous things, such as food, she took the job as a paralegal. The second thing she did not care for was that the company wanted her in the home office. True, Bartlesville was a Cherokee town, but it bordered Osage County. April did not want to be near any more Osage.

Until this second she'd had no idea that Matt worked for the same company. But he did and he was sitting right in front of her and right beside her desk. She didn't bother to flatter herself that he had found out where she was and had tracked her down.

They had shared the same campus for another two years following the farewell scene in the cafeteria, and he hadn't bothered to track her even once. That he was waiting for a paralegal to turn up could only mean that he didn't know the name of the paralegal in question. With no place to run or hide, there was nothing she could do but brazen it out. She smoothed her tight-fitting dress, prepared herself for the second worst moment of her life—the first moment having been on the day she found out that the man she was in love with was married. She walked well around him, avoiding his outstretched leg. Matt didn't look up. He was engrossed in the contract she had worked on the whole of yesterday.

"May I help you?"

Hearing that voice, Matt turned into a block of stone. It took him a moment to lift his head, and then several more moments to realize that his eyes weren't deceiving him, that he was actually seeing his beautiful tiny April. After over three long and empty years following that miserable day in the cafeteria, he had gone home to find Lucy waiting for him. He refused to speak to her, couldn't trust himself to be alone with her because he hated her so much he had wanted to kill her. The next day, he had made a new appointment with housing, put his name on the list for a dorm room for the next term. Shortly after that he saw April for the last time. She was walking across campus and laughing, arm in arm with a young man. Seeing her happy with someone else, Matt had wanted to die. And, in a way, he did. At the start of the new term, he didn't take the room in the dorm. What was the point? If he was going to spend the remainder of his life in hell, he might as well have a keeper. He remained with Lucy, kept his head in his books, and never tried to see April again.

Now here she was. And she looked so good. Just looking at her, he felt himself come alive and, in the same moment, descend further into hell. He covered the awkward moment with his usual panache.

"W-what are you doing here?"

"Working," she answered tersely.

When she sat down at her desk, he lost sight of her behind the stacks of paperwork. He shoved the stack to the side, and it waterfalled to the floor. Both ignored the mess at their feet as their eyes locked and held.

"I thought you were going to be a lawyer."

"I am a lawyer. But the funny thing is, women lawyers can't find work. Women lawyers starve. I found it suited me better to be a well-fed paralegal. Did you have a question about the contract?"

Matt looked down at the papers in his hands. "You're ASW?"

"Yes. April Sara Wilson."

Matt's head shot up. "You didn't get married?"

"I'm afraid that's none of your business. Explain the portions of the contract you don't understand, please."

Her pithy tone made him angry. Here he was mortally bleeding all over himself, and she was sounding impatient for him to get it over with and perish. "I don't understand any of it."

April leaned back in her chair. "Really," she huffed. "It's simple enough. A baboon could understand it."

"Then maybe we should run a baboon in here to explain it to me." He slammed the offending document on her desk. "All this ever was intended to be was a straightforward transaction between our company and a vendor for a load of pipe for the Wyoming development, and you've turned it into a wordy pile of guano."

April was steaming as she leaned forward in the chair and glared at him. "*My* job is to protect our company *and* company employees from opportunistic vendors. The way that contract was originally written, this particular vendor had you by the ass and was about to shove his load of pipe up a dry hole! Appreciative though I am of your disappointment, your signature is still required for the amendments."

Matt suddenly realized that there wasn't another sound in the room. Feeling the stares, he stood, grabbed a pen, and scrawled his name on the final page of the document. Then he left, with as much dignity as his awkward gait would allow. He did not go near the legal department again. In fact, he stayed out of town on business just as much as he possibly could. But he was back in Barltesville by Halloween. And since he was in the building at the end of the working day, there was no way he could wriggle out of attending the seasonal party being thrown to coincide with the giving out of achievement awards. To his great dismay, he was receiving one of the awards. Which meant that he would have to stand in full view of all the company employees. Most especially in full view of April.

Someone in Admin decided that it would be just too precious to have a few of the prettiest single women in the company dressed up as pumpkins and present the awards. When Matt saw April again, she was a pumpkin. As she stood with her fellow pumpkin victims, her little shapely legs were inside vivid green stockings. A round orange shape hid her curvaceous little body, and a orange blobby hat was stuck on top of her little head. Sitting at the bar, waiting for his name to be called, he hid his gloating smile behind his hand. But his relish of her public humiliation vanished the second she stepped forward, presented the award to the named recipient, and then fled. His name was being called, and his chosen pumpkin was standing beside the awards emcee primed to hand him the award, but Matt didn't step forward. He was no longer in the employee bar-lounge. He was in the hallway chasing after April.

If the elevator had owned a somewhat reliable nature, he wouldn't have caught her. But the elevator had a will of its own, arriving only when it cared to, never when it was actually summoned. She was sobbing as she stood at the closed elevator doors, madly stabbing the call button again and again. The elevator dinged its arrival, the doors lethargically sliding open. April jumped inside, and Matt jumped in right behind her.

"Get away from me!" she screamed. She beat his back with her fists as Matt pushed the button for the basement. When their destination was settled and the elevator sluggishly was moving, he whirled on her. Then he had to defensively hold her at arm's length as she tried to kick him.

"Not that leg!" he shouted.

Instantly, April switched feet, kicking out at his good leg. When he saw his chance to grab her, he did, lifting her up, holding her against him, his arms crushing her pumpkin roundness into an eight. Her arms around his neck, she wept against his well tailored suit jacket shoulder.

"What are we going to do?" she sobbed.

"I don't know," he choked. "I only know I can't stop loving you. And I've tried, April. I've really tried."

After that day Matt's life markedly devolved. Not only was he Lucy's doormat, now he was April's yo-yo. First she would see him, then she wouldn't. Come back, go away, come back, go away. In December, April announced that she was going home to her parents in Tahlequah. *And make confession about being in love with a married man.*

Matt missed her with every fiber of his being and he was so terrified of what her priest would advise, he was on the brink of losing his mind. He was so involved with the pain of missing April that he paid no attention to what Lucy was getting up to. And he should have done that. He *really* should have done that.

Ever watchful, Lucy noticed the day Matt changed, became more alive, and even more distant. A few days later, he began making comments about his leg, how it was severely paining him in the night. Like a complete dimwit, he believed he was fooling her. Lucy played along, acted the concerned helpmate, even helped trundle his clothing down the hall the day he moved out of their bedroom into the guest room. Then she bided. Oh, how she bided. She knew he was carrying on with some woman he worked with, but just which one would be tricky to discover. She couldn't march in and demand to see company records the way she had during the fiasco he had put her through when he'd been in college. What she did instead was become even more involved with the Petroleum Wives Club (PWC). She made it her business to become chummy with the wives of department heads, carefully pumping each wife for information of that husband's department, especially concentrating on the names of the single women in each department. The law department was next to the bottom of Lucy's hit list. It was during the last week before Christmas that she heard that despicable name again, and when she heard it, during a PWC bridge tournament, she damn near choked on a mouthful of party mix.

"My husband's paralegal, some fool girl named April Wilson," this particular wife said as she bid three hearts, "just took off without barely any notice. Now my husband has been spending nearly all of the holiday evenings doing *her* job. She's ruined Christmas for us. I've had to cancel two parties thanks to Miss Wilson. I've said it before, and I'll say it again. The company should fire every last one of those so-called career women. Then they'd find themselves husbands and stay home the way women are supposed to. . . ."

Lucy was no longer listening. Her heart was beating too rapidly, and her blood was pounding in her ears. April Wilson was back. She was the reason Matt had moved out of the marital bedroom. Because Lucy was so stunned that she again faced an old rival, one she'd believed she had reduced to pulp, she couldn't think clearly. She badly fumbled her way through the remainder of the bridge tournament.

Once she was home, she paced the Persian carpet of her picture-perfect living room. She paced until she was over her shock and was able to think clearly.

And she had plenty of time to think clearly because when Matt came home, he immediately went to his study and locked the door. He refused to come out, even for supper. Evidently he was too busy pining for April to eat. Oh, God, how she hated him. Hated them both. But she couldn't very well destroy Matt without losing the life he provided. However, she could destroy April, and in destroying her once and for all, she could mortally wound Matt. And she hoped he would suffer. She hoped he would suffer for a long, long time.

On December 23 the company threw a Christmas party for the top executives and their wives at the Bartlesville Country Club. It was the perfect occasion for Lucy to put her plan into action. In the ladies' room, a garish concoction of gilt-framed mirrors, Cupid lamps, and hideous flocked wallpaper in the colors of red and pink, Lucy sat at a dressing table squeezing out crocodile tears. And of course she timed her tears for the right women. When they noticed her distress, they crowded around her, showing their concern.

"My husband," she sobbed, bravely dabbing away her tears, "is having an affair. With a woman at work."

The women sat down in unison. This was something each of them secretly dreaded. And because this was viewed as a mutual threat, Lucy had their undying support. During the party, word reached the ears of the right husbands. The very next morning Matt was woken by the ringing telephone and advised, strongly, to come immediately to the office. Although the company was officially closed for the holidays, the president of the company, along with several concerned departmental heads, would be there to meet him.

A second call to the house roused Lucy. She became elated when she hared the female voice gush over the line, "My dear, excellent news. Your little problem has been solved."

It took him several tries as he stood before the president's desk and in the grim presence of departmental managers to fully understand what was being said. And when the violent light of revelation occurred, he felt as stricken as Saint Paul on the road to Damascus.

"Miss Wilson was sent a telegram stating that her services are no longer required. It's standard practice in cases such as these. Every female employee is well aware of our policy. Miss Wilson's termination will serve as a reminder. As for you, Matthew, you have a brilliant future ahead of you. We are willing to overlook this, uh, moment of temptation. But at the same time it is to your advantage to understand just why Miss Wilson has been terminated. You have a lovely, completely competent wife. It is our recommendation, for the good of your career, she remain your wife. From now on, Matthew, we expect you to keep your eye on the ball. Do not allow anything to impede your continuing development in the company."

Matt went home, locked himself in the study, and through the long-distance operator, called the number in Tahlequah. April answered, heard his shaky voice, hung up on him. He didn't try again. He decided that he would give her a day to calm down enough to listen to him. Besides, he had to think out just what he was going to say. All he knew for certain was that he was not about to lose her. And if that meant grabbing her and making a run for it to the other side of the planet, then that was what he would do.

He was lost in this mental fog during the early evening when Lucy drove them to his parents' house for Christmas Eve. He knew he looked and acted like a wreck, and when his father tried to gently grill him, Matt almost broke. Somehow he'd managed to keep his emotional torture to himself. He still had no idea that Lucy was the creator of this new level of hell. He was still trying to work out how to be fair to her and run off with April. That confusion ended on the drive home.

"That went well," she said, her tone oddly pleased. "Just keep up the act, Matthew, and very soon it won't be much of an act anymore."

Slowly, he turned his head in her direction. She glanced at him, a smug smile on her face. A face that seemed contorted with evil in the dim light.

"You," he rasped. "You did it. Just like you did it before."

"Yes," she said. "And I'll do it every time April Wilson pops back into our lives. You're my husband, Matthew. You will always *be* my husband. Merry Christmas, darling."

At home, Lucy went to bed. Wisely, knowing that Matt was in the living room drowning his heartbreak in whiskey, she locked her bedroom door. That lock saved her from the wrath she honestly didn't believe Matt was capable of. But then, Lucy hadn't been on the Japanese-held island. She hadn't been there to see what he was capable of when he blanked out, allowed the fury of his feral instincts to take over and free him from a life-threatening trap.

At three a.m., Lucy woke to the sound of loud crashing. She sat up in bed, fearfully thinking that a prowler was in the house. Then she heard Matt's bellowing voice and more crashing. He sounded falling-down drunk. Angry now, she switched on the bedside lamp, grabbed her robe off the nearby chair, and rushed to the door. Her hand was on the lock when she heard something hit a wall downstairs and shatter on impact.

"I hate you, you bitch!"

Horrified, Lucy backed away from the door. Matt wasn't falling down, accidentally breaking things. He was intentionally wrecking her house. And from the sound of it, he was being very thorough. The wrecking escalated as Lucy hurriedly dialed the operator and yelled for the police. Because it was Christmas, it took a good deal of ringing before the telephone was answered. During that time she heard Matt shouting his hatred for her and smashing everything in his path. And his path was leading him to the stairs. She was so terrified, she was screaming when a male voice finally came on the line.

"Bartlesvil—"

"Help me! For God's sake, help me! My husband's destroying my house, and he's trying to kill me!"

Chapter Fourteen

On the morning of December 26, Jake was cold and covered with drilling mud. He was standing on the rig amid the noise and grime involved with drilling a new well when a county sheriff's car drove onto the sight. None of the drilling crew heard or saw the car until the sheriff and one of his deputies tried to climb the platform. Spotting them, Jake started yelling his head off, ordering them back because they weren't wearing hard hats.

The sheriff cupped his hands around his mouth and yelled, "I need to speak to the Rainwaters!"

Jake gave the high sign that he understood and quickly put the grab on his two brothers. The three men climbed down from the platform and stood in front of the sheriff, the man still trying to shout over the noise. Giving up, he yelled, "Is there some place we can talk?"

Jake nodded and led the procession to the trailer house that served as a field office. The trailer was cramped inside, containing one desk, two couches scrounged from the Goodwill, four metal folding chairs, one field telephone, an electric coffeepot, and a tray of grubby coffee mugs. The men took their coats off in the confining space, the small heater combining with their body heat quickly stifling the air inside the trailer. Jake sat on the edge of the desk, removing his hard hat and earplugs. His brothers went for the coffeepot. None of the Rainwaters seemed overly concerned that the law had shown up on the drill site. It happened occasionally when a renewed hunt for Allen was launched. Mostly the hunts were because the police didn't have anything else to do. At any rate, every halfhearted search invariably began with the questioning of Allen's three brothers.

"I guess you know why we're here," the sheriff began. He was a robust man, in his mid-fifties and a quarter-blood Cherokee. He had a head full of curly hair and a luxuriant mustache. He stroked his mustache as if the three full-blood Osage men should be envious.

"Yeah," Jake nodded. "And I'll tell you the same thing I've told all the guys before you. None of us know where Allen is. And none of us gives a damn where he is."

"Allen?" the sheriff barked. "Who the hell's talking about Allen?"

"Aren't you?" Jake asked. His two brothers, stirring their coffee, came to stand beside him.

"Hell, no," the sheriff scoffed. "We're here to talk about your other brother."

"Matt?" the three cried in unison.

"That's the one," the sheriff said flatly. "Just thought that maybe you boys would like to know that he's in jail." Three mouths dropped. "I could use a cup of that coffee," the sheriff said, sitting down on the couch. "An' you boys might as well make yourselves comfortable. You're in for a mighty rough ride."

Sipping the cup of coffee, the sheriff treated the Rainwater brothers to a brand-new Christmas carol.

"Your brother's wife called up on Christmas Eve. Well, officially it was Christmas Day, seeing as how it was after three in the morning. Anyhow, she was all hysterical an' shit, screaming about how her husband was trying to kill her. So a couple of the boys roll over there, an' damn if she wasn't right. Hell, he'd already killed the house. Looked like a damn tornado'd come through but just on the inside. You wouldn't believe the mess. Your brother was actin' as crazy as a starvin' tick on a dead dog, an' as big as he is, my two dep'ties knew they weren't gonna stop him doin' nothing if he didn't want them to. At that time he didn't want anybody to stop him 'cause he wanted to beat his wife's door down and stomp the hell outta her.

"Now, my dep'ties knew that officially they couldn't let him do that, so they ran outta the house, jumped back in the patrol car, and yelled for more men. In the meantime, the whole neighborhood was awake and standing around watching Miz Lucy hanging out the bedroom windah yelling, 'Save me! Somebody save me!' No offense, I'm sure Miz Lucy is a fine lady an' all, but there wasn't exactly what you'd call a rush of neighborhood volunteers.

"Anyhow, more of my boys showed up just about the time your brother had that bedroom door battered down an' Miz Lucy was running around like a rabid squirrel, an' they all jumped on him before he could get her." The sheriff paused, scratched the back of his head. "I'll say this for him. When your brother goes on a tear, it's a real wing-dinger. He liked to have killed just about all my boys while they were holding him down. Anyways, he quit kicking after they pistol-whipped him just enough to haul him out. Once he was behind bars, his wife filed charges for attempted murder, an' he hasn't said nothing. We offered to call him a lawyer, call his folks, anybody he wanted us to call. He still ain't said boo. He's in a whole bunch of trouble an' he needs some help from somebody, so I figured I'd come talk to you boys. Ask maybe if any of you might know what set him off."

Overwhelmed, Jake looked at his dumbstruck brothers, then looked at the sheriff. "We, uh, haven't been what you might call close to our brother Matt for quite a while. I mean, he's kinda like our boss. Hard-hatters and suits don't socialize. Not even when they're brothers."

"That's too bad," the sheriff sighed. "He could sure use himself some brothers. I talked to your company's top lawyer this morning and was told that under the circumstances Mr. Rainwater was no longer suited to the company. In other words, as of this morning he's fired. Guess now he's gonna have to get himself an outside lawyer 'cause the company lawyer ain't touchin' him with a twenty-foot cattle prod." The sheriff rose, placed his Stetson hat on his curly head. "I'll tell you one thing for free. If he was my brother, I'd sure do something for him pretty damn quick. Otherwise, he's going to prison."

The sheriff left the trailer, Jake, Wil, and Walt in a line behind him. The brothers stood shoulder to shoulder as the sheriff's car left the site. Jake deeply inhaled the frosty air to clear his swimming head. As was their habit, his twin brothers turned toward him, waiting expectantly. And as was his habit, Jake thought out loud, his words carried on quickly fired puffs of cloudy breath.

"We can't call Momma yet. Not until I've talked to Matt, found out what the hell set him off. Then I guess I'd better talk to Lucy, find out for sure what she's gonna do. If I can talk her out of pressing the charges, then maybe we won't need a lawyer." He looked at his brothers. "You two, get over to the refinery. You're gonna have to talk to Dad before he hears about this through the company grapevine. Go on with him to the house, and if he decides to tell Momma, don't try to stop him. He'll be doing me a favor. If he does tell her, don't let Momma call Lucy. Sit on her if you have to, but don't let her do anything until you hear from me."

"Okay, Jakey," the twins said.

Jake signed himself and his brothers off the shift, and they all left the site just ten minutes after the sheriff. The twins went for their father while Jake broke all speed laws on his way into Bartlesville.

Matt wasn't trusted not to put up more fight, and the deputies were afraid of him. His ankles were shackled, his hands cuffed behind his back. Being heavily chained made it difficult for him to walk the long corridors to the interview room. Once he was inside and he faced Jake, Matt lowered his head in shame, said nothing as the deputy unlocked the handcuffs. Then he meekly shuffled toward the chair the deputy indicated and wearily sat down. His eyes never left the Formica tabletop while the deputy spoke to Jake, heard his brother ask for coffee.

"He hasn't eaten nothin' either," the deputy said. "Think maybe if I brought in some sandwiches, you could get him to eat?"

"That would be very kind," Jake said, emotion breaking his voice.

"Ain't no trouble," the deputy said gruffly. Then he left.

Jake went to the table, sat down across from Matt. He stuck two cigarettes into his mouth, lit them both, passed one to Matt. He couldn't help but notice how badly Matt's hand shook as he took the cigarette, smoked it like a demon.

"Talk to me, Matt."

"I don't want to."

"You've got to. Something's been makin' you nuts for a few months now and—"

Matt laughed loudly and bitterly. "*Months*! Oh, Jakey, try years!"

Jake's face drained. "Talk to me, Matt. Really talk to me."

Matt started talking, and once he started, he couldn't stop, couldn't even pause during the time the deputy reappeared with coffee and sandwiches. Matt continued to talk while he drank the coffee and ate the sandwiches, without realizing he was eating or drinking. And he smoked. For a man who rarely smoked, Matt worked his way through an entire pack. He enjoyed the cigarettes about as much as he had enjoyed the food and coffee.

When Matt finally finished the most incredible tale of suffering Jake had ever heard, he said, "I've got to get you a lawyer just in case Lucy wants to go ahead and press charges."

"Oh, she's gonna want to press 'em. I messed up

her house. I lost my job. Now that she's got nothing left, she's going to want to punish me in a real big way."

Jake was so angry he wanted to go after Lucy himself. "Damn it, Matt, you've got to fight her. You can't let her win anymore."

A new cigarette stuck into the side of his mouth, Matt squinted against the curling smoke and stared at his brother. He took the cigarette away, spat out a tobacco fragment. "Okay. I'll tell you what, you get me a piece of paper and a pencil, and I'll write down the name and the number of the only lawyer I want. But if she won't take the case, I'll just go to prison. One hellhole is just as good as another."

The name and number in his pocket, Jake drove for his parents' house. He wasn't even tempted to visit Lucy. He was afraid that if he did, he would quickly find himself in the same cell with Matt.

May Rose was beside herself, flying around her kitchen like a sightless bat trapped in an unfamiliar cave. Her entire family was in attendance, none of them trying to stop her as she made pot after pot of coffee, produced piles of turkey and cranberry sandwiches which no one wanted, and yelled and wept while she did all of this. To prevent the two little girls from getting in her way, George kept them in Toya's bedroom, reading stories as the girls sat at Toya's play table playing with modeling clay. George started when she heard May Rose shrieking in the kitchen, "Jakey's here!"

"I want *Dabby*," Sally immediately said. "Dabby" was the name Sally had called Jake from the time she was two years old. She especially wanted her

Dabby when she was feeling put upon. And having to sit still and play with boring old clay had her feeling more than a little put upon. Sally bolted from the little chair and rushed to the bedroom door. George propelled her pregnant body after her spoiled child, wrenching Sally's hand away from the doorknob. Sally responded to the rough treatment by throwing a tantrum. George's hand soundly smacked Sally's squirming bottom.

The instant he walked into the kitchen and the family fell on him for news, he heard his daughter crying from the back of the house. Under normal circumstances, the sound of Sally crying would have him rushing to her rescue. The only real arguments he and George ever had were over the disciplining of Sally. Jake didn't believe Sally needed any, and George knew their daughter was playing Jake like a violin. But because today's circumstances were beyond normal, Jake ignored his daughter as he slogged his way through his family, his mother hanging on to him, heading for the kitchen wall phone. His mother was yelling full voice as he dialed the long-distance operator and shouted the number for Tahlequah.

A man answered, and over his mother's racket he yelled, "I have to speak to April Wilson. It's an emergency."

Her father hovered nearby as April listened to the voice on the phone. She could plainly hear the commotion in the background. She knew without a particle of doubt that this call was genuine. Matt was not using devious means to entice her back to Bartlesville. Her heart sank as she listened and realized just how much trouble he was in.

"I'll be there as quickly as I possibly can."

"Do you want directions to my folks' house?"

"No. I'll meet you at the police station." April hung up, charged off to her bedroom to pack her bags.

Cradling the receiver, Jake turned to his hysterical mother. "Momma, you'd better get a couple of bedrooms ready. Matt and his lawyer are gonna need a place to stay."

"You were talkin' to his lawyer?" May Rose cried.

"Yes."

"Is he any good? Will he get my boy out of the jailhouse?"

"She, Mom," Jake corrected. "His lawyer is a she. And yes, she's very good."

"A *she!*" May Rose screamed. "My boy needs a good lawyer, not some old she. What judge is gonna listen to a she?"

"Trust me, Momma. The judge is going to listen to this she because *this* she is going to take Lucy's head off."

May Rose trembled as she wrung her hands. In a tiny, teary voice she said, "Do you promise, Jakey?"

"Oh, yeah. I promise, Mom. Now, you'd better get busy. You're gonna have company."

May Rose visibly brightened. "Then I'd better cook the New Year's ham."

Jake began to have his first serious doubt when April Wilson bustled into the police station. *Crap! If that's her, she's no bigger than a minute!* His father voiced the same concern.

"That ain't *her*, is it?"

The question was answered when, briefcase in

hand, April Wilson marched straight up to the four, very tall Rainwater men. As in their own individual way they shared the same height and face Matt owned, she knew the four men waiting in the outer lobby were his closest relatives. She extended her hand and introduced herself.

"I'm April Wilson."

Jake shook her hand, introduced his father, his twin brothers. April shook hands with each in turn; then her attention snapped back to Jake.

"Have they set the arraignment?"

"No. They couldn't do that until he agreed to an attorney. He only wanted you. He said if you wouldn't come, he'd rather stay in jail."

"Leave everything to me," she said in a crisp tone.

The lumbering men tagged after the quickly striding tiny April Wilson like four long-legged hounds. Jake was almost tempted to lift her up so that the policeman at the desk could see her properly while she spoke. He kept his hands deeply in his pockets to ward off the temptation. Within seconds he was glad he had, because April Wilson was busily slapping that cop with a ream of papers she had pulled out of her briefcase. Then she was led off by another policeman to the interview room to consult with her client. She didn't even glance back as she walked away.

"What the hell are we supposed to do?" Claude grumbled.

"We wait, Dad," Jake replied.

And they did. A half hour later, April Wilson came steaming toward them where they sat in the lobby. Seeing her, they rose.

"The arraignment has been scheduled for nine a.m. tomorrow."

"He's gotta stay in another night?" Claude wailed.

"It's the holiday season, Mr. Rainwater," she said brusquely. "Things move a bit more slowly during the season of goodwill toward men. But you'll be happy to know that he's in better spirits. He's ready to fight this. In the meantime, I have to use the lag time to our advantage. I've someone I need to see immediately."

"You're not gonna talk to Lucy, are you?" Jake worried.

"Good God, no. I have someone far more important in mind."

"Well," Claude shrugged, "if you'd care to follow us, we'll lead you to the house."

"Just give me the directions, please. I have to go to Pawhuska."

"*Pawhuska*?" they chimed together.

But April Wilson would not be drawn, would not tell them that she had already made a half dozen telephone calls to Pawhuska and that the person she had alluded to was waiting for her. Because there were no guarantees this person would do anything more than listen, it was best to keep her mouth firmly shut on the subject. Finally, Jake gave up asking questions she would not answer and wrote the directions to the Rainwater home. Without a word of farewell, she left.

Watching her leave, Claude spoke to Jake. "What the hell are we gonna tell your momma?"

"We tell her Matt's got himself a little killer fox terrier, an' that she should just stand back while the terrier cuts the she-wolf a new asshole."

*   *   *

C. R. Jones was something of a living legend. Not only was it rumored that he had once been an outlaw with the infamous Starr Gang, he was also one of the few independent oil company owners that had not gone belly up in the Depression. He was also something else. C. R. Jones was a full-blood Osage. It was solely on the basis of the nebulous blood tie to Matthew Rainwater that he consented to meet the persistent little woman lawyer in his closed office. Languidly smoking a cigar, he listened as she made her case for the defense. It was a very weak case, and he tried not to laugh.

"I've heard of your client, of course. I'm fully aware that until this misadventure he'd had an impressive record. But if he's gone over the edge, he's become a dangerous liability. And wouldn't I look the fool if I picked him up?"

April leaned across his desk. "Yes, and wouldn't you just love it?"

C. R.'s eyes were smiling as he smoked his cigar. He blew the smoke to the ceiling as he studied her earnest little face. This little woman knew her opponent very well indeed. C. R. Jones thrived on controversy, absolutely loved slander, the dirtier the better. Especially when it was directed at him. Having a publicly branded renegade Osage engineer on his team would suit him all the way to the ground. And there was something else he decided that would suit him even more.

"I'll make a deal with you. We'll call it two for the price of one. I'll agree to your promissory contract for the employment of Matthew Rainwater, if you'll agree to a promissory contract that you will work for me in my legal department."

"I'm sorry, but I'm a bit fed up with using my training in a paralegal capacity. I prefer being a starving lawyer to a well-fed lackey."

"Who said anything about being a paralegal?" He smoked again as the full weight of his offer registered on her face.

"You—you'd have a *woman* attorney on your staff? Mr. Jones, think of the opposition and—"

C. R. Jones smiled widely, showing the teeth that clenched the cigar in his mouth. He thrived on opposition most of all.

April straightened. "Where do I sign?"

"A handshake will do nicely."

April extended her hand. C. R. Jones stood, towered over her as his huge hand swallowed hers. "In times of great hardship, our women were warriors too. Kindly remember that whenever I call on you to use your considerable legal skills."

"I will, Mr. Jones. I most definitely will."

May Rose damn near suffered a cataleptic fit when Matt's lawyer walked into her living room. How in the world was this tiny little woman going to do anything for her son? But like her men, concerns about her sex and her height disappeared when April, with no mincing of words, fully informed them of her recent actions. May Rose was more than satisfied with what she heard. Not only had this little woman set the arraignment, she had worked to guarantee that Matt would be released on bail on the basis that he was actively employed within the immediate area. And she hadn't found him some stupid job just sweeping floors or digging ditches either. He would still be a respected engineer working for a highly esteemed company. Just how April Wilson had managed this major miracle, May Rose did not ask. She bustled the little woman into the kitchen, sat her down at the table, and served her huge portions of ham, sweet potatoes, black-eyed peas, and rice.

"This is New Year's food," April said.

"Sweet girl, the minute you walked in my house, the new year started. Now, you eat every bit of food on your plate."

She did. And after she finished eating, she casually threw the household into a new whorl of activity. May Rose stepped back and let her do it.

"What the hell do you have in this suitcase?" Jake cried, using two hands to haul it in.

"Oh! Those are my books. Just take that case to the kitchen." Then she bossed Walt and Wilber. "The other cases can go to my room." April then took over the kitchen, changed it within minutes into her office, her books and notepads all over the table. Walt, Wilber, and their wives drifted off home. George packed up Toya, and they left. Only Jake remained in the living room with his parents, May Rose calmly knitting as they listened to April on the telephone.

"I'm really not concerned with the hour," she said tersely. "I happen to be Mr. Rainwater's attorney of record. I demand to speak to my client. Yes, I'll wait." There was a pause, then April shouted, "My client has walking difficulty. If you shackle him, impede his walk to the phone, possibly cause him to endure a fall, I will file suits for pain and suffering and mental anguish. Then I will see to it that each and every officer involved with the shackling is sued on the grounds of the base torture of a helpless prisoner."

Claude rolled his eyes, made a soft *oooooh* sound. May Rose clicked the knitting needles more rapidly and pressed her lips together in a pleased smile.

"For your information," April was heard to say, "his medical records clearly state that he is quite incapable of your overblown fears of violence." Another pause. "Well, of course you're perfectly free to trot out as many witnesses you may have to the contrary, but in a court of law, just who do you think a jury will believe? A team of certified doctors or a load of backwater cops?" April's voice became light, surprisingly pleasant. "Yes, I'll be more than happy to hold. Thank you for your consideration." Then under her breath, "Dickhead."

Dissolving into a fit of giggles, May Rose melted in the wing-backed chair.

Matt's voice came on the line. "Hey, baby."

"Hey, yourself. Are you shackled?"

"No."

"Handcuffed?"

"No."

"Damn, there goes an easy million bucks."

"What?"

"Never mind. Just answer one question. That furniture you wrecked, how was it paid for?"

"By checks."

"Who signed the checks?"

"I did."

"Thank you."

"Didn't you want to ask me anything else?"

"Such as?"

"Such as the question about me loving you. Didn't you want to ask that?"

"I never ask the obvious, Matthew. And by the way, I love you too. Get some sleep. I'll see you in the morning at the arraignment."

"Will I get bailed out?"

"Oh, it's going to be better than that."

"How?"

"You'll see."

The Rainwater clan sat on one side of the court, Lucy on the other, her eyes burning holes in April Wilson's back as April stood at the defense table. Matt was wearing his best navy blue suit, white shirt, and tie. His three brothers had appeared at the house at seven in the morning, bullied their way in. Then as she sobbed and cried about how she could not understand why it had all come to this, they'd packed up every garment Matt owned. Now he was wearing the nicest suit she had chosen for him and was standing beside April as the charges against him were read. When the court clerk was heard to call the first charge of property damage, April voiced an objection.

The clerk stopped in mid-sentence, and the judge looked at her.

"Your Honor," she said in an even tone, "my client cannot be charged with property damage."

"And just why not?"

"It was his property."

Lucy gasped sharply. Then she stood and shouted at April, "It was mine! Everything was mine!"

April turned her head, lifted her upper lip in a

snarl, turned again to face the judge. "Your Honor, the house and *all* of its contents were purchased by my client. If this case goes to trial, the evidence of cancelled checks will show that all payments were made by Mr. Rainwater. The present"—she heavily stressed the word—"Mrs. Rainwater signed nothing. As the state of Oklahoma does not have a community property law, the current Mrs. Rainwater has no legal claim on the house or its contents. Therefore, the property in question was Mr. Rainwater's to legally destroy if he chose. He so chose."

"Objection," the prosecutor shouted.

"Overruled. Next charge, please."

The clerk barely managed to read attempted murder when April piped up again. The judge slapped a hand to his face and peeked at her through splayed fingers.

"Counselor, if you're going to object to every charge, we may never get around to setting bail for your client."

"Agreed, Your Honor. But if there are no charges to answer, the question of bail will be moot."

"Point taken."

"Objection!"

"Overruled." The judge leaned back in his chair. "I kinda want to hear this one. Proceed, Counselor."

In the back of the court, C. R. Jones was grinning like a possum.

"Your Honor, the weighty charge of attempted murder needs just a bit more evidence than that of the victim experiencing a bad fright. On the night in question, the police arrived as Mr. Rainwater was lawfully destroying his own property. He was then physically subdued by an entire bevy of policemen

361

before he had so much as an opportunity to lightly tap Mrs. Rainwater on the shoulder. Then, totally against his will, he was forcibly removed from his own home. If this case is pursued, I plan to subpoena each and every one of these officers on Mr. Rainwater's behalf. I also plan to subpoena the Rainwaters' medical doctor. Not only will he testify that Mr. Rainwater, because of a slight disability, suffered undue force while being subdued by these officers, he will also testify that in his medical opinion, Mrs. Rainwater endured nothing more life-threatening that a few stray hairs from her stylish coiffure. If this charge is pursued and a precedent is set that a wife's mussed hair is grounds for attempted murder, then every man in the state of Oklahoma will stand in fear of going to prison. As you are noted for being a happily married man, I'm afraid, Your Honor, that this will include you."

The judge roared with laughter. So did the Rainwaters and C. R. Jones. Matt looked up at the ceiling and laughed soundlessly. When the raucous sound faded, the judge looked at the clerk.

"What else you got on the list, Ned?"

Ned looked worriedly at the judge and said in a whimpering tone, "Drunk an' disorderly. Assaulting the police. Resisting arrest."

"Objection," April merrily called.

"And why," the judge replied, "does that not surprise me? Proceed, Counselor."

"We agree that Mr. Rainwater was drunk. We also agree that he was roaring drunk. But please note for the record that he was drunk in the supposed safety of his own home. People are allowed to be safely drunk in their own homes. On the charge of assaulting the police, we contend that the police came into Mr. Rainwater's home and assaulted him. As for resisting arrest, I find it hard to believe that one lone man could resist almost a dozen men for more than a few seconds. Especially since these men were armed with guns, clubs, and chains."

"Your client's a mighty big fella," the judge drawled.

"Indeed. He is also partially lame. Granted, he might put up a healthy fight against two or more of these armed men, but the number of men he faced on this occasion was a case of overkill in anyone's view. If the State proceeds with the charge of resisting arrest, I'm very much afraid I will have to counter charge with a case against the State for police brutality. Which will be a sad indictment on the state of Oklahoma, since Mr. Rainwater is a decorated war hero and holds a prominent place in Oklahoma's continuing oil development."

The judge furrowed his bushy brows. "I was given the impression that Mr. Rainwater was dismissed from his job."

"Mr. Rainwater was given the *opportunity*, Your Honor, to change companies."

"And just where did this opportunity take him?"

"To Mr. C. R. Jones of Redbird Oil."

Matt's head spun on his neck and looking down, he stared at April.

"I, as one of the practicing attorneys for Redbird Oil, am present only for the arraignment of Mr. Jones's most valued employee. If the State pursues this matter further, brings these trivial charges to trial, the State's prosecutor may rest assured that the entire legal staff of Redbird Oil will enter the fray, sparing my learned colleague the embarrassment of arguing the case with a mere woman."

The prosecutor became very pale. In a stammering voice he said, "Permission to withdraw all charges, Your Honor."

Lucy stood and screamed again, "He's guilty! He's guilty! He tried to kill me."

The judge banged his gavel. "Since the prosecution has withdrawn the charges, the defendant is free to go and with the court's apology for any inconvenience he may have endured."

"You can't do this!" Lucy ranted. "I want him in jail!"

"Your Honor," April shouted, "move to file a petition for divorce on behalf of Mr. Matthew Rainwater."

"On what grounds?" the judge shouted back over Lucy's ravings.

"Extreme mental cruelty, false arrest and imprisonment, public humiliation and harassment."

"We're going for overkill again," the judge chortled. "But you have this court's permission to file away, Counselor." He pointed the gavel toward Lucy. "Bailiff! Control that woman. She's giving me a headache."

While the bailiff physically ejected Lucy from the courtroom, April had Matt sign the divorce application. With the ink still wet on the forms she rushed to the judge's bench and stood on tiptoe to hand them up to him.

"You gonna handle the divorce for him?" the judge asked with a wink.

"Yes, sir."

"Well, I hope the *current* Mrs. Rainwater gives her

soul to the Lord 'cause I got a feelin' you're going after everything else."

"Yes, sir, I certainly am."

The judge glanced at his calendar. "Hearing for the interlocutory will be six months from now, July ninth. I shall look forward to seeing you in my court again. Counselor. You're one hell of a lawyer."

April's little face radiated pride. "Thank you, Your Honor."

He waved both hands, shooing her away. "Counselor, kindly go back to the defense table. I suddenly feel the need to make a magnificently sweeping retreat."

Matt and April were standing and holding hands when the court's clerk called for everyone to stand and the judge and his black robes sailed out. Then Matt whooped, grabbed April, lifting her off her feet.

C. R. Jones watched them briefly, then he slipped out. *Two fast trackers for the price of one*, he thought as he descended the courthouse steps. *That's the best deal I've cut in a lot of years.* He was still smiling as he drove back to Pawhuska. Matt, in a convoy of Rainwater cars, rode with April in her car.

Matt sat very close, his arm around her shoulders, kissing the side of her head. "I knew you could do it!"

"Matt! I'm trying to drive."

"Oh, yeah." He leaned back against the car seat, stared out the windshield at Jake's car traveling just a few yards ahead. "April, you have to marry me."

"Oh, I do, do I?"

"Yes, because I can't let you go."

April chewed the inside of her cheek and gripped the steering wheel. "I've been thinking too, Matt. It's

365

going to take a year to get you divorced. I don't think we should talk about marriage or anything else until your present marriage is dead and properly buried. And in the year that this will take, you can use the time to become the man I thought you were when we first met."

Matt's expression changed from happy to apprehensive.

"When I first met you," she continued, "I thought you were free, independent. I admired you for not allowing a slight disability to get in your way. The day I met Lucy, I lost more than simply you. I lost half of the image of the man I believed you were. As much as I still love you, I won't settle for half a man. If you're really determined to ask me to turn my back on my faith for you, then you're going to have to be *all* of the Matt Rainwater I fell in love with."

"W-what do you want me to do?"

"I want you to take charge of your own life. Become independent of everyone. Be brave enough to fall down and pick yourself up without reaching out for someone else's hand. When you're standing on your own two feet, when you don't need me, when you don't need anyone, then you can talk to me about your feelings. I promise I will gladly listen."

"When do I start my new job?"

"I don't know," she said with a light laugh. "C. R. Jones is in the phone book. Give him a call."

"April!" Matt cried. "You can at least tell me when you think I'm supposed to call him and—"

"No. No more, Matt. I am not your servant, I am not your nurse, and I am not your mother. From now on, you do everything, even the little things, all by yourself."

Chapter Fifteen

Taking care of himself was not as easy as he hoped it would be. In fact, it was a lot of work because problems, big and small, were constantly cropping up, getting in his way. April wouldn't even listen to him talk about his problems, never mind offer suggestions. Besides, she was busy launching herself into her chosen career, setting up her own life. She had a swank apartment on the other side of Pawhuska. She could have that because one, all of her money was her own—she wasn't losing half of her paycheck down the crapper to a separate maintenance payout the way he had to pay out on Lucy—and two, April had a car to drive herself back and forth. She did not offer Matt any rides because along with not being his maid, nurse, or mother, she was also not his chauffeur. During the first three months of his employment at Redbird Oil, Matt lived in a boardinghouse and walked to and from the office. In the fourth month, he was given a shock.

The woman from Administration, with a personality about as engaging as a gutted fish, stood before his desk and spoke to him in a clipped, irritatingly nasal, monotone voice.

"Here are the keys to your car. Gears and brakes

comply with amended specifications. All company cars are Pontiacs. Mr. Jones prefers the Indian—excuse me, the *Native*—scare head. All company cars are ash green. It will be convenient for you to memorize your license plate. If this isn't possible, always refer to the identity number on the key ring to avoid confusion. Please sign here and here." She pointed to the appropriate lines on the document she placed before him. Matt signed. "Your car," she said in conclusion, "is in the garage. If you've any questions, do not hesitate to contact Admin." She picked up the papers he'd signed and left his office.

Matt stared at the keys left lying on his desk as if they were a live, deadly snake. Finally, he gathered the nerve to pick them up and went to have a look at his new car. When he found it, by reading the identity number and examining row after row of ash green cars, a black man was polishing the hood.

"This your car?" the man asked.

"Y-yes."

"Sure is something."

Confused, Matt looked out over the lines of identical cars. "It's just like all the others."

"No, it ain't," the man laughed. "This here car is special. Mr. Jones ordered it hisself. Get yourself on in, an' you'll see just how special it is."

Seated behind the steering wheel, Matt looked at the floor. There were no pedals. The black man ("Percy, ever'body calls me Percy") leaned in through the rolled-down window.

"Ever'thing is on the steering column. You got your brakes an' gas right there. Fat flat one's gas, the roundy one is brakes. You know, Mr. Roosevelt used to have him a car kinda like this. Mr. Roosevelt was a crippled man. Did you know that? Most folks don't. I always remember that man standin' an' walkin' around. Newsreels always showed him drivin' his own car. He had braces to help him stand an' walk, an' he had a car almost just like this so's he could drive. I guess that's how come folks didn't know about him bein' crippled. He didn't act crippled. No, sir, he didn't act crippled a'tall. You thinkin' about takin' this car out for a test drive?"

"Uh, yes."

"Mind if I come along? I'd pay money to watch the way them hand pedals work."

"I think I'd better warn you. It's been a long time since I've driven a car. I'm very nervous."

"Well, drivin' a car ain't no big thing. You learn one time, you know for life. Besides, this here car's an automatic. But I'll come with ya while you're learnin' them hand pedals. That's sure gonna be somethin' to see."

Matt quickly realized that he could keep his hands on the steering wheel and work the brakes and accelerator with the tips of his fingers. It took awhile to coordinate steering and maintaining the proper pressure on the accelerator, but after only three trips around the block, he had the system down cold. After he parked the car in his designated space, Percy thanked him profusely for the drive. There was a new spring in Matt's step as he entered the elevator. He rode to the third floor.

He rapped his knuckles once on her office door, then entered. April looked up from her desk of paperwork.

"I'm driving," he proudly announced.

April's mouth twitched with a smile. "That's great.

Do you drive well enough to take me to dinner this Saturday night?"

"Yep."

"Fine. Then I'll see you at seven."

Matt turned and *swaggered* away.

Lucy hired a private investigator. So far all that she had for the money she could barely spare were pictures of Matt walking in all weathers and photos of him going into the boardinghouse where he lived and not coming out again until the next morning. She knew April Wilson worked in the same building, but April never gave Matt rides to or from work. Nursing the hope that Matt and April's relationship had dissolved, become purely professional, and that once he tired of trying to make it on his own, he would come crawling back to her, Lucy put the house up for sale. They would need the money to buy a new house in Pawhuska. Lucy decided she much preferred Pawhuska over Bartlesville. Besides, she'd become a social pariah in Bartlesville, the PWC's having closed ranks against her.

She tried to mend the fences between herself and May Rose, but Momma-May was a tough nut to crack. She was always civil when Lucy telephoned, always listened while Lucy cried about how much she loved Matt, but she never offered advice and she never invited Lucy to come out to the house. Lucy hated May Rose for that. Especially when she remembered the way May Rose used to literally beg her to come for a visit. Next, Lucy tried to become close again with her own mother. The minor snag on that one was that her mother was nearly as senile as a bug and had to be reminded exactly who Lucy was whenever she telephoned. Neither did she find any joy with her estranged sister. Irma's husband, Buck, was a thoroughgoing no-good, and whenever Lucy called Irma hoping for a little sympathy, she invariably ended up listening to Irma's latest tale of woe. Finally, she simply had to admit the facts. Without Matt she was totally alone. And July was coming much too quickly. In July, Matt would have his interlocutory decree. Which would mean an end to her separate maintenance money. After that, all she would have would be whatever the court decided was due her for alimony. Since she was young and capable of supporting herself and divorcing a man who had been her husband for less than ten years, her lawyer said to expect the alimony to be somewhere in the region of thirty dollars a month and the monthly payments to last for only two years. She would be poor again.

Lucy panicked.

She panicked even more when the investigator turned over new photos. Matt was driving! Not only was he driving all by himself, he was driving April Wilson to restaurants. They were dating!

"You might want to take a look at this next shot," her private investigator said.

Lucy took the photo, examined it blankly. It was a picture of a silly little house. "And just what am I looking at?" she asked sarcastically.

"Your husband just bought that house. It's where he lives now."

"It's a dump."

"I think that's why he bought it. He's spending his weekends fixing it up."

"Matt?"

He showed her another photograph. Matt was on a ladder, applying a paint brush to the clapboards. Lucy's lower jaw dropped. She was shown more photos: Matt hanging his washing out on the backyard line, Matt mowing the small lawn, Matt repairing the fence separating his property from his neighbor's, Matt shopping at a nearby grocery store. Which could only mean that in his very own little kitchen, Matt was cooking his own meals. He was completely independent of her, and the proof was glaring at her in black-and-white. Matt would not be crawling back to her. It was too late for any of that. There was only one thing left for her to do.

She turned angrily to the investigator. "I want you to start following him only at night. I want photos of my husband in bed with April Wilson."

"Ma'am, I can't make any promises that I'll get the kind of pictures you want. What goes on behind locked doors is kinda hard to snap."

"I don't care if you have to change yourself into a fly on the wall. Get me some photographs I can use in court!"

It was one week away from the court date. Matt was so excited he was beside himself. April knew all about his house, how he spent most of his time repairing and painting, but she had never set foot in the place, said she wouldn't until after the interlocutory hearing. But that was only a week away. What harm would it do to invite her over to his house for barbecued steaks?

April needed a lot of convincing. She argued that being so close to the hearing meant that they had to be extra careful, that Lucy would be getting desperate, and a desperate Lucy would be as ugly as a Medusa. Matt wouldn't listen.

"All I'm offering is to cook a steak for you. I want you in my house, sweetheart."

"Why?"

"Because then I'll be able to feel you there even when you're across town. My little house won't be just a place I happen to own anymore. It'll feel like home because there'll be some love in it."

April chewed the eraser on her pencil as she thought for a long moment. Then she tossed the pencil on her desk. "Will I get a baked potato and a salad?"

"Yeah," he laughed. "And a bowl of ice cream for dessert if you're very, very good."

"Strawberry?"

"Oh, hell, I'll push the boat out. We'll have matching paper plates and napkins *and* Neapolitan ice cream."

April rolled her eyes. "Ooooooh. A classy barbecue."

"So you'll come?"

"I wouldn't miss it."

Lucy's investigator, Richmond Bruckland, was a wiry man in his late twenties. He was a nondescript person with thin mud blond hair, the hairline prematurely receding. Richie Bruckland blended with his surroundings very easily. He especially blended in this lower-middle-class neighborhood. Since this was the summer vacation season, many of the families were gone from their houses, having driven off to show the kids the sights of the Grand Canyon or something. Richie had his choice of backyards to hide in as he spied on his quarry. Today he chose the backyard of the neighbor angled to the left because this neighbor had a nice high redwood fence, not the Cyclone net metal fencing that was becoming so popular—and revealing. Behind the redwood fence, Richie kept an eyeball on Matt through a knothole. A knothole Richie had made himself. The plank in the fence was irreparably damaged, but so what? This job would be over and forgotten by the time the owners discovered the damage and then they'd only blame their kids, probably give them a whipping or something. Richie giggled as he thought about the kids screaming their innocence as their father chased them with a belt. When the fantasy faded, he propped his other eye against the knothole and continued to spy on Matt Rainwater.

Some Indian, he thought. *He doesn't even know he's being watched. Indians must lose a whole lot of their survival instincts when they live in a house and go to work in a suit and tie.* Richie giggled again. *What a big, dumb jerk. Why would such a great-looking broad even want him back?* As it wasn't part of his job to wonder about the whys of anything pertaining to his client, Richie concentrated on watching his prey barbecue slabs of steak.

Matt Rainwater called out that the steaks were almost ready to Miss April Wilson, who was still inside the house. A moment later, she came out of the back door carrying a bowl of green salad and set the bowl down on the trestle picnic table. Then she walked over to Matt, placed her hand on the small of his back. Richie readied his camera. Matt turned, smiled down at her, leaned in and kissed her mouth. Richie clicked the camera.

Rainwater on the White Road

It was the first real kiss she had allowed him to give her in months. All of his love, all of his repressed need, could no longer be denied. Matt forgot about the steaks sizzling above the coals. He lifted her and kissed her. April's arms went around his neck as she kissed him back. His hands captured her little rump, and he pressed her hard against him. They moaned in unison. When Matt tore his mouth away from hers, he spoke in a heated rush.

"You're going to marry me?"

"Yes."

"And we'll make love forever and ever?"

"Oh, yes."

Their mouths collided again, and they hungrily devoured one another. Then April's little nose smelled the burning steaks. Still kissing Matt, her eyes fluttered open. She saw a strange little man with a camera stuck to his face hanging over the back fence. April screamed in her throat.

Matt came out of his moment of lust just as Richie Bruckland disappeared behind the fence. Matt dropped April and ran with a speed April could barely believe. Within seconds he was scrambling up and over the fence. Then he was gone.

Trying to haul ass with a camera and a heavy camera bag is a hard thing to do, but Richie wasn't concerned. He was halfway across the backyard, heading for the shaded side of the house which would take him out the front and to his car. Besides, what could Matt Rainwater do? He was a gimp. Gimps couldn't climb fences and chase after nimble, wiry guys, even if this particular nimble, wiry guy was hampered by camera equipment.

Richie was more than satisfied by the photos he'd

managed to take. Photos of passionate kissing were even better than photos of screwing. Blatant screwing offended straight-laced judges, and in a divorce court a picture of the kind of kiss he'd managed to get had to mean that some screwing in the grass had quickly followed. Nearing the shady side of the house, Richie was planning his testimony. He would testify that although he'd seen the adultery with his very own eyes, he hadn't taken pictures of the couple while they were rolling naked on the lawn because he'd wanted to spare the tender feelings of his client. He was planning his expression and just the right inflection in his tone when a hand grabbed him at the back of his neck and he felt himself being lifted off his trotting feet. Then he was shaken like a rag doll until the horizon became a dizzying sight. Richie dropped the camera, and the strap of the heavy camera bag slid off his sloping shoulder. Then he was thrown. He stopped flying when he impacted with the brick wall of the house belonging to the people with the ruined redwood fence. Richie blacked out.

Matt checked his victim's pulse. The little creep was still alive. He turned away from the sprawled, unconscious body and picked up the camera, opened it, pulled out the film, exposing every inch of it to dappled sunlight. Then he went through the camera bag, opened the many little metal canisters, exposing all of those films. Further search of the bag produced cheap name cards.

RICHMOND BRUCKLAND—PRIVATE EYE

He thumbed through the cards, tossing them to the ground. He paused at the penciled note on the back of one card. Mrs. L. Rainwater. Bartlesville 8-3938. Matt pocketed the card, left Richmond Bruckland, Private Eye, to come to and scurry away in his own good time. Still propelled by rage, Matt made easy work of climbing back over his neighbor's fence. A worried April was on the other side to greet him.

"Did you catch him?"

"Oh, yeah."

"Who was he?"

"A private investigator hired by Lucy."

"Oh, my God. Matt, what are we going to do?"

Matt dusted himself off, wrapped an arm around her quaking shoulders. "We don't have to do anything. The pictures no longer exist, and he won't be taking any more. Let's eat, I'm starving."

They ate the burned steaks, shriveled baked potatoes, wilted salad. April's nerves couldn't face the ice cream even if it was Neapolitan. She drove home before sunset, and she and Matt stayed away from each other until the day they met in court.

His parents turned up for the big fight scene, but the final showdown between Matt and Lucy was over before it began. The fireworks never happened. April and Lucy's attorney held a sidebar with the judge, the same judge Matt had faced six months before, and after a lot of whispering, the judge banged the gavel, granted the interlocutory, relieved Matt of a separate-maintenance penalty of four hundred dollars a month. He awarded Lucy the family home and car and a temporary alimony of twenty-two dollars and seventy-five cents per month for a period of not longer than six months.

"You can't do that!" Lucy hollered.

"Madam, I just did." The judge banged the gavel again—divorce court was over.

For all legal intents and purposes, Matt was finally free. But as he sat there relishing his freedom, he realized that for the past months he'd actually been more free than he had been before he'd enlisted in the Marines. He'd answered to no one but himself, taken care of himself as well as his mother or Lucy had ever taken care of him. And he'd excelled rapidly in his job as his confidence in his own abilities to fend for himself grew.

April came back to the table where Matt sat. Shuffling papers into her briefcase, she raised a hand, smiled, and waved to Claude and May Rose. Lucy was at the next table shouting to her attorney.

"Miz Rainwater," Lucy's attorney said with a patient tone, "it was the best I could do. The judge didn't want to give you anything more than the house and the car. He said you were a young woman with a determined personality, that he felt you could support yourself if you wanted to. You don't have any children, and twenty-three dollars a month is more than enough to keep you fed while you sell the house and get yourself a job. I would advise you do just that."

"I'm not paying your fee," Lucy snapped. "I'm not paying a dime for slipshod service."

"Your husband has paid my fee, ma'am. By order of the court. Now, I bid you good day."

Lucy glared at Matt. He smiled. "Best money I ever spent."

Livid, she stormed over to him, and Matt waved April away. Lucy pulled out the vacant chair and sat down.

"I can't believe you would do this to me. Not after all I've done for you."

"Luce," Matt said dryly, "when we first married, I cared for you. I cared for you very much. The sad part about all of this is that if you had helped me learn how to be strong again, we would probably still be married. While I might have looked twice at April, I would not have tried to get to know her. But you wanted me weak. You wanted me under your thumb. It was around the time when I first met April that I realized I couldn't breathe under your thumb. Then I fell in love with her. I was going to leave you when you wrecked everything. But you knew that, which is why you did what you did. When April wouldn't have anything more to do with me, I went back to you. My doing that made me weaker and made you stronger. Then I saw April again, and I knew I couldn't take it anymore. But I was still going to be fair with you, Lucy. Treat you right."

He pulled a small white card from his pocket, tossed it on the table. Lucy's lips parted as her eyes widened with horror.

RICHMOND BRUCKLAND—PRIVATE EYE

"You don't ever want to cross me again, Lucy. I swear to God, you really don't."

Lucy's mouth puckered, her nostrils flared. "I suppose you're going to marry your precious April just as soon as you can."

"Yes. And if you want to call your Mr. Bruckland, I plan to make love to her just as soon as I get her back to my house. If it will make it easier for him, I could always leave the curtains open."

379

Lucy jumped up from the chair, yelled at him in a hissing whisper, "You're disgusting. You've always been disgusting. I don't envy Miss April Wilson the 'treat' you have in store for her. The sight of you naked and then having to endure you groping her like a drooling gorilla will probably turn her off you forever. It certainly did for me."

He was amazed as she left him, walking away for the very last time, that she still had the power to hurt him in the most wretched way possible, snatch away the one thing he wanted more than his very soul. The joy of finally making love to April.

"Matthew," April said, her tone patient but angry, "tell me what's wrong."

He slumped on the couch in his living room, a glass of scotch in his hands. He swirled the drink, watched the cube of ice melt, leave a visible silver trail in the amber liquid. April was beside him, sitting with her legs curled to the side, her arm slung around his shoulder.

"N-nothing's wrong."

"Then why aren't you all over me?"

"I-I don't want to be."

"Bullpucky. You've been threatening me over the phone for days, had me really looking forward to being molested, and now you're just sitting here like a lump. If this is your idea of rape, I have to be blunt, it's missing something."

He choked back a laugh. April took the glass out of his limp hands, placed it on the coffee table. Then she crawled into his lap and pressed her nose against his.

"Tell me what has changed my lovely late-night obscene caller into a cringing coward."

He couldn't answer.

"It was something that bitch said, wasn't it?"

"Uh, yeah."

Breathing fire, April slammed her hands on his solid shoulders and, craning her head forward, pressed her forehead against his. "You'd better talk, buster. If you don't, I'm driving to Lucy's, and I'll find out from her what she said."

Matt believed her. "She-she said she felt sorry for you."

"Why?"

"Because you," he struggled for breath. "Because you would see me naked."

"Oh, that does it," April seethed behind gritted teeth. She began to scramble away from him. Matt caught her arm.

"Where are you going?"

"To have a word with the former Mrs. Rainwater."

Matt believed that too. He tossed her onto her back and kept her pinned with his superior weight. "She's not worth fighting."

"She is if she can go on keeping us apart. I've waited years to be with you. Years. I can't stand—"

His mouth closed over hers. When he finished kissing her, he looked down at her and spoke with a raspy voice. "My leg. It's really ugly, April."

"Matthew Rainwater, the first moment I saw you, you took my breath away. But I wouldn't talk to you because I loathe perfect men. Your one minor imperfection made my loving you, made us, possible. To be ashamed of your one flaw is to be ashamed of the love I feel for you." She ran her fingers through

381

his thick hair. "Now, would you mind carrying me to the bedroom?"

Matt's heart overflowed with joy. "April, it will be my greatest pleasure."

Epilogue

Two years had passed since the Christmas Matt and April were married in the living room of the Rainwater home. The whole family, including Jake's four-month-old son, James Peter, and April's parents, were in attendance. Now Matt and April lived in Tulsa and had busy careers. Lucy married the doctor she worked for as a receptionist. Word had it that she was now the full manager of her new husband's clinic and running it with an iron hand. No one was surprised.

Wil and Emma had a new baby, and Tara was expecting her second child. May Rose was more than content now that all of her sons were happy in their very individual lives. Toya was growing like a weed and spending a lot of time up at Jake's place, learning to play the piano. Toya practiced every day. George didn't mind hearing the scales a million times, but when Jake came home, the scales ended and Toya would then come slumping down the hill.

"I hate Jake," she always said as soon as she entered the kitchen.

"It's not right to hate your brother," May Rose would answer.

"Jake's too old to be my brother."

May Rose did not argue further. Toya was the left-out sibling, and when the family gathered, she keenly felt her exclusion, especially when early family memories were shared and laughed over. Sally did not feel this because, technically, Sally was the third generation. Toya didn't feel as if she had a generation. She was lost somewhere between the generations.

May Rose worried about Toya as she stood on the back porch, listening to the muted sound of scales coming from Jake's house. Claude came driving into the yard. She opened the screen door as Claude came up the steps.

"Hey there, love muffin," he said, pausing to give her a kiss. "What's for supper?"

"Fried chicken."

"I got time to watch a little television?"

May Rose shook her head and laughed. Since the television had come into the house, Claude watched anything that moved on its magic screen. "Yes, you do."

May Rose was turning a drumstick in the sizzling oil as Claude switched on the television and sat back in his favorite chair. The news was all about the up-coming local elections. Everybody on the television seemed very excited. Claude wasn't excited. He hadn't felt well all day. Damn indigestion was playing up. The smell of frying chicken wasn't making him feel any better, but he didn't want to hurt May's feelings. He was worrying how he was going to manage to eat the chicken that was making him ill just smelling it, when a gripping pain seized his chest. It hurt so much, all he could say was a low "Oh". Then the pain went away, gone as quickly as it had come. And suddenly, he felt wonderfully whole. Better than he had in decades.

He turned his head to the side, looked through the opened front door, through the screen door. The colors outside were so brilliant and lovely, he just had to go see them. A form of Claude rose from the chair. This form was a young man, his upper torso bare, his lower torso wearing a pair of old jeans and boots. A long ponytail trailed down his spine. He walked out of the living room, leaving the front screen door ajar behind him.

May Rose was transferring the chicken from the pan to a plate when a fat blue bottle fly bombed past her. "Oh, my goodness!" she cried. "How did that get in here?" She turned the fire off under the skillet, grabbed up the fly swatter, and chased the fly all over the kitchen, finally subduing the little winged beast with a fatal blow. She was returning to the stove when yet another fly shot past her and she went on another kill mission. Two of its cousins zoomed in, and May Rose became frenzied trying to swat them all.

"Claude!" she yelled. "Claude! Did you open the screen door?"

No answer. She heard only the voices from the television.

"Claude! Please close the front door. The house is filling up with flies!"

Still no response.

In a snit, she threw down the swatter and marched into the living room. Claude was asleep in front of the television, and the front screen door was practically wide open.

"Oh, you," she growled. She went to the door, banged it shut good and loud. Normally that was enough to wake Claude with a start, have him jump in his chair with a "What?" This time he didn't move. She stared at him. His body looked relaxed . . . and empty. And she knew he was dead. She lifted a shaking hand to her mouth.

"Claude?"

Tears were flowing as she slowly approached and touched him, sank to her knees and laid her head against his legs. She wept softly for a good long time and then, staggering to her feet, she walked blindly for the front door. After passing through the screen door, she slumped in the nearest rocking chair.

Claude leaned against a support post, watching her, fascinated that her middle-aged form was little more than a dull aura surrounding the lovely girl-woman he could see quite clearly. Both forms, the dull one and the bright young one, were weeping. Claude pushed away from the post, crossed the porch to the rocking chair, and knelt down before her, placing his hands on top of hers.

"Muffin."

She didn't hear him with her ears or her mind. She heard him with her breaking heart. "Claude," May Rose mewled. "Please. Don't leave me. I love you so. I've loved you all my life."

Claude smiled warmly. Here was the little girl he had fallen in love with. The same little girl who had tracked him down in Delbert's barn. For a long time he had been wondering where she had gotten to. All this time she'd just been hiding behind a lot of useless outside stuff.

"May," he whispered. "Thank you for loving me. It was the nicest gift you could ever give me. I'm sorry I have to go now. But don't be sad, okay, muffin? It'll only be for a little while. I'll come get you when Toya's all grown up. She's so special. You're going to be real proud of her. She's going to be an artist, the best artist in the whole state. She'll grow up fast, sweetheart. It won't take her long at all. Then you an' me, we'll be together again. I promise." He leaned forward, pressing his mouth against hers.

She felt his kiss. She closed her eyes as his kiss lingered. It felt just like the very first kiss he had ever given her, and she sat very still, praying the sensation would never end. And then she felt him leave. Her eyes still closed, tears streaming down her face, she could almost hear the clogging of his boots as he walked away.

After stepping off the last step, Claude found himself standing on a prairie of rich blue-stem grasses spangled with buttery yellow sunlight. The next step took him an incredible distance. He turned, looked back. The house seemed very small and May Rose still seated on the porch, smaller still. He cupped his hands around his mouth and called to her.

"I'm gonna be just over this hill, muffin! Okay? I love you, May!"

She had no idea how much time had passed when she became dimly aware of Jake's truck passing the house on his way home. She gave him a few minutes, then she rose from the rocker. She couldn't bring herself to go back into the house and telephone him.

Mardi Oakley Medawar

So she left the porch, walked around the side, and as the setting sun cast an ocher hue on her graying hair, she slowly walked across the field of breeze-soughing, waist-high buffalo grass.

Coming Soon!

DEATH AT RAINY MOUNTAIN
A Tay-Bodal Mystery

"More than a mystery…a beautifully
written, life-affirming, heartwarming
story…Masterful and moving."
—*ALA Booklist*

AWARD-WINNING AUTHOR
MARDI OAKLEY MEDAWAR
author of *The Glory Days of Buffalo Egbert*

For more information
visit: www.SpeakingVolumes.us

On Sale Now!

Sheriff Lansing Mysteries
Books 1 – 6

For more information
visit: www.SpeakingVolumes.us

On Sale Now!

HOWARD MOON DEER MYSTERIES
Books 1 – 5

For more information
visit: www.SpeakingVolumes.us

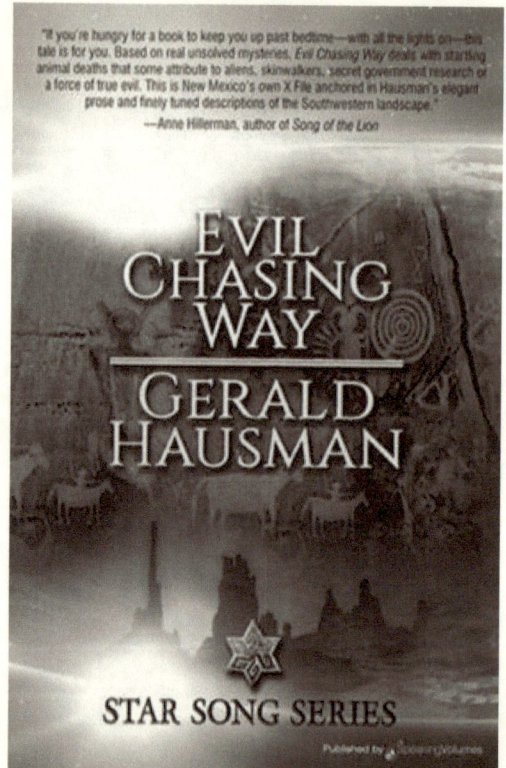

Sign up for free and bargain books

Join the Speaking Volumes mailing list

Text

ILOVEBOOKS

to 22828 to get started.

www.ingramcontent.com/pod-product-compliance
Lightning Source LLC
Chambersburg PA
CBHW021331070726
47496CB00016B/239